D1381560

EX LIBRIS

BEFORE my ACTUAL HEART BREAKS

Tish Delaney

HUTCHINSON
LONDON

1 3 5 7 9 10 8 6 4 2

Hutchinson
20 Vauxhall Bridge Road
London SW1V 2SA

Hutchinson is part of the Penguin Random House group
of companies whose addresses can be found at
global.penguinrandomhouse.com

Penguin
Random House
UK

First published in the United Kingdom by Hutchinson in 2020

www.penguin.co.uk

A CIP catalogue record for this book is available from the British Library.

ISBN 9781786331984 (hardback)
ISBN 9781786332370 (trade paperback)

Typeset in 12/17.5 pt Sabon LT Std
by Integra Software Services Pvt. Ltd, Pondicherry

Printed and bound in Great Britain by Clays Ltd, Elcograf S.p.A.

Penguin Random House is committed to a sustainable future
for our business, our readers and our planet. This book is
made from Forest Stewardship Council® certified paper.

MIX
Paper from
responsible sources
FSC
www.fsc.org   FSC® C018179

For Neil Paterson, artist poet.

And for Madge, 1922–2016. Much missed.

May the road rise up to meet you.
May the wind be always at your back.
May the sun shine warm upon your face;
the rains fall soft upon your fields and, until we meet again,
may God hold you in the palm of His hand.

Traditional Gaelic blessing

2007

THE ROAD RISES UP

1

People drown because they have to breathe in, they can't not. Granda Ban told me that at the wake of a fisherman over thirty years ago. His voice tickles my ear and I'm back in that room with him and my Auntie Eileen and the fascinating remains of the blue-lipped Bart Macroom. I've never forgotten those words. When that night floats close, I hold my arms out and hug it to me, and I am once again that eleven-year-old girl, a girl who was out of reach of her mammy for the first time ever, a girl who thought the local fortune-teller would finally confirm her wildest dream – one day, maybe that *very* day, she would grow wings and *fly*.

– Poor auld Macroom! He'd worked that river his whole life dreaming of landing the perfect fish and now he'll never know there was a fine salmon on his line when he was found. Isn't that the saddest thing you've ever heard, wee Mary?

I put on my best pious face and sighed. I wanted Granda to be in no doubt that I was all grown up, but my chance to shine was ruined by Auntie Eileen who tutted and phutted at him before she hustled me away. She didn't want anyone, including her father, egging me on. Even then I had a reputation for whimsy.

I was not supposed to be in with the big men puffing on pipes and telling tales. They were enjoying the respite of a nearly natural death in 1970s Northern Ireland. The Troubles rumbled constantly overhead like a thunderstorm, only tonight there would be no visits from the RUC or the British Army because it wasn't a wake for anyone involved in the IRA. There was every chance one of the big men would have one whiskey too many and lift me up to kiss Macroom's dead cheek, just for the craic.

I had been designated to help the ladyfolk with the tea because Auntie Eileen only had her daughter Bernie, and Bernie was not well enough to navigate kitchens or corpses. There was no shortage of help, kettles were boiling, big steel teapots were being filled, a production line of bread butterers, fillers and slicers were arranged around the table, knives and tongues moving at speed. A lot of good, strong tea is drunk over Northern Irish remains. The mourners are sorry for your trouble while they eye up the quantity and quality of the ham sandwiches flying round on the fine-china wheels of borrowed cake stands. It was already past nine o'clock but the wake wouldn't thin out until after midnight.

I was employed to cut up a heavily laden fruitcake that someone had baked and brought to feed the mourners. For some reason – kindness or madness – they had fashioned a *fish* out of candied orange peel on the top with an alarmingly large glacé-cherry eye. It looked up at me, succulent and pink, and begging questions.

– Auntie Eileen, what happened the salmon?

- What salmon?
- *Dead* Macroom's salmon! The one he caught?
- For God's sake, Mary! You wee spook! You're *worse* than Granny Moo! Get that cake on to a plate and get round the wans in the front room. Tell them fresh tea's comin'!

I'd run on, laughing at the swipe of the tea towel on my backside. Auntie Eileen had never hit me in her life; she was the reason I knew it was possible to spare the rod and not spoil the child. She was the reason I knew I wasn't nothing though Mammy had told me I was in every way, every day.

I remember watching her as I have a hundred times since. She was a fair beauty with her wild black hair in a high knot and our famous Ban Rattigan clan 'white' eyes which are in fact a pale grey-green. She moved from one person to the next with a sunshine smile at every step.

She put her arms around my neck when the fortune-teller, Decker McHugh, blew in, stinking of pigs and drink. He always pitched up at a wake for the free fire and free food, and later the free whiskey. His services were in demand at the height of the Troubles when most people didn't make it through a week without a threat to body or soul. He read the leaves, and all the tea drinkers crowded around him because he only ever allowed *one* lucky person the chance to know what dangers or delights lay ahead.

With a light tap of his middle finger on my forehead I was picked. I was the one! He sat back to settle himself for the task ahead. Oh, I was made up! A special girl at last.

I supped up my milky tea and watched Decker swirl the cup in his big hand. I knew what I wanted to hear – that my bony shoulder blades would break through my skin, covered in feathers – long white feathers sweeping the floor like all the best angels from St Bede's. I would take off as soon as I'd shook them dry. I'd leave the muck of The Hill behind. I'd be away in a matter of minutes, over our hill, over the next hill and the next, across the border, along the steely grey stripe of the Cloon River, the green grass shivering below me as I swooped through the valleys. I'd be out of Mammy's reach *for good*.

I chewed my fingernails down to the nub in pure excitement. Decker spun my cup dry and looked into the brown leaves, his bushy eyebrows drawing together in a frown. Auntie Eileen pulled me closer, I could feel the rosary beads in her apron pocket and the smell of the Coty talc Bernie was always doused in. We both leaned in for the big news.

  – There's naught but rough seas for this wan, said the sorrowful showman.
  – You could say that for any woman young or auld, Decker McHugh, you buck eejit, snorted Mrs Johns who lived down the back lane.
  – What else would you expect in the Six Counties? roared somebody else.

It took Eileen a long while to settle me that night. I thought of the white waves rolling over the sand at Bundoran on our one-Sunday-a-summer seaside outing. How cold the water was off the coast of Donegal, how easy it was to get a lungful of salt and burny eyes, how the waves dragged you back even when you were running as fast as you could to get to the beach, the watery fists wrapped tight around your ankles, your mammy not caring, your daddy too far away to notice. Was that the rough seas he meant?

  – You'll *travel*, said Auntie Eileen to placate me. That's all it is!

– Do you really think so?

– Sure, you have to take to the sea *rough or not* if you want to get as far away as America one day?

Auntie Eileen was a big fan of America. She was a big fan of *anywhere* that wasn't Carncloon. She'd already been to New York – that's where she'd got married and where Bernie had been born. I feasted on her tales of true love, of adventure. I was right by her side as she walked down Fifth Avenue describing the dresses she saw in the windows, imagined the coffee places where she tasted her first proper cup ('it's not even a *bastard cousin* of that Camp shite, don't ever forget that, Mary'), watched her learn to eat spaghetti by twirling it on a spoon.

Her stories were the best boiled sweets ever invented, changing colour and getting sweeter every time I rolled one round my tongue. They tasted of *freedom*. My head fairly bloomed with its *possibilities*. If she could do it, so could I, we were the same blood. It was Mammy who first called us two rotten peas podded thirty years apart.

The hum of Macroom's wake had carried on below us. Decker, safe in the knowledge that there would be no unnerving British Army Saracens on the street, took a fit of singing 'The Boys of the Old Brigade' and Eileen went back downstairs to see if she could hide the whiskey. I lay listening to Bernie choking on her wet snuffles and wondered if I could take her with me, back to her own country where she could breathe in without drowning.

The stormy seas first hit when I was a green girl of sixteen, but they did not carry me off. My life has been landlocked except for the times the Cloon burst its banks and the water let itself in like an old friend. The five children I reared looked forward to the floods like a day out, splashing through the kitchen like ducks. They are all gone now, grown up too fast, and my silly dreams of *sleeping in*, of being left alone for just ten straight minutes, have been realised.

When I think my voice is going to crack on the phone to them, I remember those days of wanting to be up, up and away from here, so I smile and laugh as they check again and again that I'm *alright*, that I'm *coping*, that I'm keeping *busy*. It's because I've lost their father.

I lost him three hundred and seventy-two days ago, so many sunrises and sunsets with not much light for me in between. He isn't hiding behind the barn or fallen down a bog hole. He's not dead, just taking a break, and I feel a white-hot poker of regret from my womb to my throat when I recall that it's *me* he's taking a break from. He did well to last as long as he did. Not many men would have survived a mother-in-law like his, never mind a marriage like ours.

I blamed *him* when I failed to fly because it was *him* who clipped my wings. That's the lie I told myself at sixteen and I repeated it so often that it came to be true. I fashioned a cage out of self-pity and slipped it over my head like a boned corset to hold myself together and to keep him out.

Wouldn't it have been great altogether if Decker McHugh or anyone else at Macroom's wake had been sensible or sober enough to tell me that rough seas make the best sailors? Wouldn't it have been even better if I'd figured it out for myself before it was too late?

2

I *have* travelled – two bumpy miles from The Hill where I was born to where I live now. If you had to *crawl* with a pig on your back it would *seem* like a big journey, says Auntie Eileen. She has an eye for the bright side.

The Hill is my father Frank Rattigan's place, known as that because it sits on Dergmoy, the highest of the five pudding-bowl hills of the Cloon Valley. The other four are Muckle, Sessiagh, Aghabovey and Glebe, each with its own patchwork quilt of greens, brown and purple. The house is a big square pebble-dashed, two-storey affair with many barns and sheds at its back. It's also a landmark. Strangers looking to cross over the border into the Republic of Ireland are often advised to turn right at the Ban Rattigans', which makes it sound like a mighty mountain range when it's only a farm.

I had sixteen years at The Hill. I learned to pray there and I learned to give up on prayers there. I learned how to keep my mouth shut, to not let a single thing show on my face though my insides churned and burned. I learned that I was nothing.

I learned how to take a slap and to never forget that it was no one's fault but mine that I'd needed it.

I only have to close my eyes to see the way the light caught the corner of the sofa in the Good Room and eventually bleached a pink triangle on the red material. The way Daddy always left his wellies with the toes pointing towards the back door as if he couldn't wait to be outside again. The way the kitchen always smelt of fresh scone on a wire that was *not* to be touched. The way there was nowhere to hide. The way my dream of leaving it came true so quickly that it took my breath away for years.

There are pictures of all seven of us Rattigan children, nailed to the wall in Baptism, Communion and Confirmation clothes. Mammy only framed the sacraments. There are no memories of seaside smiles or weddings. There's not a single photograph of Frank Rattigan in The Hill, though images of God hang in every room. He was the man of the house, not Daddy. He was firmly on the kitchen wall with His Sacred Heart all ablaze outside His body, reassuring her with His big sad eyes that she was doing just fine. He was in the kept-for-best Good Room suffering the little children to come unto Him. He was in the back scullery in a lovely pink robe shepherding sheep. He was in her and Daddy's bedroom with moonbeams bouncing off His head as He's borne aloft by doves to keep His toes out of a powerful waterfall.

Upstairs He's peppered about the place on crucifixes and in pictures which shimmer and shine and are lit up by electric bulbs in the shape of candles. When Mammy says, 'Good Holy God is watching you,' you cannot doubt her. He will condemn you on her behalf.

Alongside Him she has my particular favourite, No Siree Bob, the firebrand. On her scale of fury, o being mild rage, 10 apoplectic, No Siree Bob sat at around number 7. Good Holy God was a 9 and then it was straight to the perfect 10, the Virgin Mother herself, the Bo Derek of Catholic retribution. It was a busy house, though we rarely had visitors.

The weather in West Tyrone doesn't help any mood, melancholy or otherwise. The wind and the rain batter us all day and all night for what feels like weeks on end and that's just the summer. The Hill fairly rattled through every season. The tiny gaps at the windows sang like saws when the gales flew at us from the Blue Stacks on Donegal. The width of the block walls was all that stood between us and death by exposure – and *not* because Mammy cared about us freezing in our beds – she cared only for the health of our souls.

To help us get ahead in the race to Heaven, she made time to clean the chapel. It was a privilege, we were a chore. When she had scrubbed us, every room in The Hill and the doorstep clean and cooked three decent meals, she cycled off with a light heart to do it all again for God.

She polished the brass plaques, she mopped the marble under the altar, she swept the wooden floors and dusted the pews and she fed the priest whatever titbits he had a fancy for. She ripped the flowers from our garden and put them in vases under the dead-eyed statues. She looked like the perfect Catholic woman with her big family, her immaculate house, her devotion to the Church.

When peace broke out in Northern Ireland on Good Friday 1998, she was far from happy. She missed the daily battles and being duty-bound to sneer at any Protestants who crossed her path. Her and the Troubles have been on the back foot now for nearly a decade. The government of *us* and *them* – depending on what side of the barbed wire you were on – had bounced back to London for a while, but now we are *power sharing*! And surely anything is possible when the Chuckle Brothers – the Democratic Unionist Party's Reverend Ian Paisley (hate preacher) and Sinn Féin's Mr Martin McGuinness (former IRA commander) – still haven't kicked ten bags of shite out of each other?

    – There was a photo of those two fuckers in the *Tyrone Constitution* the other day, says Auntie Eileen, smiling at each other. Smiling! At each other! Imagine it, Mary? *The fuckers!*

It was nice that Auntie Eileen was more engaged with current affairs these days. When poor Mo Mowlam, God rest her resolute soul, was battling with both of those wonderfully dedicated public servants in the 1990s, Eileen only had one eye, one ear and evidently only half a brain on events unfolding on the BBC's *Inside Ulster* programme.

    – That poor woman has to fairly tear her hair out to be heard.

    – Eileen, she has cancer.

    – Who?

    – Mo Mowlam!

    – Mo Mowlam has cancer? No! Mother of God, what is she doing here wastin' her time on those dickheads? She should be at home lookin' after herself. She'll understand the benefit of rest one day!

Ah, Auntie Eileen and her one day, one day! If she has one fault, it's her one day, one day! 'One day' has been hanging over my head like a noose for as long as I can remember and even now I can't outrun it. She kept me so firmly focused on all the good things that would happen one day because so many bad things happened every day. But that meant I missed out on a thousand gems that were right under my nose. High on the list is him, the missing husband.

The September sun is dipping and the chill that it will leave reaches me where I sit outside the house that I long to call my own. I must check my hens, I must check the gates, I must check some rat traps that I have set in the barn. A lonely woman's work is never done. When I stand, my cat stretches himself, ready for the plod around the perimeter. His creaky yawn tells me that he doesn't have a care in the world except his supper – lucky little rascal.

I wake up every morning to the deafening noise of a deserted hearth. I turn in every night with the ghosts of a life not well lived. If I could go back to being sixteen again, I'd do things differently. Everyone over the age of forty feels like that, you total *gom*, says my best friend Lizzie Magee. Auntie Eileen advises me to up my intake of sweets. When I was small, she often saved me with barley twists and chocolate limes because there was nothing she could do about the welts on my body.

I never could protect myself. I didn't even open my mouth when my father gave me away. I thought it was the worst thing by far to befall me until I was taken by force. Those thoughts can drown me faster than black clouds.

To settle the heart banging painfully in my chest, I list the things I *do* know. I know my father loves me, I know my mother does not. I know that I have to reap what I have sown, it's only fair. I am the mother to five children grown and gone in the blink of an eye. I am the sitting tenant of one farm, the wife to one husband, the fool to one lover. I have an empty nest, an empty lap, empty arms, a hollow heart.

The wind suddenly barges through the big sycamores at the bottom of my street. The crows rise up in a rage and a flurry of seed parachutes twirl to the ground, God's confetti. I can see myself walking beneath them when we were all a lot smaller but equally green. They mark the entrance to the river field where the Cloon bends to make its journey to the town ten miles away. If I run, can I catch the little girl that was me and press my face to hers? You'll be alright, I'll say, one day. I could point out the holes in the road ahead where she might fall. She fell a lot. Even in this moment of seeing her again she has scabby knees. She's too thin by far. It's the week before her First Confession; she has a terrible thing to tell the priest. *Stay away from the water*, I whisper but she can't hear me. If I'm quick I can at least hold her hand.

1973

THE WIND AT YOUR BACK

3

My big sister Kathleen is leaving me here soon. I will have to sleep alone in the dark at The Hill. Lights cannot be left on to burn perfectly good electricity for stupid little girls who should know that there is only *one thing* to fear and that is losing the love of Good Holy God and His Virgin Mother. I am seven but she is seventeen so it's past time she had a proper job and stopped getting under people's feet, way past time.

She's worked every Saturday at the chemist's but there's a danger she will develop airs and graces behind the counter so she is going to scary Derry to be a nurse. She looked after me when I was sick so she will be a good nurse but people die in Derry all the time. I've seen it on the TV. She's going to wait until I've made my First Holy Communion, she promised.

Auntie Eileen says I am not to worry my bee-ya-ootiful wee head about her going to Derry. I am her Mary-Moo. I worry anyway because Kathleen is the only one who can shush my bad dreams away.

God is Jesus and the Holy Ghost all rolled into one and very soon I'll get to eat Him for my Holy Communion. He's a wafer about the size of a ten-pence piece and made out of flour and water not flesh. I've checked and He's entirely different from the wafers in ice-cream sandwiches. Auntie Eileen says that's the best way to think about Him, like a very holy biscuit, and Kathleen sniggers and tells her to try and behave even if it's only this *one* time. I've already *heard far too much* for a seven-year-old.

I just have to make it through my First Confession and get all the black marks wiped off my soul before I am allowed to take Communion. One of the black marks is as black as coal. Mammy put the coal under my nose so I could picture the blackness. Afterwards there will be a Sandwich Tea in the parish hall. The tea will not be strong enough for Mammy or hot enough or sweet enough but she'll suffer it in silence because she's a better class than some people around here. Some people around here shouldn't be allowed out in broad daylight. I'll have to ask Mrs Johns down the back lane *how much badness* it would take to have somebody shut in. I can ask her anything and she will never tell on me, she promised.

Auntie Eileen is the only person I know who isn't scared of Mammy. She even knows Mammy calls her 'a one'. 'A one' is bad because it means T.R.A.M.P. When Mammy sees Mrs Cohan going around Carncloon in her too-short skirts she always says, she's *another one*. We all know she's a T.R.A.M.P. because she goes up to the big barracks to see British Army soldiers and you're not even supposed to *speak* to soldiers. We were trained to not even look at them and their *bloody* rifles on the main street. They hang out of the doorways and watch the bombed-out shops for people with stones in their hands. They walk in the road because cars go slow in Big Town because of the ramps. The ramps are there to stop the bombers on both sides. Bombs go bang if they get shaken.

Mammy barges past them because they don't belong here. No harm to them, they're all someone's son, says Daddy. One day there will be no English boots on Irish soil, No Siree Bob, and that day can't come soon enough, says Mammy, who stands like she has a broom up her arse when the National Anthem comes on the wireless after her ceilidh programme. Auntie Eileen *is* bold to say things and Kathleen's never done telling her to behave because I have 'ears like a bat'. I'd never tell on them, though, in this house we don't carry tales.

Daddy says the worst boots aren't English at all: they are the boots of the UDR who are just as bad as the USC because the UDR is made up of the lately disbanded B-Specials. It's not hard to keep up because Mammy goes over my letters with me and I write them in my rough jotter and learn them by heart every time the men add a new set – the RUC, the UUP, the DUP, the IRA, the PIRA – into the mix. Maybe it's because bad things have to be spelt out?

Mammy always spells out B.I.T.C.H. when she's talking to her sisters, Auntie Vi and Auntie Harriet. She thinks I don't know she's talking about Auntie Eileen who did something *terrible* in America. She swanned off with an Eye-talian and came home with my Cousin Bernie who's not well. Bernie's never spoken a word and she's older than me by a year. Good Holy God has a way of making sure some people pay for their dirty sins in *this* life, says Mammy.

When you marry out of sight you must have something to hide, especially when you come home with your tail between your legs and no husband. Auntie Eileen says he died but Mammy says, pah, I'd be surprised if he ever *existed*! But sure, he must have *existed* or where did she get Bernie from? It takes a husband to give you a baby.

We went to Carncloon to buy a brand-new pair of white knee socks for the Communion. Daddy stayed in the car because the army blows up *unattended vehicles* so I carry the bags for Mammy. Shopping is a woman's job. She made me look at a wall where someone had painted the words: UP THE PROVOS! I don't know why I had to look or what it means but if she smiles, I smile too. It's safer.

My head bounces from Belfast to Derry to Dublin and back to Bloody Westminster, which I know now is a big castle in London. Granda Ban says it's called the Houses of ParleyMint. I'm glad there are only two sides in this war. The Loyalists are *them* and the Nationalists are *us*. The Loyalists have King Billy the Dutchman on a white horse from Orange, the Queen of England and the red, white and blue of the Union Jack which flutters on every tree and telegraph pole for miles in the Protestant areas.

The Nationalists want the border to be taken away so that the Six Counties can join back up with the other twenty-six counties of Ireland and we can be a nation once again because we already have a song that says that. Our flag is green, white and gold. It flies from every telegraph pole lining the road in from The Hill to Carncloon. We have had to *pay dear* for the civil rights.

Auntie Eileen caused a load of bother when she left Bernie with us and headed off to Derry last year because she wanted to march up and down for the civil rights. But marching is not allowed and the British soldiers shot at us. Not all of the bullets were rubber. Daddy made us say extra prayers when it came on the news and Auntie Eileen still hadn't appeared. Her day out is called Bloody Sunday now because loads of Catholics died.

In Carncloon, Mammy blesses herself if the RUC cross in front of her. RUC stands for Royal Ulster Constabulary and anything with the word 'Ulster' in it is not good for us. She makes out that they smell, holding the corner of her headscarf across her nose and mouth. Never forget, as long as you're spared, Mary Rattigan, that these so-called policemen are little more than poodles for the British Army, she says. I don't know what a poodle is but I do know she *really* doesn't like the British Army. It has come here to keep *us* in line and she doesn't like being told what to do in *her* own country, No Siree Bob.

I have to be a good Catholic because of the Troubles, better even than Mammy and she is a top sayer of prayers. I am the next generation and I must be ready to fight because my grandfather, Captain Sean McPartland, gave his *very life* for Ireland. He was a patriot.

The sounding of the Angelus bell on the wireless at six in the morning, midday and six at night is devoted to him and his sacred memory and we all must stop to pray. Mammy drops to her knees like a pig hit on the head with a hammer and knocks out a dozen Hail Marys and a few Our Fathers double-quick time before getting on with her day.

She likes us children to be quiet. Empty vessels make most sound, she says if she catches us talking. Talking is best left to adults who understand the world like she does although she

21

would never blow her own trumpet, that would be a sin. The name of that sin is pride. I have the sin of pride to confess. I thought I could keep a S.E.C.R.E.T. in The Hill. Mammy does not allow secrets.

My brother Mick thought we could fool her too. I worry about him. Even though he's older, he's softer than me. He wets himself now since the bad thing happened and it's my job to strip off the sheet and tell him not to cry over spilt milk. Crying is for cissies and Mammy would rather lose *all* of my brothers to the UVF than rear a cissy. UVF stands for Ulster Volunteer Force.

He has the same scary dream as me. We dream of drownings, of choking water and little lungs being shut down, of Mammy laughing as we cry, but he tries to do the job of a big brother. Just screw your eyes tight shut, he says, until you can see nothing but blackness. If it doesn't work for you, Pish-the-Bed, why would it work for me, says I, and we both snigger even though it's not funny.

Auntie Eileen does that, laughs when stuff isn't funny. Might as well, she says, if you don't laugh, you'd cry. I am not allowed to stay with her because she is a bad influence so she comes to me at The Hill, bold as brass. This is *my* brother's house, Sadie, and don't you forget it, she says.

Their mother, my Granny Moo, could see people walking down her street when they were actually heading straight for St Peter at the pearly gates. Her second sight was so sharp she could have the priest with the dying for the last rites, a sacrament which gets you into the Kingdom of Heaven even if you've been bad all your days. You don't need a doctor because bodies come and go but souls are forever.

I've been comparing sins with Lizzie Magee for our First Confession. I'm saying I've lied and been disobedient and she's going to copy me. I've not told her the really bad thing in case she copies that too and gets me into *more* trouble. One day, we're going to be missionaries and go off out to Africa and save the heathens from themselves so that they get to go to Heaven. Otherwise, their unclaimed souls'll be wandering about, maybe in some other horrible place like Limbo where all the little babies with Original Sin have to float in the pitch-black nights that never turn back into days.

Pray for Purgatory, says auld Miss Lynch as she twists the chalk until it snaps, when you're in Purgatory you're in with a chance but in Limbo you're lost for all eternity!

4

Daddy takes me into Carncloon for the First Confession. He has to ease the car over the ramps because the Chapel Road is where the barracks is and the ramps are extra high to stop anyone with a bomb in the boot. My big brother Matthew has come with us, he likes to be out of The Hill. His quietness grates on Mammy's nerves. She's never done telling him to open his mouth while she tells the rest of us to shut ours. He's going to wait in the car with Daddy. They both look happy. Mick walks me to the chapel with more advice.

– Don't be scared of the box, he says, it's not totally dark inside and Father O'Brien can hardly see you anyway through the grille. Keep your voice down and just say two sins, that's plenty.

Mick still feels bad that he didn't take his fair share of the blame for the S.E.C.R.E.T. He cried a lot when I got sick afterwards. In the end Mammy had to get the strap and that got him stopped. He has a lollipop saved for me for after today's penance.

I skip on up to wait by Lizzie Magee and the rest of the class after Miss Lynch ticks me off the list. I hope you're ready to be made *clean*, Mary, she says and I nod. I am ready.

The priest isn't too sore on me in the end. I thought he might drag me out of the confessional and throw me on the floor of his chapel but instead he sighed and blessed me before he closed the grille. I was shaking. I never thought I'd have to *tell* what I did but Father O'Brien asked me to explain myself. How in the name of God have you come up with the sin of pride, he says, so I had to speak up. You can't say no to a priest.

I was glad to get back into the light of the chapel with my penance: an Our Father and three Hail Marys and the Prayer for Peace. Lizzie Magee says the Prayer for Peace isn't about being extra bad but that there's an extra need for it in Northern Ireland. She doesn't know what I've done.

I'd told him the story of what happened after Mick and me found a stray cat sleeping in an old bucket in the barn about two months before. She was fat and skinny at the same time. We gave her some milk and before long she was waiting for us in the same spot every morning.

One day we had to hunt around for her and we found her in an old tin bucket with three kittens who were too small to even have eyes yet. We knew we had to keep them a S.E.C.R.E.T, cross our hearts and hope to die. Mammy does not like pets. We're not even allowed to give the pigs and cows names. They are food.

There were two black and white ones and a tabby. The tabby had a bright ginger belly and white paws. I thought I had never seen anything so gorgeous in all my life. I loved it the way I loved my Blue Ted and I called it Angel because angels sit on your shoulders and make you feel everything is going to get better. Mick wouldn't jinx his with names.

They were balls of fluff in no time. We let them sit in our hair and hang on to our jumpers with their soft claws. Mick was always upset when we had to leave them alone but I never looked back in case Mammy would be watching. She would figure it out for sure and try to give them away. Matthew begged us to be careful. If I've seen, she'll see, he said. He didn't need to say any more.

I knew I would *die* if they were given away. The thought of anyone but me and Mick burying their faces in the kittens' soft furry sides made my head feel funny, as if I had water in my ears. It wouldn't happen, it couldn't happen. I had been so careful, so very careful.

Mammy stopped Daddy at the back door before he got his wellies off. She spoke low to him. He nodded and turned. When she came back through the kitchen without looking at me, I knew she knew and I knew where he was going. He was going to put them in a bag and leave them on the linkbox of the tractor until he could drive them deep into the Cloon Valley. They would be wandering around, hungry and scared and thinking that I had let them down.

Maybe I could make him take them down the lane to Mrs Johns – she'd look after them for sure? I ran for the door before Mammy could stop me. She collared Mick who was already crying. He was shouting for me to run, run quick! RUN, MARY, RUN! Kathleen wasn't there and Liam, Dominic and Brendan were too scared to move. Matthew was crying too. He'd pay for that later.

By the time I got to the barn I was blinded by tears. I knew Daddy wouldn't be rough with them. The mammy cat was crying; the low auld sound of it went straight through my guts. But it was okay, there was no bag, there was no bag, just Daddy, sitting, stirring, stirring, stirring.

He had filled the bucket with water and near the top a swirl of black and white and ginger went round and round with his stick. I ran for them, knowing that it couldn't be too late, it just couldn't. Before Daddy could stop me I had one in my hand, my little ginger-bellied Angel, but he was soaked through.

– You'll be alright, you'll be alright, you'll be alright! Wake up, wake up!

– Mary, don't! Mary, don't! Mary, don't!

My kisses weren't making it better – maybe it would take Auntie Eileen's kisses but she was far away. I couldn't breathe. I couldn't speak. I couldn't ask him why or how could he? To my Angel? The scream got out of my head and tore around the barn.

Daddy carried me back from the barn. *Why didn't you tell me the waynes knew about the wee crayturs, Sadie? Why wasn't I told?* His voice cracked and his body shook but she didn't answer him, she was busy making the tea. He was a cissy and no mistake, crying over a handful of rotten cats, pah! She pulled me out of his arms and threw me into the back pantry. I landed on the cold concrete beside the enamel buckets of apples and damsons and all I could think about was their wet little bodies lying still on the straw. I cried myself out in the musty smell from the fruit skins.

I was on fire by the time she remembered about me the next day but she didn't call Doctor Loughrey until a whole week went by. I had The Bronchitis, he said. I went down like a ton of bricks, said Auntie Eileen. She'd never seen a wayne so sick. It was thought the fever would break but it didn't because I am stubborn.

- This child must be kept better, the doctor said. She's too thin, Mrs Rattigan, too thin by far. She'll have to have a jab now to try and bring her temperature down or she's for Omagh Hospital tomorrow.
- If you weren't made of such *weak material*, Mary Rattigan, she said to me when he slammed out in a filthy mood, our whole business wouldn't have to be broadcast to all and sundry.

I hoped she wouldn't find out about the scaredy dreams when the mammy cat clawed my face off. She was right to hurt me. I'd as good as killed those kittens myself. It's hard to dig stuff like that up but I had to tell the truth to the priest.

I said the little cats got put in the bucket because of me. They drowned because of me. The mammy cat would be pure lonely now because of me. The doctor was called because of me. Daddy cried because of me – now he's a cissy. Mammy hates him even more because of me.

- So it was all my fault, Father. I should have known I would get caught.
- Aren't you one of Sadie Rattigan's waynes?
- Yes Father!

Mick said he wouldn't know it was me! I didn't want to be punished again. I'd learned my lesson. My mouth was dried up after all the talking. I could hear Father O'Brien sighing and rubbing his face somewhere in front of me and I prayed that it would soon be over. I needed to get back to The Hill, I had *jobs.* Mammy would be watching the clock. In the end he just handed out the penance and asked me to remember one thing. He sounded kind enough but it's the one thing that scares me the most.

 – God is watching you, child. He *hears* everything. You're never *truly* alone. Never forget that. He has eyes everywhere.

5

I had just stopped rattling after The Bronchitis when Auntie Eileen told me I would be looking after Bernie on Saturdays. The thing was, she'd only gone and got herself a job in Crawford's the newsagent. I nodded through the blue smoke she puffed out from her Embassy Regal and the joy shining in her eyes. I was her best hope of freedom before she went off her rocker. She needed the money and the craic and the company before she took Bernie and headed for the deep water of the River Cloon with rocks in her pockets, ha ha ha.

Kathleen wasn't so sure – it's not *safe* to leave Bernie here, she said – but Auntie Eileen was full of plans. She was going to rope Mick in too and pay the both of us with sweets, as many sweets as we could eat!

She reminds me that Bernie is a china doll; she's delicate and in need of careful handling. If she has the odd accident or some such, don't be bad to her, just remember she wouldn't hurt a fly and if there's sweets she's to have as many as she wants as long as they're not toffees. A strawberry bonbon got stuck in her once – Bernie, not the T.R.A.M.P. – and she had to be rushed to hospital. Hospitals must have bloody little to bother them these days, Mammy had said when she got back, wasting time on a wayne who will never be able to serve Good Holy God's purpose.

Kathleen is still not sure I'm the best girl for the job. Bernie *is* more than delicate and she *is* hard to watch, she says. What if something goes wrong? What if Mammy has to be called? We need to make sure that *nothing else* happens to Mary!

I was dreaming about the jars and jars of lovely-coloured sweets lining the shelves at Crawford's right up to the ceiling. I kept my eyes on the pinks and purples, the reds and greens of pear drops, rosy apples, kola kubes and fruit rocks. My mouth filled with spit at the thought of them being handed to me in a brown bag with twisted paper ears on the side.

> – Sure, what could go wrong? says Eileen, lighting another fag with the butt of the first one. Sadie'll have no part in it, the bad-tempered auld F.U.C.K.E.R.! Mary'll *do grand*, won't you, my wee Mary Moo?

I nodded and peeled another toffee.

We played piggy in the middle way out in the back field behind the barn on the first Saturday. It's safer not to be seen from the kitchen window. Mick was shouting, get the ball, get the ball, Bernie, the ball, over there, look, look, Bernie, look, her just laughing her big, gurgly laugh. She'll never get the ball but she likes to watch it sailing over her head. We picked mulberries when she got tired, dropping them into old jam jars to have later. But Mick and me didn't watch her properly and she ate a mountain of them straight off the bush. Her whole chin was purple. She had an accident and there was mess all down the backs of her legs.

Mick started crying before he could stop himself. I wish he'd stop beating me to it. We checked the barn for rags. Nothing. Mick rubbed at her with a fistful of straw that made it worse. We had to try and sneak her into the bathroom without Mammy seeing us. Bernie started to howl as soon as she saw the house. I wasn't going to get a turn at crying at all today. We tried to shush her but it was no good. Mammy was waiting. Bernie bit her too-big tongue when Mammy was shouting at her.

– Hopeless, good-for-nothing article! What are you?

She wasn't going to answer but Mammy kept at it, she never gave up. She prodded her in the chest with every word. Poor auld Bernie started to moan and dribble and rock, any minute she might have a fit.

– Well? Can you not even manage to get yourself to the toilet!

Born idiot! Do you even know what a toilet is? IDIOT!

Leave her alone! Was it Mick or me said that? No matter, it was me that got the wallop! The tracks of her fingers lit up my face, hot and cold, and her wedding ring burst my lip. Mammy stripped her right in front of us even though we know it's a *sin* to show someone your bottom or to look at anyone else's bottom. She slapped Bernie all the harder when she tried to wriggle away. Whack, whack, whack.

After Bernie was washed down and dried and shoved into an old pair of trousers to make sure Eileen knew she had to be changed, we were told to all disappear, disappear clean out of Mammy's sight until teatime! She was sick of the sight of us! And it was no one's fault but mine that I had got myself another clout, No Siree Bob!

32

We went back behind the barn, shivering and shaking and hoping Daddy would find us this time, just once, please Holy God. But he didn't show up, too busy with the beasts as usual and as like as not to turn if he saw us standing in a miserable clump. Liam, Dominic, Brendan, Matthew and him were moving the cows to the far edges of The Hill. I thought he would stick up for us one day but Kathleen says that's nonsense, he never will. I had an emergency humbug in my pocket that I peeled and gave to Bernie. She needed it more than me.

China dolls definitely don't shit themselves, Mick said to cheer me up and to make Bernie laugh again though she was gone pure white in the face. A hot sob was rising up from my guts but it came out as a hiccup and we giggled. There's no use crying over split lips. We know we'll still get the quarters of clove rocks and pink elephants.

When Auntie Eileen came back with Kathleen from Carncloon, they found us in the barn. We got so, so tired that we went to lie down in among the bales of hay. Mick went in the middle because he's the man and me and Bernie put our heads on his chest and I suppose we all nodded off. It was Eileen sobbing that woke us. She just stroked my face and kissed Mick's head before she pulled Bernie out and held her as if she would snap in half.

Kathleen wiped at my mouth with her hanky but she couldn't really see what she was doing through the tears. Mick doesn't like to be left out so he got under her coat and hung on to her waist. That's how Mammy found us, and she blew her top because we were being so mucky. She doesn't like hugs, hugs are worse even than talking. A big fight got up, all three of them were shouting and roaring 'til Eileen put Bernie in the car. The door banged shut and they took off. The sudden quiet was weird. I swear I could hear everybody's heart beating, not just my own.

Kathleen stormed into the house and me and Mick ran after her like orphaned ducks. She had me in her arms by the time Mammy caught us, telling me for the hundredth time that I would be alright, to not cry, to be brave, it wasn't forever. One day we'd be gone. Seventeen or not, she wasn't safe, not yet. Mammy rounded on her.

– Get away from her! The problem with that wayne is she's spoilt! Spoilt rotten by that idiot aunt of yours with her boiled sweets and her dotey-this and darlin'-that! Pah! Who does she think she is? Ruining my waynes because her own is soiled?

– You didn't need to hit Mary in the face! Don't you think she's been through *enough* lately? Eileen says she's going to get *the priest* out to you!

– She wouldn't dare get the priest out to *me*! That *tramp*?

– She would and you know it!

Kathleen had stood up now to face her. Mammy was taken aback but she was not beaten. Mammy couldn't be beaten but even I could see that she had a worm of worry. The priest comes because we don't have policemen. We don't speak to the RUC because we're Catholics. He will tell her off bigtime and everyone will find out. It's even worse because he has God on his side not just a gun. His housekeeper, horrible Mrs Byrne, goes straight across to the parish-hall bingo and tells whole rows of women who's in the clabber. I've heard about this before, it's called 'losing face'. Mammy usually really enjoys it when other women have lost their faces.

She'd likely fed the priest enough times to keep him on side. He always dropped by almost exactly at dinnertime and had to be persuaded that there was enough food to go round and he must stay – 'shame not to, Father O'Brien, when it's my *own* chicken roast.' Mammy's *own* chicken roast was famous throughout the whole townland and she threw open the windows even in the fierce winter frosts so the smell of it, stuffed to the gunnels with sausage meat and scallions, drifted down into the Cloon Valley to fill every mouth with water and nothing else.

The butter bubbling under the skin likely made it all the way to the parochial house on Aghabovey and the poor men of the cloth, suffering the skinny shin stews of Mrs Byrne all week, would be like lambs to the slaughter. If he tried to back out of the kitchen she would follow him with a roast potato on a fork ready to feed him like a baby bird if he opened his beak.

– Father O'Brien will understand I'm rearing waynes who
   will honour their father and their mother, Kathleen
   Rattigan!

She knew she was safe. What happened inside the walls of this house stayed within its walls. Whatever Father O'Brien threw at her wouldn't stick. That she had hit such an innocent as Bernie would be passed over as an accident. She'd be able to make him see that it *needed* to be done. He wouldn't care that she had hit me, I was hers to hit.

When Mammy moved down the hall pulling Mick behind her by the ear, Kathleen bolted for the bedroom. She was sitting on the bed pretending not to cry but she had got out her suitcase again. It had been packed for weeks and sat to the side of the dressing table like a bomb about to go off.

She patted the stuff with shaking hands: the towels, the wash-bag, the new clothes from Auntie Eileen, stuff she would need to live somewhere else, somewhere I couldn't see her every day. I climbed on to her lap and wrapped my arms and legs around her like the stupid, petted baby that I was. She rocked me as she cried.

– It's not forever. One day we'll be gone, she said.

We clung on to the magical 'one day' because it was the only raft we had. One day we would get married or just leave home. One day we'd be away to college in Derry or Belfast or America. Kathleen was close to escape but I still had years to go and very soon no one to take my corner. I wished Daddy would come home.

I listened on and on to Kathleen crying but my own eyes were dry; somewhere deep down inside me was a big hollow. I tried to imagine being all alone in our room but I couldn't. Mammy ripped open the door and jerked her head in the direction of the kitchen. Kathleen walked past her without a word. The tea had to be made. You're to stay in bed for the evening, Mammy said to me, I don't want you appearing down those stairs, do you hear me? I heard her. Wild horses couldn't have dragged me down there.

That night the pan hissed as usual, the salmon and brown onions were fried in butter, the boys and Daddy came in, their socks trailing the smell of the byre, cowshit mixed with Indian meal and tobacco smoke. I heard them all at their tea, knives scraping plates in the silence. By the by, Mammy brought me up a bit of cold fish and bread. She'd come to tell me why I had a sore lip. It's because she cares, she says, cares that I grow up to know right from wrong.

She wouldn't be doing her job, and it's a *very serious job* being someone's mammy, a calling straight from the Virgin Mother Herself, a *vocation* almost. If she took her eye off me for one minute I could be ruined. Children *can* be ruined in a minute. Look at me, I was *nothing*, a slug under her boot, but still she would never give up on me.

She leans in, and with sugar on her tongue from a confiscated bag of barley twists, tells me how vital it is to be good because even when she's not in the room, Good Holy God is always watching. He can see through doors and around corners and into the very soul itself where all the black marks live. I must always save my sins for the ears of the priest and the priest alone, never *breathing* a word to another person in case they figure out what a bad girl I am.

Did I remember what happened the last time? The time when I committed the sin of pride? She smiles when I nod. I'd done well, learned another lesson. I just had one more thing to remember. Auntie Eileen must never know exactly what went on today, no matter who asked. Even if the priest asked, it was alright to tell a white lie this time. It was better for everyone to keep this S.E.C.R.E.T. After all, Bernie could have been badly hurt, *much more* badly hurt.

- You don't want that on your black little conscience *as well*, do you, Mary Rattigan?

6

My sister is leaving right after Father O'Brien has been. She's going to miss my Holy Communion. She won't get to see me in my dress. She has to go because Auntie Eileen *had* dared to go to the priest. Mammy was in for a good scolding and Kathleen had been told to get her ungrateful carcass out of The Hill and to never come back for her part in it. She is not to darken the door until she remembers her catechism: honour thy father and thy mother. Daddy didn't say anything.

My brothers scattered and Kathleen took up her chair in the Good Room when the sound of the priest's engine stopped on the street. Her face is very white and her eyes look like mine after I came out of the fever, like they were pure dry and pure wet at the same time. I watch her smooth her skirt down and then she smiles at me. Goodbye, says the smile. We'd already done all the crying and we couldn't risk speaking to each other. I was being sent down the back lane with the excuse of a bag of spuds to our neighbour, Mrs Johns at Johns Farm. Mammy didn't want me to be called on. She couldn't rely on me to lie and tell Father O'Brien that Bernie had really needed a walloping.

– Keep that mouth shut, Mary Rattigan.

– I will, Mammy.

– Run!

And I did run, Yes Siree Bob! I didn't want to see or hear what was about to happen but the lane is rough and long and I tripped and fell and skinned my good Holy Communion knees. Jeepers, they stung! I held my hands over them 'til they calmed down a bit then I picked up the spuds lying one here, one there and carried on. I had to make it past the white wall at the end of the orchard at the back of Johns Farm, then I'd be safe. Mammy never crossed that point. When I got indoors I got hugs and kisses and even a plaster from Mrs Johns.

I loved getting a plaster. At home I got iodine. Mrs Johns has a big roll of plaster and cuts off a piece the right size for each cut. She saw my poorly lip before I remembered to suck it in. Ages ago, I told her about the strap that is kept in the scullery even though I know I shouldn't have. Once I showed her the kind of mark it can leave on the back of a leg. I got a second slice of cake that day.

She's called Poor Bridie Johns because she's had TWO husbands and they're BOTH dead and she can't *cook*, she could burn water. It would be nice to have her as my mother. Mrs Johns has only one child left because, like Mammy, two of her sons died as little boys, so she would have room for me. I could sleep in the Lower Room at Johns Farm, I'd be no trouble.

I imagine all four of the little baby boys flying about as angels in Heaven because THANK GOD they were all christened and didn't have to go to Limbo. I close my eyes and watch them roar about with their goldy angel wings, swooping around the chapel like swallows in spring and hovering at our backs when we stop to pray at the graves. Frances Rattigan, 23 March–30 April 1955; Declan Rattigan, 7 January–10 February 1964; Eugene Johns, 20 April 1953–7 September 1958; and Daniel Johns, 24 November 1956–21 November 1960. If I'm not careful I can think about the muck hitting their little eyes the same way it did when Daddy buried the kittens.

Mrs Johns plants a jokey kiss on both of my cut knees to make it really, really better so I wrap my arms around her neck and she hugs me back and says, what we need now is a treat!

Her last boy, John Johns, is the luckiest boy in the world. She thinks the sun rises and sets on him. He never takes his head out of his books. He's so bright, that John Johns, he's for college, says Mammy often, if only we could figure out where the brains came from. She'd also like to figure out where those long legs and fine shoulders came from when his *father*, Dan Johns, was nothing more than a drunken little squit!

– That's enough of that now, Sadie, in front of the waynes, says Daddy.

– They know well not to repeat what's said in this house, she always says, slamming the pan on to the range.

John Johns was in the same class as our Liam and they still pal together. John Johns doesn't say much. He's a boarder in Omagh so the few times he's been at home all I ever see of him is the door closing to the Upper Room where he sleeps. He obviously doesn't like little girls stealing his biscuits.

His eyes are black and bore into you and out the other side. I've only ever seen those eyes on one other man, says Mammy, and it wasn't on Dan Johns, No Siree Bob! John Johns knows not to cross the threshold at The Hill. He walks on past in his Christian Brothers uniform which makes Mammy spit on the ground.

Mrs Johns knows not to ask me about the lip. Instead we get chatty over a big mug of cocoa and a packet of Bourbons. Johns Farm is the same as The Hill in only one way: what happens inside it stays inside it. I ask her things about my Auntie Eileen because I know she'll never tell on me. What did she do that was so wrong in America? Is she really a T.R.A.M.P.? Can you have a T.R.A.M.P. as a relative or are they only for other people's families? Is Bernie really a sure sign of sin? Why did God give her a tongue too big for her mouth if He's so great?

Will Ireland ever really be free? Will we ever be a nation once again? Why is Mammy always cross? Are you supposed to hit children *every* time they do something wrong? Does Daddy speak when he's in Johns Farm? How bad is it that the priest has been sent for to tell Mammy off?

Mrs Johns says that Eileen is no worse than a lot of people. She says Bernie's an innocent unfortunate soul. She says that other people's families are not as much cop as they let on and she says don't fret so much, sure one day you'll grow up and Mammy can be as angry as she likes when her house is empty.

Maybe the priest will be able to make her see sense? He is the shepherd and we are the flock, even an ornery auld sheep like Sadie Rattigan has to be dipped once in a while! Oh, and I'm not to worry about Ireland, people who fight over a strip of bog are apt to fight about anything. She doesn't say whether Daddy talks or not. She says what everyone says about him: Frank Rattigan is a modest man. She whispers that there'll be other cats.

She would have *loved* to have a little girl like me, she says, just like me to the tips of my toes. She could eat me up and she wouldn't even need sugar! I love her saying stuff like that when she tucks me between her knees to fix my mad, bad hair into bows. I lean in to the homely smell of her as she gets the sections just right for plaits on either side.

I wonder, as I reach for another biscuit, would anyone even notice if I just stayed here safe and warm?

Mammy wasn't in the kitchen when I got back. The priest had been, the best china was still on the tray in the back scullery. My brothers had come back in and were sitting about like snared rabbits. We had no chicken dinner when Daddy finished his work and no Kathleen. He told us all to get to our beds after we had a bit of scone bread and tea. I must have slept because Mick had to wake me up to change his sheet.

Mammy was back in the kitchen in the morning making the porridge. She filled the six bowls for my father and brothers and looked right through me as if I wasn't there. Daddy pulled on his cap and stuck his pipe in his back teeth when he was full. He said nothing about my empty bowl. Auntie Eileen says he's easily led. It makes me think of the big auld bulls who have to walk after you when you pull the ring in their nose, they're not so big then.

Mammy hands out the packed lunches to the boys. I don't get any sandwiches either so I buckle my satchel and try not to run out the back door. The boys look scared. I thought Kathleen being sent away was the end of it but she's going to take another swipe at me. The priest must have really made her mad.

Mick's eyes fly wide open and even our Liam looks worried but he tells all the boys not to look when she pulls me back at

42

the last minute. They walk on with their heads down. She gets a good handful of my hair to march me into the hall.

Her special *Mother* plate with its gold-painted hearts is lying in pieces. How did it fall off its hook? She is picking up each one and reading the sacred words but only to herself. The *Mother* plate had come from Donegal, she'd bought it for herself on a day out: *To one who bears the sweetest name and adds a lustre to the same. Who shares my joys, who cheers when sad, the greatest friend I ever had. Long life to her, for there's no other can take the place of my dear Mother.*

I want to scream that I didn't break the plate, it wasn't me, it wasn't me! It's not the boys, boys don't touch plates, and Daddy moves so careful it can't be him, which only leaves Kathleen. She'd always hated washing it. This plate is a lie, she'd say.

The cuk, cuk, cuk, cuckaw of one of the laying hens makes me blink. I have a lesson to learn though I'm not sure what the lesson is. Don't cry? Don't bleed? Don't doubt I'm made of weak material? Don't forget I'm nothing. The next lesson will hit harder; my sister's a million miles away and even Auntie Eileen won't brave the back door for a while.

Mammy knows I'd rather have a hundred slaps and get it over with so instead she stays on her knees and smiles at me, the broken bits of *Mother* now all in one hand. She's talking low but I can hear her plain as day with my bat ears.

– You know I'll take this out of you in lumps, don't you, *Mary Moo*? You have my word on that, Yes Siree Bob!

I need to say it wasn't my fault. None of it was. I didn't break the plate. I didn't get the priest to come out to The Hill. I didn't mean to end up looking after Bernie, Auntie Eileen talked me into it with toffees. I didn't mean to make Daddy look like a

43

cissy. I didn't mean to gather up the little cats. My mouth is open but none of the words I need to save myself come out.

The first bit of plate flies past and tinkles against the hall wall just below the Sacred Heart. He died for my sins. I mustn't move, not yet. The second is a better shot. It slices my cheek. She smiles when she sees her handiwork. I wipe the blood away with the heel of my hand and run for the kitchen and the back door. But Mammy's too fast and she's on me before I can reach the latch. Her nails are just as sharp as I remember.

1982

THE SUN ON YOUR FACE

7

There are two great hours in the day. The first is the hour on the bus from Carncloon to school in Omagh when I watch the lush fields and the trees rolling past and I have the weight and warmth of Lizzie Magee slumped against me with her twin smells of greasy hair and too many sprays of Impulse. She is the dividing line between the strain of The Hill and a kind of giddy happiness that settles on me as soon as we click together. We are convent grammar girls and along with the Christian Brothers boys, the lucky ones, the 11+ passers. A good education is the sure door to the dream of living in England or America and no one ever misses a single long, hard day, despite how much we grizzle.

The other hour is the one at the end of the day when I have to wait for the workers' bus to get back out to The Hill. This is the hour I get to spend with *My Boyfriend*. Lizzie says it's enough to make her boke the way me and Joe Loughrey moon over each other. It's not normal for sixteen-year-olds to behave like auld wans, holding hands and a ton of other soppy goings-on.

– Hi, yous two! Get a stable!

Joe and me were used to the stable joke. Being called Mary and Joseph is far from unusual in Tyrone, but it isn't all that funny either when you're an item. As usual it's big Scrumptious Connolly who's shouting, he never knows when to quit. But he's like everyone else that goes to school with Joe and me, they know even at sixteen that we are really *something*. We go together, two halves of a biscuit sandwich. It makes my head swell and my heart sing to hear them all at us. We're the centre of attention, Doctor Loughrey's son and me.

He had picked me. ME! Every girl on legs fancied him but it was *me* he asked to go steady. It was the best minute I'd ever had, couldn't believe my luck. Joe Loughrey? And ME? He has relatives in America, more doctors who could sponsor him until he got his Green Card. He's just the ticket, Auntie Eileen winks, and I think my God, she's right, he can get me *out* of here.

What's wrong with us, the other wans want to know? Do we dream we won't get bored soon? Didn't Joe Loughrey ever think of going out with somebody else, somebody who didn't look like a white witch? Somebody whose granny didn't see dead people?

Joe only ever smiles and shakes his head as if they are all missing something but he's no intention of telling them what. Lizzie tells all interested parties to fuck right off, all the way off, it saves time in the long run. It's nobody's business but Mary's and she's not in the business of explaining herself, she says as snotty as she can manage. I don't know where she gets half the cheek she has. I'd love just a tiny slice of it. She's a great friend, the best.

– What are you doing hanging around with *that* wan?

48

- She's my friend, Mammy!
- Your friend? Your *friend*? Well! You're easily pleased, I'll give you that!
- She's my best friend, she said so!
- Did you have to pick one of the Dirty Magee breed? Did you? Did you?
- I like Lizzie Magee.
- You like Lizzie Magee! *You like Lizzie Magee*! Well, you'll live to regret liking Lizzie Magee, her mother's nothing but a T.R.A.M.P and her mother before that wasn't much better! And to cap it all she married into the Dirty Magee breed! But you carry on, carry on when the Virgin Mother Herself would look the other way!

That's a lot to absorb when you're only five and the first day of primary school's been over for ten minutes. It didn't sway me then and it doesn't sway me now. Lizzie Magee and me would never be prised apart. From the very minute she'd reached for my hand, I felt like I'd grown a second skin, one that was harder to bruise.

She was coming out of Crawford's with her two favourites – a Curly Wurly and a quarter of Fizzy Colas.

- See ye tomorrow, Lizzie, alright?
- See ye, Mary, don't do anything I wouldn't do, given half a chance!
- Funny!
- I'm hilarious, didn't ye ever notice? And fuckin' gorgeous to boot!

I smiled as all the wans lining the front of Crawford's cracked up. Even one of the young British Army soldiers was laughing along as he walked two by two, rifle across his chest. He wasn't

UDR – no green beret or gold harp pin. He'd likely learn soon enough not to think of us as just ordinary people.

I hope he understands that we aren't fighting over religion. We only use the labels of Catholic and Protestant to indicate minority and majority rights. Did he know that the English government that had sent him here didn't *want* the Six Counties, that the punchline to the big fat joke was that Dublin didn't *want* it either? I hope he doesn't take a bullet because he's as caught between the two as we all are.

Him and the rest of the troop were spinning and turning every few yards, trying to get back inside the big barracks before anything kicked off. The barracks with its massive square cast-concrete watchtower is opposite St Patrick's chapel spire, the two hives of activity like a set of tall-pillared gates to the Republic. What did the English boys make of 'the situation', stuck in all the little grey towns along the border? Carncloon looked grimy in the winter light: the main street missing a shop here and there where a bomb had gone off, grubby windows with drawn curtains or sheets of corrugated tin. Only the broken glass glittered where it had been swept into the gutters, blood diamonds.

The 11+ Protestants who went to the academy were hanging about outside Crawford's too. They wore their uniforms with the same pride. We are put on separate buses to get to our separate schools even though both the schools are in Omagh, but when we get back to Carncloon we all have to get the same bus out to the hills. Nobody dies. We're all friends anyway when the hay has to be got in.

We all have the same Christian God, hearts, lungs, spleens and animals to deal with. We just deal with them in separate churches, separate doctors' surgeries and separate vets'. We're told from the cradle that they're land-robbing bastards; they're told we are vermin who don't know when to stop breeding. They like marching about after bands playing 'The Sash My Father Wore' battered out on drums; we don't march about so much since Bloody Sunday. They drink in their own pubs on St Patrick's Day; we drink in ours and we largely stay indoors for the Orange Parades on the Twelfth of July so they can burn their Pope dollies and enjoy the heat from the flames licking their white gloves and bowler hats. It was a brilliant system right up until it totally broke down.

Joe and me walked away from the laughing and giggling and the odd whoop and whistle to the back of the Long Lounge. It had been firebombed a year ago; some people said it was an insurance job, others said it was an Ulster Defence Association job. The UDA was set up to battle the *disease* of Republicanism and operated under the banner of the Ulster Freedom Fighters when they had to carry out any violent acts.

– *We are not a disease*, says Mammy, don't you ever forget that, Mary Rattigan.

I just nod but I think to myself, you *are* a disease, a plague! It's how I test if she can still read my mind. I'm getting better: no slaps now for nearly a month.

The owner of the Long Lounge, Gerard Hickey, had hidden some IRA men one night after they made a hit on the barracks in Strabane and getting his pub burnt down was the payback. I was sad I hadn't got to see it in its heyday. Auntie Eileen says the craic was mighty when the band struck up and the tables were pushed back to give people space to shake a leg.

Mammy's battle for *us* over *them* bangs around The Hill all day; her dream of a united Ireland has been with me for as long

51

as I've had ears. Joe Loughrey can be like that when it comes to politics and I don't like it one bit that he reminds me of her in any way. He knows all about *our* side, why *we* all had to be on it and why it mattered – boys always did. We've stopped talking about the 'incidents' because otherwise we could get huffy with each other. Without Mammy to scare me, I'd argue that one of the sides had to stop their nonsense first and he'd just say, aye, aye, as long as it's the Loyalists. It always had to be *them* not *us* that got sense.

I smile and change the subject when Joe squares his Republican shoulders. I shut his mouth with kisses and don't bite his lip even though I dearly want to. Talking things out wasn't an option for either side; from the top to the bottom of both crews, some eejit would always rather plant a bomb or pull a trigger. It was the same for Joe and me: I held his tongue with mine to keep the peace.

I always got a packet of cherry drops as soon as we landed at Crawford's. I ran the sweets around and around my mouth when no one was looking. Lizzie knew what I did and she thought I really needed to catch myself on. I sucked in my lips and bit and licked them to make sure the cherry juice stained them perfect confectionery pink. I thought it made me look nice and that maybe Joe would think I always tasted like cherries.

The Long Lounge, wrecked as it was, was a top-notch kissing place and Joe and me had been using it for months. It's hidden from the main street and keeps the wind and the rain off us. Joe stands to one side to let me through the blackened frame like he's opening a door to a ballroom and I smile and bow as I go through and he grabs and tickles me from behind. I squeal and shout at him to stop but we both know I don't mean it for a second. It worries me how little I mean it.

I so loved being touched and held. My world and its bother fell away when I was locked against his chest. He was dark like me, but not so nearly black, and where my eyes were grey, his were blue. I'd never be able to give Joe Loughrey up. He would get me *out* of The Hill and *away* from Carncloon, away from the Troubles; him and a grammar-school education were the tickets I needed. It was like a winged dream I could hardly wait to fall dead asleep for.

We both knew he had a hard-on because it was held between us but we never let on it was there. I couldn't *stop* thinking about it but I couldn't *imagine* doing it. My face went on fire and I was convinced that everyone could see inside my head. Maybe even the nuns could see my unclean thoughts running about like Wile E. Coyote after Road Runner?

But more and more, even though I *knew* I was being bad, I wished Joe Loughrey would put his hands on me, anywhere, everywhere, all over me, inside me. If he ever pushed I would cave in. I was hollow from between my legs to my heart.

We knew what went where from the dismembered body parts in *Girls Growing Up* when Sister Dolores had braced herself to teach us about reproduction. The picture of the willy was just that: a side-view of a willy by itself on the page, not attached to a body. The outline was solid when it was hanging down but a series of dotted lines had been drawn to indicate how it would get up, so it looked for all the world like it was moving up and down like a pump handle. How do you get on it if it doesn't stay still? I whispered to Lizzie Magee who'd snorted so loud she was sent out to the Mother Superior's office to explain her 'bestial proclivities'.

The wombs floated on the page, the fallopian tubes keeping them aloft. The opening sported one down arrow that said 'vagina'. I just couldn't imagine it. The whole *act* seemed impossible. Mammy avoided all things below-waist. She had tutted when I got my period. I wasn't to complain as the Virgin Mother Herself would have had to tolerate 'monthlies' too. Oh, and I mustn't use too many sanitary towels, they were very expensive. Don't bleed on anything; a towel should be put down if I couldn't be sure. Don't tell another living soul: disgusting things are best kept to yourself.

Auntie Eileen had bought me a bra after she'd caught me squashing my new boobs down with my palms. The blinking things are going to grow anyway, she said, might as well enjoy them. Anyway it's *lovely* being a woman!

Mammy didn't think so. Women were not up to snuff, we were degenerate time bombs waiting to go off like Auntie Eileen had as soon as no one was watching. To lead Kathleen and me by example she kept herself braced. Monday to Saturday, she squeaked and creaked and strained at the sink, the cooker, the mangle as the very big bra, from shoulder to waist, and the very big girdle, from waist to mid-thigh, only allowed her to bend a certain painful amount in the middle. She was always rubbing her mid-section. She must have had welts as red as a bishop's cape.

For Sunday she had an even tighter set of pristine white underpinnings. She would appear with sweat on her lip, trying not to look as if she was being pounded in the stomach. Every day called for nylons, her American Tans. The fact that long dark hairs cowered inside them never bothered her because she was 'decent'.

Every month, one or other of the sets would be handwashed in Daz before anyone got up in the morning and pegged on the line inside a decent layer of tea towels and dishcloths in the summer. In the winter they were rolled in towels and coiled like a snake on the rack above the range.

Even kissing the most sought-after boy in town can't keep her and her madness away for longer than five minutes. Everything about her – everything she does, her smells, everything she says – makes me want to take off at such a pace that one day she'll go to hit me and all there will be is air.

8

After *hours* of analysis, me and Lizzie Magee admitted it seemed a very tricky business getting Body Part A into Body Part B without injury but she reckoned if *my* horrible mammy and *her* daft mammy had done it, we would be able to manage too as we were far smarter. It was hard to argue against that kind of logic. They had definitely managed it a few times. We were walking, talking, biscuit-eating proof of it and Lizzie was going to test her assumptions by allowing me to go first. She was too gracious.

She had big plans for my virginity during the school's retreat in April at Gortnahook. I didn't bother mentioning that I felt sick with nerves; she would have shot me down in flames. The nerves made me want to do it, the nerves made me not want to do it, I just wished it could be a bit less *mechanical*.

I wanted it to be romantic and floaty and painless. If it made you into a woman, it should be enjoyable? Afterwards, when Joe and his willy magically disappeared from the picture, Lizzie and me would compare notes on the event just as we had compared notes since we were five. We were best friends for a reason: she was forward, I was backward and we'd always known that about each other. I was the sheep to her Judas goat with my eye on her dainty little hooves always a step ahead of me on the mountain.

The same week we had our rubella booster jabs, the nuns wrote home about Gortnahook. Every Easter the convent sixth form was sent to the old monastery near Belfast for a week with the corresponding class from the Christian Brothers.

We would be thrown together for an 'exchange' and evidence that we were from the same species after all. We would 'discuss' whatever we want, as long as it's in line with everything we've ever been fed by said Church, society at large, the newspapers and our families who don't ever question anything they hear.

The rest of the weekend would be taken up by feeling embarrassed, the overwhelming desire to be anywhere but under the eyes of teachers playing trendy hymns on the guitar, *Kumbaya, my Lord, kumbaya*, sponsored walks in the rain or shine and long-boiled cabbage. Oh, and if Lizzie Magee gets her Easter wish, my deflowerment.

The Six Counties was boiling over. The IRA's Bobby Sands MP had starved himself to death in the May of 1981 and the other nine hunger strikers had followed him within months because they wanted to be documented as political prisoners.

We watched them on the TV, wandering around their prison cells like filthy beggars in dirty blankets. It was too sad to bear. They were someone's sons and brothers. As each one of them passed away Mammy crowed that it was another six feet of clay closer to freedom for *us*.

In common with towns across the Six Counties and indeed Europe, when Bobby Sands's death was announced, Carncloon erupted into rioting and hadn't stopped a year on. It was littered with rocks that bounced off the Saracens as they tried to pull into the barracks. Margaret Thatcher said his death was a choice that his *organisation* – the Irish Republican Army – did not allow to many of its victims. Crime is crime is crime, she said, it is not political. He was only twenty-seven and it took him sixty-six days to die. Sadie called down every curse she could think of to land on Maggie's iron head!

When the letter home said that the Troubles and our duty as *Catholic youth* would be high on the agenda, she refused to sign it. She did not want me out in the world debating the pros and cons or forming any alternative viewpoint. She tore it in two and put it on the fire with a pah! *I* was going nowhere without *her*.

When I had to explain myself to the Mother Superior, Sister Pious, I stammered through a too-long speech on how I was needed at home because there's always so much work on a farm. I watched as she wound a new piece of paper on to her type-writer to produce a special letter to make Mammy release me from The Hill. Sister Pious wrote that I was entering a very dif-ficult phase in my young life and this retreat was vital to my development.

– If your mother wants to *debate* this further, tell her that
    I've sent a copy to your parish priest, says Sister Pious.
This time, Mammy punched a hole in the paper over the 'i' in Sadie with the biro. She was livid and she didn't even know what was on Lizzie Magee's agenda.

With the signed release paper submitted, something shifted inside me. My head was light! I was getting five whole days OFF from The Hill! A door had opened, a door I could reach to get out of the kitchen. The reality was that men had starved themselves, that the Six Counties was being watched by the whole world, that we rarely made it through a week without running for cover. Yet all me and Lizzie Magee could think about was the fact that we'd be away from Carncloon and all this bloody nonsense TOGETHER for the first time ever and that Joe Loughrey would be there too. It seemed set down from God.

– It's way past time, Mary darlin'! What are you keeping it for? Next Easter?
– Lizzie! Jesus' sake. STOP, will ye? I'm scarlet!
– I can't stop! Every lad that looks at me is a minger and I'm not givin' mine up to a minger!
– What if I get pregnant?
– Oh what if, what if! I'll nick a rubber johnny from Dessie's stash. It's your one chance, Gortnahook; if you don't take it you'll be forced to give it up round the back of a cattle shed in the summer up by Brooky Hay. And SURELY you don't want to give it up standin' in cowshite?

She was right; she was always right, damn her hide. I definitely didn't want to give it up standing in cowshite.

Brooky Hay was a clump of sessile oaks that grew in a hollow and apart from all the other trees in the wood halfway between The Hill and Joe's house. We met there on a Saturday for a precious hour. I loved it; it was a different world. The bark on the trees was bumpy with silvery lichen and the gentle pale green slope all around it grew wild with sunshine-yellow dandelions and darker green ferns. No one could see us unless they marched all the way and stared into the dip. It was here, cocooned, that

Joe and me had managed to float the idea of taking kissing to a whole new level.

When it came to home time, we pulled apart. I hated the way the wind hit my front where the warmth of his body had been just seconds before.

– Alright?

– Alright.

– You were doin' some serious smilin' just then ...

– I've things on my mind, Joe Loughrey, funny business.

CHRIST! Why had I said that? I hadn't meant to say that! I was not bold! It had been weeks since we'd had the guts to refer to it. It had been born in Brooky Hay and that's where we'd left it.

– Is that so? And it's no time at all 'til Gortnahook ... just a few weeks.

He was thinking about it too! He was thinking about getting his Body Part A into my Body Part B. He said he wanted me and I wanted to be wanted. I couldn't have been happier if he'd pulled a box of Milk Tray out of his back pocket. We used the word 'love' instead of all the other words we knew for it. We'd try to make this love in a monastery with nuns and priests checking the perimeter. They'd set dogs on us, massive Alsatians like the army had, to run us down when we broke for the barbed wire. We must be out of our tiny minds but needs must where the Devil drives.

– We better go, I hear the bus. Father Yankee Pat is coming to tea.

– I'm not too keen on him ... or his son.

– Joe! He couldn't be John Johns's da; he's a *priest*, for God's sake!

60

We'd all heard the rumours over the years that he was meant to be Father Yankee Pat's son. Now the good Father had decided to come back from San Francisco to Carncloon to celebrate thirty years in the Church and so for the first time in a quarter of a century they could be compared side by side. The apple doesn't fall far from the tree, we say around here when we don't want to use the word 'bastard'.

– If he's not Father Yankee Pat's, whose is he?

– I don't know. Mammy's boiling over about it.

– Well, she hits the boil easy, doesn't she?

– Yeah, I suppose she does.

We both had to look away then. Joe couldn't bear talk of my mother or her methods. Her moods sat between us like a rotten egg that had to be handled with care in case it cracked and poisoned the day. He could never understand why I couldn't stand up for myself. Talk to her, he'd say. Tell her to back off. How could I explain how frightening she was, how much power she had, to a boy as *mollycoddled* as he was?

His parents were sickeningly sweet. His father said I should call him Dermot but I couldn't say Dermot if he paid me a million pounds. They called each other and Joe 'darling' and they couldn't get over the fact they were so chocolate-box perfect. I was all darlinged-out after an hour. Inside that house, he was someone's baby and I needed him to grow up and run away with me, as fast as his soft-lad feet could carry him.

The whole house was choked with air freshener. Mrs Loughrey went about from room to room spraying away any of the air we could breathe. She sighed a lot. She had a woman in twice a week to clean up and do the ironing. She had a job at the post office 'to pass the time'. Plenty of women would have liked that job 'to pay the bills'.

To me, a *home* was a version of Johns Farm. Bridie's little house is ancient, with long, low, thick walls made of granite blocks; the lintel over the half-door is granite too, a pinkish slab that was unearthed and left exposed where it gathers lichen. The walls are whitewashed and the roof is red tin. When I'm inside it, I feel I could sit out a hurricane. But I knew my life would be lived somewhere else, somewhere I won't be able to hear the rush of the Cloon River and its spinning gravel.

I'll miss it and Mrs Johns when I leave with Joe but I'll send her postcards and maybe even dollars to pay her back for all her kindness. I'll write interesting things about my marvellous set-up and if John Johns happens to see them he'll wish he'd spoken to me when he had the chance.

We'd just settled ourselves on the bus when John Johns sat down in the front seat so he could chat to Petey McGovern, the busman. He had been away in London working with our Liam on the building sites; they'd shared digs in Cricklewood then in Kilburn for a while but now they were both back. I was glad for Mrs Johns; she'd been in tears over a letter he'd written to say the woman he had fallen in love with had disappeared. This woman had been mentioned in several letters: the amazing Catherine who was all he had ever dreamt of, now he understood what it meant to have a soulmate.

Now, though, Catherine was *never* to be mentioned again; he did not want to hear her name. He would be home, he said, he'd stay home on that condition. It was just like him to insist on carrying the misery all alone, sobbed Mrs Johns. He'd always been wary of letting anyone get close and the very first time he'd let his guard down, he'd been gutted.

I was desperate to read that letter, to see written evidence of *soulmates* and *true love*, but she kept it balled up in her fist. What happened with this Catherine? What kind of a woman could steal John Johns's heart and then give it back? She'd have been a model or something, an actress maybe, someone with golden skin and *pure straight* golden hair? There's no cure for a broken heart, Mary, no cure, Mrs Johns said as she blows her nose and pockets the precious letter in her apron where I can never lay my hands on it.

Will my heart break if Joe Loughrey tires of me and my million excuses? I have to be home, no, that's not *another* bruise, I don't want your father to say *anything* to my father, I can't get out again this week, don't mark me. I was a litany of don'ts! He might think I'm not worth taking to America? He might not want to tangle with Sadie Rattigan for the rest of his life?

I look over at him and he's just a boy, a boy already flicking through one of his jotters to see what homework he has that night. I'm putting a lot of weight on those little shoulders but they're the only shoulders I have.

I look from him to John Johns's red lips pulled back in a smile at something Petey McGovern has said and I feel the blush burn my face before I even realise that I'm embarrassed. I'm roasting from top to tail! I don't know why just seeing him has such an effect – he's not even close, he's twenty seats away. After all he's just a man, as Tammy Wynette says, and she should know as she's on her fifth husband. Tammy doesn't get much further than the opening bar at The Hill. Mammy doesn't like the strains of THAT SINGING TRAMP infiltrating her clean kitchen.

John had started at the agricultural college Greenmount in Enniskillen a few days a week and Bridie was never done worrying about him travelling through checkpoints. The problem always was, and always would be, that he stuck out; it was impossible to miss him. He *looked* like a soldier, the kind of soldier who could lead rebels. Bridie swears he's not involved. He'd promised her years ago that he would never risk his life for Republicanism when he was all she had left. It seems almost impossible that little round Mrs Johns had produced such a handsome creature. He stands head and shoulders above the entire congregation at Sunday Mass and is stop-the-traffic gorgeous.

Like so many stories, the story of Bridie was handed down by Granda Ban. She had married a Thomas O'Neil when her mother finally died after being bedridden with a stroke for four years. Alas, Thomas O'Neil died after three years, leaving her childless. Then at thirty-eight she married Dan Johns in the rare year that he was sober and had buried her two sons from pneumonia not long before Dan fell off the long road home one cold winter night when he'd had too much whiskey. He was found dead in the ditch by morning. Granny Moo had seen Dan wave goodbye to her from the foot of the bed before the sun was up.

The young curate Father Pat O'Connell had started calling round as part of his priestly duties to check that Bridie was alright. Tongues had wagged as soon as she was spotted in the town, dry-eyed at last but definitely in trouble as her only coat strained at the buttons. But she was forgiven by all and sundry because she'd had *the good sense to suffer*!

First she did her duty by her mammy, then she lost two husbands plus two children, which all adds up to a get-out-of-jail-free card in Northern Ireland. When you suffer you can be tolerated even if you've broken every rule in the book and ripped it up and used it to light a fire. There's no fool like an old fool, says Mammy, who doesn't approve of Catholic women who lose Catholic husbands for any reason. It's slipshod.

When the bus stopped and John Johns and me stepped down into the dark damp of a country evening, I begged the grey sky above me to not let him speak but he did and I fell into the trap of trying to answer him.

– Hello, Mary.

– Hi, hi, I mean hello … J-J-John, I'm fine.

– Well now, thanks for letting me know.

Bloody Nora, what a gormless wreck! I hated how *young* he made me feel and me nearly a *woman*. I hung back to get out my torch to put some distance between us. The Hill is a mile from the crossroads and Johns Farm is a further two. There was one narrow road in and the same one out.

John Johns was ahead when a car stopped and asked me if I wanted a lift. It was none other than Father Pat O'Connell and even by the dim glow of the car light there could be no doubt whose daddy *he* was! I managed to say no even though a soft rain had started to drift in off the river. He drove on, slowed down to a stop when he passed John who had stepped on to the grass verge. He must have said no too as the car moved on, heading for The Hill.

– Why didn't you get in?

– My mammy says I'm not to take lifts off strange men!

Christ alive! Had I really just started a sentence, perhaps the first sentence I had ever spoken to John Johns, with the words

'My mammy says'? I was SIXTEEN! I was certainly more worldly than *her* already. She doesn't get invited to take tea in the doctor's house. She doesn't know other people's parents *speak*. She doesn't know such a thing as *smooching* exists. She doesn't know that some people actually *like* their children. John Johns just snorted at me because he can spot an idiot when he sees one.

A longed-for hole does not open up to swallow me and I have to trudge after him in the rain all the way home. My hair is soaked and clings coldly to my face but it's like watering a bush; tomorrow it'll be even thicker and harder to wrangle into a ponytail. The car is there, and the lights of the kitchen at the back and the Good Room at the front throw yellow squares around the darkening street. John takes his 'good-night' with him.

When I come in quietly and shake out my coat in the back hall, I can already hear my mother and her special priest voice booming from the passage between the Good Room and the kitchen. She is dressed in her pure-white linen apron that is kept for such occasions. It serves to make her look very clean and tidy even while it lets everyone know she is dressed in her work clothes because her work is never done.

Father Pat has his buttocks in the ordained wing chair. My father is wearing his Sunday shoes over his thick wool socks and hasn't managed to change his cowshit-spattered trousers. The brackish smell of them mixes with the dust heating on the plastic log fire. Matthew is also pinned on the sofa hoping to be rescued from providing conversation. How did Liam escape? She is making much of the fact that Mick is up at Queen's University, studying to be a vet, no less. The subtext is that two out of seven isn't bad although Mick and me have been warned silly books are a poor substitute for the Common Missal.

- And this is my *youngest*, Father! Mary! Say hello, Mary! *She's with the nuns!*
- Hello, Father!
- Hello, Mary, although I think we have already met!
- Mary! What? What was that, Father?
- Oh, I offered Mary a lift a minute ago but she very sensibly refused!
- Oh, right. Well, sit down, *Mary darlin'*! You must be frozen! It's a long day for them, Father, down at the grammar school but it's worth it! Education is easily carried, that's what I *always* say!

She backs out of the room so she can never be accused of showing her backside to a priest and we all wait for the sound of her tin biscuit box of doilies being taken out of the cupboard like the chalice from the tabernacle to know she's at a safe distance. With that, Father Pat O'Connell turns his attention to me. His face has a fair few liver spots like all the Irish I have met coming back from America but the black eyes don't give you much time to inspect the sun damage. He locks on and I have to answer up about my subjects, my hopes, my friends, their hopes, my response to the recent *bit of bother* in the town.

Some Loyalist men and some Nationalist men had resorted to the use of fists and feet when enough Guinness had been drunk on both sides and a Protestant had ended up with a bottle in his face. He was in a terrible state; he would be scarred and worse. There were fears for his eye. Father Pat O'Connell asks me to tell him what I think of these ongoing sectarian skirmishes. Don't stutter, I thought, please don't stutter, not now! Maybe both sides should try behaving themselves, I managed to stutter; we'd tried the auld bombs and intimidation and kneecapping and it wasn't going that well. I said we were being taken to Gortnahook to discuss just such incidents. I wished Joe Loughrey could hear me now! I wished he could see a worldly-wise man nodding his agreement with me! ME!

My father looked puzzled that I had an opinion and that I could voice it. I was quite surprised myself but Father Pat was so easy to talk to. I was *desperate* to impress him; he must have been powerful in the confessional. I would have told him anything just to keep his eyes on me. I kept jawing nervously and he kept nodding.

I put forward my theory that one of the sides would have to break first or the Six Counties would never change; even though I knew Mammy would be able to hear me, just having Father Pat in the room made me bold. I'd take the slap later.

    – That's very interesting, Mary. It's always good to feel the pulse of the youth at times like these. Of course, I know you're an exceptionally smart girl; I've heard a lot about you over the years.

    – Thank you, Father.

    – I must say, you're not what I expected.

And that's when I grasped what was going on. This was no visit to pander to my Mammy and her need to feed priests so that she could report it to all and sundry at Wednesday-night bingo. This was a visit set up by Bridie Johns, a revenge attack. I could imagine her taking him by the arm and dropping a few words in his ear. She would have gone too far; she would have risked being indiscreet about Sadie Rattigan and her idea of mothering. She might have told him about bruises and belts and welts.

I met his eye. He *knew*. He knew about the auld bitch; he knew what went on in this good Catholic house. He knew Daddy had no backbone. That was nearly the worst of it, seeing him there in his dirty work clothes while a priest observed him as the coward he was, married to the bully she was. Father Pat smiled beatifically at us all, waiting for my mother to bring the pot of good strong tea to the turkey shoot.

Despite several attempts, she could not get him to swallow a mouthful of cake. When she'd settled herself and explained how many eggs were in the perfect Victoria sponge she was slicing up – *six* – he treated us to a history lesson of his life in San Francisco. He worked with derelicts and drunks, men – and women, by God – who had lost sight of themselves and of the fact that God saw everything even without the cold light of day.

– People, good *Catholic* people, can put God and His wish
   for us to live kind lives to one side. God sees everything,
   every deed; He hears every word spoken in anger. I've seen
   women *abuse* their children, Sadie. Not a thing you would
   understand, eh?

– No, Father …

He waxed lyrical about the power of redemption, the desperate need for truth and confession and penance! She knew she was exposed and she kept a terrifying lipless smile glued on to try and hide the fact. Daddy bobbed like a noddy dog being driven too fast over ramps. Matthew picked at his ragnails.

Father Pat preached on about souls saved, souls lost, about beatings and cruelty, unkindnesses visited and revisited on the children of those who had strayed from the Christian path. He had seen children nearly starve to death in one of the richest countries in the world through the purest neglect.

– You wouldn't be able to conscience it, of course, Sadie! There's no shortage of food in this house, eh?

– No, Father.

– Ireland still has its deep Catholic faith, despite its troubles. Shall we pray before I go?

– Yes, Father.

We all bowed our heads then, and the smell of the strawberry jam and buttercream accompanied us for the rosary. She'd used too much vanilla essence to try and impress the Yankee and must be regretting it now that she'd been taken down by the horns and branded! He blessed us all when we'd hurtled through it like a train.

Daddy asked Father Pat would he say the 'Salve Regina' before he left? I was delighted that he had asked for *something* at last. He had been in my Uncle Peter's house for the Stations of the Cross when a car bomb had gone off. It killed a girl call Maeve McFadden; she was in Kathleen's class at school. Her hand had flown in through the window and hit the television set. Daddy saw it fly past and land on the carpet among the broken glass. It was sewed back on and they buried her in her wedding dress. He's been even quieter since then.

Kathleen says she'll never be able to put the tiniest pinprick of dark brown blood on the lace cuff out of her mind. Mammy doesn't care that the car bomb that took Maeve McFadden was the work of our very own IRA. It had gone off by mistake in a Catholic neighbourhood. Someone high up in the chain of command and probably sitting safely on his sofa had hired some boys to do a man's job, they drove over a ramp too fast and BANG, they never looked back or forward again.

When Father Pat finally got up to leave, Mammy didn't hang on his handshake for far too long as she usually would. He dipped his huge blunt fingers in the Holy Water fount in the back hall and made the sign of the cross on our foreheads. I waited for Mammy to sizzle but she didn't. She dropped an uneasy genuflect before she took her uneaten sponge back to the kitchen and set about cutting it up. Cake doesn't throw itself into Tupperware, y'know?

Daddy kicked off his shoes and pulled his wellies back on and preceded the good Father out, back to his cattle who wouldn't tax him. I did shake hands with my new favourite priest and he folded my hand in both of his. They were cool and warm and strong and a shiver ran up my spine and across my breasts as his fathomless black eyes bored into me.

   – I really hope to see you again, Mary! Keep at the books; *education is very easy carried*, after all!

   – Thank you, Father!

I had seen that lovely sarcastic smile on only one other face. And it was on the one other man around here who didn't abide hypocrites, a flower among cabbages, John Johns himself.

An hour with Pat O'Connell did me more good than a thousand of Joe Loughrey's kisses. I was *happy*! I had to work hard to squash a smirk which started in my toes. It was the endearing way he had kicked my mother in the teeth while he kept a steady hand on his cup and saucer. I wanted to share the joy of it with Matthew but he was blushing, growing more like Daddy every day. Something was wrong.

   – Liam went back to London this morning, he whispers looking upset, he says good luck with your exams.

Why couldn't Liam have said goodbye? I might not have cried. I might not have clung on and begged him not to go. I might not have told him I missed having a brother who was too big and strong to get hit. His loss wouldn't help Mammy's mood. She didn't like the thought of him thriving in England, it was a betrayal of all she held dear. Dominic had run to Dublin, Brendan had fled to America – all three of them were rats and each of their departures had made it harder for us ones left behind on the sinking ship.

I knew I'd better move quickly to see if she needed any help clearing up; she could blow at any minute. The cake had been dispatched and she was wrapping sandwiches in tinfoil. She saw me by the door and gave me a good eyeballing, trying to read if I had understood what had just gone on. I kept my face dead straight and she finally looked away. No slaps for a month and counting. She settled instead for the last word.

– What did I tell you, Mary Rattigan? Bridie Johns was nothing more than a T.R.A.M.P. in her day!

9

I only coped up at The Hill without Kathleen because I had Lizzie Magee and the precious few nights when I got to stay with her and her bonkers family. It only happened if there was a bomb scare that would keep the work bus out of town and I couldn't be picked up in the Austin Maxi because the roads were blocked with Saracens. Me and Lizzie were delighted by Unexpected Acts of Violence! I would *never* have been allowed otherwise.

Mrs Magee, Lizzie's mammy who said that I could call her Sheila, bought me a toothbrush and I couldn't have been more chuffed if she handed me the night sky and every star in it. Just seeing it in the mug in the bathroom swelled my heart.

Their house was *light* and not just because Sheila had painted nearly every wall a different shade of peach puke. I loved everything about them, from their shop-bought bread to their cheap lino that you weren't afraid to walk on because you knew it hadn't been washed in a month. We jumped on the sofa, we lay on the floor. We could watch cartoons and *Coronation Street* without even begging. It was heaven.

When Dessie came in from the garage he fell to smooching with Sheila right in front of us! I was always delighted when he had a word for me too. I soaked it up.

- And who's this? Eh? Is that Mary Rattigan, youngest contestant on the Miss Donegal parade? Is it? It's somebody bloody lovely lookin' anyways, that's all I have to say. Mind you, it's a bit like a beauty pageant every day in this house!
- Dessie Magee, you've all the charm of a snake, says Sheila with an eye-roll.

We all laughed like he was the funniest man on the planet. I dreaded the minute that always came when I had to leave them.

My mother had given them a strict list of all the things I was not to have: fizzy pop, baked beans, Fray Bentos, Vesta curries, Swiss rolls, biscuits, sweets, everything delicious and everything that they actually lived on. She had hoped it would put them off me, make me look fussy, but no, they rose to the challenge. Sheila did not invest in fresh vegetables, peas and chips came from the freezer, beans came from cans, cabbage was minging, Smash was the greatest thing ever invented, she was never going to wash or peel a spud again. She was sure nobody really *needed* carrots, fish was always fish fingers – only a lunatic would deal with bones when there was no need.

When Sheila made us baked beans on toast with cheese and brown sauce for tea – *for tea* – we'd break into our routine and try and get through it with straight faces. Dessie would take a big slurp of his lager, Sheila would slap him when he belched in pure badness and then he'd hold up a spoon of baked beans to begin.

- Now, Mary, what is this?
- Cabbage?

74

– Very good. Correct.

Sheila would point at the enormous white loaf that was more air than flour when it was her go.

– And what's this, Mary?

– Potatoes. Potatoes with butter and not margarine which will be the undoing of good Holy Catholic Ireland!

Afters was always a box of Quality Street. Sheila, Lizzie and me all fought over the hazelnut whirls but Dessie and Darragh would eat any of them 'til the box was empty and we all felt a bit sick.

We all understood it was a sin to encourage a child to lie to her mother but we weren't bothered. God didn't feature so heavily. He was there on the kitchen wall but He was sort of hidden by a big calendar from Dessie's garage which had a picture of a shire horse pulling a cart on it. *Magee's – where your car's the star*, it said. The Angelus bell tolling on the wireless at six in the evening had no effect on Sheila; she talked louder 'til it was over, gesturing this way and that with a fag held between chipped scarlet nails.

Once, Lizzie got her mammy to scrub her back in the bath – I nearly passed out! She was *naked* and her mammy could see her and her father didn't even bother to lift his face out of *Jackie* magazine even though he must have known. I suppose it was the only chance he had to ogle it in peace. They all behaved like it was *normal*. Lizzie called me Modest Mary and assured me my stupid auld hairy ha'penny was just the same as hers.

She had no shame but then this was a house where Dessie would often be seen sitting astride a chair stripped to the waist while Sheila tended to his back spots armed with a bottle of Dettol. In front of the waynes? Who didn't bat an eye? I was so mortified the first time I stumbled upon this level of intimacy my whole face, ears, neck and innocence went up in flames. I swear, you're more motor oil than man, Dessie Magee, she'd say and he'd nod to please her while he winked at me.

We were leaving on the Sunday for the retreat at Gortnahook and I was up at 6am. We were allowed to wear our own clothes when we got there and I wanted to pack mine fresh in the morning so they would be perfect. Lizzie and me had the five days planned. We were going to sit in the middle of the bus, away from the swots and the nuns at the front and away from the stupid loud girls at the back who would be drawing fire the whole way there from Sister Pious.

Lizzie was even more excited than I was, unhealthily so as she was further down the fingering stage than me. She'd had a handful in all so was a pro, I was a rookie, she reminded me daily. I, therefore, had to listen to my elders and betters because she knew what she was talking about. I was going to skip being a novice and go straight to the sisterhood. Time was precious, time away from home was priceless, I had to make the most of it. On my life, at sixteen, Lizzie Magee could actually make me blush *inside* as well as out.

The gardens were in the middle of the compound, the old monastery wrapped around it; we would sleep in one wing, the boys would sleep in the other. They were arriving the same day, on a different bus. They were on a different bus from the same town, and not because they were Protestants, just because they were boys. It made no sense when the nuns and brothers were going to mix us all together later that we couldn't be trusted to sit on a bus together beforehand. Lizzie and me laughed over that one, giddy as we were about what we were planning for the gardens. It was always 'we' even though 'I' was going to have to go it alone quite soon.

I still hadn't even tried to explain to her that I was panicking. It was a big step and the doctor's son might just decide that I wasn't worth the bother. I had been staring into the bathroom mirror every chance I could. I wasn't getting any better-looking. The black hair was too black, the white skin was too white, the grey eyes looked alarmed – I should do something about myself but I didn't know where to start. I wished I could put my head in a raffle box and pull out a better one.

Daddy dropped me down to the town to pick up the bus and all he said was 'watch yourself'. He headed off in the Austin Maxi to do the big circuit around the checkpoint and straight home. I kept my eye on him as long as I could but he didn't look back. One day, Daddy and me would be able to bowl along, windows wound down, loving the fresh smell of the green thorny hedgerows running riot with honeysuckle and foxgloves, nettles and briars, and we wouldn't have to slam to a stop because an armed soldier was standing in the middle of the road.

Daddy always gives the car registration number and shows his licence without a word while the soldiers wait with a roll of spike strip ready to throw across the road in case he drives off. He's like the wild birds who keep up their sweet song from the trees while the walkie-talkies hiss and click, untouched.

The bus as always smelt vaguely of sandwiches and wee and stale smoke. I was sitting framed by a big circle of clear window where I'd wiped and wiped with my glove to get rid of the sweaty condensation. I saw Joe getting out of his daddy's much nicer car. My heart flipped.

His daddy ruffled his hair and gave him a kiss. My stomach flipped, a cissy *in public*. For God's sake, couldn't they have got that mushy nonsense out of the way at home where no one but themselves would have to tolerate it? I waved just once and he gave me a funny little salute before he turned away with his smile and a blush to get on the bus set aside for the boys. He's alright, I told myself, he's just different like Lizzie Magee is different and I love her. Neither of them had been trained to walk to heel.

At the very last, Lizzie puffed aboard with a suitcase. What could she need with a suitcase? It travelled in front of her, part armour, part battering ram, until she got to me where she collapsed pink-faced and sweaty-haired.

– What's in the case?

– Mostly biscuits and other essential items!

We were still laughing at how mad in the head she was when I looked up and saw the convent's French *assistant* Jacques Bernier standing on the pavement staring straight at me before he started to make his way through the cars to get on with us. Lizzie Magee had been madly in love with him from day one. This would tip her over the edge.

– Jesus! Mary! Is that ... is that *him*?

– It certainly looks like *him*!

– Mary, this is set down from God! You won't be the *only* woman on the bus home!

Oh dear Christ alive. We were allowed to call him Jacques because he was only a few years older than us and was employed by the school in an exchange programme to help French teachers with their English accent and Irish teachers with their French accent. Lizzie fancied the pants off Jacques because he was a bit exotic, all long hair and bright clothes, the anti-Irish boy. He must have had twenty pairs of coloured socks; we'd never seen anything like it in our lives when he sat *on the desk* with his legs crossed. Yellow socks on a man, *trop chic*!

He could wear glasses and not look like a geek. He was so French he could gaze directly at a teenage girl for minutes without blinking which had us all in a state of total panic. You couldn't look away and you couldn't think of the words you needed for the two whole classes of French pronunciation and conversation on a Wednesday afternoon because he held your eyes with his big brown sleepy ones and as a result your brain turned to mush.

We heard him explain to Sister Pious that the PE teacher, Miss McElroy, was sick and he had been roped in to help supervise us for the week. Sister Pious did not look best pleased; she had needed big beefy Miss McElroy to help her herd thirty-five hormone-riddled eejits and now she had someone who would stoke those hormones to catastrophic levels.

Lizzie was speculating on the chances of her being taught French kissing from the horse's mouth. She always made such a *mess* of herself when he was around, it was excruciating. She couldn't understand that she looked like a fool, a fool with verbal diarrhoea. Like her, I really *did* fancy him but I denied it every time she questioned me. I crossed my heart and hoped to die that he did *nothing* for me. I had to put a lot of effort into not drooling over him; she would have thumped me or anyone else who got in her way.

Lizzie had opened the suitcase of dreams to bring forth a bagful of egg and onion sandwiches with cheap margarine on nasty sliced white bread, a packet of chocolate digestives and a pile of sweets: Crunchies for me and at least five or six Curly Wurlys for her. I had homemade bread with jam: dull.

  – Oh, Mary! I think I *actually* love Jacques! I can't stop thinking about him. Have I the skinniest, weeniest, teeniest of chances of pulling him before he disappears back to France?
  – Stranger things have happened.

I had to have the egg and onion in case Jacques suddenly saw sense or saw her with the light behind her and fell head over heels squealing her name and begging her to snog him! She couldn't risk having breath like a farmer when he *finally* came to his senses and leaned in.

The bus to Gortnahook took us from west to east through a series of small towns, most of which had at least one chapel, one church – usually Mr Paisley's Free Presbyterians of Ulster – and one barracks, all on A-roads. It nearly got stuck and had to reverse and turn, reverse and turn a few times. Each episode was an excuse for sitting up at the windows, pointing and waving at the locals and being annoying. Jacques stayed *très* calm throughout despite several attempts by the tenacious Lizzie Magee to engage him in conversation.

  – Sir, sir, Jacques, do you see we nearly crashed into that pub then, sir? Do you drive, sir, back in France, on the left like?
  – Jacques, what do you think of Ireland?
  – Sir, is there more than one word for green in French, sir? Or is it just plain *vert*?

Jacques never cracked, just stayed staring ahead at the forty shades of green hills. Sister Pious eventually told Lizzie to stop being so bold and to leave poor Mr Bernier alone.

  – Sorry, Sister, I just thought I'd work on my vocabulary!

Sister Pious pointed out that she knew very well what Lizzie was working on and told her there was to be no more attempted intercourse between her and Jacques. Which blatant bluff-calling shut even Lizzie Magee up. The rest of us sniggering on the sidelines followed suit. She slumped against me so she could sulk in comfort. We watched the grey April skies ripple and roll as the clouds raced each other to let go their soft rain. When I glanced back, Pious caught my eye and frowned. She'd warned me that Lizzie Magee was not the most suitable friend a girl like me could have, how I should make sure that I kept my mind on my studies as I was bright enough for As in nearly all my O levels.

What was a 'girl like me'? I tried to figure it out by staring at the back of Jacques's beautiful neck but he picked that instant to turn around and look directly at me. I wanted to scream and point and say I wasn't the one being bad but instead I blushed and he smiled a bit smug and turned around again. I could *not* wait to be grown up. Women don't get reddeners, and they only cry when they've had a drink.

The countryside rolled past us and I read the signs saying how close we were to Lough Neagh and every mile nearer to it was a mile further away from The Hill. I let my shoulders drop and smiled at myself in the glass of the bus windows. In Cookstown, we got stopped at a checkpoint; the army walked down the aisle of the bus with their guns on their hips. The Six Counties had been bombed from Armagh to Ballymena, Derry to Magherafelt and back, and everyone was twitchy. One of them had a tattoo of a flag on his forearm; it was blue and faded but must have meant something to him at some stage.

Around mid-morning the bus turned right for the signs pointing to the monastery and we all pushed our faces to the glass to

81

get a look. The driveway was tarmac and flanked on both sides with cypress trees which framed the main entrance, up a set of stairs. A priest waited to welcome us, his arms spread wide. We piled out and stood about waiting for instructions. He got as far as introducing himself as Father Kevin before Lizzie Magee took off with me in tow.

– Come on! This way, Mary!

We pelted for the stairs to cries of 'no running' with thirty-three other girls hot on our heels. We got a great room, at the front of the block and just a few feet away from the double doors. There was a single room between us and the stairs; Sister Pious would probably sleep in there or maybe one of the two Holy Joe local women who had been rustled up to help corral us.

We'd a sheet of paper with the retreat's events listed. Most of Sunday afternoon was eaten up with a lecture called *The Contemporaneity of the Bible*. It could be interesting as not a one of us had ever even *opened* the Bible. We only ever read what was in the Common Missal and that was only during Mass. Monday was a Mass with loads of readings and bidding prayers. Tuesday was the sponsored walk before a nice big dinner and then more late-night-vigil stuff in the chapel.

Wednesday was going to be set aside for the counsellors from Belfast who would want to know how we *felt* about Northern Ireland and all its woes while we listened to how they had been made homeless, intimidated and firebombed and then we were to write up what we thought of the show so far.

Thursday was miracle day when I would do IT with Joe Loughrey. After a big hike through the woods around the southern tip of Lough Neagh with the boys and their chaperones, we would stop for lunch, more prayers and talking in 'groups' – the word of the week. The groups would be mixed so we could hear what boys our own age, from the same religion, and the same class background for the most part, had to say about the Troubles and how they affected life in Carncloon, and what we had to say back. Fascinating stuff.

Then after dinner, when we'd settled the cons and cons of people blowing ten bags of shite out of each other on a daily basis for twenty years, we were going to have a sing-song. Hymns and popular folk songs as Father Kevin, apparently, was a dab hand on the guitar, a nun on piano and seventy highly bored teenagers trying to ignore that they were trapped in a version of every wedding they'd ever attended.

Dinner would be done and dusted by 6pm every day. Joe and me fixed on 10pm for our meet-up which we'd taken to calling a rendezvous for some strange reason. I suppose it sounded a bit more exotic. Two hours for everyone to settle down and stop acting the maggot. Another two hours to make sure the nuns and priests were done patrolling the corridors and checking the toilets before they risked boiling the milk for the cocoa and uncapping the sweet sherry.

I would go home on Good Friday as a woman. I beat down the desire to write that on the schedule – 10am: Mary Rattigan emerges from the dark side of her life and takes her seat on the bus. Her classmates notice she is different but not how. She sighs and shakes her head at their childish simplicity!

Lizzie and me unpacked. She had brought a red polka-dot gypsy dress and black plastic high heels even though we had been told to bring something 'modest and comfortable'. She had just hung it on a hanger at the back of the door when Sister Pious clocked it and said no chance, no way, under no circumstances was it to be worn inside the walls of a monastery! Had she anything else? If not, she was to stay in her school uniform. This was a retreat, not a *dis-co-theque*.

Lizzie burst into tears and locked herself in the bathroom. I had to talk to the door. She only opened it to quiz me on whether I'd thought any more about the practicalities of gettin' a ride?

- Lizzie! Jesus! How can you go from suicidal to saucy in thirty seconds?
- I'm a quick healer. Now, the path to the ha'penny must be clear to avoid any fumblin' ...
- Christ. I'm scarlet. I can't listen to this. And what *are* you talking about?
- You can't wear your knickers, you dafty! What'll you do with them?
- Lizzie! For Christ's sake. Will you *stop*?
- You have to plan it. God is in the detail.
- I swear to God, I'm gonna lump you one in a minute!
- You've not time to be abusin' me ... you need to decide if you're wearin' yer knickers or not for the romantic interlude of the week. Picture it now, folks: a boy, a girl, an open door?

Lizzie drew stars in the sky with her hands and then clutched her chest and fell down on the bed, sighing and writhing about shouting.

- Joe, Joe, me darlin', don't put your whole foot there, Joe, or at least take off your hobnailed wellies first!

I tickled her until we both nearly wet our pants and had to lie still in a mess of limbs 'til we got our breath back. At that second in time I'd have been hard-pushed to decide who I loved best in this world, Joe Loughrey or Lizzie Magee?

*

Lizzie Magee didn't let up for a minute the whole five days. When she wasn't discussing the finer points of me and *our* plan, she prowled the corridors looking for Jacques. Her 'love' knew no bounds and she lost at least two nights' sleep by sitting up at the windows to see if he would come outside for a fag and then she would pounce. He, in turn, was able to block out the space she took up when she was bobbing about in front of him. I had never seen someone so unmoved; it was as if she was speaking a foreign language even though we knew his English was perfect.

Where many a girl would wilt from the constant scorn, the remoter he became the more Lizzie clambered after him. Every time she went too far, it was *me* he looked at, *me* he seemed to blame for the fact that she had no shame. I blushed deeper and deeper and tried to drag her away. It would be easier to rip a bone from the teeth of a starved dog.

The week went in somehow between a shocking long Mass or three, several nerdy boys and girls crying and talking about the effect of having brothers in HM Prison Maze and such, cups of luke-warm tea and terrible bowls of roasting-hot vegetable soup. I talked to Joe a few times, enough time for us both to mumble something about Thursday night – I reckoned we'd both left it to the last night in case it was a disaster! Being away from Carncloon had made us shy; we were too exposed without the Long Lounge. With no one watching the clock we had no cut-off point.

Father Kevin took a fit of playing the Beatles on his guitar on the Thursday afternoon and the whole assembly snivelled along as he plucked and warbled his way through 'Yesterday' and 'Eleanor Rigby'. Why would an apparently jolly priest on such good terms with Good Holy God single out numbers *designed* to make us

85

cry? I *hated* sad songs. It took such an effort to hold tears *in*, anyone daring to force them *out* of you on a precious week off from The Hill should be shot.

When we were done drying our eyes, Father Kevin rounded us up like sheep. We had to hunker down in a circle of ten: five boys and five girls. Because we were hanging around each other Joe and me ended up in the same discussion group. Father Kevin wanted us to discuss a recent horror, what it meant to us, what it meant in the world, what it meant in terms of our faith. Two of the lay counsellors, one whose dog had been hanged by the UDR and one whose house had been torched, were on hand to tell us again about turning the other cheek when 'confronted with acts of terrorism'. There were no Protestant representatives to chat about any horrors they'd lived through. Maybe they were all busy?

A British soldier had just been sent to the Province; it was his first tour. He was young, only nineteen, and was earmarked for Carncloon on account of its hotspot Tyrone border-town reputation where IRA men could run for the Republican hills of Donegal and from the jurisdiction of the Crown in a matter of minutes. When the Chinook landed he had jumped up, straight into the blades which were still spinning to allow for a swift take-off. The top of his head was sliced away and he near bled to death with his kitbag still around his shoulder.

The sirens had got up and the ambulance rushed him to Omagh with an RUC escort at full pelt but he died just this side of Drumquin. The news had been everywhere within hours. We had to tell each other what it meant while we sat cross-legged on the floor like children. The bulk of us said it was sad, nobody deserved to die like that, we were sad he was young, sad for his poor mammy in England, sad for all the people who had seen it, sad for the fact we knew he wouldn't be the last. But Joe, *Joseph*, said something that blew a hole in the wall of high regard I had built around him.

– The Brits have no right to be here, Ireland should be united. He wouldn't have died if he hadn't been in the wrong place at the wrong time. It's all he deserved when he was coming here to help keep us down!

I don't know if he was trying to look smart or grown up or what, but by the time he realised he'd made a mistake it was too late to turn back. Father Kevin was a bit teary – and what of the sanctity of human life that Jesus teaches us? he asks. I couldn't speak. I couldn't look at Joe. I had cried over that story, cried more when Mammy had hooted as she read it out of the paper, delighted that they had lost one of *theirs* and one of *ours* hadn't even had to risk themselves. But Joe couldn't back down, he would lose face, and that face was working so hard to look macho and uncaring that it was ugly to me for the first time. His sneer was slipping and his ears were on fire but he held on to being smug even though a few pals were shouting at him for being such a DICK.

Father Kevin put a stop to it eventually and took Joe aside for a talking-to, calling in Sister Pious and one of the Belfast men as they withdrew to a side room. A few of the girls looked at me, *me*, and tutted and rolled their eyes in disgust before they turned to walk away. Why was it always my fault when someone else was being a dick? I only *loved* Joe Loughrey and Lizzie Magee, I didn't *operate* them! I wasn't their keeper! And then I was looking at Thursday night.

10

Lizzie reasoned that he had had some sort of conniption fit, brought on by all the blood running to his willy. I scolded her for making light of it and she backtracked with stories of how young lads get all wound up listening to the men at home and in the pubs and how they're apt to repeat stuff they've heard even if they don't mean it. I didn't like my voice, it sounded like Mammy.

– If you don't mean something, you shouldn't say it!

– He was showing off! Trying to look hard to impress you! He's never been a dick before! Come on!

– He doesn't know me too well if he thinks I'd be impressed by that bullshit talk. I hate all that 'us' and 'them' and who's to bloody blame. We have to live in the middle of it, do they ever think of that? I mean, for Christ's sake, when did somebody dying get funny or have I missed something?

– You haven't missed anything, but just *calm down*, Mary! Joe was just being a knob, he wouldn't have meant it.

– He's a tosspot!

– Aye, he is, but he's still *your* tosspot!

Damn her for making me smile. From the first moment I met her, she could crack me up. Everything about her is *warm*, from her red hair and rosy freckles to her huge brown eyes like Ginger Nuts. I loved being near her. She made me feel *coloured in*.

I saw Joe collecting his dinner later. He'd been crying, I could tell, even though he still had his Provo face on. To make up for the blotchy neck he carried his tray in one hand and kept the other one in his pocket, like he had a grenade in there and could throw it at any minute to set the whole of Ireland free. Bloody stupid little dickhead; if I wanted an idiot I'd get one anywhere. I expected more of him. He was supposed to be better than me and my weak material: a better class, a gamble worth taking.

It took Lizzie Magee nearly three hours to wear me down. She brushed my hair as she talked me into it. He was just flexing his political muscles, this was his first time away from home too. He was probably a nervous wreck at the thought of the night ahead. Sure he was only young, as young as us? He was just being a lad. With every repetition it seemed a lesser crime; she kept telling me I knew him, that I knew he wouldn't know how to be unkind, and I found myself nodding, yeah, yeah, he was a good boy with a good heart. He had been good enough to pick the likes of me, I should be grateful. And tonight was my first step towards America; we'd be bound together before we got to the boat.

I waited 'til nearly 11pm. I hoped he'd wait for me. I hoped he'd give up and go to bed. I hoped I wouldn't be sick with fear. Lizzie and me watched Sister Pious cast one last glance into each room. She was secure in the knowledge that, with her by the exit doors and the French *assistant* helping two Christian Brothers keep guard on the other side of the compound, all was well: our reputations would make it back to the countryside intact. Lizzie held out a cherry drop and I let her put it on my tongue like Holy Communion. She spun me round and kissed me on the back of the head and after a quick hug propelled me forward. I was instantly lonesome. She pulled me back and tucked the rubber johnny into my bra, choking on her giggles. I promised myself I'd get even one day.

I tiptoed past the closed door of the staffroom. There was a low murmur of contentment. They knew that boys and girls would always try to meet but for a start they were watching the well-known sly girls and had already put them at the end of the long corridor furthest away from the exit. Mhaire Doherty was one they had their eye on because they had already lost her big sister's virginity to a freshly ordained priest, one Father Martin O'Hara. As soon as the poor girl was pregnant, the Bishop suddenly decided that Father Martin O'Hara was urgently needed in the next parish along for a few months. Dymphna Doherty was left without so much as a blessing. When she wheeled her baby boy up to the convent to meet Mhaire, Sister Pious had sailed forth to shoo her back out of the school gates.

She could *not* be allowed to stand on Church land. She was a bad example, a reminder that you can't trust a young girl around a young priest. But Dymphna cracked and got her by the back of the neck and shoved her face into the pram! An indignant Pious had had to wrestle herself free, re-pin her habit and storm away without a word.

– He's just as good as you, better. He's innocent, just a wee
   babby, not all covered in sin. Where's his da? Eh? Where's
   Father Martin O'Hara? Where's the da, Sister Pious? The

boy could use a few auld nappies and such. Can you hear me? Where's the da? *Where's Father Martin O'Bloody-Hara now?*

I put the image of poor abandoned Dymphna out of my mind. Tonight was my night to fly. It was so beautiful: cool for April, dry, the air still sharp with cut grass like a hayfield only it was a lawn. I had on Lizzie's red gypsy dress and no knickers or shoes so that I could creep out and I felt fantastic. I was loose!

She'd done a great job on my hair; it hung down like *real* hair. The anger I had felt earlier was largely gone, leaving me tired, but I had been tired for as long as I could remember, tired and lonely. I wanted him again, I wanted to be touched, to be held, to be somebody's. My mother was miles across the country. I was free of her and The Hill and him, my modest father. I liked the taste it left in my mouth, my mouth that tasted of cherries.

Over the garden walls the tops of the cypress trees stood still against the light sky. There was a crescent moon. I had arranged to meet Joe just past the confines of the herb garden. There were some old table gravestones in an alcove on the back wall and the whole place couldn't be seen from any of the windows. A blind spot full of healing plants, ha ha ha.

Should you make jokes when you're about to throw away your virginity? Or when you wanted to punch your boyfriend in the teeth but you couldn't risk being like your mammy? Or when you felt so brittle you could break at any minute? Or when your heart was swelling because your mother was a coach trip away for the first time in sixteen years and couldn't hurt you?

I wished Daddy was beside me though he'd be unlikely to put his arm around me and tell me I was safe. He might manage another round of 'watch yourself, watch yourself'. It was the only advice he ever had. It was always said with concern, maybe even love if he knew what that was, but I'd lost count of the number of times I wished he'd do the watching. He was a hopeless guardian. I adored him all the same. He had shrunk a bit every time he lost one of the boys. Like me, he was probably as glad as he was sad that Matthew would never have the courage to escape.

I strolled across the edge of the lawn. I should have brought a cardigan but Lizzie said it would spoil my 'whole look'. I hardly ever wore dresses, Joe would be so surprised! I'd never had anything red before. Mammy said it was too flashy but it was absolutely my colour.

The chilly air felt good. Goosebumps raced up my bare arms. The tang of rosemary came above all the other herbs growing there along with lovage, which we had had in handfuls in the soup of the day and which we'd still be tasting at Christmas. I wanted to cry when it was the first time for ages I didn't feel sad.

I looked to see someone coming. He was strolling too. He had come. He had waited for me. I did love him, he did love me! We had loved each other for years, hadn't we?

– Joe! Joe, over here!

He came towards me and I nearly passed out. It was Jacques Bernier. I was in deep trouble.

– 'ello.

– Hello.

– Who is Joe? Your boyfriend, I think?

– Yes, no. He's more a friend really ...

– He must be a very good friend if you cannot wait to see him tomorrow, *non*?

– Yes, a very good friend. I'll just go back now ...

- It's okay. I found your Joe and locked him away! It's a beautiful night, don't you think?
- Yes, sir, and it's not even raining.
- *Non!* It is not even raining. Which is strange for Ireland. Such ugly weather and such beautiful girls. Is it the rain which made you so beautiful?
- I don't know. I better go in now before I get caught?
- You will not get caught. All the good sisters are asleep. A little too much sherry and other intoxications involving the company of Father Kevin. They all went off giggling like schoolgirls. You know all about giggling, don't you, Mary?

I was stuck. What could I say? He was laughing at me and teasing me at the same time. I felt like I didn't have a dress on at all, never mind no knickers. I shivered. I bet he would tell Pious. He was looking at the stars; there were fewer here than at home because of the light pollution from Belfast. I looked too, just to join in and try to feel like it was okay. He wouldn't know that they'd be reflected on the water of Lough Neagh, lying dark and vast close by. I hardly felt him move next to me. He backed me on to the cold slab.

- You are cold?
- I'm grand.
- Grand?
- Fine, you know, fine.
- Yes, very fine.

He was moving his arms from my hands up my bare arms to my shoulders and back again. I didn't breathe. He leaned in for a kiss and I just sat there. He lingered a few inches from my mouth so I kissed him. If he wanted to play games with me, fine, grand. I can play. He was a good kisser, a great kisser, but then so was I, I'd had years of practice.

He moved his hands back down my arms and kept moving 'til he had his hands on my knees, kissing me all the while, deeper and deeper. He stroked my thighs, higher and higher and then he reached my ... oh! He pulled back then and looked at me. His face was impossible to read; it wasn't shock or disgust. I'd totally taken him by surprise and I was delighted. He was firmly on the back foot!

His mouth was still open but he didn't need to speak; I knew how it seemed and strangely I didn't want him to stop. I wanted to be on *his* level, I was tired of being a little empty girl. I wanted to be exotic, I wanted to be louche. I wanted to be worldly. He smelt of cigarettes. He tasted of them, too. I'd put my tongue in his mouth and he suddenly didn't seem so far above me, *me*, Mary the weed!

I looked over at the boys' dorm but there was no one coming, there was no Joe, he was locked in. Jacques turned my face to his with one finger and kissed me again. He pushed my hip bones with his thumbs and I lay back on the cold granite.

What happened next cut me to the bone. He bent his head between my legs and started kissing me *there*. I tried not to make a sound. He was kissing me so softly, French kissing me, and I didn't even have to join in. This was NOT in the *Girls Growing Up* book! Sister Dolores had definitely NOT mentioned this kind of carry-on inside or outside holy matrimony! What chapter would it have been in? A clean mind in a clean body? Did I miss that class?

I felt a pulsing start in my legs, I thought it was because I'd held them rigid for so long but, when I looked down, my legs were actually flopped out to the sides and Jacques's head was still moving slowly over me. His hair tickled my stomach. I was lost. I felt something inside me break free and start to swirl and swirl. And then he was inside me. Just like that, no real pain, no fear and no way back.

He moved slowly at this too and after a while when he put his thumbs on me down there I crashed on to him like a wave while he cried out and threw his head back. I didn't make a sound. He wiped his mouth with the back of his hand and kissed me briefly on the lips before he rested his head on my breastbone. He seemed happy, content. I felt like I'd been handed a gift, a beautiful gift which even now was turning cold as it ran out of me. All the girls fancied Jacques Bernier but it was me, ME, who got him in the end!

I put my arms on his shoulders and moved him away. He zipped his trousers and lifted me on to the ground, light as a feather with a ton of guilt already starting to pull at my heart. I had just cheated on Joe Loughrey. I had replaced him in a heartbeat after years of longing. I was a T.R.A.M.P. after all.

Maybe it was because Jacques was more manly, someone who didn't give a fig for the Six Counties, the sickening see-saw of *them* and *us*? He was lighting a cigarette. He blew the smoke up and away but it blew back. His hair flickered around his face. He picked at a bit of loose tobacco which was on his tongue. His tongue, my tongue. My God. For a second that rush ran through me again. What had he *done* to me? I hugged myself tight and started to look around. How long had we been there? I couldn't grasp the time. I thought I might cry. But something between my legs was still happy, still open. I had been *touched*. I was a woman at last.

– Your boyfriend, 'e doesn't have to know, yes?

95

– Joe?

– Joe, yes. His loss is my gain, I think, Merise?

I wanted to run but women don't run so I walked away without even saying goodnight. I was already cheekier and it had only been minutes! Joe would never know. He hadn't made it to the gardens so he wouldn't know if I had been there or not. I'd say I'd set out and then got frightened. I hadn't waited long, it was cold. I knew somehow, *somehow* that he wasn't coming. I wouldn't tell a soul. Not even Lizzie Magee. Never.

She would kill me anyway; she would kill me just for *looking* at Jacques! She thought she loved him. Imagine what she would do if she knew I'd tasted his tobacco? Christ alive, she'd stone me in the street! I consoled myself with thoughts of secrets. I was an expert at secrets, even better than I was at kissing. I had been taught by the best. I was trained from the cradle to keep quiet. I would take it to my grave.

I closed the big monastery door on the night and felt the relative warmth of the old flagstones as I tiptoed back to my life. Lizzie Magee was asleep! Miracles do happen! She'd swore she'd stay up 'til I got back but she didn't stir even when I put the light out. I pulled off her red dress in the bathroom. The rubber johnny fell on the floor, intact. I put it in the bin. I wanted to wash myself. I looked in the mirror: my lips were swollen and I liked the look in my eyes. I wasn't totally ugly. I wasn't nothing any more.

I knew what the big fuss was about. I knew it didn't hurt and I knew that no one in my class would know that French boys liked to do kissing way south of the border, properly in bandit country! I didn't know anybody else who could dream about those things! I was clever now. I knew I'd never get caught. *Never.*

I wiped myself with a flannel; it was cold which I was glad for. I put my nightie on and slid into the bed. Under Lizzie's scrutiny I might have slipped up. She had a knack of rumbling me; she would know I'd been kissed but not *how* this time. I nestled down and waited for the warmth on her side of the bed to reach me.

Joe Loughrey would be none the wiser. He hadn't been in the right place at the right time, that was all. If he had been in the right place at the right time he could have had me for himself, we would have been united. I would have been his and he would have been mine but now it was too late.

I'd done it. I'd done it and got away with it. I was over the moon, I'd broken out, had slipped Mammy's net. I smiled in the dark 'til my cheeks ached. Auntie Eileen was right: it was *lovely* being a woman.

The next day it took Lizzie Magee nearly an hour to get rid of her rage at Joe Loughrey. He was useless, a waste of bloody space! I had been right all along; he *was* a tosspot, a wanker, a bollix! Did he not know how long *she* had planned this week. I shushed her and soothed her and told her it would be alright – there was plenty of time for me to dodge the virginity bullet. She would not promise to cross her heart and hope to die that she would not under any circumstances say anything to Joe about how LONG I had waited. So long *she* had fallen asleep! Oh, she was frothing at the mouth!

We both saw him at breakfast, all saucer eyes over the bowls of porridge, and he caught up with us as we set off to tidy our rooms.

– Mary! Mary!

– Wanker, tosspot, bollix!

– Yeah, thanks for that, Lizzie! Mary, *wait*!

– What is it, Joe? The bus is going to be here in a minute.

– I tried to get out but that French bloke got in the way! I waited, Mary, but he stayed out in the gardens! Did he see you?

– No, of course he didn't!

– We'll talk about this when we get home, aye?

– Aye, sure!

For him, home was a safe place: two darlings to dote on him in a rose-scented box. Memories reared up of Doctor Loughrey ruffling his hair like a pet dog. Joe got smaller in my eyes, and my heart ached. For the first time I could see past him but I still didn't want to; I wanted him to be my whole horizon because I needed to keep my eyes fixed on something.

I saw Jacques on the bus home. Instead of running his eyes all over me, he glued them to a spot just past my head. I didn't mind in the slightest. I drew a line under it and moved on. I could block things out as if they had never happened. I added Jacques and the cold granite, the sliver of moon and the smell of rosemary to my cache and threw away the key.

We were all subdued on the way back to Carncloon; we'd talked and talked and resolved nothing. Britain was at war with Argentina, we were part of Britain and we didn't want to be; our own little war was ticking away, like a bomb. Lizzie was gloomy that she had had five days to pull Jacques and failed. She snivelled the whole way home.

She was going to ask her mammy if she could have chips *and* spaghetti hoops *and* loads of ketchup for her tea in a desperate bid to cheer herself up. I watched her wander off to the housing estate, her red hair swinging from a ponytail making her look even more dejected.

Joe called Dermot Darling from the phone box to pick us up and take us back to the hills. He wanted to get us sweets to pass the time; I didn't want any. He wanted to step into the Long Lounge; I didn't want to. He wanted to know if I was alright; I wasn't but I told him I was. I was standing on the ground right beside him but with an army-issue riot shield between us. His questions bounced off me; I was untouched.

My heart was floating on a salty sea, burning and freezing by turns as it bobbed this way and that. I pulled back from Joe Loughrey and the more he whined the more I wanted to smack him. If only you hadn't taken your eye off me, I wanted to shout at him, I wouldn't have ruined myself in a minute.

For once Mammy and her temper proved useful. I said I knew I wouldn't be able to get out after nearly a week away from chores; I said I'd be under lock and key. I practically tied a bonnet on her head and gave her big eyes and big hairy paws all the better to batter me with. He nodded that he understood.

Dermot Darling finally eased his car over the ramps at the top of the town, all teeth that Joseph was back. He'd been missed; bungalow land just wasn't the same without him. Mrs Loughrey (*Mummy* Darling) had made a cake, a cake with chocolate sprinkles to welcome him home sweet home. When I was dropped on the street at The Hill, I stood and waved and waved 'til they were gone then I walked around to the back door and let myself in.

– Hello, Mammy …
– Oh, it's only *you*! Get changed into your work clothes now you're done gaddin' about! Spuds don't dig themselves, y'know?

11

Joe and me tried to talk about Gortnahook but both of us nearly passed out with embarrassment. He thought I was being cold because he hadn't made it into the gardens. I couldn't stand to talk about it because it made me feel like a bitch in heat who'd been locked in a shed and Joe couldn't win because he was the useless randy dog who failed to dig himself under the tin.

Poor Joe, who even though I said no, no, no, thought I hated him because he'd been a dose over the poor dead soldier. He was showing off. He hadn't meant to say that shitty thing about being in the wrong place at the wrong time. Father Kevin had insisted he make a confession and he had, he had made a heart-felt confession right there and then in the retreat and he had been forgiven for his malicious words. He'd done a fucking *ton* of penance! Why couldn't *I* forgive him?

I lied and swore that I did. When we tried to get the kissing back on track the taste of pineapple cubes on his tongue made me gag; it was too sweet. My tastes had changed. I craved bitter things and lied to myself about why I had a stash of them under the bed.

Lizzie Magee and the rest of the class were devastated when Jacques went back to France without so much as an *au revoir* a month before summer term ended. I wasn't bothered; I had enough on my plate with my nine O levels and the growing numb terror that not all of him was going home.

The fear grew with the sickness as I dashed for the loo before anyone was up in the morning. Back under the covers, I hoped against hope that the low dull ache in my guts was the start of a period but I knew it was just the fear growing eyes and legs and arms. My stomach was still as flat as a pancake and I thought I should be able to hide it 'til 'it' came out and then I'd leave 'it' somewhere. 'It' would not last long at The Hill. 'It' would need somewhere safe, somewhere where 'it' would be cuddled and cared for and told that 'it' was something.

The newspapers had stories of girls who had done that and not many of them bled to death although one of them had and the poor little baby had died of cold in a graveyard somewhere in the Republic. I vaguely thought that Auntie Eileen would take 'it'; she loved children but she couldn't get any more because men who liked the look of her didn't like the look of our poor Bernie. She could finally have a little girl who could talk! She would love that!

When I realised that I had allowed 'it' to turn into a girl I ran all the way out of The Hill and down the back lane, past Mrs Johns's half-door and all the way to the big pool of deep water where the Cloon arced towards town. I knelt on the bank and stuck my whole head under the icy rush to see if I could clear it. I needed to be able to *think* even if it was only for five minutes.

I was blue-lipped and shivering when I finally ran out of time and had to sit up gulping and gulping for air. That's when I saw

John Johns standing on the high ditch of the river field but he didn't move a muscle as I jumped up and nearly went arse over in the mud.

Should I say hello? Tell him not to worry? Tell him I'm not trying to do away with myself? Then I remember that he doesn't give a bucky for me or my troubles. He's known for being level-headed, a safe pair of hands. The man every other man calls on in an emergency. He's only ever going to think that I'm a half-wit, a halfwit who doesn't have enough sense to jump straight into the Cloon and float away as far as it flows before it's too late. If only he would say one word – just a 'hello' would take the sting out – but he doesn't.

My only option was to act as if nothing at all was strange. I stood a minute to squeeze the water from my hair, just a nice normal girl on a nice normal outing to cool herself down before slowly turning for home. Halfway up the field, the marsh mari-golds all sunny in their butter yellow, I checked if he was still there and he was, his big dark silent shape picked out against the thin blue sky, unmoved. I took off like a hare, any hope of a dignified retreat down the pan as I stumbled and scrambled away. I should have known I'd not be able to dodge Mrs Johns twice in a day. She was at the half-door begging me to come in.

I was soaked through and she was all fuss and bother, trying to find out what in *God's name* had happened to me at all! Had I been *interfered* with? Was there British Army about the place? RUC? God forbid, was it one of our *own*? The big brown teapot being slammed down on the range made me look up and meet her eye at last. I had no answers for her but when she stroked my face, I knew she knew but I knew she would never tell on me.

*

I studied and studied and studied; my head was crammed with words that outsang the whine of worry. I worked so hard that even Daddy noticed; he told Mammy he was going to take us to Bundoran the first Sunday after my last O level. A blast of sea air was just the ticket to put the roses back in my cheeks. He'd never taken in that I don't have roses in my cheeks and never would. It was a particularly lovely June; every tree seemed to swoon under the weight of its green leaves, every branch housed a songbird at the top of its game. The beach would be beautiful.

I showed up for every exam prepared, strangely calm and put down every word I knew on paper. As the last O level approached a feeling of panic had space to move into my head. How would I soothe my nerves when I could no longer study? I was forming a plan to talk to Auntie Eileen so that she could help me. In the wild event she wouldn't, I would get the bus to Derry and throw myself on Kathleen's mercy. Maybe Kathleen could hide 'it' in the nurses' home? Nurses loved babies, didn't they?

I broke up from school on Friday. Thirty-five of us covered in talc and eggs and marker pens rampaged through the corridors spraying Crazy String at the teachers. We fixed our ties around our heads and roared along with cassettes played too loud in the common room. Mr Spears, the science master, took a few snaps of us draped over each other and promised he'd have copies in September. You only get to be sixteen once in every lifetime, he says.

The drill for 'a nice day out at the seaside' was rise early, get to the first Mass in St Bede's, make enough ham sandwiches to withstand the next famine, half with mustard and half without, load the gas ring and gas tank into the boot where it slid dangerously around for the forty-mile trip because tea had to be freshly made if we ventured away from the range for a *whole day*. Mick agreed to come along but Matthew made noises about cows and feeding and slipped away without a word.

Mammy creaked into the front seat in her Sunday-best under-pinnings and we got in the back and off we set over the back roads through Pettigo, crossed the border at Belleek and on through Ballyshannon to the coast. The guilt and gloom lifted a little as the blue of the ocean came into view.

It was fine and warm, the light soft over the water. The beach was packed and the sweet smell of ice cream, toffee apples and candyfloss was burnt into the air. Mick and me ran off to the wee-smelling huts on the front to get on our cossies, leaving Mammy and Da to walk around the noise and promise of the penny arcades before we could get at the sandwiches. In the heat, the butter would have melted into the cottage-loaf bread and they would be the most delicious things we'd ever tasted after an hour in the freezing Atlantic.

When we were blue with cold we ran up the beach; we ran straight past them once and when we doubled back neither of us knew where to put ourselves or our eyes. My mother was in a bright yellow swimsuit which she had 'improved' by inserting a large red modesty panel to cover the line between her breasts. She started handing out the sandwiches as if nothing was amiss. Sadie could never be described as fat because she was solid; her flesh, even uncontained, did not wobble but she was substantial, tall for a woman, broad at the hip and shoulder, buxom, bun-ioned, absolutely not built for bright yellow.

Some young girls laughed and pointed and we all heard the words 'scary canary'. Slowly she covered her feet, then the terrible legs and finally her torso with a towel, which she tucked into the scarlet modesty panel to still it in the breeze. My father managed the word 'dodgems' and he and Mick showered us in sand as they legged it to the amusements. I sat burning beside her, letting my salty hair swing forward to cover my face so I could take her in.

Until that day her skin had been her arms from her elbows down and a small white V at the base of her throat. When I got to her face she was staring back just as hard. She held my eyes for an excruciating minute or two before they dropped to my chest and travelled on slowly, so, so slowly, to the chipped nail polish I had on my toes, a forgotten bit of fun at Lizzie Magee's. We were new to each other.

I waited for the insults to fly, the cry of how I would have to look about myself, the warning that Lizzie Magee was a menace, but no, all was silence bar the seagulls. Why wasn't she shouting?

That night I was putting my uniform away in a clothes bag to keep the moths off it 'til September when she stepped in and closed the door quietly behind her. I knew by the folding of her arms I'd been caught before she even opened her mouth.

– Well, Miss. Have you anything you want to tell me?
– No. Like what?
– Like what you've been up to? Have you been makin' free with that mollycoddled Joe Loughrey?
– It's nothing to do with Joe Loughrey!

That shut her up but she was calm, too calm. Maybe she didn't hit pregnant girls? But maybe she was only gathering steam.

– What do you mean, 'it'? So there is a baby on the way? You little T.R.A.M.P.! Can you imagine what your father will say?

Ah, the killer blow: wheel out the daddy and the terrible thought that *this* might be the thing that makes him speak. My face was on fire so I kept my head down and my hair over the whole sorry mess. I was exposed, I was a bad girl, I was going to break my father's heart. I had forgotten to watch myself. I had become a T.R.A.M.P. like Auntie Eileen, the original bolt of weak material. It was nothing to do with Joe Loughrey, although in that minute I had never missed him so much.

   — And what do you mean this has nothing to do with Joe Loughrey? I thought that was who you were steppin' out with? Who HAS it to do with, Mary Rattigan?

I would never tell her. I knew that I would never own anything again so completely and I didn't want to give it up.

   — No one, it was no one!

   — It had to be someone!? Did someone interfere with you? Mary, talk to me, did someone force you?

Mammy wasn't shouting now, she was whispering. Who did she think was going to overhear her? Good Holy God or His Virgin Mother? And did she just suggest that I *talk* to *her*? Now was not the best moment to fall down in hysterical laughter but I couldn't guarantee I'd be able to control myself.

   — Mary! Did someone make you *do something* against your will?

I thought briefly of how I'd felt myself take off courtesy of Jacques Bernier. How far away she had seemed. How the stars shone into my eyes and into my heart and how much I wanted to feel like that again and again and again.

   — No, I wasn't forced. And it was nothing to do with Joe Loughrey.

My mother breathed out and the air whistled slowly through her still-pursed lips. She was trying hard not to lash out and it was costing her. She couldn't believe how brazen I was, neither could I. I braced myself for the slap that would help her get her point across, but she was at the door before she turned.

   – We'll see about who owns it tomorrow when we take you
     to Doctor Brown.

He'd make no difference. He wouldn't be able to help me. And Joe's daddy worked in the same surgery; he would be bound to find out. I could feel the vomit rising to burn the back of my throat. Joe would kill me when the news got back to him. I should have kept him happy, should have kissed him again while I had the chance. And Lizzie Magee: she would definitely kill me for not telling her that I'd done it.

And Daddy? Oh Jesus, my daddy. Would he stick up for me? Would he be the man of the house at last? How could I explain to him that I had *handed* my mother another stick to beat him with? I hoped that he wouldn't cry anywhere where I might see him; my heart wouldn't take it.

I sobbed myself to sleep after that. I was glad for the first time ever that Kathleen was away in Derry so I didn't have to waste any energy trying to hold it in. I let it all out. Knowing that I'd let myself down, knowing that Lizzie Magee might bin me, knowing that Joe Loughrey would have to forgive me, having to face the consequences of one stupid night, not even a whole night. Twenty minutes? Thirty minutes? I didn't even know how long it took to *make love* – it couldn't be less than baking a sponge cake, surely?

12

Monday dawned with a brilliant-red sky. Daddy was a robot eating porridge. Mammy rubbed at her stomach where the kept-for-best underpinnings pinched her hard. Matthew looked from him to her to me and was finally told to get out and see to the beasts. *Your* father has to take *your* sister to Carncloon this morning, she spat, and I have to go too whether I like it or not. With that she took the mug of tea out of his hand and smashed it against the sink. I hardly moved but Matty and Daddy leapt out of their chairs as if they'd been whipped. They both looked at me for the first time that day.

Doctor Brown confirmed my worst fear and sealed my mother's loathing of female creatures: we all should be spayed. She asked him to repeat it twice and four times to tell no one and he nodded six times. I let out a giggle when he asked when I'd had my last *cycle*; it sounded so funny but Mammy fetched me a good hard wallop across the back of the head. I didn't laugh again.

I sat dumb while my mother talked dates, deliveries and vitamins. I was to take an iron tonic for the baby. There was no talk of where it would live when I had to go back to school. By what they were saying I would miss the first term when I should be starting my A levels which would be a disaster. I'd have three whole months to catch up on.

My father was waiting for us in the car park unaware of the news he was about to receive. I sat in the back seat looking at the necks of the two people who would hate me for the rest of my life and I burst into tears.

– What's wrong, girl? asks Daddy.

– Ha! Wait 'til we get home and you'll hear all about your *lovely* daughter! says Mammy.

And he did. Mammy made me stay in the kitchen while she explained that I was in the family way to someone who wasn't the doctor's son and someone I didn't care to name. She stoked the fire with her 'tramps' and her 'disgraces' but he didn't rise to it. He chewed the inside of his cheek.

– She's only sixteen.

– She might only be sixteen but she's only sixteen and carryin' a baby that's come from Good Holy God knows where! Pah! We'll have to get the priest. He'll find out soon enough! Do *the Dirty Magees* know?

– No. No one knows … Daddy?

– I've to see to the beasts, Mary. Do as your mother tells you.

He left us inside where we belonged, ashen-faced, for the outside where he belonged. He would probably have a toke or two on his pipe after news like that. It's not every day you find out that your daughter is a T.R.A.M.P. I just wanted to tell him I'd only done it once, just once, but then I'd have to say to my daddy I'd done it.

– Get to your room and don't come out of it unless you hear me say otherwise. You're not to even come down the stairs, d'y'hear me? You're not fit to stand in my kitchen!

I was formally sent for the next night. I was instructed to make myself look 'decent'. I didn't laugh. Daddy, as always, was already in the car waiting. He said nothing when I got in the back. The lush green hedges slid by, a few early lights glowed around the foot of Aghabovey, then we were under the steeple at St Bede's. We passed the big wooden cross that stood by the entrance to the graveyard. As we drew up outside the black and white parochial house I wished myself asleep again and alone on my side of the bed. A telling-off from Father O'Brien was all I needed. He was from the days when girls like me were disappeared to Dublin and the Magdalene Laundries and often never seen again.

The housekeeper, Mrs Byrne, opened the door and looked at us all like she'd found a dog turd on the step. She stood behind it for protection as she told us to go into the big sitting room at the front: Father would be with us in a moment. But within seconds I saw it was going to be much worse than a sermon from Father O'Brien. Joe was in the big sitting room and so were his parents. Seeing him there, I was suddenly overwhelmed by what I had thrown away; my key, my happy ending, thrown away with both hands.

I stumbled to the chair nearest the door. My face was mottled and so was his; he was hunched over, grinding his teeth to keep from crying, a picture of misery.

Our parents were going through the motions of greeting each other but Mammy was a bit bristly; thinking she had the doctor and his snooty working wife cornered, she tried to get the smug smile off her lips as Father O'Brien came in.

– Well now, well now, here we are, Doctor ...

– Father ...

– Frank, Sadie ...

– Father ...

– Mrs Loughrey ...

– Father ...

Oh, that didn't please my mother when Joe's mammy got a 'Mrs' and she just got plain old 'Sadie'! Joe and me didn't get a greeting of any kind.

– Well now, well now, this is a very sorry thing, a very sorry thing.

I must be the very sorry thing he was talking about; he was looking straight at me. I pressed my knees and ankles so tight together that I thought the bones would break through. Mrs Byrne wheeled in the hostess trolley and a fruitcake the size of a breeze block. It had a fish picked out in orange and lemon candied peel and a glacé-cherry eye. I was instantly back with Granda Ban at Macroom's wake: the salmon fisherman who had no option but to breathe in the river he loved. A cloud plump with rain settled over my heart.

Mrs Byrne took an age to pour milk first and add sugar to five sets of cups and saucers. Joe and me weren't going to get any kind of refreshment either, it seemed. God, she was really stringing it out, the horrible auld bag, hoping someone would break rank and start shouting.

With chinaware to civilise them they started. The good doctor wanted to know if I had been forced? Only he had discussed this with Joseph and Joseph had assured him that he had nothing to do with it? His good wife wanted to know if I was alright, sweetheart? She knew in her heart that Joseph Darling would not tell her a lie, isn't that so, Dermot Darling? The good priest wanted to know where the daddy was and my mother wanted to know why we all couldn't admit it was Joe so that we could be married off as soon as possible. My daddy didn't want to know anything. He kept both his eyeballs glued to the swirly carpet.

It all fell apart when the tea ran out and my mother made a jibe about Mrs Loughrey surely not being able to keep track of *her* children when she was gadding about in high heels and tights and *paint* behind the counter at the post office. Joe's mammy retaliated with details of how she only worked part-time, *part-time*, which left her ample hours to look after her family and Joseph and how dare my mother insinuate that she had taken her eye off the Catholic mothering ball!

It took the professional men in the room to keep them apart while my father stayed in his seat, a spectator. The parochial house was dripping with poison and Mrs Byrne was as happy as an apple-fed pig. It was Joe who restored peace. He was on his feet and shouting.

– I NEVER TOUCHED HER, OK? IT WASN'T ME! IT WASN'T ME! I never laid a hand on her, I swear on my life. It wasn't me.

When he had their attention and finally caught my eye he broke down and cried, a bubble of snot unnoticed at his nose. Mammy would call him a cissy and, may Good Holy God strike me where I sat, I would agree with her as the tears ran down his face. Could he not wait 'til he got home? Instead he stood and let his shoulders heave and we all had to sit and stare at him falling to pieces. When he finally realised that no one could rescue him, not even the Darlings, he turned his misery on me.

– I'll never forget what you did! Never! For as long as I live!

With that he ran, past me and away out of the front door. The cold air he let in brought the adults to their senses. Father O'Brien agreed that no more must be said about the matter: the Loughreys – *hugely* respected family that they were – were obviously not involved; my parents must come to some sort of decision on their own on what was the best way forward. I saw my father shake hands with the doctor; the women kept their fists in their laps.

– Frank, I don't know what to say, truly.

– No harm, no harm.

Daddy was already backing away, wanting to be outside. The priest asked me to stay behind as Mrs Loughrey's high heels clicked along the black and white tiles in the hall towards the front door and freedom. Dermot Darling and Mammy followed and Mrs Byrne wished them all safe home and God bless as the glee of seeing them all exposed warmed her through. She hated my mother; they had often battled over the flowers for the altar and now she would be able to arrange her sad dahlias without fear of intervention. Sadie Rattigan would be *banished* from the rota. When my shepherd and me were alone I got my little homily.

– Mary, if you were *complicit* in this – and it seems you were, it certainly is your intention to make us think that you were – then you will have to answer to God in this life and in the next. Do you understand what I'm trying to say to you, Mary?

– Yes, Father, I understand.

He was saying that it would have been more palatable all round if I'd been raped. I'd probably get off scot-free if I said I had been raped by a British Army soldier or, even worse, an RUC man. It would help everybody if I'd simply been blown to bits in a bomb. I was worn down from not ever being the right girl at the right time in the right place. I felt my temper rise, finally, finally it rose! I'd tell him what had happened. I'd make myself *right*.

– Would you hear my confession, Father? I want to confess.

– Of course, my child, kneel here.

He picked out his forgiving ribbon and placed it around his neck as he kissed the crucifix on his rosary beads and adjusted his buttocks so that he wasn't sitting on his balls. I saw him glance up at the clock. Mrs Byrne was frying him a nice bit of haddock and I was in danger of eating into his teatime.

– Bless me, Father, for I have sinned. It's been a month since my last confession.

– Go on, my child ...

– I'm worried, Father, worried about what I did.

– And why is that, Mary?

– Father, I do know who the father is. But I'm not sure if I should tell you; I'm not sure if I wouldn't be putting myself in more trouble with God?

– Speak freely, Mary, you have the secrecy of the confessional to protect you.

– It was Father Martin O'Hara, Father, but I hear he's been posted to another diocese now and surely he's not going to be *able* to marry me and make it better in the eyes of God? What do you suggest, Father? Father, are you alright? You're looking a bit green around the gills. Shall I get Mrs

Byrne? No? Tell me, Father, do you have a phone number or an address for Father Martin, at all? I'd love to let him know. He was always so *kind* to us girls.

I left with my absolution firmly in place and Father O'Brien's word that not only would he make sure that no one, *absolutely no one*, would ever be informed but that he would talk to my parents and try to make them understand that young girls are apt to have help when they make such big mistakes.

The look of dread I'd managed to nail on Father O'Brien's face and the way he placed me outside his front door like an incendiary device was all that was keeping me in one piece. I'd got the Salve Regina as part of my penance, my daddy's favourite. Tomorrow I would escape from the house and run all the way to Brooky Hay and I would run on to Joe's house. I would pound on the beige bungalow until I got in. I would have to find the words to explain that I wanted to be touched by someone other than him when I hardly understood it myself. I'd make him understand that I hadn't set out to get myself into trouble. I knew he'd forgive me; even Father O'Brien had forgiven me.

Tomorrow, I screamed silently, tomorrow I'll tell you *everything* and you'll come to see how it was. You'll come to see it was just a mistake, a silly mistake, I'd never do it again. Wait for me, wait for me and I will wait for you. Tomorrow, tomorrow, please wait for me to come tomorrow.

I didn't get out the next day because Mammy was on the warpath. Father O'Brien had been early that morning and managed to unhinge her unshakeable faith in the vengeance of the Church. She wouldn't have liked to hear that there are two sides to every story and that she might think of practising a bit of Christian forgiveness when it came to her poor besmirched daughter. I even heard her raise her voice, unheard-of behaviour in front of a priest.

— How? How EXACTLY would I do that, Father? How do I get over the fact that I've reared another Rattigan T.R.A.M.P. when I did everything in my power to keep her from harm? This would NOT have happened if she hadn't been sent home with a begging letter from that do-gooder Pious!

— Sadie, there is no evidence at all that this ... this *incident* happened at Gortnahook, no evidence at all!

— There'll be plenty of evidence in a few months' time! PLENTY!

It was to be a day of traumatic events. When she had cleared away Father O'Brien and his tea tray and custard creams, my father came crashing into the kitchen covered in blood. He had sliced through his hand with a scythe he had been sharpening and needed taking to the town or a doctor fetching. He stood with his arm in the air while Mammy tried to find tea towels she could bear to part with to stop him from ruining her clean lino.

I would have to run to Johns Farm and see if John Johns was there. And I did run, I ran as fast as my legs would carry me, taking no care, jumping and leaping over puddles and muck. Bridie was on the stoop with a cup of tea and she called out for John Johns to come quick. He dropped everything and came at once. I rode with him in the cab of the tractor and I kept slipping and sliding as we joggled up the long, bumpy lane. I had to touch his shoulder to steady myself; he was wearing a thin shirt and I could feel the heat of his skin through it and I pulled my hand back as if I'd been burned. He never opened his mouth and neither did I.

I was knocked up, alone, in the doghouse with both parents, and I was hard-pushed not to look at John Johns's red lips and the ridges of muscle running from the back of his neck to his shoulders. When we got back to the street, John revved up the Austin Maxi and got Daddy in and settled while Mammy roared at them to watch the good upholstery.

With the men away to the town there was no escaping Mammy who had recovered from the sight of Daddy's poorly hand as if it had never happened.

– What did you tell Father O'Brien? Hmmm? What? He showed up here today in a very different frame of mind. Did you spin him some sort of a sob story when you saw your chance?

– I told him nothing. There's nothing to tell.

With that, she finally hit the boil and was up and after me, swiping and swiping at me with a bloodied tea towel, when the front door knocked. I ran for the stairs while Mammy tore through the pantry to roar at the person to come round to the *back* door. It was Lizzie's mammy, Dirty Sheila Magee. Sheila wanted to know if I was alright, only Lizzie hadn't heard from me and they both knew how prone I was to bronchitis.

– She's grand. Just a chest infection so she's laid up and can't come down. Best she stays where she is 'til she gets better, don't you think?

– Aye, of course, but tell her we were askin' after her? Maybe she can come down and stay for a night when she's well?

– We'll see. Good day to you now, Mrs Magee.

Would the Magees want to see me when another few months had gone by? What would they do with my toothbrush? Would Dessie still think I was gorgeous?

I heard Daddy coming back with John Johns and unusually John came into the house. I don't think he'd been through the back door in the past five years, as men had their chats outside, leaning on gates. I heard all three of their voices speaking low in the kitchen. I wanted to know how Daddy was but I couldn't sit in the *same room* as John Johns. What if he guessed that I was in trouble? What if Bridie had broken the habit of a lifetime and dobbed me in?

They droned on and on, mostly my mother's voice and the sound of my father clearing his throat over and over again. John's voice was a rumble under the floorboards. Finally my mother made a sound which I had thought I wouldn't hear again for a while. She was laughing, the resentful cak, cak, cak like a machine gun beneath my feet.

By the by, John Johns left and when the phut-phut of the tractor engine faded a little I heard my mother on the phone, sounding altogether too cheerful. She never called anyone except Vi or Harriet and then only if someone had died violently. They loved a good wake. Ham sandwiches don't criticise themselves, y'know? The stairs creaked as Mammy made her way to me.

– Well, lady, I have news. Don't you want to know what it is?
– Yes, Mammy.
– Joe Loughrey has been sent away to his uncle in America, went this very happy mornin'. Your father just got it straight from the horse's mouth at the surgery. And as for you, you're to be married – this Saturday, in fact, which will give us just enough time to find some clothes to throw on you

and might even mask that you're way too far gone to be married in a chapel, but Father O'Brien is willing so why not? He's even going to skip the reading of the banns.

– What do you mean, he's away to America?

– Just that. The doctor and his perfect wife thought that he would be better away. A sure sign he's as guilty as sin! But no matter. Put Joe Loughrey out of your mind; he's obviously not thinkin' of doin' the *decent* thing and it'll be too late for you before he comes to his senses.

– How can I marry Joe Loughrey if he's already *gone*? Where's Daddy?

– Never mind *cryin'* for your daddy! Do you think he wants anything to do with *you*? You are gettin' married ... and this Saturday coming, no other day and no more delay.

– Who's going to marry me?

– Well now, the real boy next door, John Johns himself!

Ordinarily she would have stuck around to enjoy how flummoxed I was but she was too busy. Shotgun weddings don't arrange themselves, y'know?

Blood hammered at my ears and roared around my head, getting hotter and hotter with every circuit. Thoughts of Joe scalded, thoughts of John blistered; every member of my family floated by to drop burning embers on my skin. Even Bridie stood in the shadows with a branding iron. I thought I would melt from the heat.

John Johns had been called to kill a calf at The Hill a week ago. It had been born with its guts all outside its body. I wasn't supposed to see it but I couldn't stay away. She was beautiful, a roan heifer, her soft hooves destined never to harden. Her mother called out from where she was tied up in the next stall, swollen with milk that wouldn't stop coming. He stepped past her with his bolt gun and the poor little thing was dead in a minute. Was I nothing more than the next ruptured animal on his list?

I must have slept because I dreamt that I was running, running, running through a cut cornfield, the rough stalks scratching my legs. Someone or something was after me and I knew that if I turned to find out I would be wiped off the face of God's good green earth. When I finally stopped, gasping for breath and daring to look over my shoulder, a huge blade came spinning out of the dark and took the top of my skull off. The blood ran down my face and into my eyes; the metallic taste of it coated my tongue.

It had the feel of a dream that would stick with me for years and years. I woke up in a panic of being in the wrong place at the wrong time. I'd bit my lip and the tinny taste of blood pooled in my mouth, reminding me that it was no one's fault but mine that I had hurt myself again.

13

I was up sitting dry-eyed at my window by 6am after the longest Friday night of my life. I watched the light gather itself behind the three hills to the east. Muckle, Aghabovey and Sessiagh are smoky blue as the mist starts to lift. I chant the names and places, the ground I have been standing on for sixteen years, like a prayer. We are on top of Dergmoy and Glebe is to the left. The mighty River Cloon still runs down between us and forks at the point of the river field in Johns Farm before it flows steely and cold under the Castle Bridge in Carncloon ten miles away. Nothing's changed but everything is different.

The deep-scarlet sky fades to pink then to streaks of gold. Red sky in the morning, tramp's warning. The warning doesn't last long. After an hour all the pretty colours have been wiped out by the daily pigeon-grey sky that brings the promise of soft rain, the only constant in the churning of the days.

I see my father walk around the end of the barn on the way to his cows, his pipe already lit. He doesn't blink. What will he be thinking today?

I am thinking he will not rescue me but *I will be rescued.* Someone will come for me and pull me from this latest wave of Mammy's madness before I am washed away. I will them to come: Kathleen, Eileen, Bridie, Sheila, Kathleen, Eileen, Bridie, Sheila, Kathleen, Eileen, Bridie, Sheila. One of them will stop her with a silver bullet.

Out of the fog comes Father Pat O'Connell's face, the face of someone who has seen much worse things than an unmarried pregnant girl and who might be able to prevail upon my mother to just let me have the thing so I can give it to Auntie Eileen and get back to my A levels! But with his face comes the face of John Johns.

He was going to marry *me*? ME? A knocked-up girl he looked down on when there were a hundred women like moths smashing their faces against the light from his Tilley lamp and him oblivious to the stench of burning wings. He must have chosen to do this; Daddy would never have asked, Sadie neither. I realised it must have been Bridie; she must have begged him to step in for now to help the scandal blow over.

I would have to get to John Johns and talk sense to him. Didn't he understand that he was spoiling his own chances of a proper marriage? I could get married again if I abandoned my faith; I could cross over and turn to be a Protestant divorcee otherwise how would Joe and me manage when we made up?

No one came to rescue me. I hadn't really believed for a second that they would. I had already been dealt with. The decent thing was about to be done. I was only a prisoner 'til then. Then I would run. I would run from the chapel if I had to, oh Yes Siree Bob! Wouldn't that be a nice little bit of icing on the cake? After

Mammy had dropped the bomb of John Johns, I begged Mick to get Kathleen or Eileen. A red welt below his left eye let me know he'd been caught on the phone. My sister and my aunt came together on the Thursday night and battled through to my bedside. All three of us pretended we couldn't hear the abuse that trailed them up the stairs. I had been made by *them*, she roared, and now look at the mess I was in. Pah! I was their doing, not hers.

I don't know what I thought they would do or could do and they only had another whole day to do it in. But they were both too upset to think straight. They checked and double-checked that no rape had occurred, no drugging, no blackouts or other fits or seizures that might account for the fact that I had ruined myself. When they finally understood that I was to *blame*, that I'd been *awake*, that I was complicit, they had nothing to say, no words of comfort.

- What *possessed* you? Kathleen cries. Now you're never going to be able to leave this bloody place!
- Mary, I can't imagine what you were *thinking*, Eileen wails.

Why couldn't she, at least, understand that I *had* been thinking after a fashion. I'd been thinking this is the first chance I've had in sixteen years to do what I want. I'd been thinking I wanted to know what making love felt like. I'd been thinking that being joined to someone else would stop me from floating up out of my body. I'd been thinking that just for half an hour I could stop watching myself.

They had to leave me with no hugs, no kisses, no swearing, no boiled sweets, no reassurances that it would be alright, one day, with just one gift. Granda Ban had been told; he had nothing to say, no words of wisdom or condemnation, but he sent me Granny Moo's ancient brown handbag. When she was still with us, it was used to transport her unopened packet of linen handkerchiefs, her rosary beads and a bottle of smelling salts. Auntie Eileen and me managed a giggle over it. If one fails, try the other, she said before she set herself and Kathleen off crying again and they both had to run out. I'm left holding the bag 'til I feel a sort of tremor from it that would normally scare the bejesus out of me but which is oddly comforting as I let it travel through me, a sort of feathery hug from beyond the grave.

The ceremony had been set for 3pm to keep Mammy's dreaded gawkers to a minimum. My family were pinned behind their paper roses: white for the boys, red for the girls. Kathleen, Matthew and Mick were there but Liam, Brendan and Dominic weren't coming back. Auntie Vi and Auntie Harriet had shown up nice and early to enjoy Sadie's disgrace and were corralled in the Good Room.

Mammy had gone as far as Derry to get herself an outfit, braving the petrol bombs and rubber bullets, to secure enough polyester to cover her arse as the Mother of the Bride. I hear it rustling against her petticoat as she comes up the stairs.

- Why are you not dressed yet? It's nearly time.
- Are you going to make me go through with this?
- Yes, I am, no better woman for the job!
- I can't marry *John Johns*! We've not spoken more than two words to each other our whole lives.
- So? You should be grateful there's *anyone* willing to take you at all.

– But I'm only sixteen! Sixteen! I can't get married. Please, please, I'm begging you to see sense! I'll give it away! I'll give it to Eileen! Anything ...

I didn't think she'd slap me on this day. It would ruin the photos. I was wrong. Bam! I held my face; it was on fire. It was always worse when you didn't see it coming. Mentioning Auntie Eileen was like waving a red rag at a bull.

– Babies are from Good Holy God. Your father will do his duty today; he will walk you up the aisle, which is a lot better than throwing you out into the street where you belong, Mary Rattigan, do you understand me? You're getting off lightly. Now dry your eyes and get dressed.

I was to wear a pink suit. It was heavy wool, a box jacket would hide the bump, the skirt was knee-length. It had been bought in Harper's, the Protestant drapers in the town, so that no tales could be carried to Catholic neighbours. There was a pair of pink plastic shoes. The only white was the tights.

– Try your hardest to do something with that awful hair? Even *you* should make the effort to look nice on your wedding day!

The shoebox was on my lap. I pulled them out and put them on the bed. Wasn't that bad luck, new shoes on a bed? I dragged the tights on and over the tiny bump and got into the itchy, scratchy suit.

The track of my mother's fingers still showed on my cheek. In pure badness, I combed my awful hair into two high pigtails and tied them with big white bows so that everyone could enjoy them. White, pink, pink, white, different pink – that was better. If you can't wear pigtails on your wedding day when you're knocked up, lonely, broken-hearted and sixteen, when can you wear them? What was Joe Loughrey doing today, far, far away in the US of A?

I put on too much black eyeliner with a shaky hand, and a big slash of pink lipstick, and tried to ignore the fact that my chin wouldn't stop wobbling and no amount of swallowing hard helped. I hung at the door for a moment, both hands steadying me in the frame. The bed had a dent in it where I'd lain all morning. I couldn't wait to crawl back into it and pull the covers over my head. If the monsters can't see you, they can't steal you. The clock ticked. I had to go, ready or not.

The effect on Mammy was just what I wanted. She looked away in disgust and tutted as if to say let her have her snotty way just one more time and then we'll deal with her later. The effect on Daddy was not what I wanted. I still wanted him to love me, to look after me.

– Mary, he says flinching, I think that might be a bit much.

A bit much? A bit much? I was being married off to a man who barely acknowledged I was alive and who didn't even have anything to *do* with the bump, but black eyeliner and pigtails was a bit much?

– I don't think it is, Daddy, I think it's just fine.

He nodded and I knew then that I would go quietly, I'd never be bold enough to act the blackguard when Daddy was doing his duty. He'd not said a cross word to me. I couldn't hurt him again.

My heart lurched at the chapel where I had been christened, made my First Confession, First Holy Communion and my Confirmation. I had white dresses for all of them except this. My mother hooked my arm under my father's and stayed behind me to block the exit.

At the altar there was the shocking sight of John Johns in an immaculate suit and white shirt. I knew I'd never see a more beautiful man. Not a single thought showed on his face as he was presented with a pregnant tart in pigtails. He could hardly miss the welt on my cheek. He could have anyone he wanted, *anyone*; why had he hobbled himself for me? I'd never have took him for a man who would willingly enter into a farce. I stumbled but Daddy kept me on track and gave me away. It was his job.

Father O'Brien gathered us all together in the sight of God and all but galloped through the ceremony; there was no Mass, a first for me at weddings. It was only a few minutes before we arrived at the exchange of rings and I suddenly understood that this man, *this man* who was respected by the whole townland for his honesty and frankness, had gone somewhere and bought these two rings. He had carried them in his pocket for three days and he had allowed the lying, two-faced priest to bless them. Now he was going to swear in front of Good Holy God that he meant it all? He had never spoken to me.

I'd always known that Catholics had a gift for hypocrisy, I'd witnessed that first-hand, but this was breathtaking. In that moment, I hated him more than I had ever hated anyone, Mammy included. He hadn't asked how I felt about being handed on like a broodmare. He hadn't saved me; he had saddled me. I started to shake. Mammy's neck craned forward, Father O'Brien squeezed my shoulder. My palms were sweaty. John's fingers were cool and dry as he cupped my hand to pass me the ring. I pushed it on; it was a perfect fit. The gold band he'd bought for me was too big.

A huge sigh went up after as my mouth said "til death do us part.' I hadn't kicked, screamed or bitten and now I was right again in God's eyes and so everyone relaxed before they were herded out and into the parish hall by my mother to have a sandwich tea.

The parish hall was bare apart from a long table hung with a brown gingham cloth. The sandwiches all had lettuce, even the tinned salmon. A tower of butterfly cakes quivered in the cold. The faded brown velvet curtains on the empty stage were tied back with a tasselled brown rope so we could enjoy the single vase of cheerless flowers standing there. Mrs Byrne got the party started by cranking up the urn and trying not to look like she'd die of happiness.

Auntie Eileen's eyes were glazed open and her smile was nailed on; Bernie looked upset, ever sensitive to moods. Kathleen stuck close to both of them. John Johns went over to talk to them and Bernie flung her arms around him. He hugged her back and kissed the top of her head. If she but knew it, she had just outstripped every woman in the room except me. My hideous aunts told me how lucky I was to land such a handsome man. Somehow I had become someone who other people patted. You look lovely, grand, pat, pat, pat.

A photograph was taken of the whole group, then one of me and him standing side by side, close enough to have our wedding suits touch, one of me and him with Bridie between us, but when it came to me and him and Mammy and Daddy, I walked away and sat down. Bernie jumped up and got into the photo so for evermore, amen, Mammy would have a shot of herself looking at Bernie in total disgust. John linked arms with her and told the photographer to go ahead. Bernie beamed her biggest smile and Eileen finally laughed.

Alright? says Mick. 'Alright' didn't really touch it. Poor Mick! This awful afternoon wasn't good for his nerves. I hated that I had upset him. He was holding a cup on a saucer like it was a chalice.

– Don't cry, Mary. Please, for God's sake, don't cry.

– How am I goin' to get out of this, Mick? How?

– This'll blow over. John Johns is a decent fellah to do this. At least it'll get you out of the doghouse now that you're legal and all?

– As long as I can get back to school, I don't care so much!

– Ah, Mary! You always did love the auld books!

Mick was trying to wipe a load of black eyeliner off me when John Johns came over. He's my husband, I thought to myself, but I'm not his wife, not now, not ever, so help me Good Holy God and His Virgin Mother.

– We'd better make a move. There's a ceilidh here tonight.

Soon people would be dancing through this cold empty place and I would be at home, confined to my room for months: no Lizzie Magee, no Joe Loughrey, no school books. The party was dissolving as quickly as it had been forced together. Auntie Eileen had already taken Bernie outside, first time either of them had left a party willingly. My sister's eyes begged me not to say good-bye, as if I would ever have found the strength. My father checked his watch: the cows would be waiting for him at the hill gate.

Poor Bridie was standing alone wringing her hands. She looked ridiculous in a big navy-blue lacy hat that she'd bought or borrowed for the occasion and her broken down-at-heel Sunday shoes. It had made my mother tut loudly. She herself had on a much more fetching green felt hat with a jaunty feather tucked into its darker-green ribbon.

Father O'Brien was walking around with his arms wide as if he was nailed on an imaginary crucifix, but really he was just herding us all out of his parish hall and away back to our lives. His duty was done, Father Martin O'Hara had been successfully painted out of the picture, and he wanted us gone before the fiddle and tin-whistle players showed up to get the craic started.

There was a kerfuffle at the cars. I had turned to get into Daddy's car only to be intercepted by Mammy who hissed at me to get sense, what was I doing with everyone *watching*? Trying to make eejits out of us all? She pointed at a blue car that John must have borrowed to make it nicer for his mother.

— You get in with Bridie, says John Johns.

— That's right, darlin' girl, you pop in here beside me. There now, there now.

She put her hand over mine and we were driven away like we were the happy couple and he was the chauffeur. I looked back to see if I could see Mammy and Daddy or any of the boys following. The house would be locked in case the UDR paid a visit and I didn't want to be stuck out on the street. The same trees counted me home too fast but John Johns didn't stop when we got to The Hill. He was driving me down and down into Johns Farm. The potholes juggled us this way and that. I started to panic.

— Stop! Let me out here. I don't want to have to walk back. Stop, stop, stop.

I pulled at his shoulder, even though I never wanted to touch him. He didn't even turn round, just changed down through the gears to keep the car from crashing into the wall by the orchard at Johns Farm, his knuckles white on the wheel.

— Oh, Mary, sure you're to live with *us* now. You have *to live* with your husband, that's how it works!

130

– No. No. No, that's not what's going on, Mrs Johns. This was just for show. I'm not really going to live down here. Please stop!

We were on the street at Johns Farm. It was two miles to get home and I was wearing stupid plastic slippers. I thought I was going to be sick.

– Please can you take me home? I didn't know I wasn't going home. Please? Please? Please take me home!

He didn't answer me but got out of the car and took an overnight bag that I recognised as Kathleen's out of the boot and walked past me into the house. Bridie was crying; her auld dog, Brandy, was whining and jumping around her feet. I saw the Tilley lamp come on in the kitchen. The weak yellow light hit the ground outside where the three of us stood in various states of distress. The big clump of leafy sycamores by the entrance to the river field were dark against the dusk sky and one small blackbird belted out its cheery song. Two miles away, my bed with its blankets and sheets that smelt like me was empty. It didn't have me hiding in it. I didn't have it to keep the monsters away.

By the time I walked to the half-door, John Johns had taken off his suit jacket and was unbuttoning his shirt cuffs. I was struck by how big he was in the little kitchen, how very tall. He didn't speak but the set of his mouth said it all: he was far from happy with what he'd taken on. My bed called out to me, the only spot in the whole of The Hill where I'd felt safe.

– Are you going to take me home? Please? Please can I go home now?

– You *are* home.

He walked away from me to the Lower Room, carrying Kathleen's bag. I looked at Bridie; she was still crying. She tried to pull herself together.

– You see, darlin', your mother had it all arranged. The few things you'll need tonight are in the bag; John picked it up on the way to the chapel. She knew you wouldn't have thought of it, don't you see?

I tasted the vomit before it reached my mouth, just making it to the side of the house, where it sprayed all over one of the rose bushes. As I wiped my lips, John walked out and past us, dressed for the feeding. A farmer's work is never done. I saw the disgust on his face.

– She's in the Lower Room, he said to his mother who nodded.

– Come on, sweetheart, come inside and I'll get you a cup of tea? How's that, eh? A nice cup of tea to heat your stomach? I was as sick as a dog every day I was expectin'. Come in, come in, sit down and I'll get the fire up to boil the kettle.

I was shepherded inside and made to sit on the old sofa which was parked in front of the range. I had always loved this house but now its four walls tilted towards me, crushing me into the leather. Bridie banged about, shovelling coal and wood and rising smoke. I was home, for better or worse, in sickness and in health. A wave of the purest hatred rose up inside me for my mother. For my father I had a deep well of disappointment. They had washed their hands of me. They had sold me down the river and the bump with me. I drank the tea that appeared in my hand. Bridie had put a spoonful of sugar in it and she was right: it did heat my stomach. I felt it travel through me, warming as it went.

I had become someone's wife. I had left home without even knowing it. Joe Loughrey had abandoned me and I couldn't even hate him for it when it was my own fault. Kathleen and Eileen must have known but they hadn't understood that I could be this dense with all my book learning. I was home – but only for tonight. One night only was all I would give to this sham; tomorrow I was going back to The Hill. Mammy couldn't make my life any more unpleasant than it already was.

I'd always wanted to get away from The Hill but now I'm not ready. I want to be just along the hall from my brothers. Who was going to make Matthew milky tea when he was sad? Who was going to look after Mick if not me? I hadn't said goodbye; I hadn't told them to watch themselves. I'd be good; I'd not be seen or heard for all the months it took the bump to go away if Daddy would give me another chance, just one.

Daddy wouldn't stand for me being left down here to rot. I would promise him that I wouldn't be seen or heard and this time, *this time* he would stand his ground. After all, he was the man of the house. Mary's come home, he'd say. I'd hide behind his back while she banged the frying pan on the range in fury at his impudence. This is where she belongs, he'd say, and that would be the end of it. I'd be home and he'd look after me; he wouldn't let her hurt me any more. Mary is not to be hit again, he'd say. Mary's been hit enough. Yes, yes, Daddy would make it better. I'd get through that first night on my sliver of hope that I would step back into my life one day.

The Lower Room was what would be the living room in a normal house, the Good Room, like the Good Room where we kept the framed reminders of our sacraments at home. It had a flowery sofa, covered in huge burgundy flowers, a sort of rose or

133

peony maybe, and it smelt damp. There was also a brown leather chair that was a match for the sofa in the kitchen, but which had split open to show its horsehair stuffing, and a heavy wooden wardrobe with an oval mirror running the full length of it. The walls were painted brown to waist height, cream on top.

The ceiling was painted wooden boards that might have been white at some stage but were now faded to grey with smoke stains. Several large holes told the truth that there were rats living up there. There were windows at either side of the room, one looking out to the orchard at the back, one looking on to the street. The back window had a rose bush growing too close and the thorns hit the pane and screeched and scratched when the wind blew. As I stood there, a fall of soft rain started a gentle drum on the red tin roof.

On the back wall, a makeshift bed had been set up. It was behind a clothes horse that had an old cream blanket edged with blue hung over it. The bed was just a base; it would seem that John Johns had made it from rough wood he must have had lying around the place. The fact that he had *prepared* for me made me rage inside. Who makes a bed before speaking to the bride? The mattress was brand new, covered with linen sheets folded neatly back. A stained feather pillow in striped black and brown was sticking out of the clean pillowcase. There were at least three blankets on it and one of Bridie's quilts.

John had made the bed very high. I had to climb on to it and when I settled myself my legs dangled over the edge in their stupid pink plastic shoes. I was too lonely to cry. The holdall had my toothbrush, a nightie, a facecloth and a bar of Camay soap from the set of three that Mammy had got from Auntie Vi the previous Christmas. I was spoilt.

My eyes were dry balls as I stared into the darkness settling around me. Now and then I switched on the torch that Bridie gave me, in case I needed to 'go out' in the night to the dreaded Tin House. But she had also told me to 'go easy on the torch because batteries were very dear'. Good Christ, I couldn't be expected to live in a house with no running water, no toilet that wasn't a walk away in the dark and no electric light? Home had had plenty wrong with it but at least had those!

I'd give my mother such a piece of my mind when I went back to The Hill. I didn't care how much I would have to pay for it, how many slaps I would have to take for my own good. When I lay down in my wedding suit and pulled the blankets over my head I could still hear the deft clip of the rats' nails.

14

I felt ridiculous when I finally walked into the kitchen the next morning still dressed like a French Fancy. John Johns wasn't there, thank God. Bridie was bustling about asking me if I'd slept alright and saying that I mustn't worry. Everything would be grand given enough time. Sit down and she'd get me a cup of tea. Would I take a drop scone? A pancake? Don't worry, they're *not* home-made! Would I like an egg? No, I wouldn't like an egg.

– Mrs Johns, I need to borrow some shoes to go home in.

– Oh, there's no need, Mary, your father'll be along today. And for heaven's sake call me Bridie!

– Oh, well, that's okay then …

– Yes, yes, that's okay. D'you know, I think I will make you that egg anyway, you *must* be starvin'.

I was starving. I ate the egg after I'd picked a fleck of blood out of it, and two slices of shop bread with a big mug of tea, and I felt better. It's hard to beat a boilie was one of Auntie Eileen's favourite jokes. I must wash my face before Daddy comes to get me. Bridie is pottering about, washing up her few auld cups and such, so I wait for him outside in the scent from Bridie's much-tended roses.

The countryside is so beautiful viewed from the stoop at Johns Farm. From the river valley I can see the purple hills of Shanagh Bog which wraps around the middle of Aghabovey, the roundest of the five hills. To the left of the bog are the swathes of pines planted by the Forestry Commission. Combover Hill is art, the Forestry only planted half of it, and the border is a widely exaggerated 'S' shape that sweeps its dense green in a wave to meet the purple bog and the rushes on the other side. It's called Comber Forest but it's been Combover as long as I can remember. Its light and dark emeralds sit at a respectful distance from the hill field which is behind the red of the roofs on the milk house and the big two-storey barn where the hay is kept.

The other two-storey barn is attached to the house and it's where the cows are wintered – as a result the cow muck has to be wheelbarrowed to the midden past the front door, not something which helps the smells about the place. All of the buildings and the little house have been whitewashed recently; some of the whitewash still speckles the grass along the edges. The river carries the sounds of other lives from the road which is two fields from the far bank. In the soft light of morning it looks benign, even homely.

He comes about midday. I hear the noise of the tractor on the lane and Brandy barking right up until he recognises who it is. Will I be in trouble if I get any grease or dirt on the pink suit? Daddy's tractor isn't the cleanest and Mammy always wants to keep things good or to pass them on with some strange alteration. She might even have plans to take it back to Harper's and get her money back? She'd like that, sticking it to a Protestant business. I suppose Daddy's thought of it and he'll have a bag or old coat for me to sit on.

I'm already outside when he arrives, waving and waving like I haven't seen him in a lifetime. I'm showing far too many teeth but I can't stop. He waves back, just the once, and looks away as he turns round on the narrow street. I'm just about to tell him that I'm ready, so Bridie won't start fussing and making tea, when I see he has a suitcase with him. It's an ancient brown leather thing that's been sitting around the house for years.

– Frank, will you take tea?
– No thanks, Bridie, I must be getting on. I've a lot of ground to cover today.
– Daddy? What's in the case?
– Did yous hear the terrible news from last night?
– No, Frank, what happened?
– Daddy? What's in the case?
– Podgie McCourt's son is dead, shot through the head in front of his mother!
– Oh, God save us! God save us all! Mind, he was often warned not to sell *An Phoblacht*, but Lord alive, his poor family!

They both try to ignore the fact that despite Sean McCourt's execution I've started crying again … for myself. We all know what's in the case. My stupid life, or what's left of it.

– Daddy?
– I must be going, Mary.

He swings himself into the tractor and fires it up and I feel a kind of river running through my head. I'm so tired. I run to him and start to plead.

– Please, Daddy! Take me home, please. I want to go home. Daddy, please, please don't leave me here, please don't do this, please stop, please stop …

Then he looks at me, crying and begging and trying to stay his arm. We've been here before. We've been here before and we probably both thought that that was the worst thing that could ever take place between us. We only recovered because we pretended that it didn't happen. We never mentioned it again. The wet little bodies of the kittens were still lying between us. How heavy they had been when they were dead! Twice the weight of when they were skipping about. But now we were standing over something that could never be forgotten. There wasn't a carpet big enough to sweep this under.

– Mary, don't take on … this is the way it has to be!

– You lousy bastard. You rotten lousy *cowardly* bastard! I hate you for this! I hate you! And I hate you for the last time, too! I'll never forgive you, never!

– You'd better run on, Frank, you can do no good here, says Bridie.

– Aye, run on, Frank, run, run, run, run! It's all you've ever done!

I don't know how I got the words out. I felt like someone had tied a rope around my neck and was pulling, pulling, pulling. He gripped his pipe tight in his teeth as he slammed the tractor door shut and started back up the hill. Bridie helps me off my knees. She manhandles me into the Lower Room and lifts my legs off the floor. I sleep but today is not a good day to sleep because I am already dog-tired. Today is the kind of day when bad dreams just let themselves in and smash the one or two good memories you have hidden to smithereens.

*

When I jolted awake later that afternoon the suitcase was standing by my bed. I'd never had a suitcase before. I'd never been anywhere except Gortnahook. I had to open it. Inside was my toiletry bag and my clothes in their various shades of navy and white. I took them all out and put them on the bed. There was a brand-new towel, bath-size, and two brand-new flannels. What a treat! I put my unopened Camay soap on top of them and my toothbrush. Blue Ted was lying face down in the bottom.

I dearly wanted to scrub myself clean but there was no running water at Johns Farm, and no bath. How would I wash? Where would I launder my clothes? What would I do with myself all day without school for a *whole* term? How would I read a book in a house with no electricity?

I stripped off and changed into my jeans, a T-shirt and boots. An ex-bride, I balled up the itchy pink suit and the stupid pink slippers and wrapped the white tights round them to make sure they'd never escape, then I closed the case and slid it under the bed. I hung up my things on the wire hangers in the wardrobe and shoved Blue Ted to the back of the shelf. Unless he had a ticket to America stitched inside his belly, he'd be no use to me in the days to come.

Joe hadn't even tried to find me. How did he feel knowing that I had been with someone else, someone that I had to admit didn't force me? How had I gone from being *his* back to being nothing so quickly?

Bridie was waiting for me, wringing her hands, just outside the door. She was still crying. What a sweetheart! I had so often thought it would be *lovely* to have a mammy like her and now I did. I hugged her close and told her that it would all be okay.

Not to cry. I called her Bridie to her face for the first time. Bridie, put the kettle on and make us both a nice cup of good strong tea.

She was right: I would be grand, given time. I knew I had to be punished. Tramps have to pay. Auntie Eileen was still paying. I could go home sometime, not like Sean McCourt who only sold a Gaelic newspaper, the printed voice of Sinn Féin. He was never going home. Try as I might, I still felt sorrier for myself than him. I was a hateful girl.

Bridie must have sent word with Daddy that she needed a lift to the wake and by the by Auntie Eileen trundled down the hill and on to the street. We made tea and none of us mentioned yesterday's wedding, the bump, the fact that I had a face the size of a football, that I had left home without even knowing it. I wanted to bring all of those things out and lay them on the table right beside the biscuits but I was too ashamed. I hoped Daddy wouldn't tell his sister what I'd roared after him. I hoped nobody would ever be told that I'd behaved so badly on the day another family would be waking their murdered son.

They were discussing the horror ahead of them. Bridie was worried she wouldn't be able to look his poor mother in the face. She was bringing four rounds of ham sandwiches: good ham off the bone not washings. Auntie Eileen had two dozen scones, a box of teabags and an emergency bottle of Lourdes water. They were part of the advance army of women who would show up to try and console Mrs McCourt. The remains were being released from Omagh Hospital to O'Carolan and would be back in the front room by night-time.

As they wittered on about washing teacups and boiling water, Auntie Eileen asked if I was alright and I said, yeah, I'm grand

and she seemed pleased enough though I'd never seen such a strained smile. She hates wakes, especially the wakes of young men. She wants no reminding of her lost husband, Nicky D'Angelo. She still longs for him. She's always been furious that there was hardly a mark on him after he crashed his motorbike. He looked as if he was sleeping. His lips still sang to her. His eyes shone behind the dead lids. She won't have that problem tonight. The violence that has taken Sean McCourt will be on full display.

It was a given that I would not be going with them. I was to be hidden away, me and my bump of shame. I was too scared to go anyway, afraid of what I might have to see and hear.

They were gone for hours, hours I spent watching the dust motes spin in the last of the light from the kitchen window. That's how John Johns found me when he came home, staring into the middle distance. Bridie had left his dinner in the oven – brown fish and spuds. I was to fetch it out and put it on the table for him and not to forget the butter from the cold press and the coleslaw. Only the coleslaw wasn't burnt. When he ducked to get in through the door he looked put out, like he had forgotten that I now occupied the Lower Room. We stared at each other, perfect strangers. We didn't even manage a hello.

He sat down at the table, leaving his long legs stretched into the room. As he reached down to the enamel bucket for a mug of water, I got his dinner and put it on the oilcloth in front of him. He looked at it and then back at me and I'd no idea what to do next. A giddy part of me wanted to say bon appétit just for a laugh but I wasn't sure what would happen if I dared to open my mouth. Something was bubbling inside. Instead I stood there twisting the tea towel around and around my fists, astonished that the thousand songbirds in the trees outside hadn't held their beaks to hear what our first conversation would be.

He kept his eyes down and I held my breath. We needed to know where the border was drawn between what had happened and how it was going to be now that we found ourselves stuck in the same spill of treacle. He finally looked my way – what did he see? A girl left alone to keep house – his house – but he couldn't stop himself for long from looking at the bump. The bump was always going to be hard to negotiate. He cleared his throat and asked if there was any butter. It was such a polite request, softly made. I'd forgotten it! If I'd committed such a crime at The Hill I'd likely have a clout round the ear by now. I should have tried harder on the first day of being someone's wife.

The reality that he could ask me to fetch and carry for him just like I'd been made to fetch and carry for *her* all my life made me bold. I didn't have much more to lose by letting him see he hadn't got a bargain.

- I'm not going to be your wife! I'm not, you can't make me do anything I don't want to do, you can't. If you come any- where near me, I'll tell Daddy ... or ... or ... Eileen or the priest! I will!
- I have no intention of coming anywhere near you! You're hardly more than a child! Anyway, I'm not in the market for a wife. My mother's fond of you – you'll be company for her when I'm out and a bit of help around the place. So you need have no fears, *Mary darlin'*; as of this minute, you've never been safer! I have no interest whatsoever in you, although it's nearly funny you're so ready to defend your honour? Shame you weren't so sensible with Doctor Loughrey's boy?

Why did he have to mention Joe? Why did he drag him into the room and remind me that I'd thrown away my chance of being free of Carncloon one day? Why had I been foolish enough to forget that Joe was the best match I could ever hope for? I imagined him being pushed on to the aeroplane by Dr and Mrs Darling, protesting, begging to be allowed to come home and hear me out. He said he loved me and I still believed he was telling the truth as I stood crying in front of my brand-spanking-new husband.

– You can't speak to me like that! You don't know what went on between Joe and me, you don't know, *you* could never understand ... anything!

– I don't want to know! I *never* want to know. I don't want to *hear* from you. I don't want to *see* you more than is absolutely necessary to keep Bridie happy. I don't *care* what you think of me, Mary. I don't care what any single idiot from Carncloon thinks. What you have to realise is that it's done. You and me are done, *a done deal.*

With that he barged past me, got the butter out and cut great slices of it to try and make his dinner easier to eat. I didn't like the way he was clenching his jaw. I ran to the Lower Room and sat on the torn horsehair chair shaking like a leaf. I thought he was supposed to be a quiet man? Seems he had plenty to say when he was in a mood. I shouldn't have pushed him because now I knew he hated me.

I had been right. I was little more than a bauble for his mother. As long as I gave him no trouble, we would get along just fine. I would stay down here, untouched, and he would stay in the Upper Room, untouched. The problem was that we had to stay together.

Of course, he didn't want me! *Me?* He never could have wanted me in a million years. His soul still ached for the golden Catherine. I was just a stupid lacklustre girl and he would never have to stoop to wanting a stupid lacklustre girl. My vanity embarrassed me. I'd never felt such humiliation – even being dissected in the parochial house hadn't been this bad. I was an idiot and I burned with the shame of letting him see that for a good two minutes I'd thought of myself as someone worth having.

I heard him in the washroom at the back. He had to go to the McCourts' house, respects had to be paid. The half-door swung shut and the lights of the tractor swept around the little room before he headed up the hill and left me all alone again. Around this time up at The Hill, Daddy, Mammy, Matthew and me would be saying a few decades of the rosary and a Prayer for Peace before she makes the last hot drink of the day. Will they miss me? Will they wonder how I'm doing? I can live without the prayers but I venture up into the empty kitchen and put the small milk pan on the yellow range. When it hit the boil I poured equal measures of sugar and Camp Coffee into it. It's the only way it can be swallowed.

That night when I lay in the pitch-dark it floated down into me and took up residence in my chest. Daddy had given me away and now here I was, all by myself. There was someone living inside me and I still felt alone. She – I *knew* she was a girl – had been with me for nearly three months and she was no company at all. John Johns's words hit me like stones again and again until I felt bruised. He didn't want to know me, he didn't want to hear me, he didn't want to lay eyes or hands on me. He had managed to make me feel less than nothing. He'd outdone Mammy's lifetime work in five minutes. That was good going. *He* had nothing to lose by marrying *me* because the amazing Catherine had his heart in her back pocket and he hadn't stopped to consider that he had ruined my chances of landing Joe Loughrey.

How do you turn back time? Or at least fold it so you can shout out some warning to the poor crayturs who don't know that when they walk past a particular bush on a particular day things will never be the same again? How do you get to just be someone's girlfriend again and stand about giggling and eating sweets? The rug that was your life could be whipped from under your feet and you'd be left standing in the same spot, totally different backdrop. For me it was Johns Farm; for the poor McCourts it was six foot of freshly dug clay. The thoughts ran around and around until I was dizzy watching them. There was no way out.

The next morning, I was altered. I was a bad rooster who had flown up out of the pen one time too many and now I was hobbled. Even the lowest branch would prove too high. I made a promise to myself that I would take John Johns at his word. It worked for my father: say nothing, show nothing, do nothing, feel nothing, be nothing. John would never hear another word from my lips, he would never catch me alone again. He might tell me some more truths. I'd had enough of them from Mammy to last me.

I started that very day telling myself the story of how badly I had been treated; mine was a sad story and I would make sure I never forgot that. I had the foundations dug and the rocks lined up to make a start on my House of Pity when our Protestant neighbour Arthur Rowley rocked up with a few cans of beer to toast our happiness and to celebrate the birth of a son for Prince Charles and Princess Diana over in England. I was fetched up out of the Lower Room and Bridie slammed the door double-quick time behind me. Farce or not, no one was to see my lofty bed standing as evidence that I was not married in any real sense.

Arthur had to fall back on us to wet Prince William's head because he hadn't been able to get into Carncloon and the craic in the Protestant bars. An RUC roadblock had stopped him at the crossroads. The local Orange Order were having a practice march because they hadn't quite got the hang of walking up and down with banners after two hundred and thirteen years and the whole town was on lockdown.

Cheers, we all said as we pulled the rings on the cans of Harp, and I hoped against hope Mammy couldn't hear us wishing the best of health to the next in line for the throne and face of the 'English Crown forces' that haunted her every waking hour.

The atmosphere had changed as soon as the door knocked; we all pulled our public faces on and made out that we were living in a happy home. Here's to you young wans, may your children be many and your worries be few, says Arthur, all sombre. John was friendly and nice and took Arthur's wish for our fertile future in good humour though he was careful not to catch my eye when I choked.

15

Every single morning I ask Bridie if the postman has come, if there's anything for me, and every single morning she says no. She knows I'm relying on a letter from America to stop me from going to pieces. The Darlings probably wouldn't have told Joe I'd been sent to Johns Farm, they mightn't even know, but he could write to me care of The Hill. I need his address: he must be able to understand that? I can't believe that he will just let me disappear from his life without even finding out why I was so stupid? Does he not at least want to know that I've not been drowned in a bog hole by my mother? What kind of love was it if it can be thrown away like a rag? That he's gone forever without a backward glance stings.

Bridie's handed over her writing pad with its lined sheet underneath to keep the words straight. I've scribbled a thousand words to Lizzie Magee on rough jotters, but every time I try to commit them to the pristine paper I hesitate. There's lots of 'sorrys' and 'should haves' and 'one days' but I can't put them into an order that makes me feel less than a total eejit. How can I ever explain to her what's happened? Or why?

Soon, I'll get over myself and get a note to her. It's just a question of what to say and what not to say. The news of the wedding will have got around the whole townland by now. I hope she won't give up on me. Without the vibrant colour of Lizzie Magee bleeding into me, I'll disappear again.

Bridie tells me that it's fresh air I need. There's no shortage of fresh air at Johns Farm. When she finds me clinging to the four walls of the Lower Room, she rousts me out and pushes me through the half-door. It always seems too bright but I leave the cover of the little house and walk the ditches. I'd always loved it down here in the hollow but the thought of The Hill just two miles away has wiped out its pull. I imagine that my bed has been stripped down to a baldy mattress. Mick is gone. Daddy is up there, Matthew too, carrying on as if nothing is wrong when nothing is right or even close to it. I look at the end of the lane where it starts to climb past the orchard wall but I can't step too close. It'd be easier to fly to the moon.

I spend a lot of my day listening to Bridie pour her heart out about dead husbands and dead children in a bid to show me that things could always be worse. The teapot never cools. I've not told her that it's my job to listen to her now. I'll never mention it because I love her so much.

She hasn't told me outright about Father Pat O'Connell but it won't be long. She's already assured me she knows *exactly* just how it feels to be in my boat. Does she remember calling Decker McHugh a buck eejit when he forecast my rough seas? I wonder how he got it so wrong then I realise that maybe he got it absolutely right.

*

I was married a month when the IRA set two bombs in London: one in Hyde Park, one in Regent's Park. Bridie and me listened to it on the wireless; both were military ceremonies guaranteed to have a lot of civilians gathered around. In the end they killed eleven soldiers, seven of them musicians, and seven horses. It seemed terrible that they were just all on a bit of a day out in the sunshine. Bridie insisted that the three of us kneel down together to say a decade of the rosary. John and me looked at each other alarmed. He had kept his promise to show no interest in me and I had kept myself hidden away as best as any person could in a three-room house. This was being too close for comfort.

John didn't argue with his mother and bowed his head as we chewed over the familiar words. The daily bread, the forgiveness of trespasses, the dodging of temptation and the delivery from evil floated into the greenery outside. We didn't bother with the Prayer for Peace. It was all going well until he had to help me off the floor when I went limp, a dizzy whale out of water. He was behind me with his hands under my armpits before I had time to burn with embarrassment. He wiped his palms on his trousers and got on with his day.

All the hundred pinks of the apple blossom were gone and the fruit was on its way. The soft, sweet scent of the orchard with its damsons and apples ruffled the draught curtain at the half-door. Brandy dog lay in a panting heap in a pool of shade at the foot of the biggest tree at the end of the street. I was going to take him to the river later on for a dip, he loved that. I might beg Bridie to come with me if her pains weren't too bad. She was my only company. There was no word from Lizzie Magee.

*

I was nearly five months pregnant when my mother summoned me to get my GCSE results. She told John to drop me off when he was passing next time. I had to be up very early as he left by 6am. We both tried to ignore the fact that the bump kept hitting him on the side as we joggled up the hill in the tractor. I hadn't seen my mother since the day I got married off and instead of being angry with her I was pathetically grateful that she had, at last, asked to see me. Daddy still hadn't.

John dropped me off and informed me that I would have to walk back as he wouldn't be home 'til the usual time. I told him it was okay as it was all downhill and then we stared at each like goms. It passed for the third longest communication we had ever had because the 'I do's' and the first-night row don't really count. I blushed and he cleared his throat and we parted company.

Mammy greeted me at the back door, arms crossed, the smell of Jeyes Fluid letting me know the floors had been washed in the last hour. I was honoured.

– Well, well. And how are you?
– I'm fine.
– Sit down and I'll make us some tea.
– I don't want any tea. Living with Bridie, I'll be the colour of tea before long.
– Well, she never did have any sense!
– I said she makes a lot of tea, I *didn't* say she had no sense!
– Don't you answer me back, madam! Don't you dare! I don't see you for months and the first thing you do is cheek me?
– Well, you knew where I was.

She turned away, neck on fire, to set a tray with the good china that only ever saw the light of day for priests and

Christmas. I was a visitor, without a shadow of a doubt. I would always be a visitor from now on and *I would take tea.* The hope that I'd be let home when the baby was born faded. I'd not be going back to school. I clamped a big lump of my cheek between my teeth to stop the tears and I lifted the cup by the lip not the handle and put it down too hard on the wooden table instead of on the saucer. She winced but didn't say a word. Out came a plate of Mikados on a paper doily, hang the expense.

   – So, how's it all going down there?
   – Married life, you mean?
   – Well all of it? How are you finding … the conditions?
   – The conditions are not good.
   – Well, it's a rough house, always was. John could get a grant
     to modernise, you know; you should talk to him about it.

Talk to him? Talk to John Johns? Was she insane? That would mean sitting in the same room as him, not shaking like a kicked dog under a table.

   – We don't exactly *talk.* And even if we did, I'm not sure he'd
     be too interested in what I had to say.
   – What do you mean, you don't talk to him? He's your
     husband.
   – I know, you picked him out for me, remember?

She was a class act. She hadn't *talked* to my father for years! He *talked* to the cows, if indeed he *talked.* For all that, my little dig didn't go down well. I could see she was fighting to keep her temper. She'd married me off with a bastard on board and I was still churlish. I would never learn. She'd done her level best over the course of my childhood to get me to see sense but my damned Rattigan weakness just couldn't be remedied.

– Mary, it doesn't pay to be so brazen. Have you no shame at all?

– None. Have you?

The sweet coconut and jam smell of the Mikados wafted between us in the silence. The clock ticked on. Finally, Matthew came in and nearly passed out with the shock of seeing us together over the teapot.

– Jesus, Mary! How are you? You've come visiting then, at last, wha'?

– Don't take the name of our Lord in vain, Matthew Rattigan!

– Aye, I'm just visiting, Matty. I'm off in a minute but I'll be back soon. Mammy was just sayin' how much she's lookin' forward to helpin' me with the baby.

It was then that poor Matthew realised he was standing in a kitchen that was about to explode; there'd be brains and marshmallow on the ceiling and he could see that I was enjoying the idea of it. Matthew gave a little nervous laugh and asked me if I wanted to see a set of chicks he had just incubated. He needed to get back outside quick; kitchens with two women at war in them, were not for him. He was wired the same as Daddy. I eased myself out of the chair and made for the door as my mother turned the knife.

– Your exam results are there by the Holy Water fount. I don't know what all the studying was about when all you were going to end up with was a houseful of waynes. Nothing can be made of *nothing*!

I never failed to disappoint her. I waddled out into the hall where a gaudy new picture of the Sacred Heart gleamed inside a plastic gold frame. It went beautifully with the *Mother* plate she'd replaced herself. She'd put a lock on the telephone so the one small chance I'd thought I'd have to phone Lizzie Magee was gone. I took up my results envelope and walked past her in the kitchen without another word. She'd have to ask if she wanted to know how smart I was!

Matthew's babble about chicks and about how he hoped Daddy would back him up took us away from the back door to a safe distance. He'd an idea of starting a chicken farm, intensive rearing; it was all the rage nowadays.

– Listen, Lizzie Magee's been phoning … and writing.

– Where's the letters? Did Mammy read them?

– She did, just before she put them in the fire!

– Jesus! Try and save one for me, Matty? Please?

Matthew looked back at the window and the finger he chewed when he was worried flew into his mouth. Mammy was framed between the net curtains, not looking best pleased that we were talking. I broke out in hives at the thought of what Lizzie might write, not knowing it would be read by Sadie Rattigan. He patted me on the arm and said he'd try to get a message to her even if it meant him having to suffer a night out in Carncloon. Then he left me to slip behind the barn. Mammy smiled before she disappeared behind the white lace. The postman's tea tray doesn't set itself, y'know?

I turned for Johns Farm and was halfway down the lane before I opened the envelope. I'd got six As, two Bs and a D in maths – even better than I'd expected. One of the As I'd got was for French. *Félicitations à vous, Merise*, I thought to myself, as the tears ran down my face. How would I let my daddy know that I'd done so well?

16

Summer turned quickly to autumn as August slipped away: green into orange and red. The Troubles rumbled on, a bomb here, a shooting there, all of it pushed to the back of our minds as Bridie and me picked fruit and made jam and got ready for the winter. The Tilley lamps with their delicate mantles humming made me so droopy when their paraffin wicks were lit I seemed to sleep for days on end. The bump got bigger; I worried it would be studded with lumps of sugar when it came out, I had eaten so many Paris buns. John never mentioned it, never looked at it or me unless he was cornered. I pulled all my limbs in and away every time he walked too close, as if he was a bed of nettles.

Bridie didn't talk about anything else but the bump and had her ear to my stomach every chance she had. She had told it a thousand times how much she loved it and I swear it stretched itself with delight! I was getting to know its every movement and in my mind I always called it 'her'. She had my heart in her tiny hand and I was glad. Someone needed to take care of the silly broken thing. I'd keep her away from John Johns; he didn't strike me as a man who'd go wild for cooing into a pram.

I was getting used to not having electricity, not having TV, though I missed Bob Monkhouse and Hughie Green, even Val Doonican and his bog-awful jumpers. I really missed *Coronation Street* and Betty Turpin with her face like a bulldog. I had a sense of slipping into the past. Bridie banked the fire to keep it going for the morning pot of tea and the smell of turf clung to us all. I watched the sky with her for night to draw in. Carrying water in buckets now seemed normal even though I would never get used to braving the outside toilet which we only ever call the Tin House, to how cold it was, how full of things that crept and wriggled and bit, how bad the stench.

Washing my hair in cold water if at all, having a small bowl of hot from the kettle for my face every day and a stand-up wash at the Belfast sink that Bridie called the jaw-box every week. The bump liked to do a few auld somersaults when I rubbed my belly with the facecloth. Would it be very forward to ask Bridie if the bump was supposed to be covered in blue veins? In the end, I didn't ask in case she would need to see it all sticking out and terrible.

I always washed during the day because I felt more at ease when John Johns was out. I knew his routine and made sure I was away to my bed before he came in, exhausted and quiet. He never asked where I was because I couldn't be anywhere else when the rain was pounding down. Bridie never tried to get me to stay put. We both of us hurried through the last chats and chores of the day, wordlessly going our separate ways before the half-door opened. He was out all day, only coming back about seven o'clock for his dinner which Bridie always had ready and half-burnt in the oven. He never complained, just sat down and ate, trying to soothe Bridie who he handled with care at all turns.

– Is that alright, son?

– It's fine, Ma, fine.

– I burnt it a bit; I forgot the oven was on too high for bread on the other side.

– It's fine, fine.

– These spuds are grand ...

– Those are Podgie McCourt's spuds, they're very good again this year.

I smiled from my perch in the Lower Room. Irish people the world over must have the same conversation a hundred times a week. To me spuds were spuds; I didn't know how to decide between the degrees of flouriness that made one crop better than the last. All I knew was I'd love some chipped. Having a lovely big deep-fat fryer was something I really missed.

I was getting through the stack of romantic rubbish that Eileen had given me to pass the time. I read a few pages before my eyes started to droop. All the women were letting on they were looking for love but they never fell for anyone who wasn't rich. There was a lot of 'heaving bosoms' and 'velvety hard-nesses' which made me all pink even though I knew there was a bit more to making love by that stage. I wondered very often how I'd ever manage to do it again. Longing to be touched like that made me more desolate by the minute.

I rarely sat down in daylight. I did all the light work outside, leaving Bridie at the range to burn the dinner. I gardened and cleaned out the hen house, measured out buckets of meal for the calves, carried water. By the time I was nearly eight months pregnant, Granda Ban had a stroke and had to be put into the old people's home, Lisnagh House, so Auntie Eileen and Bernie started coming down every week. John had bought her old navy Hillman Hunter now that he had two passengers and, soon enough, three. She had got herself a mint-green Opel Kadett so it took her an age to get down the lane. She was terrified of the potholes damaging her paintwork.

Bridie made such a fuss of Bernie, but Bernie was only interested in one person at Johns Farm and that was John himself. She would wander about outside hoping to see where he was working and usually he would show up if he heard their car. Bernie was on a mission to collect as many hugs as she could and John would often have to walk off when she was still clinging to his back.

- Don't throw her to the cows instead of a bale, Auntie Eileen would shout after him, smiling even with her gums.
- I wouldn't part with my Bernie that easily, Eileen! he would laugh. Watch this!

We'd watch as he'd get Bernie to stand on his wellies and he'd let on they were jiving even though he was doing all the footwork. God, the smile on Bernie could have been spotted from the moon! He's a dote, Mary, Eileen would say to me all misty-eyed and dry-mouthed as if I was remotely interested. That *man of yours*, look at him! A pure *dote*!

I never told her he wasn't *mine*. I never told her the sunny smiles and chat only came out for visitors: with me he was still cold as ice. I could tell by her envious sighs she assumed we'd slept together. The thought of being with him *like that* made me reel. No one would ever see the Lower Room with its secret bed hidden behind the clothes horse and I was too embarrassed to come clean and ruin Mammy's brilliant scheme when everyone was so jealous of me and my good fortune.

I smiled along with her instead, reaching for the biscuits she handed round to dunk in my tea, imagining what she would say if she knew what my life was really like. What would she make of me lying awake through the scurrying of the rats at night, the bushes needling at the window, the sound of the rain on the red tin roof which made the rats run even faster, the curdling laments of foxes? In the blinding dark, my only thought was: I'm here, I'm here, I'm still here.

We'd started to chat about Christmas, ignoring the fact that it would be my last without a baby, when eleven British soldiers and six civilians were killed by an INLA bomb in the Droppin Well disco in Ballykelly, County Derry. It was a time bomb left beside a support pillar on the dance floor and most of them died when big lumps of masonry fell on their heads. Three of the young people killed were teenagers like me. Christmas celebrations faded back into the gloom of a freezing Northern Irish winter.

We brought the cows in and tied them up in the stalls and the sound of them rattling their chains and splattering the groop added itself to the rats and the howling wind when the sun went in. It was dark by three o'clock and we were often in bed by seven after Bridie stoked the fire.

Eileen came down with Bernie for Christmas Day. She didn't have time to do a whole big fancy dinner and visit Granda Ban. We were so happy to have them to talk to. John surprised us all by cooking the turkey and making mash and carrots and even gravy and he didn't look like a cissy for a single second. Bridie burned some stuffing to go with it and we had a jolly time with my aunt spinning yarns and filling the kitchen with fag smoke.

I got a baby blanket, a baby's hairbrush set and a packet of white Babygros just in case I forgot the massive dome in front of me was a baby. I got nothing for me.

Me and the bump only went to town when I had to see the doctor. John dropped me off right beside the door, not from concern but because I still had to be concealed as I was far too pregnant for the few months I was married. I always went in alone. John made out like I wasn't in the car the whole way to Carncloon but his hand with its big blunt fingers resting on the gearstick always felt too close to my leg so I made myself as narrow as I could just in case he remembered I was there. I saw Doctor Brown and he always had the same word for me.

– Textbook.

That was nice; it made me think that I was still good at exams. I was as healthy as it was possible to be. I got plenty of Paris buns and my iron tonic and plenty of exercise. I was due on January 4th: an ambulance would pick me up about two days before that and take me to Omagh. I was almost looking forward to it because I knew that hospitals had magazines and books lying around and *surely* I'd get chips if I was there for a whole week?

On my very last check-up, disaster struck. Doctor Brown was off with shingles and I had to wait for Doctor Loughrey. Dermot Darling was the last person on God's blue planet that I wanted to see. The nurse made me wait anyway because I went white when she told me and she said there was no way I was getting out of there without a blood-pressure check. I sat under the posters covered with blackened lungs and others asking people to speak out against terrorism and hoped that no one would ask me how I was or, even worse, be kind. I did not want to be crying when I got face to face with Joe's daddy. When I finally went in, after I'd nearly chewed the nails clean off myself, he looked just as put out as I was.

– How are you, Mary? Please, sit. I see from Doctor Brown's notes that you've had a textbook pregnancy. No problems at all and nothing to report?
– Nothing.
– Good, good. Well, let's have a quick look at you, shall we?

He listened to the bump and he listened to my heart which was banging. He had Joe's ears when he bent forward and Joe's smell: the same washing powder and soap. He was all red. I was embarrassing him. I could feel the tears rising and rising even though I tried to swallow them down.

– Your blood pressure's a little high, but perhaps that's understandable ...

I heard the words break free before I could bite them back. I sounded pitiful and pleading. I'd never stop showing myself up.

– I'm not a bad girl, you know? I'm not a bad girl, I'm not!
– Mary, no one ever said you were a bad girl. But for God's sake, can you tell me what happened you? Now, here, with my word that I won't tell a soul?
– I can't. I just can't. How's Joe?
– Were you forced?
– No. How's Joe?
– He's working hard, he's a different boy these days. His mother and me were at a loss as to what was best but he's doing fine in America. Please, Mary, don't cry like that, it's enough to break the hardest heart. You're going to be fine, just fine. Here, dry your eyes. What are you hoping for?
– I'm hoping it doesn't hurt and that I can go back to school ...

He blew his cheeks out and rubbed his forehead like he couldn't think of a word he desperately needed to finish a sentence but it escaped him. There was no point in asking him to carry a message to Joe. He would never mention that he had even seen me.

John Johns was tapping the steering wheel when I came out. I was late and I was in a state. He just looked at me in the rear-view mirror as I slid into the back seat. I knew he had to be over at Arthur Rowley's to help with a cow being de-horned and daylight was burning. The small saw he needed was on the passenger seat. He didn't have time to waste on this nonsense.

I lay down as he pulled out of the car park and must have slept because when I woke up I was still in the car on the street at Johns Farm. I was freezing cold and it was dark and pouring with rain but there was something else wrong. My whole body was in motion; it was turning and splitting from side to side. I got to the house between pains and Bridie knew as soon as she clocked me.

– Oh darlin', I was just about to waken you … Oh my! Is it time, is it time?

– Help me, Bridie! Help me!

She got me from the half-door to the Lower Room and on to the bed. We both knew we were alone. Bridie would never make it to The Hill and the phone in this terrible weather and I wouldn't let go of her anyway. We both thought that John would be back and he could run for help but he didn't appear. She checked several times for his tractor headlights sweeping across the window and tried to cover her fear. She stayed with me for every one of the eight hours it took as I screamed and cried and howled my way through it. The rain drummed on the red tin

162

roof as Bridie told me over and over and over that I was going to be alright. She was all I had, so I had to believe her.

My little girl was born at 2am and the rain stopped when Bridie had given her a bit of a rub-down and handed her to me. She never made a sound. She had a crop of shocking-black hair, a real Rattigan. I never wanted to leave her out of my arms, not even for a second. I knew that I was going to be alright only because, all of a sudden, I wanted to be. I was glued to her tiny, serene face, I kissed her all over and promised her that nothing bad would ever befall her delicate head.

– What will you call her?

– Serena Bridget, after you, if you don't mind?

– Mind! I'm delighted! But what about your mother?

– What about her? Where was she tonight? Where has she *ever* been? You're the closest thing I've ever had to a real mother, Bridie, and don't think I'll ever forget it!

– Oh Mary, Mary, you're a darlin'! And so's she!

We all three cried then 'til we had to laugh again. I was learning that too. It was never that long before you had to laugh again. Crying was so dull; it fixed nothing really and it only served to ruin your good face and brine your eyeballs.

When Bridie was clearing up, I went in to the kitchen to show Serena the coloured paper chains that Bridie and me had made and strung across the brace over the range and to put the kettle on for tea. It's Christmas-time, I said to her but she just yawned with her perfect pink mouth and got on with burrowing her way deep, deep into my heart.

17

There was hardly time to think after Serena landed, never mind feel sorry for myself. Everything to do with a baby took so *long*, especially at Johns Farm. The fire had to be stoked for night-time to heat the bottles and to boil the nappies. I tried to feed her myself but I had no milk to speak of so I gave up and anyway Bridie loved bottle-feeding her; that way we could share her.

I was in love again, totally smitten with Serena's tiny fingers and her soft-as-silk hair. I couldn't stop kissing her. My mother came to call. It was the first time she had crossed the threshold of Johns Farm for years.

– John tells me it's a girl you have? Better luck next time.

John Johns's mood and mind seemed changed with Serena's arrival. He had been lifted the night she was born. The RUC figured that errant Paddies might be afoot in the terrible rain and had set up a checkpoint. He had nearly ploughed straight into them with their one stupid torch and they had taken exception and he spent the night in Carncloon Barracks.

He looked stricken by the fact that she had arrived in his absence and he kept telling Bridie over and over how I must go to hospital anyway, how *the baby* should be checked out. But the district midwife had already been and said that I was fine to stay put. Popping out babies was a young woman's job and I'd done it well. She hadn't seen me wailing like a banshee. He peered in at Serena where we'd put her to nap outside in her pram wrapped up in a green blanket against the frost, just touching her chest with his fingers as if she was made of glass.

– I like her name.

– Serena Bridget suits her, I think?

– Serena Bridget Johns. Yes, that suits her fine!

Until that moment I hadn't even thought about her surname, I was such an eejit! The next day, he came into the Lower Room when I was settling her for bed. It was the first time he had set foot inside it since I had come to live there. He made it look small. I didn't like him standing between me and the door.

– Is she alright?

– She's fine!

– I'll leave you in peace … unless … could I hold her?

– Surely! Take her!

John gathered her up and a smile broke across his face, the like of which I would never be able to describe. It was as if he *knew* her and she knew him, as if he had been waiting for her all his life. He was so beautiful and with my baby in his arms he looked like an angel when he tipped his lips to her little, dark head and kissed her over and over again, lost to her, lost to himself, oblivious to me as ever. He was a man in love.

He came in every night, smiling, happy, wanting to hold 'his girl'. I could give him nothing but Serena could give him everything. He changed nappies, his big fingers struggling at first with the pins. He brushed her hair and wrapped her up in her blanket so he could sit with her in his arms and admire her. Her eyes shone up at him. Clever girl, he was all *hers*.

He was still a switch in my day, but for a different reason, a reason that made me hate myself. I'd be happily chatting and laughing with Bridie and Serena but if I clocked him even looking at us through the window I bolted for the Lower Room, like a mink in a drain. I wanted to keep Serena from him. It was mean like Mammy was mean and I didn't want to own up to a single drop of *her* poison. If he ever figured out what I was doing he couldn't have guessed at why. I was jealous of their love. I couldn't have been greener if I was the grass on the other side of the fence. Bridie knew, though. I couldn't hide anything from her. When she questions me I try to explain that *he's* not keen on seeing *me* about the place. *He* banished *me*. I'm just doing as I'm told, I tell her, trying not to make it sound like a whine. I'm the eternally innocent party. She doesn't buy it for a second.

The world outside the street at Johns Farm – my family, the gossip from Carncloon, the Troubles – all faded as if a bulletproof bubble had settled over the little house. Life became about what Serena had eaten, what she'd drunk, what she'd tried to say. Thank God, she was proving interesting; she had to fill the lives of three love-struck adults. John Johns turned into the Good Provider and I had to let him even though it killed me. Did Serena need anything? Anything at all, name it and it would be hers? He bought her clothes in Woolworths when he was in Strabane. She had frocks of every colour and every single colour suited her. Oh, she was perfect!

She slept in with me; I bolstered her with pillows against the back wall in the Lower Room so I could feel her breathing, perching on the edge in case I harmed her. I was so *tired* but I could hardly bear to sleep in case I missed one tiny yawn. I fought the idea of a cot, a cot right beside the bed would have been too far. She was all I had to call my own, I would not risk her being beyond an arm's-length away.

As there were so many little dresses and Babygros and terry nappies, I felt I had to take over washing the clothes from Bridie. I've never seen a woman move aside so quickly. The laundry included John Johns's stuff and my heart lurched when I knew I'd have to deal with them and where they had been. I grabbed everything he owned and submerged the lot in Daz as if they were contaminated. I left them there 'til I figured they were clean and I couldn't smell his mossy smell and rinsed them all out in the big water barrels in the scullery. There wasn't a pair of man's pyjamas – brazen. And I had looked for them, Yes Siree Bob!

Drying weather doesn't come along too often in a Northern Irish winter. The clothes had to be hung above the rack on the range and turned and turned like Mammy had turned her underpinnings. Usually John grabbed his clean stuff from there but he'd been so busy, it built up and had to be shifted so I took a deep breath and packed it all under one arm. Is it strange to be afraid to go into someone's bedroom when that someone is the man who can call himself your husband?

I had never been in the Upper Room. It ran parallel to mine with just the kitchen to divide us. Standing in it would make me feel like the total stranger I was. Man up, Mary! You've wrung out his undercrackers, you can put them in a drawer. I reached out and turned the handle and stepped in.

The room was immaculate. A fire was set in the grate of an old black fireplace that had a bit of gold paint outlining it. The brass bed was neat, one of Bridie's brightest patchwork quilts pulled tight across it. I slipped my hand under it, past the wool blanket to the sheet. Did John Johns know about undoing a girl? Did he know about kissing way south of the border properly in bandit country? Probably not; probably it was just something they did in France where it was warmer.

I blinked the thought away to see that the whole back wall was a bookcase! The joy hit me full in the face. It was like being back in the utter peace of the convent reference library, breathing in the smell of paper that had been through a thousand hands and minds.

I read the spines in the gloom. There were books on horticulture, design, some on photography, Thomas Hardy, Frank O'Connor, Henry Fielding, Patrick Kavanagh, Oscar Wilde, James Joyce, Shakespeare, Wilfred Owens, somebody called Rimbaud stood just by Seamus Heaney. Where would I start? I would start with Heaney, my old friend from school. I pulled it from the shelf and sat down on the bed which let me know it was made of springs. On the inside front cover it said *To John from Father Pat O'Connell on the occasion of your 16th birthday.* Father Pat's boy was emerging from the shadows.

- I thought you weren't going to be my wife?
- Jesus! John! You scared the life out of me! Where did you come from?
- That's a strange question to ask a man when you have evidence in your hand?
- Oh! I meant, now, *now*? I wasn't expecting you back and this stuff needed putting away. I didn't mean to pry ...

- I know you're not prying; you've had months to pry if you were remotely interested in me.
- I'm *not* interested in you and you're not interested in *me*, remember?

The black eyes narrowed. He couldn't argue that the stand-off had been instigated by him, so he left. I'd just dropped my shoulders and sat back down on the bed when he reappeared in the doorway to scare me afresh. Jesus, how did he *do* that in a house where every bloody floorboard creaked? I shot off the bed like I'd been electrocuted!

- You're welcome to borrow a book if you want, Mary. After all, what's mine is yours!

He could even make letting me read sound like something I might have to pay for, somehow. I put Heaney back on the shelf, he was the O-level me. Walter Macken, Sean O'Casey, some American novels – *The Great Gatsby*, *To Kill a Mockingbird*, some Steinbecks – all sat happily cheek by jowl; none of those had been on the syllabus. I pulled out T. S. Eliot's *Four Quartets*; it had been on the reading list for A-level English. *Footfalls echo in the memory/ down the passage which we did not take/ towards the door we never opened/ into the rose-garden.* I would carry it to the Lower Room and soak up the words from better, brighter lives, like a blood-starved tick.

It was him who sent for Auntie Eileen when Serena was about six months old and still not christened. He'd mentioned it to me, made it sound like my duty as a good Catholic mother and wife, and I'd walked straight out of the half-door with her in my arms. He needed reminding that she was *mine* but he wanted his name branded on her. He knew that I wouldn't be bold enough to call her Serena Rattigan and damn every pious hypocrite in St Bede's. I just didn't want it to happen yet.

She was already reaching out for him; her little face lit up brighter for him than it ever did for me. I didn't want to lose another crumb of her. Auntie Eileen and Bernie showed up one day with a mission and a fresh cream sponge. She knew all my weaknesses. I knew she'd do anything if John Johns asked her, even if it was slipping a set of reins over my head.

– Well?

– Well what?

– Why hasn't this gorgeous girl been christened yet?

– What's the rush? Why is *everyone* so desperate to toe the party line?

– *Everyone* isn't! But you have to get her christened at some stage and there's never any better time than the present. Here, take another slice of cream cake and cheer yourself up – you've a face on you that could turn an Orange Order parade!

Bridie cut me another slab of sponge and I rammed it into my mouth. I noticed she was very quiet on the subject of going back to the chapel and swearing more lies. But then she was carrying the secret of an unconsummated marriage without a single stumble; this was small beans.

The sick fluttering around my heart didn't stop as Eileen ran through the really important stuff of what I would wear, where she'd get the white robe for Serena, who would I like for godparents. Had I ever managed to get back in touch with that mad pal of mine, Lizzie Magee? Would John be able to stretch to a sandwich tea after in the parish hall or would we just come home and *make tea*? Why hadn't she asked *him* when the two of them were scheming behind my back? I swallowed my cake and hoped it would choke me. It didn't.

- We'll come home and make tea, I manage.
- Great! I've booked it for Sunday! It'll be a blast! says my faithful aunt.

I didn't sleep on the Saturday night. I lay beside the little innocent bundle of Serena snuffling beside me. I was going to let Father O'Brien, the big fat liar, anoint her head with holy oil and swear that she would be a follower of the Catholic faith. Kathleen and Matthew were standing up as godparents after Auntie Eileen had refused to renounce the World, the Flesh and the Devil. Why would I give up the good stuff? she'd asked, lighting a fag.

In the end, I got up and went out to get a better look at the moon that was shining through the curtains. It hung, a glorious silver ball between the shadows of the big sycamores at the entrance to the river field. The leaves shivered alongside me and the soil was cold and dense beneath my bare feet. The Cloon was flowing fast, washing the stones smooth by the bend. Nothing was stirring on the air except my breath. It was as if I had the whole world to myself. What if I slipped into the river and let it carry me away from Johns Farm? It was only the thought of my girl that made me turn back and get to my bed.

In the morning, I walked out with Serena draped in her long white lace dress. She was a picture and a half. Auntie Eileen had done her proud; it was a confection all its own. I kept my eyes on my girl's face for the journey up the lane, past The Hill, past my father who was standing by the door of the chapel, past my mother who was already ensconced in the front pew. I had a crick in my neck after the whole hour of the Mass but when I left my daughter was a Catholic and everyone seemed happier, especially John. He took her from my arms as I stepped out of the door and into the bright June sunshine.

She was official, she was free of Original Sin, it was safe for her to die because she would float straight up to Heaven. I had handed her over to Jesus. I had sworn to keep her on the straight and narrow path of a religious upbringing. Me, the woman who fell off the path at the first hurdle. I had named her Serena Bridget Johns when she wasn't a *Johns*, but then her stand-in father wasn't a Johns either; he was an O'Connell, son of Father Pat. The apple doesn't fall far from the tree. I had married into the Church.

I'm not mad, I thought to myself, every other person around here with a head is. I'm doing alright. Kathleen was all teary; Matthew was so chuffed he couldn't speak. Daddy came over and shook my hand like I'd run a race and won. I wiped the feel of his lovely old calloused palm on the side of my jacket before I gave in and smiled. I'd never be done missing him.

John Johns spun Serena around in the air and the lace flew round her like flower petals. Auntie Eileen and Bridie were debating whether or not to put tomatoes in the ham sandwiches, a life-and-death decision. Things were going to settle down to what passed for normal in County Tyrone, whether I liked it or not.

No one asked me if I was happy, if I was coping alright. I looked up at the sky and for the first time in a long time I didn't want to float up, up and away. I wanted to stay right here until Serena was old enough to come with me. Mammy walked over, reeking of elastic and disapproval.

– There was hardly a need for such a flashy christening robe, given the *unfortunate circumstances*, she says. You just can't seem to *learn* decency, Mary Rattigan.

I'd always have her to keep me firmly on the ground. She'd drive stakes through my feet if that's what it took.

18

Serena walked early and was such a strong little thing. She was determined from the top of her black curls to the tips of her pink toes. She wasn't quite a year old when she hung off the back of the half-door, her treat being swung backwards when John came in. When she was older still, he pretended not to have seen her and would ask Bridie and me, *Where's my girl? I can't find her!* And we'd all play the game 'til she came rushing at him, grabbing him by the knees and shouting 'Dada, Dada' before he whooshed her up in the air and brought her down squealing for a kiss. He was her whole world and she was *his*. In this way, with her to glue us together, we limped on, a three-legged race.

The seasons flew by and the sky stayed put, full of clouds by day and stars by night. My work at Johns Farm was endless and I fell into bed by eight o'clock every night hoping I'd brought in enough water and wood to get us up and going in the morning without having to brave the cold. John let me know my efforts were not going unnoticed by letting me know they were also not quite good enough. *Make sure you tie the hill-field gate properly. The chicken coop could do with a clean. Did you not notice that the new Friesian heifer was lame? Are you listening to me, Mary?* I nodded and apologised and lifted my daughter out of his arms and carried her away from him to the Lower Room and darkness. The rats took turns to watch my wonderful life from the holes in the ceiling.

But Kathleen called every time she was home and it was through her that I eventually got back in touch with Lizzie Magee. I was eighteen, no phone, no car and no money. The bold Lizzie Magee had a driving licence and was roarin' about in an old banger that Dessie had fixed up for her before she went off to university and England. She was away to London in September. She caught up with Kathleen in town one day and asked if she could see if *I* still wanted to see *her*. Wanted! I would have given an arm and a leg to lay my eyes and ears on Lizzie Magee.

Matthew had never managed to run into her. She'd not had a single reply to several letters. When she phoned The Hill, she'd been told in no uncertain terms by Mammy that she was not wanted. I was a *happily* married woman now, I didn't require the company of a silly schoolgirl. She'd be best to not forget that; better still, she was not to dial the number ever again: no messages would be passed on.

Kathleen rolled her eyes when I burst into tears: why hadn't I just *asked* her to carry a message? Or why hadn't I asked Auntie Eileen? The two of them were better bets than Matthew who could hardly speak? Did I have tapioca in my head in place of a brain? I laughed along with her so she wouldn't see how embarrassed I was. Kathleen had told Lizzie how to find me. She couldn't get lost as I was at the end of the road.

Lizzie showed up one day not long after. I was standing by the half-door with Serena on my hip because I'd heard the sound of her car coming on the river. She braked hard because she was driving too fast and jumped out of the car screaming and ready to hug before it had stopped. She had to jump back in as it rolled towards the river field; she'd forgotten to pull on the handbrake!

- Jesus Holy Christ in a chicken basket! It's the Virgin Mary and Child!
- Lizzie Magee! Go easy, will you? Don't swear in front of the wayne!
- God, look at you! Look at you! You haven't changed an inch!
- You have! What in God's name have you done to your hair?
- Fuck off! Perms are in! Not that you'll ever need one with that wig! It's pure fashionable! Oh cripes … sorry … erm … Mrs …
- Lizzie, this is Bridie. Bridie, *this* is Lizzie Magee.
- Very nice to meet you, Lizzie. Sure, I'll take this little one and you two girls can run on down to the river or somewhere for a chat, eh? You must have some catchin' up to do!

And we did run! Like children, whooping and screaming and pushing each other around! We were like cows let out after the winter: half-mad and blinded by the light but still determined to kick up our heels. The downy seed heads of the dandelions danced in our wake. When we came to a stop, breathless and laughing, I just held her for an age; she was soft and warm and I drew the softness and warmth deep down into my marrow. There was too much to say and no words to say it with. But

Lizzie made a stab at it anyway as she dragged me on a whistle-stop tour of the past two years.

She'd *actually* studied, a near-miracle brought on by losing me to mess about with in classes. Sister Pious was still a dragon. My name had never been mentioned after the first week or so, when the thirty-three other girls in our class were desperate to know if it was true that the brainbox Mary Rattigan had got herself pregnant. Then they all got bored, especially as Lizzie had been 'absolutely loyal' and wouldn't even grace them with a 'fuck off'.

Sheila and her had found out about my wedding when it was a week old. They'd both laughed about the fact that I'd ended up with the most gorgeous man in town; it seemed appropriate somehow. I was a dark horse but then they'd always known that! Had they? It was news to me. Had she no problem with me getting married at sixteen at all? Had she forgotten that once upon a time I had other plans? What was so *appropriate* about *me* marrying *him*?

Lizzie had woke up one morning and her boobs had grown two cup sizes. She wasn't sure if that was a good or bad thing and had a total sense-of-humour bypass over it and bloody Dessie had told her to cool it: at least her arse had grown at the same time and to the same size so she wouldn't trip over. Sheila had fetched him a good hard slap across the back of the head for his lack of understanding. I lapped up the words and the teenage drama and never felt more isolated.

- But hang on a cotton-pickin' minute. Are you going to tell me what went on exactly? We had a deal, Mary Rattigan: NO SECRETS.
- It's the oldest story in the book. Girl meets boy, girl falls under boy, boy marries her. What did you think happened?

– Noooooooooooo! So all along it was *him* you fancied and not poor auld Joe Loughrey at all? But what John Johns McJohns-boy? I thought he gave you the heebie-jeebies? I don't know why, though, he's fuckin' gorgeous! So you love him then or what?

– Well, I married him.

– But what NOW? You're not goin' to stay out in this countrified hellhole with a sprog and an old dear and a farmer and no runnin' water for much longer, are you, surely?

Trust Lizzie Magee to reduce my life to a sentence. I had nothing to say for myself. I started spouting about how Serena meant the world to me and that Bridie was like an angel at my back. I couldn't tell her that I never went into town because I couldn't face the thought of Serena seeing soldiers and RUC with guns standing outside the sweet shop and thinking it was normal. I couldn't tell her that every penny I had held for two years had come from John Johns and I didn't feel I deserved to spend it. I wasn't able to scrutinise myself in the mirror. I didn't want to lock eyes with the startled pale face trapped there.

I only left this patch of land to go to Mass and I walked with Bridie and Serena right up to the front seat. I wanted to make sure that Father O'Brien couldn't forget Father Martin O'Hara. I blocked out the sounds of tongues clicking in the pews. My priest always had the decency to avert his eyes after the most cursory of cursory acknowledgements and he still just looked as if he was being forgiving rather than friendly.

I didn't tell Lizzie Magee that technically I wasn't married; she had no problem believing that John was the daddy. She didn't need to know that I had actually managed to fall pregnant the very first time I made love when she was sleeping not two hundred feet away. She wouldn't believe me. That it happened with her super-crush, Jacques Bernier, *on a gravestone*? She would KILL me. That I retired each night with my daughter in what should have been the Good Room, with a torch beside my single bed. That sometimes I could hardly sleep for thinking about when I would be kissed again and knowing it would be no time soon.

I didn't tell her that I knew escape was not an option. I hadn't acquired a husband as much as a new owner. I didn't tell her that most of my days felt like I had fallen down a deep well and had only the certainty of sleep to keep me from going bonkers. Any of the words I needed to explain my sad little life would have stuck in my throat like dry bread.

She got distracted then – luckily – by my girl toddling towards us, her baby bunches bouncing around on her head. Bridie waved from the entrance of the river field in defeat: she couldn't keep up. Serena was playing peek-a-boo by putting her hands over her eyes and shouting boo-boo-boo. Lizzie scooped her into the air and spun her round and round. That made me smile with my very heart, my two best girls getting acquainted.

They giggled and jostled and played tag 'til Lizzie had to get off. Dessie was still nervous of her at the wheel, she had to drive past the garage and honk every time she was on her way home to prove that she hadn't wrapped herself around a tree or ploughed into an RUC roadblock.

She pulled some stuff from the back seat of the car: a whole tin of Quality Street for me and a jigsaw and blowing-bubbles set for Serena. The jigsaw was far too complicated for a two-year-old. It was five hundred pieces and had a picture of Paris on it showing the river reflecting the city. Lizzie said Paris was where she was going the first time she felt filthy rich. Jacques Bernier might still be there pining for her at last; he was only human, after all. I grinned, secure in the knowledge she was holding the only bit of Jacques Bernier that she would ever get her randy hands on.

She was coming back and soon. How magical to be able to come and go as you pleased. It made Johns Farm seem even more like a prison, a prison with trees and hills and velvet fields as far as the eye could see. I stood in front of the half-door with the widest, brightest smile I could muster and waved and waved, bye, bye, bye, bye. Lizzie's tail lights disappeared up the narrow lane, dragging another fingernail of meat from my heart.

I had missed out on everything: all I had to my name was my daughter. My days were filled with wondering how it would be remotely *possible* to slap her beautiful little face, to light it up with stripes and tell her it was for her own good. It would never happen, never. If I was not going to be anything else, I was going to be a good mother. I would buck every child-rearing trend I'd learned at Sadie Rattigan's hands.

Lizzie'd be going home to a bit of craic, probably beans and chips and all the love she could handle. Any time she wanted to nip out and go to the shops she didn't have to think about how dangerous it was, how anything could happen to a little girl. She had university and London in her sights and her whole life ahead of her. She was out in the bars of Carncloon having a drink and a dance now that she was all grown up, all grown up and managing just fine without me.

I roared in at Bridie to put the kettle on. Poor wee Serena nearly jumped out of her skin! I needed tea to keep my stomach from twisting and my mouth from letting out the howl that was travelling from my toes. I wouldn't be letting it past my lips: someone might hear it and call an ambulance. Only someone close to losing their mind would be able to produce such a pitiful sound.

19

When John Johns had finally trained me how to look after his farm to his high standards, he went back to the building sites full-time. I was happy to work hard, it let me sleep soundly, and John was pleased he had scored a strong, biddable girl to leave in charge while he earned some decent money.

Every morning, rain or shine but mostly rain, I would walk the Friesians – my Ladies, their udders trailing on the ground – up from the river field to the parlour at The Hill where I would clean them down and set the milking machines on them. The black and white of their hides brushing against the bridal high heads of wild angelica lulled me with its sweet scent. I patted their silky auld haunches and thanked them for their company. Sometimes I whispered a line or two from a book or told them a story about Serena or Bridie because I had no one else to tell.

I lugged hay bales and cut the twine with a penknife that John had given me for the job. I broke the ice on the big water tubs where the cows drank and cleaned the crow, pigeon and rook muck out of their feeders in the summer. In the winter I cleaned the cow muck out of the byre and wheelbarrowed it to the midden. I'd asked John if we could move the midden further away from the street to help the smell about the place. He'd said fine, it's you will have to travel further. I remembered that when I thought my arms were being pulled out of my shoulders. I had no one to blame but myself.

After plenty of those days I dreamt that I would beg my mother if I could have a bath, a long, hot soak in a tub where the water came out of the tap instead of a boiled saucepan. But I kept my dreams to myself and got out the ancient wooden nailbrush and scrubbed the orange cowshit from under my nails. I often wondered how Lizzie was doing in London in that same moment. Was she thinking of me?

Indoors, Serena was centre stage at mealtimes where we taught her to count and started her on her letters. I bathed her in the old Belfast sink and John read the bedtime story. I stayed by the door so that I could close it when he left and we all pretended it was so that Bridie could hear about Cinderella and Snow White and Rapunzel from the comfort of her chair by the fire.

He had collected up every picture book about every princess he could find. I chewed my lip as he named them all, got her to repeat the colours of their dresses and eyes and hair. She had to try to count the wheels on the carriages and the legs on the horses. Sometimes the horses ended up with six legs because she was so busy showing off she forgot to stop. He'd catch my eye and laugh and I'd smile without baring any teeth and pray it would soon be over and her and me would be alone again.

I stayed mute through the rescues by the handsome, heroic men and the happily-ever-afters. Every night, Serena picked a different one to be when she grew up. I nodded at her while wishing they'd rot inside their glass coffins and wither in their ivory towers. I was heartily sick of all the silky-maned little waifs. I kept a close watch on Serena's eyelashes and willed them to flutter shut.

When he left the Lower Room he said goodnight and I said the same and I never followed him back to the kitchen, summer or winter. Sometimes I heard him and Bridie talking low in front of the range, oftentimes not. In that way, we got through the long and short evenings well enough. I'd stopped bothering to think about when it would end, about when I'd start up my own life again. I knew it would be one day.

It was Serena who John Johns was worried about, and her alone, when he decided to go back to England for a year. The money was good and, as things were hotting up between the RUC and the local boys, it was a sensible time to get out. Talks of raids and beatings and days without news of whether a son or brother was safe or not did the rounds. It made Bridie shake in her shoes and reach for her rosary beads.

The letter asking him to be foreman on a job had arrived on a Friday and by the Monday John had made his decision. He apologised to me because he knew it would be hard on Serena, she wouldn't be able to understand why he'd gone but he would be in touch with her as soon as he could. *It's best to do these things without much warning, Mary.* I said yes, yes of course. I'd had enough plasters ripped off to know he was right.

In the space of a few days he had organised Arthur Rowley to help me with the morning milking a few days a week, Matthew could be relied on for heavy work and I would do everything else. Bridie would look after my daughter. Eileen would do the shopping and collect the Family Allowance at the post office. Don't forget your father is only up the lane, too, said John Johns and I tried not to laugh. Daddy wasn't exactly my friend in need. Was there anything I wanted to ask? Was there anything I wanted to know? There wasn't so I just nodded and chewed my lip.

It was a rotten, foggy day, biting cold in the early January of 1985, when he left. I'd had Matthew take Serena over to Auntie Eileen's for the morning so she wouldn't see his bag all packed and ready by the door. It wasn't three months since the IRA had bombed the Grand in Brighton trying to do for Margaret Thatcher so it would be no picnic being an Irishman in England.

He didn't look back at me or his weeping mother, bereft where she stood on the street. As soon as he was out of sight a weight lifted off my shoulders and settled itself neatly on my heart. I put my arm around Bridie and told her we'd both be okay and she cried harder.

Serena was a different kettle of fish. A monster who could not be placated and no amount of cajoling and pleading with her helped for nearly a fortnight. She stood at the half-door every day until she nearly fell with tiredness, her little face pinched and white until she was thrown down with a fever. That seemed to burn her back to life and she emerged quieter and rather forlorn, but at least back with us.

After three weeks a huge parcel landed from England; it was addressed to his mother and in it was a teddy bear bigger than Serena and a letter saying he was alright and would send money soon. I didn't get a mention. Serena called the bear Bosco and set about covering him in leaves and muck and snot and food because she wouldn't leave him out of her hand even for a minute.

She marched up and down outside the kitchen window talking to him while Bridie burned the dinner and I washed the clothes and fed the cows and every other bloody animal with a mouth, and I worried that they were both lonely.

The radio brought us all the bad news we could ever need at home and abroad. There was an IRA mortar attack on an RUC base in Newry, County Down in February and nine RUC officers were killed and thirty-seven wounded. In May four more were killed in County Armagh by a remote-controlled IRA bomb and so every Catholic family would suffer a bit more low-level intimidation every day.

The little house wilted around us. I had always loved the bones of John's Farm, the place I ran to when my mother hit the roof and every child under it, but John's absence drew up to the table every time we sat down and made us weary, watchful. The talk was of him, our ears were peeled for news of further bombs on the mainland, any incidents that might make life even harder for an Irish boy who stuck out of the crowd.

Every two weeks, Matthew would come and get us in the car and we'd all go up to The Hill to speak to John when he rang from the hall of his digs on the payphone. He had written to explain that everyone could hear him so he would be keeping things brief – and this from a man whose brief was truly brief. It didn't suit my mother one little bit to have Poor Bridie Johns as a regular visitor but we all had to make do and mend so that we could hear his voice. I nodded at my father if he was in the house and he nodded back.

My mother eyeballed me every time a phone call came through but he spoke mostly to his mammy and then to Serena and – surprise, surprise – he would run out of ten-pence pieces as soon as it was my turn. We had the same conversation twice a month, my husband and me.

– Mary.

– John.

– Do you need anything?

– No.

– Does Serena need anything?

– No.

– There's the pips now …

– Bye.

The days, the weeks, the months flew in. Every day was pretty much like the last and the seasons came and went with only the bloom on the hawthorns in June a real highlight. Its pink and white flowers filling the air with heavy musk was so welcome. I walked out to the forest with Bridie and Serena, making sure I kept a wide berth of Brooky Hay down in its secret hollow, my auld kissing place.

John was still in London when Margaret Thatcher signed the Anglo-Irish agreement with Taoiseach Garret FitzGerald of Fine Gael in November to support cross-border co-operation between the Republic and Northern Ireland. Bridie and me had to park ourselves in front of the wireless for the translation. It meant that the politicians in Dublin would have a say in how to promote power-sharing in the Six Counties. This'll see some feathers flying, says Bridie.

Every Unionist MP in ParleyMint resigned in December because it gave the Republic a role in governance for the first time ever while Nationalist party Fianna Fáil's leader Charles Haughey said it officially recognised Britain's jurisdiction in Northern Ireland. All in all, the whole place was torn up, with

MPs baying at the moon, and thousands of people from both sides of the divide took to the streets for rallies and strikes and petition-signings and good-auld fist-fights, which was reported as 'civil disobedience' – the same dog only washed.

The Provos killed two more RUC officers in Ballygawley, County Tyrone and totally flattened the barracks by planting a bomb right inside it. Bridie and me listened to the wireless; she sighed and rolled her eyes as I tried to keep up with the marbles being thrown underfoot by the SDLP, the UUP, the DUP, Sinn Féin, the Alliance Party. It didn't take too many minutes to figure out who was at the front, shouting the loudest. It was everyone's favourite Man of God, the Reverend Ian Paisley, and the Democratic Unionist Party.

The walls of Johns Farm stayed put, the red tin roof stayed on and Bridie and me gave up on the wireless because it made our heads ache, relying instead on any pundits who stopped by for tea to fill us in on the latest screaming match. None of them could see a way out or through it, bad things happen when the Northern Irish are invited to 'talk', we were better suited to roaring and shouting and banging our fists on tables: that way none of us could be heard, nothing could be resolved and we could all accuse each other of collusion.

John had stayed away the whole year and would probably have gone again if it had not been for his reunion with Serena. We knew the date – December 23rd, he wanted to be home for her third birthday – but we didn't tell her: she would be up to high doh with excitement and probably down with a temperature before we got the pan on!

I had a kind of strange fear in the pit of my stomach. When he was back I would have to watch myself – my daddy's only

advice: watch yourself, watch yourself. I'd have to share Serena
with him again after she'd come back to me body and soul. I'd
have to take advice on what to do with Johns Farm. I was a
good farmer now, in tune with the herd, my Ladies, who walked
to me like lambs as soon as I opened the river-field gate. I'd
pulled calves from them, wormed them, dosed them for liver
fluke. They got better care than I gave myself: more love. My
plan was to present myself as a girl who had done a lot of growing up in his absence.

I washed my hair when Bridie was asleep and brushed it until
it shone. I studied myself in the mirror as I put lipstick on, wiped
it off, put it on again. I looked and felt ridiculous either way.
John Johns would never care what I looked like and still I wished
my hands weren't red and raw. Had he discovered the where-
abouts of the beautiful Catherine and sweet-talked his way back
into her heart? Maybe she had kissed him? Maybe he had
wrapped his big blunt fingers around her wrist and pulled her
close? Would she still love how red his lips were?

Somewhere towards four o'clock he walked around the corner of the barn as if he had never been away. He was leaner and
browner and his hair was long, down to his shoulders, and I
stood looking at him on the street like a mug.

– Hello, Mary.

– John.

Thank God, at that moment Serena came bowling out of the
house screaming for him. There was no shyness, no disbelief;
she launched at him like she would never let him go as the string
of gold tinsel she'd been playing with haloed around their heads
in the wind. He hugged her to him and they danced about, only
stopping long enough to let Bridie into the embrace. None of

them thought to ask me in, though John caught my eye for a second before I flinched. The frown said it all: he still couldn't *stand* me, I was a cross to bear, a bundle of nerves called Mary.

I stood aside and watched as an acid loneliness threatened to burn a hole from my stomach to my throat, a bystander. One day I'd be part of a family of my own making; it was only ever a question of biding time. For now, I was once again second on Serena's list and Dada was home for good.

John Johns had made a pile of money in England, by working all the hours and practically starving himself. I heard him now and again laughing with Bridie as I skulked about. He had finally cured himself of egg and chips by eating it every bloody day for weeks at a time! He told her about the craic in Cricklewood – it was more Irish than Ireland – everybody shot to their feet for the Irish national anthem when the pubs closed and a hat was passed to collect funds for 'the cause' – Ireland couldn't be set free for free! Any poor unfortunate English boys who didn't want to donate would like as not get a good thumping as 'Amhrán na bhFiann' died away. I thought to myself, so *we* go over *there* and beat up lads because *they* come over *here* and beat up lads? It was a pot and kettle situation.

Now he was back, he had two things on his mind: food and a better house for Serena and Bridie. That's how he announced it. I didn't figure in the plans, presumably because I wasn't young, I wasn't old and he felt no responsibility for me so I could fend for myself. Serena had all but abandoned me to stick close to his legs anywhere he went; she was not going to risk letting him out of her sight again. I missed her and tried to block out how much I wanted another child. It was my every waking thought. But it takes a husband to give you a baby and all I had was John Johns.

Auntie Eileen had asked me if 'things' were alright and I had nodded and said sure. She was likely at a loss as to how I'd got myself knocked up so easy when I shouldn't have and now that I was safely married to a stud there was no sign of another bump in the road.

He had a plan to sell off the herd for now; they were bringing in nothing anyway. He was thinking of switching from milk to beef; he might even squeeze a new huge barn for bullocks alongside Matthew's chicken house up at The Hill if Frank was amenable. My heart broke. He was selling *my Ladies*?

Then I heard the second part of the grand plan. He was going to make the barn part of the house. THE BARN? He had seen something along this line in England and it didn't seem to bother him that we would all be the laughing stock of the town. This was the kind of scandal that would be broadcast to all and sundry; my mother's head might well pop clean off her neck when she'd done sending up novenas for the return of his common sense.

Roll up! Roll up! Meet the Johns family: Poor Bridie, the Tramp Rattigan, her little bastard and the priest's son all living in a barn, happily ever after. I was so angry I didn't speak when he mentioned it first. If it wasn't for the blissful thought that I was about to be returned to a house with running water and electricity and a FLUSHING TOILET, I might have huffed and puffed until the next Christmas. We would all have to live in a big caravan while the renovation took place. Great, it would be like Bundoran without the candyfloss! I was still stewing when he spoke.

– Do you have anything to say about these plans, Mary?

– It's your house not mine!

– You may have noticed that you live here too?

– That doesn't make it my house!

– Well now! I'm sorry I tried to drag you back to life and all its tedious details! Will you miss carrying water from the well, tell me?

– No.

– Will you miss the Tin House?

– No!

– Well then, the loss of both those joys should allow for one tiny smile to ease itself on to those lips, eh?

– Ah, leave her alone, John! says Bridie. You know the girl has never been able to speak up for herself!

I wanted to speak, I was desperate to speak, but I couldn't start now because I was upset about the lovely placid old dolls I'd been tending for a year being sent away and Johns Farm being ripped apart. John Johns was watching me, willing me to give an opinion on proceedings.

My entire world had shrunk to the walls and high ditches of Johns Farm and I didn't know how to voice how important that was for me, how it suddenly seemed to be all I wanted and I didn't want it to be touched, not now, not ever. The farm was my cocoon, perfect and cosy. I didn't want it disturbed.

– It's okay, Bridie, I'm just too tired to think.

John snorted and flipped all the magazines and drawings he'd made on the floor. He slammed up and out of the room, banging his bedroom door so hard it nearly came off the hinges. Poor auld Brandy dog was whining and shaking and turning circles. Bridie looked shocked as he smashed about, shouting.

– Mary's tired, Mary's tired, Mary's tired, MARY'S ALWAYS BLOODY TIRED!

I heard some books hit the wall and I worried for their spines but he wore himself out soon enough. The night ended as they all did, with milky coffee and broken biscuits and no further discussion. Tomorrow, we'd all let on nothing had been said or done or thrown. It was hard to beat the normality of a good Catholic family life.

We spent Christmas Day 1985 in front of the range, just the four of us. Serena got some books and colouring pens and a horrible thing, a Cabbage Patch doll; its little sealed-up lips and dimple made me feel claustrophobic but it was what she wanted so Dada had wrapped it up. When we sang 'Jingle Bells' and 'O Little Town of Bethlehem' for her she spun like a top in a red velvet dress that Bridie had sewn. John Johns's voice was deep and crisp and even and it resonated through the concrete to my toes, making them curl up in my winter boots.

I cooked the dinner and everything turned out gorgeous. Even the Christmas pudding was worth floating in a pint of cream. Bridie announced she was retiring from the job of head chef. Lizzie Magee, home for the season, came up at night-time to have a drink and I watched her gassing with Bridie and John and not noticing that I couldn't join in. I poured beer for them and made turkey sandwiches and they hardly looked up from Serena, who was lying on her stomach drawing pictures of mammies and daddies in the heat from the fire.

Daddy came down on Boxing Day night to thrash out the plans for the new barn at The Hill; it would be built by February or March and we would start on the house as soon as the better weather of spring arrived. He stayed for a round of cards: him, Matthew, Bridie and John played Strip Jack 'til bedtime for pennies. I made biscuits on a whim because I wanted to keep away from the table and the talk. I came out with shortbread dusted with cinnamon that were cool enough to have with the tea before they left. The label on Daddy's vest was sticking out and I tucked it in, resting my fingers lightly on his neck for a moment. He didn't even jump but turned round and gave me a smile worth a million pounds.

– My mother always made shortbread biscuits, he says. Just like yours.

I made a cake with '3' written on it in pink icing on December 30th and John beat me to helping Serena blow out her birthday candles. I made a wish anyway. I wished I could fly, but not because I wanted to go anywhere else. I just wanted to know if they'd look up at me if I took off and did a few circuits of the kitchen ceiling at Johns Farm; there was no guarantee.

The foundations for the new barn were dug just after New Year, 1986. They were still full of icy water when my twentieth birthday came and went on February 20th unmarked bar a card and sweets from Auntie Eileen and a card with a £20-note from Kathleen: a pound for every year, she wrote in it, kiss, kiss. I took myself off for a walk to Brooky Hay the day the Ladies were walked from the river field for the last time. They had to climb to The Hill to be loaded up in trailers and taken to the mart. When I got back, the whole street was pitted with hoof marks but there was no other trace of them. I should have had the courage to say goodbye.

A storm of activity blew us towards April. I cooked for the men who were laying blocks; John just gave me the number of mouths as he dropped off the groceries. I stretched spuds and meat the length of the table and he hardly acknowledged that I was in the room. I was an apron and gloves, nothing more.

Often, Bridie and me would have to do with fried eggs on toast if too many men showed up with big appetites. Serena knew what side her bread was buttered! She had her dinner straight off Dada's plate, robbing his carrots and peas as he laughed at her antics and hugged her on his knee. The resentment wrapped itself around my neck like a thick wool sock coated with Vicks.

By the by, the shed was up, the beef cows bought and life resumed its slower pace for a solitary week before it was time to flit out of Johns Farm by travelling a full two hundred yards: the caravan was coming! Moving day was set and Bridie and me had to pack up all our worldly possessions in readiness. I pulled out my suitcase and shoved the pink wedding suit and plastic shoes into a rubbish bag without a second glance. Joe Loughrey's face materialised in front of my eyes but I shut them quickly and locked him out. Had he forgotten about me overnight or had it taken him a week or two? It didn't matter now. There was an ocean between us.

Serena laid claim to Blue Ted when he was fetched out of the gloom at the back of the wardrobe shelf; she put him in Bosco's lap and wheeled them both off in her pram. Toys shouldn't be left all alone, she said to me, cross as you please. Bad Mammy! I watched her straight little back and dancing ponytail skip away from me through the light at the half-door. She was more like John Johns with every day that passed.

When Bridie went to pack up the jams and pickles from the scullery, she says to me, you can pack John's room, as if it was nothing.

– I'm not sure that's a great idea, Bridie. Surely John wouldn't want me in there poking about? You know what he's like?

– I do, pet, I do, but there's a pile of stuff in there and I'm not able for it – so you'd better have a go. When he lands back tonight with the caravan it'll be late and he wants an early start tomorrow when Matthew and a few of the other lads show up to set the wheels in motion.

I let myself into the room and spotted the one thing out of place straight away. He'd left a book open on the bed. Helmut Newton, said the cover. I'd not seen it before. How had I missed it after all my poking about? The photographs inside were very saucy: all made-up nudey-rudey women and bare bottoms. It roasted my face to look at them and I *did* look at every single one of them, pored over them 'til I had them by rote.

To darling John, love always, Catherine. The same neat hand I'd seen printed on the inside of so many of the books I'd borrowed signed herself off with a few kisses.

What kind of a tramp must this Catherine be to give a boy a book of photographs like that? She was worldly, she was sophisticated; not like me, the farmer's daughter who lived at the bottom of the hill she was born on. She was golden-haired and golden-limbed. She was still in his life.

I ran for my empty boxes and packed up all of the books, slamming Catherine the T.R.A.M.P. right at the bottom so she couldn't be seen. I packed his clothes, shoes and coats, his radio and alarm clock. I stripped his bed, pulling the sheets and blankets off it and dragging them all to the floor in a high pile. I kicked them in their soft guts over and over again 'til I was totally out of puff. Then I folded them neat as pie and carried them to the kitchen, a portrait of calm. Bridie said, do you want tea? You look done in! I said, sure, I'll take tea.

What's another year to someone who's getting used to being alone, wails Johnny Logan from the wireless for the millionth time, what's another year to someone who's lost everything that he owns? If I have to listen to that Eurovision shite just *once* more I'm going to throw the batteries over the hedge.

The sound of the tractor towing the caravan comes to me on the river and I know I won't have long to gaze my last at the little house as it stands, my oubliette of four years. The picture of the Sacred Heart left a paler cream rectangle and the old black-framed mirror is already sitting out on the street bouncing the light back too brightly. All that remains is the kettle as the yellow range will be kept stoked until we get the gas cylinder hooked up to the two-ring cooker.

– Mammy, look, a house on wheels! says Serena.

Bridie and her and me run on to the street to see the spectacle of it being towed down the hill. The caravan brushes against the greenery and snags on a low branch on one of the big sycamores and then it's parked. It's a mint-green Clubman that's seen better days but for Serena it's paradise. She's never seen pink frilly curtains before, didn't know that kitchens could be so uncluttered, had no idea that benches could double up as beds. She holds up Blue Ted and Bosco against the back window and John kisses them both through the panes to make her scream with laughter. The track of his lips is still on the glass when I go to drag her away. I am left out of all their games.

We were over four months in the caravan in all; Bridie was on one bunk, Serena and me on the other. John slept in his brass bed in the milk house which made Serena giddy with joy. She wanted to sleep outside with him but he wouldn't let her because of the rats. To her, he said, little girls can't sleep outside in case their hair goes straight. Well! He created a monster: after fruit loaf and milky tea, straight hair was everything she wanted. I often had to go and lift her out of his bed when she was dead to the world. He kissed her dangling feet by way of goodnight and I wiped them on my side.

One night, he must have been so tired, working on the farm and building the house, that he fell asleep and when I went to collect her, they were wrapped around each other, Chicken Licken and her falling sky lying open and the yellow glow of the Tilley lamp making the whole scene look like a life I might have wanted at some stage. I should have let her alone, but I couldn't sleep without the warm smell of her beside me, so I slid her out and tiptoed back to Bridie, taking care not to look at the shape of John Johns's red lips when he slept.

I'm not yours, I said to his dreaming face once more for my own sanity, *and you're not mine.* Those red lips were sneaking past my defences, had made a few appearances in my secret dreams where they got all mixed up with nudey-rudey photos and the thought of him putting his mouth on the sophisticated Catherine. Now he was stuck back here building a better house for my daughter and for his mother and I would get to live in it too if I didn't annoy him. There was no denying that he was decent in many ways. I had to keep an eye on my anger. It was in danger of petering out if I didn't keep it fuelled.

I blame the whole caravan-living thing. It was playing havoc with my nerves. We had all had to get *closer*. Without rooms to run to, we sat around together at night. I cooked outside in the log store on the two-ring gas stove, churning out great piles of stew or chicken soup with spuds which we ate with spoons from tin bowls. We felt we could nearly touch the stars, they were so close in the low dark sky. We drank hot chocolate on the steps of the caravan after John cut a steel drum in half and used it to light a fire. The smoke kept the midges from eating us alive.

Serena loved it: having Bridie, me and her dada all on call at once was her greatest delight. Matthew started coming over more regularly and the other lads who were knocking down and putting up walls stayed for a few beers in the evening. The days were stretching into summer and there were more hours to get through all the work of the farm. Along with the light, there was no doubting it: the place had become *jolly*. I wanted to laugh too, wanted to throw myself into the joy of watching the amber sparks of the wood burning in the silvery-blue of the flames. But my laughs were stuck in my feet and by the time they climbed to my mouth it was too late.

Seeing John among his friends joshing and joking was unsettling. A lot of them had been in England with him and the tales they'd spun and heard in pubs were often repeated. Bridie had a few favourites she asked for every night and she laughed like she'd never heard the punchline before. They tried to include me but I would blush and stammer and clam up if a question came my way. The looks on their faces assured me they thought John had married an idiot out of the goodness of his heart when he could have had his pick, and they were right. The man himself answered for me so I could blend back into the whitewashed walls.

I was more shocked than any of them when one night I finally joined in. I don't know what came over me, a sort of dander maybe? It was really late, Serena and Bridie were both asleep. We'd had the usual rounds of yarns and discussions and enough drink had been taken for them all to get a bit sentimental. There were loads of things in London they missed: the buildings, the parks, the great Irish bars. None of them made a single mention of women although I knew England had them, too. The money was so good, the work maybe not so hard as they thought at the time. They kept going until they were convinced it was a great country altogether, better than here most days. At least there the police didn't have guns. I might as well have fired a shot above their heads when I piped up.

   – Will you go back, do you think?

   – We're just talking, Mary! Talking too much maybe!

   – I'd like to know. Are you thinking of going back across the
     water for any reason? Any reason at all?

   – No, I'm not going back. I've done my time there.

With that, I'd bid them all goodnight where they sat with their mouths open. When I closed the door on the caravan they all burst out laughing. I heard them ribbing John Johns about the auld ball and chain and he must have taken it in good humour because he didn't answer.

He seemed to have a new-found lightness all round and he had nearly turned me inside out when I caught him *bathing* in the river a few days earlier.

Serena was snoozing with Bridie under the big yellow tarpaulin John had strung between the milk house and the barn. I took the opportunity to stroll down to the river to cool off. I rolled up my trousers and waded in, delighted with the relief, scooping the water in chilly handfuls up my arms and over the back of my sunburnt neck.

I looked up at the pure-blue sky and saw the white trails of two aeroplanes, heading out from Belfast over the west coast to America. Would I ever get there? Would I ever get anywhere? Would I ever see more than a mile of the Atlantic where it gouged the Donegal coast?

John had stood up right beside me, buck naked but for a smile, and scared the bejesus out of me! I had run for the bank and hauled myself out after screaming like a girl. I'd never seen a naked man before in the flesh. He had laughed: laughed and laughed, not even trying to cover … his … himself up. Oh, he was brazen! In the end he lifted up his arms like a man about to ascend into Heaven.

– Can you see what you do to me, Mrs Johns, even at this temperature?

I had run through the rushes barefoot, my face on fire and other bits of me not much cooler, the sound of his pleasure ringing in my ears.

I had never thought of what I did once a week on a Wednesday as self-abuse. Wednesday was bingo night and John would run Bridie into the town and go for a jar while she gossiped and struggled to get a line or a full house for a fiver. With the house empty and my baba fast asleep, I would have a proper strip wash at the sink. When I was clean, I rinsed the rough facecloth out for the last time and pressed it over my face to block out the light. I would lean my weight against the locked door and wedge my feet on either side of the blocks that held the big Belfast sink up in the air, to keep from sliding on the lino.

Memories intruded: a really deep kiss I'd shared with Joe Loughrey, one from the early days when we couldn't get enough of each other. The look on Jacques Bernier's face when he had picked the flake of tobacco from his tongue, the thought of where that tongue had just been.

If I was extra tired, or lonely or sad, I couldn't stop John Johns's face floating past, his eyebrows knitted together, his lips burning red but still with nothing to say. Those nights I juddered to my feet and vowed I'd never do it again. It was a sin, anyway. But far from any of it making it better, far from it being a release, I might as well have been throwing paraffin at a fire instead of sand. The heat raged higher and hotter and harder inside me every time I strove to damp it out.

The blotches on my chest and neck would just have time to go down before they got home, she reeking of fag smoke and mint imperials, he with beer on his breath and a look in his eye I couldn't meet.

20

The remodelling of Johns Farm was finished by the end of August, after the hottest summer any of us could remember, and we painted the whole thing white like a giant Christmas cake. The house was further linked to the barn with a glass conservatory that looked out to the orchard. John had built out the back to a huge kitchen with room for the table and chairs, and four bedrooms in all. I didn't think about the bedrooms in case I broke out in hives.

He had made a special room for Bridie on the ground floor with her own bathroom, and the sheer excitement of it: a *second* bathroom under a skylight on the second floor. To go from no toilet to two toilets overnight is a rarely experienced joy. We kept the concrete floor in the kitchen: concrete never wears.

I was amazed by the space when we cleared out all the tools and the dustsheets; the pink skimmed walls with not a bump were the most beautiful things I'd ever seen. He had been so clever, sketching what he wanted before getting an architect to draw up the plans, and he and his pals had built a palace. I bought Serena's school uniform the same day we piled twenty cans of white emulsion into the boot of the car.

I painted the walls downstairs late into the nights. John was painting the whole upstairs but he had caved in to Bridie who had begged for a bit of auld flowery wallpaper. She couldn't look at all that white: she'd think she was locked in the Tyrone Fermanagh! She had gone straight to the rolls of dainty blue roses climbing on delicate green stalks when she was let loose in McGoran's hardware place.

I had to help him line up the slim stems and petals and our hands kept touching, our hips kept touching and our forearms. The fine dark hair on his arms was softer than it looked. My mouth had never been so dry; John kept clearing his throat and exhaling through his lips. It must have been the dust. When the last strip was up we stood back to admire it.

– Bridie'll love that!

– Let's hope she doesn't want carpet to match, Mrs Johns!

I wished he wouldn't smile at me with those teeth and expect me to say something, *anything*. I wished he'd stop calling me *Mrs Johns*. I backed away from him and made for the caravan and the last of the few nights I had with my girl before she went to pre-school. Pre-school for pre-cocious, John teases her, and she screams with laughter as if she understands she's miles ahead of the herd.

Serena took to school like a duck to water. The first day I went to collect her she came out holding hands with a little girl called Nora Reilly and I had to speak to her mammy who was also at the gate. I got the usual look: the 'oh, you're Mary Johns, the quare wan who disappeared after disgracing yourself' look.

The look I dreaded. But I kept the 'I'm just a normal girl picking up her daughter from school' face on 'til I had walked to the top of the town. I hoped to God no one could see or hear my heart flailing about.

Because it was her first day, John was picking us up in the car and we were having fish and chips from the takeaway for tea. Serena found shyness at last as the waves of loving attention washed over her. It was John's neck she hid her face in. He squeezed her tight and covered her ears with kisses 'til she had time to recover.

We had the lovely vinegary chips on our laps in the barn and we covered Serena's schoolbooks and jotters with the last of the blue-rose wallpaper. Serena Bridget Johns, she got me to write on the books, The Nursery, St Patrick's, Carncloon. My mother hadn't even marked the day with an insult.

By Friday, Rosaleen Reilly had asked her to go for a sleepover with Nora – what we called going to stay at somebody's house before America got involved. Just like Lizzie and me, they were inseparable after five days. It was the first night she would be out of Johns Farm since she was born, or out of my bed for that matter. Her excitement swept the lot of us up. Bridie had sewn her a pair of pink gingham pyjamas with a matching pink gingham teddy-bear pyjama case to put them in. She packed her toothbrush and agonised over whether or not Bosco and Blue Ted would cope without her for one night? I said they could both sleep in beside me and I'd explain: it would be for one night only and we'd all have to cope without her.

I got her to take her Cabbage Patch doll so that its weirdy face wouldn't freak me out. Bridie was off to the bingo, the two of them talking about what to wear, two little birds twittering about what would be the Very Best Outfit for such an exciting excursion.

John Johns was outside clearing farming stuff off the back seat, like it was a Sunday. His mother always sat up front for the weekly trip to Sunday Mass, with the other two women in his life in the back. He pulled round to the door to save their shoes from the mud. Serena got in and sat still, looking straight ahead while John Johns mock-inspected her. She always had to be immaculate, not a hair out of place and with her shoes shining. They both loved that game and he always said A-plus before she giggled. Bridie got in and fussed around and then they both waved and waved like they were off to London to look at the Queen instead of the town ten miles away.

I waved and waved back as the street grew dark and I was left alone with just the trees for company. The caravan glowed yellow with the Tilley lamp; a few moths fluttered their dusty wings against the light. The house stood large and dark and empty, all white and grey and smelling of cut wood. I let myself in and wandered from room to room, my steps echoing. There were no rats, no ticking clock, no kettle singing on the range, no shouts of laughter from my girl or Bridie stirring tea. There was no pretend-husband stepping lightly. There was *something*, though, the slightest agitation of dust, and when I turned I saw her.

Granny Moo stood in the new doorway between the house that Johns Farm had been and the house it had become. She put her finger to her lips to stop me from screaming and then she pointed at the kitchen. I jerked my head around as headlights swept the length of the wall. John Johns had come home and when I looked for the messenger she was gone. I was quaking in my boots when he walked in looking bigger and more alive than ever. I could see the pulse in his neck, thick with blood.

– You're back.

– Yes.

– I thought you'd probably go for a pint at O'Carolan's instead of doing the drive twice.

– I went in but Scrumptious Connolly can never let me pass. He was wondering when I was going to have some waynes of *my own*.

John Johns's mouth was dry; he licked his lower lip. Two seconds, three, four, five … I made for the upstairs bathroom and the lock on the door. He was outside by the time I'd bolted the door and slid down under the glass top to hide myself.

– Jesus, Mary, we can't go on like this – two dry husks moving around each other! Mary, open the door, please. Mary? MARY!

– I *can't!*

– Let me in, please …

I couldn't answer; what would I say? If I broke now I'd have to admit that I was fine to stay here in this day-in, day-out, every-day-the-same farming life. He could hear me thinking.

– Mary, you can't keep me out forever!

– I can and I will!

He knocked his forehead gently against the glass before he walked away.

Bridie was already up and at the old range in her new kitchen boiling the kettle when I got dressed. I stood beside her trying to avoid her eye. I had to speak, although it seemed like my voice was coming from someone else, someone who sounded like they were in a deep hole.

— How was the bingo?

— Grand, grand, same crowd as always. It's not the same without wee Serena, is it?

— No, it's not the same.

— Children are a gift from God, they really are ...

— I *know* that.

God! If only she knew how much I *wanted* to have another baby. I'd give my eyetooth for one, or two or twenty! But I'd have to do *it* with John Johns. It seemed totally impossible. Me and him? Together, *like that*? My whole body started to shake at the very thought of it. I'd probably *die* of embarrassment. He would see me with no clothes on. The very thought of his Body Part A coming anywhere near my Body Part B sent it into a tailspin. Bridie sniffed a few more times and finally got enough of a hold on herself to voice what was making her snivel, like I hadn't been able to figure it out.

— John's a good man, y'know, Mary? There's worse men. Mary? I say, there's worse men? This life ... and him ... might not be what you wanted but it's what you have?

— I know, I know. I could have done a lot worse. Drink your tea, Bridie.

Outside was bright sunshine and the oblivious fields. I stayed out all day; I did my work, cleaned the byre, swept, carried, dug and toiled 'til the sweat was running down my aching back. I stopped for dinner with Bridie; she'd made us potatoes and fried fish, not burnt, and I was delighted to have the warmth of it, I felt so hollowed out. I could hardly wait for Serena to come back.

I was waiting at the end of the lane where it dropped away from The Hill when I saw her running to me. She jumped into my arms without even a hello. As soon as I felt her I knew something was wrong. She pressed every inch of herself into me and held on for dear life.

– Serena? What's the matter?

– Nora says Dada isn't my real daddy.

– What? *What did you say?*

– I told her he *is* my daddy! He is my daddy?

She was as white as a sheet but I hadn't lied to her and I wouldn't start now. I'd always known it would come to light but I wished with all my heart that John was standing beside me for this one. He'd know what to say; he'd know how to say it to make it better. For Serena he could always make things better.

– Look at me! He *is* your daddy! And do you know why? Because he's always been here and he always will and he loves you to The Hill and back. You know that, don't you?

– Yes, Mammy!

– People love saying horrible things and this won't be the last you hear of it. Your daddy is the man who takes the job on, okay? And you don't know any other daddy, do you?

– No, Mammy!

– Well. That's settled then! When you're a big girl we'll talk about this again, alright?

– Alright.

– Shall we have a walk? I thought we'd go and see if there were any daisies down at the river?

– Alright.

We strolled on hand in hand, the guilt chewing its way through my guts. It was hateful that she suffered because of me.

Children repeat what they hear and Nora Reilly had most likely overheard her parents sniggering about it. While I got her to tell me about the good bits – eating Jaffa Cakes in bed – I replayed what I had said and found that I'd managed the truth. Her daddy was the man who took the job on and I could not fault John Johns's love and devotion to her.

He was a good man, a better man than I had had my sights set on as a sixteen-year-old. To think, I'd always hated him for having no wings, no desire to be up and away from this patch of ground, when he'd been standing over her like a guardian angel since she was born. What would I have done without him? I resolved to be kinder.

The daisies were there, stuck to the side of the mossy river-bank. Serena leaned down and picked a few for Bridie while I held on to her spindly legs. She checked that Bridie was still her granny and I told her, of course, Bridie came as part of the package with Dada. Serena was accepting, a child so full of confidence and so empty of fear, that she had already rooted herself in a new version of the truth. I just had to tell John and hope he didn't blow a gasket that anyone had upset *his* girl.

As we got to the bottom of the street, the little bit of growing up I just did was replaced with a sudden desire to be pressed against Auntie Eileen's middle with only a choice between which boiled sweets to eat. John Johns had my bed from the Lower Room on a trailer and a newly-bought pink wooden bed frame standing on the street. Serena spotted it straight away and made for it at speed. I could hear John Johns telling her that, *of course*, it was for her. A big girl who was old enough to stay away from home should have her own nice bed. It was going into her new bedroom right this minute.

– But where will Mammy sleep now?

I'd reached them by then. Bridie couldn't look at me. John Johns picked up the little bed with its wooden love heart carved into the headboard with one arm and manoeuvred it into the house. He never even looked in my direction when he came out, just started up the tractor and set off. I watched my old bed disappearing up the hill, quelling the desire to run after it, shouting and swearing, but then the trailer rounded the bend at the top and it was gone forever, leaving one tiny echo.

– But where will Mammy sleep now?

It seemed I was finally to take my rightful place beside my husband. I'd been so right for so long in the eyes of the Church and now I would be right in the eyes of the law. John Johns had staked his claim: for richer, for poorer, in sickness and in health, 'til death did us part. Life didn't come into it, or so I thought. I had to hand it to him: he had found a foolproof way to overhaul communications between us without uttering a single word. I breathed in and put the kettle on; no point in trying to swallow anything without tea.

To my mind, Serena went far too happily to her new life in the new bedroom. Bridie and the blue roses were just next door any time she wanted a natter or a hug and she unpacked Bosco, Blue Ted, the Cabbage Patch Kid from hell, her pink gingham pyjamas and few auld dollies and let me know that she'd be just grand. She knew where me and Dada were if she needed us. I blanched at my transformation to an 'us'. It had only taken John a matter of minutes to put the question of his fatherhood to bed. I'm the only daddy you'll ever need, he said, with her little face cupped in his hands, and she had nodded very solemnly and got on with piling her bread high with rhubarb jam.

While she stayed on the ground floor with Bridie I was to join my husband underneath the sessile-oak eaves. He had spent the rest of the day moving his boxes of books and they stood along the wall in the kitchen. It seemed like years since I had taped them up instead of months. He gave me an hour to get what I wanted from the caravan as it was going to be towed away that very night. I might just stay in it now that my daughter didn't want me and even Bridie had decided it was time for me to become an adult. I wanted to have a bit of a huff but no one was watching me. It was alright, no one could feel sorrier for me than I could for myself.

I dragged my brown suitcase out from under the bed and stuck my toothbrush in my pocket. I was putting my tired clothes in it when I felt John attach the caravan to the towbar on the tractor. It started to move as soon as I closed the door. He was a man taking no chances that I would have anywhere to lay my head except beside his. Having a little cry down by the river in the gathering dark did no good; the blackbirds got on with their lives, I saw a fox slink along the stone walls on his way to terrorise the chickens. I ran at him flapping my arms and shouting as if it would make any difference to his dinner plans. I was a dog with no bark; Foxy Woxy kept pace with me half a field away. Even the owls laughed in the shadowy trees.

The house was quiet, the kettle sang on the range and everything else was fresh-painted plaster. John had come back and was nowhere in sight. I got out my nightie and, despite the heat of the night, put on every stitch I had to hand 'til I was like the Michelin Man. John was reading by the brass bed when I slipped under the blankets and clung to the outside edge in case he touched me in the night. By the by, he slipped in beside me and switched the light off and I swear I could *feel* him smiling in the dark.

The embarrassment of having him laugh at me rose up from my toes and I was boiling over with it, never mind the two pairs of socks, three pairs of knickers, four jumpers, my jeans and a hat in the mildness of September.

– Are you cold, Mary?

– Yes!

– We can fix that ...

Oh, the lousy bastard! He went off and got another heavy blanket, doubled it and put it on top of me. I was going to be smoked out! Then he got back in so I could enjoy him cracking up fit to burst. I broke after about thirty minutes and clawed the soggy clothes off my back and ran for the bathroom to sponge down the heat rash. Oh, but the joy of just turning a tap! I looked more like a fresh-boiled ham than a girl so I hiccuped my way back to his room and got in beside him. He'd had his fun so he kept his back to me and we must have fallen asleep, a space between us you could have driven a baler down.

He didn't touch me in the first week but I was as alarmed by his new nakedness as I was by his total lack of self-consciousness. I was constantly struck by how beautiful he was even as my stomach twisted when he just came in, stripped off and slid into bed without a word. The whiteness of his skin only served to make his dark hair darker and he always slept naked, brazen. The deathly chill on the linen sheets didn't even slow him down. I was always there before him, eyes jammed shut and limbs clamped into a ball.

He got to me slowly, a deer stalker stepping light, breathing into my hair, inching his way closer, putting his arm around me. One night pulling me round to rest my head on his chest, another night fitting his whole length behind me and many more nights holding my hands, my sweaty little-girl hands still in fists, in his palm. He kept a pillow between me and him as if I mightn't know what was brewing.

All of these things took root in the silence we had been cultivating for years and so we came to know each other without the handicap of words. When he lifted my nightie and licked me slowly from the back of my neck to the base of my spine, I had to hold on to my nipples in case they pinged clean off me and rolled under the bed! I prayed he would never open his mouth for any other reason.

I caved in in the end: seems he *did* know about kissing girls way south of the border properly in bandit country and, damn my pedigree tramp's DNA, I rose up to meet him. He was so big, so smooth, so patient, he covered me easily. When he kissed me like that, when he kissed me *at all*, I was glad that my daughter and Bridie were far away out of earshot. I hated myself for not being able to deny my need. I was entirely undone.

The sounds of us together under the eaves made the silence of us together during the daylight hours seem less strained. We'd never be yammerers, that was for sure, but now when he stood close to me, just to reach past me for the milk or to kiss Serena when she was already in my arms, I had to concentrate on not tipping headlong into him instead of pitching back. I don't know if he felt the same pull towards me. If he did, it didn't show; nothing showed on his face and I did my best to match the lack of change in the atmosphere between us. I couldn't risk forgetting that he wasn't in the market for a wife even though now I had become one. If he wanted to be a husband, it was no business of mine.

A few weeks after the new sleeping arrangements were in place and my charming child hadn't had the grace to miss me for even *one* night, we were all in the kitchen having breakfast. Bowls of porridge all round with extra stewed prunes for Bridie. I was minding my own business and stirring the pan so I was caught like a rabbit in the headlights by Serena whose already gold-standard confidence was growing with every day at school.

– Mammy?

– Yes, lovely?

– I heard loads of noises from your room last night?

– *What?*

– Noises, like you were shouting about something?

– Must be that imagination of yours or a dream!

– NO! I heard you shouting! I did!

– I know what it was! We were saying our prayers. Your mammy dropped her rosary beads, says John smiling, somewhere around the tenth decade ...

– Did you, Mammy? Did you drop your rosary beads?

– Yes, pet, I dropped my ... rosary beads.

John and Bridie had to hunch their backs over the sink to hide their hilarity and she let off a fart that set the pair of them off in total hysterics. I was hoping it was the prunes but I knew it was me, Mrs Mary Johns, figure of fun and T.R.A.M.P. extraordinaire.

21

I had just realised that I was pregnant when pictures of Reverend Ian Paisley wearing a red beret were shown on the news. He had the good sense to wear an ordinary necktie, leaving aside his dog collar. Himself, Peter Robinson and Ivan Foster, all members of the Democratic Unionist Party, had got together to set up *another* Loyalist paramilitary movement, Ulster Resistance, because a fresh terror group was needed to tackle the aims of the Anglo-Irish Agreement. No baby step towards peace would be taken on his watch, No Siree Bob! None of it, none of the madness, could impinge on the joy I felt that I had another glorious child on the way.

I was eight months along when Carncloon's two bombs went off. It was twins I had on board and I swear both of them flipped around at the sound making me cry out and frightening the life out of Bridie and Serena. John was out and the three of us gals were snug and silly in front of the old range in the kitchen. With the electricity had come a television set (Sony Trinitron, nice) and a music centre and we had a few records already: Horslips, Van Morrison, the Undertones, Johnny Cash, Dusty Springfield.

We'd switched the telly off because seeing Gerry Adams being dubbed by another man with a Northern Irish accent made us all crazy. Margaret Thatcher was trying to rob terrorists of the oxygen of publicity but the message was still getting through; Sinn Féin had a voice.

We were playing Snakes and Ladders when we felt the windows go. They didn't break but they sort of bowed in and out again and then we heard the noise of the bomb. Like everything at Johns Farm it came to us on the river: first one and then the other. The second one only seemed louder because by that stage we were all standing on the street straining to make out what was happening. The sky over Carncloon glowed orange and was filling with smoke and then the sound of the sirens broke out of the silent night. It was impossible to tell what side was hit; we wouldn't know 'til morning. Bridie broke the spell.

– It'll be somebody's son anyway.

– Or somebody's daughter.

John came rattling down the lane in the tractor and told us all to get back inside, to get to the bedrooms, and he would wait in the kitchen for the fallout if it came. We lay for an hour, Serena with her eyes like saucers, 'til we heard something else rumbling on the river. Big blocky Saracens coming fast; I'd know that heartless sound anywhere. It was their side that had been hit, not ours. They'd have already stopped at the McCourts place and picked up the two remaining sons from there; Mammy and Daddy would get a rub but, thank God, Matthew was away staying with Kathleen in Derry. Then they would travel on to Johns Farm.

217

I got up and hugged Serena while I warned her again, no matter what she heard she was to stay in her room and away from the windows. John was eating a lump of bread and cheese in the kitchen.

- You never know when you're next going to get a square meal!
- Are you going to be alright?
- Why? Will you miss me, Mary darlin'?

I didn't have to answer because they were on us, beating on the outside door like their lives depended on it. In the dead of night they still expected you to be ready and willing to fling back your bolts. Bridie pulled auld Brandy dog away from his yapping at the door and held his jaws together; she wanted to make sure he didn't get a kick or worse. She held on to him because she couldn't hold on to John.

- Answer the door and then get out of the way – don't give them an excuse, do you hear me, Mary? Stay back and stay safe.
- I hear you.

The soldiers had RUC men with them, all armed to the teeth. It would have been farcical to think that it would take this much force to lift one man but they did it in a way that wasn't funny. No one bundled John Johns; he walked where they wanted him, head and shoulders taller than all the armed men put together. I winced when one of them pushed his head down to make him disappear inside the truck. When he was out of sight one of the English boys came over, all cocksure and finding himself hilarious as he mocked us in a cod Irish accent.

- Don't worry, love, he won't be long gone and I can always come back and check up on you, yeah? Make sure you're alright! You and yer mammy!

I don't know why he was being an idiot from Dublin when we were in County Tyrone but I wasn't about to ask. I suppose we all sounded the same? Bridie was quaking at the half-door; she motioned for me to come in without a word, let them have their fun. Neither of us wanted to make it any harder on John or the other boys.

He came back after three long days, unshaven and tired but otherwise not too bashed up. I waited 'til we were alone in bed before I reached out to touch a purplish bruise blooming on his cheek. I only wanted to acknowledge it; blows to the face can be very sore. He didn't say how it had happened.

They had kept them up for a couple of nights and given them a few thumps but they couldn't tell what they didn't know. I was only glad to have John Johns back, because having anyone snatched away like that makes your blood boil when you have to swallow everything that the other side throws without gagging. An angry Serena wanted to know why they were so mean and we had to remind her that both sides were mean.

Mammy, flying high on the drama of being the mother-in-law to a 'patriot', actually walked from The Hill to Johns Farm to announce she wanted to cook us a meal. Even Bridie was to come, Bridie who had prayed on her knees for three days that her only child wouldn't get his head kicked in behind the high walls of the barracks.

The date was set for the following Sunday and Kathleen would be allowed to attend too. It would be a celebration of sorts – not something The Hill had ever seen before. Holy smokes, says Bridie when Mammy's marched off again, all business, I never thought I'd live to see the day that I'd have my American Tans under the same table as that bloody auld trout!

Serena and me cracked up; it did seem other-worldly. I'd not had more than a cup of tea in the house that I used to call home in the five years since I'd left it without even realising.

That night, as we were getting ready for bed – not that I could sleep with two babies juggling for space right under my heart – John added to the rarity of the day by speaking to me. I stopped poking and fussing with the pillows to gawp at him where he sat stripped to the waist.

– What does she want?

– Mammy? I don't know. Kathleen tells me she's been watching the television, that terrible *Fair City* programme on RTÉ, and she made some comment about her own family being not so bad after all! She's even been a bit nicer to Kathleen since …

– The Lord works in mysterious ways.

– He does!

I thought he'd say more but he didn't. When I'd propped myself up for the night ahead, he flicked the lamp off and left us both in the dark. I felt him brush his lips against my stomach. He was soon asleep, his breathing deep and regular. His children settled down too, in tune with him already. Would we ever have a fat chat, like the ones me and Joe Loughrey used to have? Likely not as we liked to keep ourselves to ourselves. I put in the time until three o'clock watching his back rise and fall where the moon caught the shine of his skin.

The Hill was unchanged. Mammy met us in the front hall and pointed out the Holy Water fount in case we'd forget to bless ourselves on the way into her Good Catholic house. We had her 'own chicken roast', swimming in butter, sausage-meat stuffing and roast spuds done in chicken fat, sweet shallots, carrots and cabbage. The sherry trifle was loaded with fruit salad under the whipped cream. As always, Mammy had pulled the cherries out of the tin of Del Monte Fruit Cocktail and kept them to decorate the whipped-cream top. Every mouthful was delicious and we scraped the plates.

I had a sherry, even though my father measured it out very small. I don't want you to be falling about the place, Mary, he said, not in your condition. We smiled at each other. The thaw had started and it should continue unless Mammy thought of a new way to put us at odds. John had a few beers and was almost rosy as him and Daddy talked cows and crops.

I had allowed Serena to bring Bosco, just to wind Mammy up. John had backed her up when she asked if Bosco could sit with us. Mammy had immediately killed the idea – no, no, no, there's *no need* for silly toys at the table – but, straight-faced, John had said Bosco must have a chair; after all, bears must eat too. A rattled Mammy let Serena set a place for the bear at the table with a look at me, *me*, that said she's *ruined* and you're to blame! It was an unheard-of indulgence that had me and Kathleen exchanging glances and raised eyebrows.

I mouthed 'thank you' to John Johns who winked back at me and smiled and I blushed despite myself. At that moment he seemed so lovely to me but I squashed down the tiny lump of pathetic gratitude gathering in my throat. I must make sure my weakness is confined to the bedroom. I had been thinking of reaching out to him during daylight hours but every time I mustered the few words it would take to show him that I'd softened, I recalled that he only had one use for a nothing girl like me. I bit them back and let him walk on, unaware that he was appreciated. A man like him didn't need to be buttered up.

When it was time for the four of us to wander home with our torches I had a beaming Bridie hooked on one arm and the bear in the other while he carried Serena on his back, her little legs in their Sunday-best white socks hanging by his waist. Daddy said goodnight and safe home to us as a group to save his words. Mammy was too busy to bestow any kind of wishes. Chicken bones don't boil themselves, y'know?

Granda Ban passed away below in the nursing home a week later and I was sitting by the phone waiting for the call. I saw him in my dreams rounding the bend at the top of the lane. He turned to wave before he lit his pipe and the little clouds of grey smoke from it grew and grew 'til I couldn't see him any more. It was 4am and I slipped out of bed, got the range up to heat the kettle and wait. The babies swirled under my heart and poked their hands and feet in four directions at once as if they wanted to meet him before he went.

I was grand until I stood right beside his remains. I swayed a few times before I crashed into Bernie who was doling out coconut slices. It took John, Eileen and Kathleen to get me upright as I weighed a ton. Daddy was directing them from the doorway: watch her, watch her, he says, drawing tender shapes with his big hands. Being patted down and fussed over and forced to drink even more bloody weak tea was no consolation for the fact that I'd embarrassed myself once more. I couldn't even keep my wits about me for darling Granda Ban. With all four faces staring down at me, I burst into tears, got the hiccups and nearly peed myself all at the same time.

– I *told* you, you weren't strong enough for this! I'm taking
   you home right now, says John Johns, my hero.
– Mary, are you attention-seeking *again*? sighs Mammy.

I wasn't allowed to the funeral. The rain was blamed, as if I
was made of salt or sugar and might be washed away. I was
holed up in Johns Farm beside the fire; Brandy had squeezed
himself under the chair and the damp reek of his coat wafted up
to where I sat surrounded with biscuits and chocolates, bitter
and sweet.

Mick had chosen this weekend to tell me he was going to
Australia and the thought of him so far away from Carncloon
closed my throat. I might never see him again. I don't know if it
was because I was the size of a house, that Granda Ban and all
his stories were gone forever or the fact that Mick – who had
never mentioned wanting to travel – was going to get out into
the world and see it in a way I never would. The old longings to
be up, up and away, to be light enough to fly – God, to be light
enough to get out of a chair without groaning – took hold again.

The tears rolled down my face and slipped under my chin
where they tickled until they dropped. I couldn't even be bothered to wipe them clear. By this age, if I hadn't fallen off the
path, I would have flown all the way to America. I could have
been walking the streets of New York, hailing myself a yellow
cab or soaking up a bird's-eye view of Central Park from one of
the high-rise buildings. I could have photos taken of me to prove
that I'd got there, like the Polaroids Lizzie had a bad habit of
sending me from London.

Instead, I had a fresh set of shackles on the way. I blamed
John, of course. It takes a husband to give you a baby and that's
what he was whether he liked it or not. It wasn't easy to block

out my part in it. But in a way it wasn't my fault, it was breeding. Mammy was right, I was weak material. I should never have allowed him in but I didn't have the strength to keep him out.

I looked across the concrete floor of Johns Farm, my vista for the foreseeable future. Serena and Bridie were going over her three-times tables, getting faster and faster with every repetition. Three times seven is twenty-one, says my daughter. That's the age your mammy was on her last birthday, says Bridie. Happy key of the door to me!

22

The twins turned out to be two hefty baby boys and another one followed within eleven months. I didn't even know I was pregnant again 'til three months had gone by. My body hadn't lost the slight softness they had left behind before it was filled up again. Each son was more gorgeous than the last, all dark hair and wide little backs, their clavicles like the buds of angel wings. I called the twins Eugene and Marius; number three was Shane. I gave birth at home with Bridie to help me; the thought of going all the way to Omagh Hospital seemed ridiculous. John paced up and down outside the door 'til Bridie cleaned up before he brought Serena in to meet each new member of the gang.

– Do you remember *me* being born, Dada?

– Of course I do! Sure that was a *great* day!

John Johns greeted each arrival with a glow of pride and talk of having to extend the house again. He lifted them off me as soon as they were dry and kissed them over and over, anointing their perfect fingers and toes. The boys became 'my boys', just as Serena had become 'my girl'. I vowed each baby would be the last but I couldn't resist the smooth skin over the muscles in his back as he held himself above me. He always waited for me to turn back to him again in the bedroom where he was tenderness itself as he licked the pearls of milk from my nipples.

Although every one of them would tie me to Johns Farm for longer and longer, they took my heart in their tight little fists when they were born and would never let go. I would *not* have coped without my daughter and Bridie – Bridie my saviour who did all she could to help me rear them – but I still fell into bed every night exhausted. We battled wind and juggled bottles and Serena carried them around on her back to get them to go to sleep. Bridie wasn't getting any younger and her arthritis was getting worse so she took to swallowing her painkillers with Guinness to 'protect the lining of her stomach'. She was often drunk and high in charge of a toddler or two.

John did all he could outside without my help. We had fallen so easily into the roles I'd watched my parents play out over the years. The big animals were his domain, the big fields of hay and grain, the big machinery and miles of stone walls. Mine was the little house and the street, the children, the chickens, the orchard and the garden. We were so well rehearsed we could go whole days without more than a hello.

I was glad, because I needed every spare minute to worry; it was a worm inside me. Every time I looked at their delicate necks the sight of Sean McCourt's mother came to mind. She haunted the back of the chapel, bald and skeletal, reaching out to embrace anyone who had known him. She was a wreck around babies; they had to be handed over for her to hold too tightly and it was difficult to get them away from her. Her fingers had to be unpicked one by one. Both of her breasts had been removed already but the cancer was still eating her up from inside. It's amazing what the human heart and body can withstand.

Boys grew up to take sides and they had to answer for their choices. When the worry was bad enough to make me shake, I could almost feel the bullet travelling through Sean McCourt's head and keep going for one of mine. They had become targets as soon as the umbilical was cut.

The Troubles, the backdrop to my whole life, came screaming into focus all guns blazing. Northern Ireland boiled on all around us. The cocoon of Johns Farm shook to its very foundations during Marius and Eugene's first birthday party. I had made a rather sad, flat little cake and it had two candles, one each. When we blew them out a bomb went off in the town and scared the bejesus out of the two of them! They roared the house down and didn't stop shaking for an hour.

John nursed one while Serena nursed the other one. Bridie took a fit of crying and limped away to her blue roses. I had no room on my lap because Shane was trembling at my neck. He was so small still, just eight weeks old, and already his poor wee ears had had to withstand such a *bang*. We all waited for the sound of the Saracens on the river but none came; it must have been Catholic premises that was flattened.

They couldn't have been born into a worse time. Every day the television brought news of deaths: them and us. A lot of RUC officers and British soldiers were killed in the late 1980s and so were a lot of IRA. I added the SAS to my long list of acronyms. The Special Air Services took out eight IRA men who had just bombed an RUC base at Loughgall in County Armagh. By way of retaliation the IRA let off a bomb at a

Remembrance Service for military dead at Enniskillen, County Fermanagh. The bomb was meant to kill a whole parade of UDR soldiers but the timing was wrong. Ten Protestant civilians were killed and one police officer. Sixty-three people were injured. The IRA said they had made a *mistake*! A *mistake* is getting yourself pregnant, a *mistake* is forgetting to put self-raising flour in a cake because your eyes are crossed with tiredness, a *mistake* is thinking life will be what you always wanted one day.

The SAS popped up again when they killed another three IRA volunteers in Gibraltar and then, to cap it all, the UDA's Michael Stone opened fire at their funeral in Milltown Cemetery in Belfast, killing another IRA man and two civilians. We all shook our heads in disbelief around the fire at Johns Farm. We hugged our children tighter, cupping their delicate skulls in our hands as if that would save them, and Bridie prayed and prayed and prayed. We shouldn't have let her pray; God was not listening. He hadn't been listening for years.

Just days later two off-duty British soldiers were shot when they accidentally drove into an IRA funeral procession. Our jaws were on the floor and our spirits were at an all-time low. Once again the Catholics were as bad as the Protestants, and the Protestants were as bad as the Catholics; nothing was sacred any more. Bridie threw her rosary beads into a drawer and slammed it shut.

We heated milk to mash into rusks, changed nappies and washed the downy heads on our three small boys as the Lisburn van bomb killed six more soldiers in County Antrim and the Ballygawley bus bomb killed a further eight soldiers in County Tyrone.

I forced myself to check with John that 'the situation' was getting worse? He assured me it was: I wasn't just feeling increasingly panicky because I now had four precious lives to protect and I was lost as to how they would live in such a madhouse! If I couldn't get *myself* out of Northern Ireland how would I get my children to safety, to a new life?

Their arrival in my life had changed me utterly. When Serena was born, I only worried about ordinary things like nappy rash and colic, doing all I could to settle her. But with the boys, the whole world suddenly intruded. Sectarian hatred loomed at every turn, every bullet carried their names, every bomb would get bigger until the fallout landed right outside the half-door.

I took to putting them in the orchard for their naps in big navy-blue prams with hoods in case a helicopter crashed into the house. I told John that I, too, needed to be out and about; the walls were closing in on me. He nodded and let me work beside him between bottles and burpings until Serena needed meeting from the school bus at 4pm. I held posts while he tamped them in with a sledgehammer. I carried staples to secure wire. I walked back to the house for a flask of tea when we were both parched. It felt safer somehow as we worked together, cutting the binder twine, throwing bales, and pulling the musty hay apart to push it into the silos.

The victims piled up. Just when we thought it couldn't get any worse the IRA revisited the use of proxy bombs. They weren't new – both sides had stooped to use them in the 1970s – but somehow the horror of them drilled into my brain as I was breastfeeding Shane. The proxy involved tying collaborators – any unfortunate soul who associated with British security forces, maybe even just selling them petrol when they were off duty – into cars packed with explosives and setting them off on their merry way, some of them knowing that their families were being held at gunpoint as they drove to a near-certain death and murder.

Three human bombs were set up to explode on the same day, 24 October 1990. The driver and six soldiers died at Coshquin, near Derry; the driver escaped and one soldier died at Cloghoge on the border with County Armagh; the Omagh bomb failed to detonate.

Omagh was where the hospital was, Tyrone's county town, where Bridie went to get her pains and blood checked out. It was where the mart was, where we bought and sold cattle. It was where Woolworths sold Pick'n'Mix. It felt so wrong to even have it mentioned on the news. My milk dried up practically overnight and I was pregnant again by the time Margaret Thatcher was forced out of Downing Street. She had a little cry in the car as they drove her away in November.

Daniel was born in a matter of hours at home, proving beyond a shadow of a doubt that I was made to have children. I was back on my feet and back in front of the range frying eggs when he was barely dry. The bombs, firebombs, mortars, bullets and bullshit were still flying thick and fast as Daniel cut his first tooth. He was up toddling about and falling happily on the concrete when the IRA bombed the Baltic Exchange in London. The news reported the endless talks that were taking place behind closed doors between all the parties and the British government. Someone's not listening, says John Johns. He was right.

When Eugene and Marius were getting excited about going to school and practising their letters with Serena at the table, the

IRA killed two children in Warrington; the UDA killed five Catholic civilians on a building site in Castlerock, Derry; and Bishopsgate in London was hit by the IRA killing just one person, religion unknown.

Lizzie Magee married someone called Kenny McGuckin, a Derry man who was waiting out the Troubles in London just like she was. I'd tucked my invitation into the frame on my bedroom mirror as soon as I'd written to say I couldn't make it. Too busy with children and cows; she understood. I hoped I'd see pictures of her in the biggest white meringue she could find! We had promised we would be each other's bridesmaid when it came to living happily ever after, another dream dashed. We'd had a collection of frocks snipped out of magazines that peppered the mirror in Lizzie's bedroom. We changed our minds so often on which one was the most beautiful, which one we'd wear to make sure our big day was perfect. We were old enough now to know that there was no such thing as perfect.

Dessie and Sheila wouldn't cross the water. That's all she wrote and I knew that her heart was broken that they didn't make the effort. I couldn't believe that the mad pair I'd known wouldn't crawl there if they had to? They thought the sun rose and set on Lizzie. What had kept them at home?

Bridie found poor auld Brandy dog dead under his favourite tree. He got to live his life, she said and make it to being an old man. His head was on his paws as if he was only asleep. John put him under the ground where he lay and we dragged a big granite slab over the clay to mark another sadness. The children broke their hearts over it and we bent the house rules such as they were and let them all jump in the bed with us that night. Me, him and Bridie all gave up on sleep around 5am. We met in

231

the kitchen and toasted Brandy dog with a whiskey as the sky glowed orange over Sessiagh.

The SDLP's John Hume and Sinn Féin's Gerry Adams issued their first joint statement. The IRA voiced their concerns via the Gaelic newspaper *An Phoblacht*, urging the British government to stop its futile and costly war in Ireland and pursue the path of peace or resign itself to the path of war.

– Didn't they just bomb the bejesus out of London?

– They did, says John.

– And cause millions of pounds' worth of damage?

– They did, says John again.

We still weren't chatty but the boys and Serena filled the house with laughter and light that was hard to block out. We spoke through them and about them. They meant the world to the both of us so we got used to having common ground to stand on. Thoughts of an existence outside the madness of Northern Ireland still intruded with every death reported but inside the border of Johns Farm, a kind of peace descended as we did our best to give the children and Bridie a happy, natural life. Some days I had a job reminding myself that I was unhappy, that really I should be somewhere else.

There would, it seemed, be no more children because without any discussion John started using condoms. I could hardly tell him that I loved being pregnant, that I loved babies. They were the only thing I had ever produced which made me feel as if I was worth *something*. But if I exposed myself like that, John would be within his rights to point out our deal didn't extend to me having what I wanted. I had been taken on to provide *him* with what he wanted and when. Worse still, I missed the silken nakedness of him more than I cared to admit.

Much, much worse than even that, John learned to talk so that he could lecture me. I was failing him again, falling short of some standard he had set. His family was complete now so it was time I went back to the world, the world I had been so furious to give up. It was his only song and he had it on repeat.

- The waynes will be fine with Bridie if you ever want to go out? Or go to night school? No? Too happy by the fire, Mary?
- What are you going to do with yourself when the waynes go to school? Anything? Nothing? Cat got your tongue?
- Waynes don't last forever, Mary, you need to find something else to do with your life!
- Is there any chance *at all* you might leave the waynes and go off to Derry with Kathleen when she's been begging you for months? It would do you good to see something other than these four walls!

He didn't seem to understand that I couldn't leave them! What if something *happened*? What if the RUC lifted their father off the street when I was gadding about with my sister? What if I was killed in Derry, just another civilian caught in the crossfire? I couldn't risk it. I stayed at the range and cooked three square meals a day as they all careered around me. Time meant nothing as long as they were all happy. My life would start again one day when they were grown up and could look after themselves. When they could get on a plane or a boat and get the hell out of here.

My eyes never left them. My heart never failed to lift for even the faintest smile on their face. How had my mother hit us so easily for so little? Mick was given a pounding one night after he'd fallen in a bed of nettles. He was clumsy and had to be

233

shown the error of his ways. Most women would have run for a doctor but not Sadie Rattigan: she only ever ran for the stick. Daddy didn't stop her. All he had to do was open his mouth, surely?

I couldn't imagine John Johns standing by if anyone so much as looked cross at his children. They run through his long legs like pesky cats but he just steps around them. He takes the time to show them little things: a magpie feather, an acorn, a fledgling's skeleton. Serena has a whole box of treasures; she keeps everything he touches and won't let any of the boys near it even when they're wailing the house down. I should give her a lecture on sharing but I can't. Instead I think, good on you, girl, you keep whatever precious memories you can get your hands on.

John asked me every week if I needed anything but I always said no. The only thing I dearly wanted was something money couldn't buy: another baby. I'd never recovered from thinking of myself as a charity case. I didn't need many clothes; I didn't go anywhere. I'd a pair of wellies that would last me another five years. My hair was long enough to be nearly straight; I wore a lick of mascara for Mass. Eileen and Kathleen always got me bath stuff for my birthday.

He shopped for all our food as I still had no love for Carncloon and its broken windows and British soldiers. The box of groceries was left on the table every Friday evening and had the Sunday joint wedged in between the few things we didn't grow – some coffee, loose tea, flour and sugar, Bridie's dried prunes.

The waynes got an auld KitKat or a Turkish Delight for a treat once a week. Bridie got a bar of Fry's Chocolate Cream that she split with me when all five of the hallions were finally in bed and we had our aching feet up in front of the range.

I always got a bag of candy but when John treated me to a quarter of cherry drops I had to tell him that I didn't really like them.

He was astounded by the fact that I, Mary Margaret Johns, had been bettered by a boiled sweet and promised he would bring no more. Would he be safe enough if he stuck to humbugs and pear drops? Yes, he would. His gast was flabbered that he hadn't known that the taste of cherries made me sick.

The sun rose and him and me rose with it. We always had a half hour in the kitchen alone together before the day got under way. I'd get the range up to boil the kettle and we'd have mugs of tea and lumps of buttered scone, now and again with an egg, other times with jam. We might go over what one or other of the children had said, whether or not they needed anything, or we might not.

Bridie waited to hear the thud of the half-door before she got up and stirred the waynes. He'd turn out our wellies in case there was a mouse in them or a spider and we'd pull them on and wander down to feed the cows.

On a good morning there were no sirens, no Chinooks churning up the air above us. We watched the yellow light widen across the Cloon Valley a thousand times. I loved that view; it was something for us both to focus on and we always rested for a moment as one before he unlatched the wooden gate on the river field to let it swing open to start the day.

I stopped thinking about America and I stopped thinking about what it would have been like to go there with Joe Loughrey. I thought of him now and again but always as the boy who had stood crying in the parochial house, never as the golden boy, flicking his perfect hair and knowing he was the bee's knees.

I had no idea if John ever thought about England and Catherine the beauty. Every time he heard Sinéad O'Connor on the wireless singing 'Nothing Compares 2 U', he took the trouble to walk over and turn it down until she was finished breaking every heart in Ireland including his.

I often studied him when he was squinting at the horizon but he never looked at me. Why would he? I hadn't changed in the eleven years since he took me on; I was the same auld Mary only with fewer scales on my eyes. We kept the parts of ourselves we were willing to expose for the bedroom.

Life trundled on as inescapable as the five hills around us; we went from daffodils to roses and back to nothing beautiful blooming for months at a time, from haymaking to muck-spreading, and in that way the years marched on.

23

When the postman handed me two letters in the summer of 1993 and one of them was a blue airmail from America my heart nearly stopped. At last, at last I had my news from the long-lost Joe Loughrey! Time did a painful little fold and I was sixteen again and desperate to hear that I hadn't been wiped from his memory. I settled down with a mug of tea and a homily to myself not to get too worked up, when I saw that it was from San Francisco and addressed to John Johns. It could only be from Father Pat O'Connell. What had made me dream I was worth remembering?

The other letter was from Omagh, from the convent. Serena had passed her 11+ and was being invited along for an interview to see if she was the right kind of material for the nuns. Sister Pious's signature leapt off the page and punched me in the gut! Could she dream she was writing to the class of '82's famously failed virgin? That Serena was starting out on the road I had slipped off, coupled with such a fresh jolt from the past, made me think about how deep I had buried the life I once wanted.

The life of a teacher coming back to my nice clean, rose-scented home, the two perfect children I had always imagined would be enough, a fine upstanding doctor on my arm. I could have sworn I once thought of those things as *ambitious*? I left both of the letters on the table and went outside. Cows don't feed themselves, y'know?

When John came home I handed them to him. He was delighted by Serena's chance at the grammar school and he called her over for a hug. She was all blushes and giggles, still just a little girl whose knee socks didn't quite reach her knees any more. She wrapped her arms around his neck. He was the best dada in the whole townland and she was the best girl in the whole wide world and I was the most jealous mammy on the entire concrete floor.

He was less than delighted with the contents of the other letter. A pained look travelled across his face as if he had just been handed bad news. I never got to read it because, after he'd torn open the envelope and read it once, John Johns put it straight in the range where it flared brilliantly purple for a second and then curled up and died.

Bridie meets my eye from her chair where she's in danger of being swallowed by a blanket she's been crocheting since Christmas. Don't ask, she mouths, as if I would ever dare! My super-sharp brain allows me to understand that the father had reached out for the son although the son was too upset to let him try but I said nothing.

The timing couldn't have been worse for daddies with dog collars popping out of the woodwork. One Bishop Eamonn Casey had just been splattered all over the news because it turned out he had had an affair and fathered a son with an

American woman. Irish Catholics, high on the list being Mammy, didn't know what to think or what bit of the scandal was worse. Was it that he'd had the sex, that he'd wanted the child adopted or that he'd robbed some diocesan funds to pay for the cover-up?

Sadie Rattigan was convinced it was a British government conspiracy to destroy the unshakeable faith of Ireland and get us all to run to the other side. It was their way to maintain a Protestant majority and keep the union, Yes Siree Bob! She couldn't be swayed until she saw it on *The Late Late Show*, heard it from the tongue of Saint Gay Byrne as he interviewed the 'hussy' Annie Murphy, so it had to be true. She marched on Johns Farm to vent her anger in front of Bridie who had always been part of the rot.

She roared across the plate of Blue Ribands that everyone knew that priests were *just men* too, everyone knew they *had their fun*, but no one had the right to let on. If that hussy had just kept her mouth shut, like *most women who had enticed men of the cloth* to give in to their MUCKY ways, it would be business as usual instead of this devastation of the Church's power. Bridie nodded and said, is that so? I'd never been gladder that John wasn't in the room. He might have picked Sadie's head off her shoulders like a wild strawberry and popped it in his mouth.

I'd half a mind to tell her that her local hero Father O'Brien, the man she lived to worship with her dusters and mops, had played his own part in covering up another fallen soldier of God. My old friend Father Martin O'Hara had been passed along and hidden in several parishes thanks to his inability to say no to hussies but he'd served me well when I'd needed a scapegoat.

239

In another week, another letter landed. It was when I saw the postmark read Donegal that I slipped the envelope into my apron pocket before John Johns came back for the mid-morning tea. I had no big idea what I'd do with it but Father Pat O'Connell had done me a favour once. He had come into The Hill and chastised my mother when she was at the height of her powers. He had told me that I wasn't what he expected and I'd felt special for five minutes which was better than nothing.

The letter got hotter and hotter where it lay in my apron but I kept it there until John and me were alone in the bedroom. I delivered the lines I'd been rehearsing for hours.

- This came for you today.
- Why have you brought that up here? I've no interest in it and you know it!
- Why don't you just read it? It's been posted in Donegal.

There was no range up here so he'd hardly stomp the whole way to the kitchen to make a point and sure enough he didn't. Though his face was like thunder, he read it from top to bottom and turned away from me to put it on the bedside table. His big back was hunched and I was suddenly sorry for getting involved.

- He's not well …
- Who?
- Don't be *coy*, Mary. It doesn't suit you.
- What does he want?
- He wants to set things right with his long-lost son!
- I think you should go. You only get one father in this life.

Serena picked that moment to shout out goodnight to us and he raised an eyebrow at me. Her *Dada* hung in the air, a mosquito.

- What about you, Mary? Are you feeling confessional?

240

- No, I'm not!
- What a surprise! I don't care anyway; Serena's always been my girl. Maybe you're right? Maybe I should go?
- Maybe you should.

When we lay down together he kept a space between us. What was in his mind and why couldn't I just ask him? I was glad when he spoke because it was the kind of night Granny Moo might appear but, just as I thought I saw her forming in the corner, he broke the spell.

- I'll go tomorrow as it's Saturday and get it out of the way. Don't tell Bridie, okay?
- Okay.

It didn't even take the whole day for him to realise he had made a mistake. He'd spun some yarn about looking at machinery in Ballybofey and Bridie had nodded, unaware. He'd smiled at me when he left; we had a secret after a fashion. But when he came home after a very few hours only a blind man wouldn't be able to see it hadn't gone well. The children cleared out of his path when he stormed through the kitchen and up the stairs to get changed and he slammed through the half-door and stayed out in the back fields until it was nearly dark.

The boys went out after him to see if he wanted any help but he sent them home and they trailed in, a bit gloomy because Daddy wasn't acting like himself. Much later, Serena went out to ask him to come in: it was time for cocoa and stories. He didn't come in with her so I knew it was bad. I had to go myself.

I followed the sound of the sledgehammer to find him stripped to his vest though it was chilly and getting dark. He was pounding in fence poles, swinging the sledgehammer wildly and bringing it down with such force that I could hear the wood nearly splintering in two with every blow.

– John?

– Ah, here she is! My *darling* wife!

– What happened?

– The priest says I'm a bastard! Isn't that funny, Mary? But guess what? I'm a bastard for ruining *you*, not because he took an unorthodox route to fatherhood himself!

– I don't understand ...

He decided to inform me. Father Pat O'Connell was holed up in a luxury Catholic Church house called Killhatch to recover from an operation on his bowel, suspected cancer. It started out well enough, two men having a standard Irish conversation: the price of this and that compared to America, the shocking amount of rain that had fallen just that afternoon, the change in the times since his day. John was feeling *happy* – imagine that, Mary, happy after all these years of being the most famous bastard in Carncloon? Hundreds of auld bitches just like Sadie Rattigan whispering about him in the streets and snorting when he was safely past without *contaminating* them with the sins of his father? He'd thought the old man might want to reach out, that he might want to apologise for leaving his son so exposed. He'd dreamed that the shaming of Bishop Casey would give him food for thought.

I nodded and nodded. I knew just the sort of behaviour that my mother and her Catholic cronies were capable of. I would have tried to stammer out that I didn't want to be tarred with her brush but there wasn't a lot of gaps. John was beating out his explanations in time with the sledgehammer: whump, whump, whump.

Father Pat O'Connell hadn't really wanted to see *him* at all, hadn't actually wanted to spend time with his *son*. He'd wanted to tell John Johns what a mistake he'd made. He should never have married me. ME! It had been playing on his mind for years and he wanted to put it on record that I should not have been married off when I was only a child. He'd met me once: I'd seemed a very sweet, innocent young girl and I should have been given the chance to get on with my life.

I had the look of a girl who might do something with my brains, certainly I was too good to be stuck on a farm. It had been good enough for Bridie – she'd had no options – but me, *me*, I had come across as having potential. John should have seen his way to being the bigger man, maybe even just taking on the baby and rearing it with his mother's help?

Father Pat had seen things like that happening in San Francisco – he'd played his part in it himself, 'encouraging' good local families to set things straight in God's eyes, but now he's not so sure that was the way forward. Maybe the Church should focus more on forgiveness? After all, everyone makes mistakes, he'd made a few himself. His first mistake, John, was practically snarling. He'd had to tolerate being the butt of a lot of jokes as a boy because of Father Pat's human failings and there he sat telling John what to do, *preaching* to him, not trying to heal the pain of the years.

I saw how hurt he was, how angry and I knew it was my fault. If I'd kept my mouth shut I would have saved him more upset. He stopped hammering; a fine sheen of sweat had gathered on his face and his arms, soaking a dark V at his neck. It was my chance to say that I was happy enough, that I had had no big plans to change the world bar being a teacher and I got to teach my own children every day. It wasn't a terrible life. I loved them so much. I loved Bridie ... I ...

– Do you know what Pat O'Connell's parting shot was?

– No.

– He said *I* had had no right to put *you* in a cage! Is that how you see this *situation*, Mary? Like you're some sort of prisoner?

– I just wanted to travel, to fly ... I ...

– Ah, so you *are* a sorry little songbird I tied to the bed?

– That's not fair!

– That's all you have for me? After all these years? *It's not fair?* Go away, Mary, *looking* at you makes me weary! I've been stuck with you and your bloody nonsense for years but somehow I'm the bad guy. Some nights, I feel that you couldn't *be more mine* and the next day you're gone again. It's a shame Joe Loughrey didn't come back to claim you in time. He would have saved us both a lot of pain.

I turned for home. The hatred on his face burned into my back as I went. I was watching my feet moving through the long grass, seeing the tiny grey moths rise up when I disturbed them. The bats would start to fly soon; the sound of them gathering on the big sycamores at the entrance to the river field was my signal to boil the milk for the cocoa.

I had to stop by the corner of the milk house. A great ache was spreading across my chest. I wished I'd kept my nose out of his business. I *had* felt stuck down here on Johns Farm but now I understood that he was just as stuck as I was. He hadn't mentioned Catherine. He was prepared to forgive *her* everything but it was her who trashed his heart. It was her who'd cut him loose and he'd settled for second best with me because I was on the doorstop. I didn't make him do it. He didn't care enough to save himself. I hadn't been brave enough to make it stop. We'd buried each other. So why did I suddenly feel very much alive?

The yellow glow from the windows was darkened now and again by the shadows of my children running about inside, safe and warm. He had given me that roof and that life and I had rewarded him with silence. That's when I realised that Pat O'Connell didn't know that Serena wasn't John Johns's daughter. He thought *John* was the one to get me pregnant and the one to do the decent thing and marry me quickly before too much time passed. He would never know that John had stepped up and done a brave thing, foolhardy as it was. Not many men would take on another man's child; not many men could have made her feel so loved.

He hadn't disowned Serena just to save his own skin. He hadn't ratted on me as the silly girl I was who got herself into trouble. He had kept my secret even though it had earnt him a sermon from his father. He could have leapt off the hook. Why would he take the blame for me? I was hardly worth it. I would never understand what made him tick.

I was back at my post at the range when he finally came in. The waynes all ran to him, nearly knocking him off his feet. *Daddy, Daddy, Daddy! Daddy, will you read me this? Daddy, will you take me with you tomorrow? Daddy, Serena called me a gobshite! I did not, Dada!* Bridie meets my eyes and laughs at my happy houseful and all I can do is smile back. She would have loved a pile of waynes of her own under her feet.

My mind drifts back to her two boys and my two brothers under the earth at St Bede's. What a waste of beautiful flesh and blood. The sad smile that the memory brings is caught on my lips by John Johns but he is not about to give me another inch. I've had miles already. He scowls his way past, trailing the children in his wake, without a word.

He'll be biding his time until they don't need a mother stationed at the range from 6am until 10pm every day. Then he'll be able to let me go. I'll be set free but where will I fly? The very thought of it makes roots grow out of my feet through the concrete in front of the range, through the hundreds of feet of good clay and still further into the granite bedrock.

This is my *life*, I thought: children, farming, Carncloon, the five hills I feel I can touch. Even the Troubles – the rattle of Saracens and the Chinooks chopping across the cloud-filled blue skies – flowed in my veins. The joys of Bridie, Eileen, Kathleen, Bernie, Matthew; the sorrows of Daddy and Mammy. The sights and sounds of Lizzie Magee. The taste of John Johns.

This is *my* life and only a fool would keep running away from it. What I needed was a way back, a crosspiece, something to yoke me and their father together more securely so that I could stay on Johns Farm. Something that no man, priest or not, could put asunder.

24

John Johns kept his word. He would not look at me in case I made him more weary. The way he blocked me out made the children's eyes wide with worry. Bridie could see it too but she kept her counsel and talked louder and laughed more to take the edge off the hostilities. More tea than ever was stewed, more cakes bought, more treats laid on as she did her level best to sweeten the air. The boys were half taken in when their mouths were stuffed with chocolate eclairs and jam tarts, but not Serena. Serena knew something had started to rip.

She pulled us together every chance she could. She held his hand and mine and dragged us closer to her on the couch; when she was kissing us goodnight she pulled our heads together, her little muscly arms roping our necks. She insisted that every bit of the book she was reading aloud needed *both* our attention.

I could just about stand it in the daytime when I had them all as a buffer but in the bedroom he kept his back to me. The salve of our kind of loving in the nights at Johns Farm was wearing thin. The panic started in my toes and threatened to boil up all the way to my eyes. He didn't touch me for a month, a *whole month*. I longed to creep my hand across the sheet but I didn't. Instead I lay rigid, arms by my side like a demented soldier. I wouldn't buckle first, No Siree Bob! I could wait him out. This was a siege.

When the self-pity washed over me I blamed *him* for being childish, *him* for being unreasonable! How could it be *my* fault what Father Pat O'Connell had said? It was a miracle he had even remembered me. It's not my fault, I screamed at him without making a sound. He couldn't hear what I couldn't voice. I was weary too, but I was weary because I couldn't *stop* looking at him. He kept his eyes from me until I let Serena down.

She had to go to the convent for her interview but I couldn't force myself out of the house and up the lane. She wanted me to come, begged me, but I couldn't. What would I say to Sister Pious? The thought of walking through the big pillared gates, along the drive and through the glass doors to the assembly hall made me shake.

I'd be walking back to the life I once had when I'd just settled myself in this one. I hunted through my list of sad, sorry excuses for doing nothing but in the end I stuck with my most-used one: *I just can't*. Serena hadn't cried or played up; she just nodded because she still had Dada. Dada was not so accepting.

– Why can't you grow up, Mary?

– You don't understand …

– You're damned right I don't understand! She needs you today, don't you care about that? Don't you want to step up to the plate just *once*?

– I just can't …

Bridie stepped in to get him to drop his voice. The boys were milling about by the doors to the orchard, pretending they weren't listening. Serena came out, all brushed hair and shiny shoes, and walked past me to take his hand. They walked out of the half-door together but I didn't wave them off. I couldn't move because Granny Moo was standing in the shady space between it and the window. Her head was rocking violently from side to side like a metronome, tick, tick, tick, tick.

John didn't turn back to me in the bedroom. He kept himself to himself both night and day and I knew that I would have to be the one to break cover. Late one summer's evening, we waded into the water to get the worst of the dust off us after we moved the cattle from the hill field to the river field. I stumbled and soaked myself through a dress that Lizzie had sent from England in the post. A grey cotton thing – to match my eyes, ha ha ha – with tiny pink roses dancing around the hem. It came off over my head as light as a feather as he watched me but he didn't just watch for long. He picked me up and made for the shade of the big sycamores on the far side.

The last of the sun rippled around us, picking out the beads of water in his hair. I put my face in the hollow at his collarbone. I could be *yours* and you could be *mine*, I thought as we moved together. I had hung on to the news that some nights I couldn't have been more *his* and discarded all the other words that had hurt me.

I wanted a way to bind us together again. I needed it for the sake of the children who didn't like the chill in the kitchen. Bridie advised a bit of action – always better than words, she winked. I knew I was pregnant as we walked home through the river field, the last of the lilac cuckooflowers nodding in the dusk. Within weeks, the acid nausea of morning sickness, always absent when it was one of the boys, convinced me it was another little girl I was carrying.

I knew that he might not be best pleased but my head kept telling me that it didn't matter! Nothing mattered except the precious girl growing beneath my heart. That she was *his* filled me with joy. I'd give him something he'd never known he wanted: a daughter with his own blood running through her veins. I'll take the slap when it comes; she'll be worth it. She will set me back on the right road with her father, on the right path of my life. She is the step I have to take.

Then she left me.

I called out to John, screamed for him, where I lay bleeding in the vegetable garden. He came running from the river field but he was already too late. He rushed me to Omagh Hospital but nothing could be done. It was over. I wasn't even kept in over-night so we had the long drive home to suffer in the dark, just the two of us alone. We both knew it had happened when we made love on the cool of the river bank. We both knew that I knew what I was doing. We both knew that I'd planned it, I was an old hand at getting knocked up. But now our water baby was gone and we mourned the loss of her. I would have called her Roisin, my little rose.

– Why didn't you tell me? said John.

– What difference would it have made?

He would never be mine. The second-worst bout of bronchitis I had ever suffered followed on her heels and I was pinned to my bed for a fortnight. I washed the black and red antibiotics down with mouthfuls of Benylin and never refused a hot toddy of whiskey when John offered it at night. Daddy came with a half bottle of medicinal poteen that was supposed to be rubbed on my chest but I drank it as well, punched with plenty of sugar. I reckoned the best way to survive was to stay drunk. Mammy didn't come at all; she was busy cleaning as she'd got herself back on the list to hold the Stations of the Cross at The Hill. Net curtains don't bleach themselves, y'know?

I drifted in and out of sleep to find John sitting beside me in the armchair, his eyes just shadows. I wished he'd ask me how I was. I'm torn in two. Half of me is with her, the other half is here with him and everything we've made together. But he didn't ask and I didn't tell.

Bridie told me she'd found him crying in the orchard. She'd not seen him crying since he came home from England that time. He was never able to cope with *loss*, she says. He's softer than he lets on, she says, as if that makes it any easier on me. The bed under the barn eaves fairly reeked of booze and misery by the time I emerged a few weeks later into what I hoped would be a tolerably new world.

It wasn't, of course. Northern Ireland was still bubbling away but among the reports on 300-pound, 500-pound and even bigger bombs the news was eaten up by the talk of *talks*. The SDLP's John Hume and Sinn Féin's Gerry Adams were centre stage because they had reached an agreement; they had a vague way forward and everyone was sitting up and paying attention. John Major seemed to be doing his best to listen – I'd always had a soft spot for him since he kindly mentioned that we were British citizens too and imagine the outcry if people in Surrey or Sheffield took to murdering each other in the streets over political differences? The *talks* didn't stop the IRA or the UDA from killing some more civilians: old habits die hard.

The children were glad to have me back in the kitchen though I was too tired to cook anything more than eggs on toast. We don't care, Mammy, as long as it doesn't have black bits, says Daniel and the rest of them nod. I was still Mammy but emptier. John came in from the fields and sat down with them without a word of any kind and they eyeballed the pair of us for signs of improvement. There weren't any. I'd have to do something about that. I knew what growing up in a house of black moods and stony silences does for the soul.

That night, emboldened by the prospect that change was in the air, I plucked up enough courage to start our own truce.

   – The children shouldn't see us like this …

   – Like what?

   – Like we can't be … civil?

   – Civil? Civil? Mary, you're a treasure, do you know that? We've been married for nearly twelve years and have five children between us and *civil* is all you're aiming for?

   – Six!

   – Six what?

   – We have six children between us!

I picked the wrong time to tot things up. He looked like he'd been punched in the stomach. But I couldn't put her aside so easily and I was damned if I was going to allow him to. The quick, clean cry of a fox somewhere in the river field startled us both to breathe in again.

   – You needn't worry about my memory, Mary. I'll *never* be able to forget how many children I have.

   – That's good then? That's good?

– It's perfect! Tomorrow we'll get straight back on with the civilities!

When I talked I got it wrong, when I didn't talk I got it wrong. I couldn't do or say right for doing and saying wrong. I wanted to keep her alive for a little while longer but John didn't share that feeling. He wanted her buried. The sadness was like heartburn: sour and hot. We got up the next day and got on with the civilities.

Bridie taps me on the back of the neck when she finds me drooped over a sink or a table or a spade in the vegetable patch and tells me it gets easier. But it won't get easier anytime soon because John has decided to cut off any possibility of me having another baby to hold. He disappeared first thing one day without so much as a goodbye and Matthew dropped him back on the street long after the sun had dropped between Sessiagh and Glebe.

The deed was done and he had a bag of frozen peas held to his vasectomy scar the day the IRA announced a three-day ceasefire in the wake of John Major and Albert Reynolds's Downing Street Declaration which demanded that it would permanently renounce violence if peace was ever to be delivered between the main midwives of Dublin and Westminster. It was the kind of news that would have stopped me in my tracks on a normal day but this was no normal day. This was the day that he shut me out forever, the day he denied me the chance to heal my shattered heart.

Bridie was having a little snivel, cracking on that she was glad that there was a break in the Troubles, but there was to be no break in my troubles and that's all I cared about in this moment.

I had to know how he could ignore me and the rock in my chest with such seeming ease.

– Why didn't you tell me? I said.

– What difference would it have made?

I would never be his. I hid my disappointment with every ounce of brilliance as he did. I had let him down and he had let me down: we were both flat as pancakes. There was nothing to add; our rage leached into the stone floor instead of ripping the roof off. We turned our attention to the television and the talk of Gerry Adams being allowed to go to the USA at some stage: Bill Clinton was keeping his visa under review. Bridie jawed constantly from her armchair that she would never live to see peace in this ridiculous life and we had to agree with her, it seemed like a pot of fool's gold at the end of a rainbow.

After a while, John turned again to face me in the bedroom but the pleasure of it is not without its pain. He has stopped kissing me and keeps his eyes closed. He won't forgive me any-time soon for making out that he was my jailer when the half-door to Johns Farm has always been on the latch. Though I paw at his skin I am still blocked out. It's a lonely, cruel busi-ness but neither of us seems able to put it aside. We never referred to our little Roisin-that-never-was again, though she treads the air between us on gossamer wings, getting more ragged by the day. I paid for her with more than half of my heart. Does his ache as much as mine?

1998

THE RAIN ON THE FIELDS

25

The roof stayed on Johns Farm when peace descended on Northern Ireland. I don't know how, when we'd roared and danced through the kitchen like banshees! Bridie nearly broke a leg. We'd been sitting out the storm for so long that when the sun finally broke through we were dazzled by it. Tony Blair – or Saint Anthony, Patron Saint of Miracles and Lost Items as Auntie Eileen calls him – delivered the Good Friday Agreement in April. With Mo Mowlam and Bill Clinton and even the Pope wading in, he'd wrestled Ian Paisley, David Trimble, Gerry Adams and a score of other opponents on to the blank canvas.

I'd longed for an end to the madness as if it was the last boiled sweet in the whole of County Tyrone. Now it was here! Things can only get better! That's what D:Ream, a bunch of lads from Northern Ireland, were singing last year for Tony Blair as he sailed into 10 Downing Street, all dimples and pigeon toes and promises. Things are a thousand times better already.

Serena is on the edge of sixteen, my boys will be teenagers in a peaceful country, they would not have to pick a side. They could leave the house and I'd have a good chance of them coming home again in one piece. Tony Blair, Senator George Mitchell and Bertie Ahern were all teeth and gums as the governments in Belfast and Dublin ended British rule and gave us a new Northern Ireland Assembly where Nationalists and Loyalists would have to share power. We just had to make it to 1999 when the agreement kicked in.

Serena announced that she had known all along that it would happen sooner rather than later! She was so confident, she *knew* what life could be like. Her and the cherished Nora Reilly were going to take on the world. Now the Troubles were *over* the Six Counties would need teachers and doctors even more. She thought she could see the future. I remember being just like her, daft. Lizzie Magee and me had thought that life was as easy to choose as a lollipop.

I watched her a minute, lying up against the pillows in my bed with the sketch pad she never left out of her hands now tucked under her arm. I marvelled at having produced her but even more remarkable was the fact that I hadn't ruined her. We could talk, hug, kiss; we were MUCKY! There was never any talk of boys; they seemed to have been demoted in the overall scheme of a girl's experience. She didn't need anyone to make her feel good about herself. She was an open book, so when she settled herself nice as pie and tried to look casual I knew straight away she had been sent by John, sneaky.

We'd been having a look at Bono on the telly holding David Trimble and John Hume's arms in the air when they had emerged together ahead of the referendum in May. There was a joy in the image that lifted our hearts. Serena wanted to know how *I* was doing? Only *she'd* been thinking it would be great for me to go on a course. She'd been thinking that maybe I'd like to learn how to drive now that the roads would be safer? There were plenty of opportunities out there for women like me, apparently. *Women like me?* I was a farmer's wife: nothing more, nothing less.

   – Things have changed since *you* were sixteen, says my wise
     child!
   – Is that so? says I.
   – Tell me again what happened?

So I told her again her favourite story of How Serena Came To Be and for a good few years now I'd even stopped thinking of it as The End of Mary Rattigan. I played up the glamour of the whole enterprise. I painted in the crescent moon, the summeriness of the night, the feeling of freedom, and glossed over the tiny fact that I was the tramp I'd always warned her not to be.

I never mentioned Joe Loughrey. He was irrelevant to the story of her even though he was the key to the story of me. I'd first told her about Jacques Bernier on her thirteenth birthday. She never expressed any desire to find him. I was glad of that, thinking what a shock it would be for him discovering that a few minutes of pleasure had led to a brand-new person. I had days when I could hardly believe it myself.

I'd never asked her to keep it from John but she hadn't told him. She wouldn't dream of hurting Dada by even bringing it up. The words we had set down when she was tiny had never left her: John Johns had taken the job on and he was all the daddy she would ever need. She was still *his* girl, right down to her bones. She sighed and threw herself across the bed, delighted she was the result of such a romantic interlude. Jesus Christ on a pushbike!

– Did Dada ever tell you about Catherine?

– No. I heard of a Catherine once but it was before my time …

– Honestly! You pair! Have you ever thought about *talking to each other*?

I was still *desperate* to know what had gone on so I got up and started folding clothes as if I didn't care a bucky and, sure enough, Serena spilled the beans without realising she was being flipped. I'd get her to bend the main rule that John and me lived by – he didn't want to know about me and I wasn't interested in him. Deals don't break themselves, y'know?

He had told my daughter all about the English girl that he had fallen for, hook, line and sinker, in London when he was just a boy. The English girl that I had never quite measured up to. She was the loveliest creature he had ever met, kind and decent and good. And funny, so funny, they had shared so many laughs. *They had what?* I closed the wardrobe door on my hand and bit back the yelp! She was a Protestant girl so they would have to get married in a registry office. John didn't mind not being married in the eyes of God. He had sort of given up on God after his pal Shimmie Tollund was kneecapped for no reason.

Catherine's parents would go mad but she didn't care a jot because *he* was what she wanted. It was only about six weeks to the wedding when he thought there was something wrong one night. Her head was exploding; they both held on to it to try and keep it together, but the pain made her scream until she couldn't scream any more.

The ambulance hadn't come, bogged down in James Callaghan's Winter of Discontent. She was trembling in the bed; he had held her close to make her feel less scared but she was still terrified and wide-eyed, looking straight at him, as she died in his arms. He didn't know what it was that took her away so suddenly. The doctors didn't tell him anything because he wasn't next of kin.

He'd only known about the baby for two months, the best two months he had ever lived. He would finally have someone with his own blood running in their veins, the start of a family at last. My heart split open. Catherine and him had lists of names; she'd had time to cast on the stitches to knit a white wool blanket. His hope was that it would be a little girl – Bridie would have loved a little girl – but she had stayed with her mother, both of them gone in a flash as the pigeons circled outside.

Her parents wouldn't talk to him, wouldn't tell him anything after they found out that their daughter was shacked up with a Papist and a spit-on-the-ground Irishman to boot, living in sin. English people were still raw years after the Birmingham pub bombings. They didn't care that he wasn't *involved*, that she hadn't been alone at the end, that Catherine had been *loved*. He was banned from the funeral for want of a piece of paper saying that he was the husband. He hadn't been given the chance to put either of them to rest.

His heart was broken. He had never seen her face again after the ambulance men had taken her away. When Catherine died he had wandered every inch of London looking for peace and when none was found he came home to Johns Farm and Bridie but he couldn't bear to tell her or any other living soul the story.

He had come to understand how someone could take their own life; the blessed relief beckoned more than once. He just buried Catherine and the baby whole and untouched in his memory and hoped the years would make it bearable. Maybe one day we could agree on the number of years? *And then I was born,* says Serena with a flourish, *and the clouds were on the back foot for him forever. He got to have a perfect daughter after all!*

— Mammy? Don't cry! It was a hundred years ago!

— Oh, I'm not crying about *me*! It's just so sad the many things that can happen to a person in one lifetime!

I hate to lie to her. The tears *are* all for me. They should be for him, only him, and the fact that he got stuck with a foolish girl who never took the time to realise that he was hurting. Did he never tell me about Catherine? Why would he when he knew I wouldn't listen? I had stuffed my ears with self-pity the day that Daddy left my suitcase on the street. I had been comparing myself to a ghost for years.

I thought of his face as he drove me home from Omagh hours after the miscarriage. I had been inconsolable, so much so that I had selfishly thought that my loss was greater than his. Had we *ever tried talking to each other* I might have known that he was the one person who could understand, the one who'd already been on that lonely, bloodied road.

Now *Serena* thought that I'd been hiding down here in Johns Farm long enough; *she* thought that I should get back to my books. I nodded and nodded, hearing the sense being preached and feeling the panic rising. I would soon be out of excuses for hanging around the house.

John was obviously sick of me. I was dead wood so I would have to go. Back to school because he couldn't think of anywhere else to send me. If I could make a living, his responsibility for me would be over and, anyway, in a matter of a few short years all of our children would be grown and gone, no need for a mother then and my days as a wife were numbered.

– Come on, Mammy! Northern Ireland is going to need all sorts of people! Tony Blair is going to be *throwing* money at us!

– I'll certainly think about it, says I to my daughter.

I'd not an ounce of intention of thinking about it! Imagine *me* trying to sit in a classroom when I was her age the last time I'd studied. I would look and feel ridiculous! She didn't need to know that and she would report back to her father that I was considering a change in my circumstances. I must be such a disappointment to him after Catherine. He'd likely dance a jig in the street if he came home to find I'd flown away. The only thing weighing me down was my heart so all I had to do was find a way of cutting it out and leaving it behind. I'd have no use for it.

26

I tried not to soften too quickly towards John but even Bridie
noticed when I lightly touched the back of his neck at the dinner table. She raised an eyebrow as if to say, 'Well, now this is
a *real* breakthrough,' and the children all looked up in time to
see me go bright red when she guffawed. He was telling me
that peace was breaking out in the countryside a lot quicker
than it was in the cities. There was no fanfare in Carncloon
but slowly roadblocks disappeared and there were fewer torn
Union Jacks and ragged Tricolours hanging from every tree
and lamp post.

The edges of the pavements which had always been kept in
pristine red, white and blue or green, white and gold were
allowed to fade. The weight of all those colours drifted away
like a rainbow of smoke and I found myself walking taller and
breathing easier. I put it down to the joy of my family being
safer than it had ever been. It had nothing at all to do with the
fact that I had smiled at John Johns – only once so far – and he
had smiled back. *Nothing at all to do with that*, No Siree Bob!

We limped on to the Northern Ireland Assembly elections and we got the UUP's David Trimble as leader and the SDLP's Seamus Mallon as his deputy. It felt as if the Six Counties might just make it if everyone played by the rules. We planned what fields we'd change from hay to corn the following year, what walls needed strengthening, what fences needed repair to keep our beasts protected.

What none of us could have predicted was the hellishness of the first Twelfth of July after the peace deal. The brand-new Parades Commission banned the Loyalist march down the mainly Catholic Garvaghy Road in Drumcree as it was likely to be contentious. *Contentious?* Where had *they* been for the last few decades? As we watched, Drumcree imploded again. Lizzie Magee called us to check that the Irish news was the same as the English news because she couldn't believe what she was seeing. She rang off in tears but said that her and Kenny were still thinking of coming home, one day.

What she could see and what we could see was a battle raging between the Loyalists and the Nationalists on either of the barricades made of steel, concrete and barbed wire. It had only taken three months for violence, threats of execution, roadblocks, attacks on security forces and Catholic homes, gunfire, blast bombs and plastic bullets to be back in the headlines. So this was peace? It's only sixty miles away, Mammy, says Eugene, and we all hold still a minute in case we can hear Saracens coming on the river but the mighty Cloon was silent. We thought it couldn't get much worse and then it did.

Three little boys, three Catholic brothers, died in a fire when their home was petrol-bombed by Loyalists. Bridie slammed her rosary beads back in the drawer before she went outside for a cry. Marius went after her to tell her the lie that it would be alright, that it would get better one day. What kind of God lets things like this happen, Dada? Serena managed as the tears tripped down her face. John had nothing to say because he would never lie to the waynes.

John followed me from bed to bed that night as we kissed and kissed our precious boys and our precious girl. We were so blessed, so very lucky. Without a word we ran back to the bedroom. His skin was so cool it burned me. Just as I was about to cry out he silenced me with his lips and I latched on to him, back in the fold at last! We made love for what seemed like hours but still we lay wide-eyed side by side, staring at the eaves. The windows were open and the blackbirds picked out their bright song and every time the breeze threatened to cool us too much, he reached for me or I reached for him.

Sleep must have come for I dreamt that helicopter blades were scything through the darkness. I felt the breeze as first they moved towards me and I braced for the agony. As they came close they stopped and veered away, making straight for John Johns. He was smiling, a smile that could light up the hedgerows, when they sliced the top of his head off like an egg. His eyes, his lips, his teeth ran with blood and there was nothing I could do to stem the flow.

We knew that something even more terrible was brewing. We could feel it in the air. The clouds settled once more over Carncloon and over every small and big town in the Province. Protestant neighbours were as shook up as us as we set about getting in the first crop of hay together. It was heartbreaking that the extremists on both sides could cause such damage in our name. We had no control over the mad bombers, the murderers; we knew they would be impossible to stop – if three dead children couldn't stop them, what would?

The waynes had grumbled a bit about working on the farm; they had wanted to go to the last day of the carnival week in Omagh. It was *summer*, it would be busy, fun, *loads* of people would be there, Serena could go *shopping*! Nora Reilly was allowed to go, why couldn't Serena go? It was unlike her to keep on long enough to get the boys to join in. All five of them were convinced they were missing out on something special.

– It'll be a day to remember, Mammy!
– Every day you get to live healthy and free is a day to remember, Serena Bridget!
– Oh Mammy, *puh-lease* don't even start up with your fluffy nonsense about us all being *together* and all being *safe* and all being grateful that we have *eyes* to see the grass with!

It made me smile to hear that she had taken in my daily prayer. John smiled too but she carried on with her tutting and pouting a bit too long and he told them all to remember their manners and they knuckled down.

I drove the tractor, pulling the reaper, and the men and Eileen piled the cut grass into windrows. When it looked like rain, we got Daniel to drive instead so we could double up. The children were fine workers; John praised them up the field and back down it again and they worked faster and faster to please him. Bernie and Bridie were in charge of the tea-making down at Arthur Rowley's place and they brought us a box of flasks around midday. We sat at the foot of an oak and let it burn our thirst away.

Serena, long dark hair shining, was leaning against my daddy; they sat back to back to hold each other up and I ached to feel or to be close to him. She was sixteen. She had my face, my body, but not my sin. She had my father's love in spades.

I bit back tears and stared hard at the high white clouds hung in the blue sky over the valley. There was hardly a sound aside from the chirrups in the blackthorns; the swallows swooped and soared, picking off the exposed insects. No one wanted to talk about anything other than making hay.

Shane took his turn on the tractor and we made good progress, getting through two more fields before Arthur called it a day and insisted we came in for a beer; the waynes could have lager shandies and he'd even bought in a few auld packets of crisps for them. I'm game, says Eileen, very, very game! Every cell in our bodies was tired; the sweet smell of cut grass clung to us, its juice staining our legs and hands green.

The boys ran on ahead, making for Arthur's water. John walked with his arm around Serena's shoulder and I risked another inch of my heart to link mine lightly through Daddy's. When he pulled me close to him, I thought I would burst. I could feel his lean old body through his shirt as he fumbled with his pipe and baccy before he lit up and bathed us both in sacred smoke. We strolled on, the evening gently folding in on itself as it swam in my eyes.

– Mammy! Daddy! Something's wrong!

All the boys were shouting at once. We all started to run towards the street and the house where Bernie was standing. Her arms described big circles, her face all pulled out of shape; she pointed at the door and drew more circles. We knew that sign: it meant Boom Bang Boom. Bridie was dry-eyed in front of the telly. The six o'clock news was showing a town ripped up by a bomb; nothing but dust, grey dust, registered at first.

– It's Omagh, says Bridie, stunned.

We all looked and saw the familiar high street, the spire of St Columba's Church of Ireland still standing in the background, but to all sides there was destruction. People were lying on the street wounded; some of them were not moving. How had the television people got there so fast? The fire brigade showed up in their yellow jackets; ambulance crews picked up one, two, three from the tarmac. Everyone was running with horror on their faces and bits of cloth in their hands as if they might be able to clean up.

– Whose side did it, Bridie? asks Arthur.

– Nobody's saying, says Bridie.

Not that it mattered a pile. We let the images roll on while Arthur pulled the rings on the cans of Harp and put out the Tayto crisps for the waynes. They all looked a bit peaky. There was nothing to say except prayers for all the poor families who would never be whole again. God save us all, says Arthur, his voice catching. He raised his can and we raised ours, clinked and drank deeply to the hollow toast.

It seems that Ulster Television had been given a warning, the Samaritans had been given a warning, and the army had been given a warning. But the car had been parked on the *wrong street*, not in front of the intended target of Omagh courthouse, so the RUC were actually moving people *on* to it when it exploded. It was just another mistake in a swollen sea of mistakes. Omagh, our county town, was once again in the news.

It's hard to adjust to such a sickening scene when you've just come in from fields swamped with buttercups and daisies, growing lush and perfect and impossible to make any sense of it. It would be days before we knew how many were dead, how

269

many were injured, but we knew from experience it would be a lot. There was nothing to see but damage. Fear grew back into a knot in my guts: would I *really* have peace to finish rearing my sons? Would they be safe? It was only a few hours earlier that we'd made the decision not to let our children go. It would be a day to remember.

I look at them all now, white-faced and staring, speechless like John. Bridie, Auntie Eileen and Bernie are crying but they too are silent. Arthur had stepped out to mourn in private. Like everyone we were watching, picking their way through the shattered glass from blown-up shops, covered in dust and blood, Serena had only wanted to go out shopping and laughing in the sunshine.

I realise that she's left my side. I hear her on the phone sobbing. I know she's finally got through to the Reilly house. She shouldn't have to have this conversation, I think to myself. No one should ever have to have this conversation, never mind a sixteen-year-old. She's hardly done being a child, although she doesn't know it. I want to be back, back, all the way back through the years, holding her against my waist and kissing her face until she squirms away to see to her dolls and teddy bears and their many picnics. Her pain and her words tear through me like shrapnel. I can't keep any of us from harm.

– Oh Nora! Thank God! I thought you were dead! I thought I'd lost you!

Even the worst of nights go in eventually. We had drifted about until I got everyone around the fire with a slice of bread on a fork each. We need toast for these fried eggs, I said, and we all managed a small smile. Bridie mashed the tea in the old brown teapot and we sat at the table together. John was raging inside but that's where he kept it, inside and away from the waynes. I touched his neck; it was hard as marble but he breathed out and the atmosphere cheered up a notch.

The next day we found out how many had died. It was twenty-nine. The news kept saying 'civilians'. Over the next few days we found out how many were injured, over two hundred – some left without limbs, others blinded or disfigured. Men, women, children all chewed up by sectarian violence. A young woman who had been shopping with her mother and her little girl was killed. She had been pregnant with twins – all five of them wiped off the face of the earth. It could have been me, Bridie, Serena, Eugene and Marius. Then we found out who was responsible: it was our very own Real IRA. Would my darling mother's rampant Nationalism be robust enough to spin this one?

We'll soon find out. She's been invited down for a slice of cake to celebrate Serena's GCSE results and her A in art A level that she did 'just for fun'. I didn't invite her but my much more forgiving child did. Bridie groaned and Auntie Eileen announced that she, for one, would *not* be doing the party sober, No Siree Bob! Daddy's coming too, although he won't stay long. Serena's done well, and her and the beloved Nora Reilly have their eyes on Belfast. I can't bear to think about it but I nod away as she explains they want to get to Queen's University to study law. There's no flies on my girl. I should never forget that as I see her frown at me where I stand decorating today's main attraction.

- Why have you made a coffee walnut? You know that's *Dada's* favourite, not mine!
- You like it well enough. Don't mither!

- I always get a coconut raspberry sponge; that's *my* cake!
- Serena, one more word and I'll scrape the whole bloody thing into the bin and you can explain to your Auntie Eileen that's she bought a load of silly fizzy wine that won't exactly go with plain biscuits!

I can feel my whole 'When I was your age' speech coming on when she stomps away but I swallow it down to not ruin the day. The last few days haven't been good for any of our nerves. But when I was her age I had a baby and no running water to contend with! When I was her age I had no idea what life would throw at me next! When I was her age I had successfully shut every door that I thought would be open to me! When I was her age my O-level results resulted in a big fat nothing and Mammy gloating over it like a cat swimming in cream.

I hear her on the phone again to Nora Reilly, complaining like a champion, and I think, yes, today is as good as it gets! The *pure joy* that we were arguing over a cake and not a coffin bubbled inside me and I put every ounce of love I had for her, for them all, into arranging the walnuts around the edge. It had to be perfect.

Mother dearest arrives to darken the half-door. She's early, not because she's polite but because she's trying to catch me out. She has no idea how well-prepared I am today. I've been scheming all night. All the death of the last week has made me feel foolish for wasting so much of the life I've been given. She scans the kitchen and can't find a single thing to complain about: a first.

The sound of my father's tractor rounding the bend before he gets to the street brings all the children running and I hear the gate to the river field whine open and clang shut. John Johns is coming. I watch for him to appear in the far window. I know he will stop by the water butt and wet his face and hair with the still-cool rain. He will wipe his hands on his jeans and turn back to look at the river field before he ducks to get into the kitchen. He will smile at me today. I hold myself absolutely still so that he can't miss me.

I have scrubbed this house from top to bottom. I have even polished myself. I have made a perfect cake. I have laid a perfect table. Everyone he has ever cared about is in this room except Catherine. I can't do anything about her but there must still be time to do something about me? I'm *here* and well and living right under his nose.

He has stopped to talk to my father. I hear the rumble of their voices and the shouts of the waynes. The wait is agony. Any minute now Bernie might start swiping scones or messing up my napkins and the whole thing will be ruined! I need to be viewed in the scene that I've set, the perfect wife and mother at large. Eugene runs in screaming. We're all going to the river for a swim and then a picnic! Auntie Eileen's delighted; she can smoke her guts out in peace in the fresh air. My mother's eyes roll so far back with rage that I'm shocked when they roll back again.

Before I can stop it, every child has grabbed an armful of the food they want to eat and Eileen and Bernie follow them with a bottle of fizzy wine under each arm. I remember seeing a wildlife programme once where a cloud of locusts covered a field of grain in seconds. I was the last ear of corn standing, bewildered. Mammy was so happy! The whole place was trashed, so she satisfied herself by just laughing at me and my cake when she stepped out into the sunshine.

John has been in the milk house gathering up the rough rugs we keep for the fields. He sees me standing alone, chewing my lip.

— Aren't you coming?

— I'd set the table ... I made a cake ...

— So? Bring it, or leave it and we'll have it when we get back!

— No! It's all ruined! The whole thing's ruined ...

— Oh for God's sake, Mary! Only you could cry over something so trivial! After everything we've seen this last week, it's just typical of *you* not to learn the lesson! It's a beautiful day! Life is short and when it's gone, it's gone!

He walked off without me, shaking his head. It was nothing to him, all that effort. I watched the set of his shoulders as he jumped the gate before striking for the river. I wanted to call out to him, to ask him to wait, but he was moving fast and soon disappeared behind the big sycamores. It *was* a beautiful day. The shadows of the high clouds raced along the ridge of Combover Hill and Shanagh Bog was a purple jewel in the clear, bright light. I loved it here. I loved Johns Farm and everyone on it. And I had learned a lesson – a hard one, one I would try not to forget the next time I got a soppy notion in my head. Girls like me just don't get smiles handed to them on a plate.

Autumn brought my favourite shade of red in the shape of the bold Lizzie Magee. She kept her promise and started to come home more often when the retaliation we thought was inevitable for the Omagh bomb never materialised. With her to pick me up and keep me company, I started to go into town more. She was around the week the steel barricades were taken away. The sparks from the grinders flew silver as they chopped through the metal poles and every barrel of concrete was lifted on a fork-lift and put in the back of a van. Carncloon looked naked without them and when we were able to walk from one end of the town to the other it just didn't seem right. We kept meeting Protestants who looked as lost as we did, all of us like pigs going to hoke.

Cars could be left unattended, they could be parked right outside shops, there were fewer and fewer roadblocks. All the shops in the Diamond, a triangle of buildings which had been used to bookend the security gates in and out to the bottom of the town, were demolished: Carncloon was going to have a village green. Lizzie Magee and me nearly wet our drawers! Why would a town need a tragic patch of grass when five green hills loomed around it?

The Long Lounge was finally going to be rebuilt and I had stammered a 'yes' when John Johns suggested we might go there together when it was finished. I thought of all the kissing I had done with Joe Loughrey in the burned-out dance hall at the back but the next time I set foot in there it would be to stand at a bar and have a drink with the man who had become my husband. Life was a strange beast. I'd never thought we would *go out* together when all we had ever had was the *staying in*. Not that I was complaining; the *staying in* was a high point of every day.

The barracks remained, huge and grey at the top of the town, but the rest of the place started to look normal: a few shopkeepers even licked on a bit of paint, a lot of green and white appeared at our end, a lot of red and blue at the other – old habits die hard in Northern Ireland. By Christmas, even a cheery string of white bulbs survived the season, strung across the air above the marks of the border, casting a weak festive light between *us* and *them*. Progress was being made!

Life took on a different rhythm, with Lizzie coming and going. She was jolly when she was at Johns Farm, fussing over the children and making John laugh at the stuff she got up to in London. When they started comparing tube-train rides and pubs, I tried not to look jealous even though a little green-eyed maggot was chewing through my heart. I wanted to be the worldly one; I wanted to be ordering drinks at bars and hailing black cabs. I wanted to be the one he was paying attention to, just once. Sometimes it felt as if the fabric of the sofa had grown over me and no one had noticed.

We refused the invitation to have our Christmas dinner at The Hill for the sixteenth year in a row and we didn't extend an invitation for them to come to us. The hostility was burning a hole in me and I resolved to try harder. My father showed up; as usual he wasn't 'stopping', just dropping by to wish us all the cheer of the season and he had a pile of stuff for the waynes, including a selection box each. The rain was beating down and he had on his ancient drover's coat, gone shiny round the pockets and buttons. I managed to get him past the half-door where he stood in a puddle of his own making. Would it be alright if himself and Matthew came down on Boxing Night to play cards with the waynes and us as usual? Of course it would, Daddy, I said as the boys and Bridie took the stuff and put it under the tree. There was a bottle of whiskey and another of sherry, all wrapped in the cheapest paper Mammy could find.

When we were on our own he reached into one of the huge pockets and handed me a damp little cat that had been soaking up raindrops. That's just for yourself, he says before turning back for The Hill. I thought my head would burst. It was a kitten of every colour: black, white, brown and orange with little amber eyes! I buried my face in her furry belly. She wasn't much but she was mine. I called her Ginger after Lizzie Magee and, before the day was out, she had every claw she owned lodged in my buttery heart. I told you there'd be other cats, says Bridie as she wipes the tears off my cheeks with the heel of her hand.

27

I saw in 1999 with Ginger in my lap and a whiskey in my hand. Auntie Eileen and Bernie had come with beers and we laughed the night away, playing Scrabble until the children got sick of us cheating and dancing until they nearly passed clean out with embarrassment.

I only spotted Serena whispering with Auntie Eileen a few minutes before she ripped another hole in my heart. Tell her, go on, it's not going to get any easier, says Eileen, I'm going out for a fag. Serena had changed her mind about finishing her A levels and following Nora Reilly like a duck. She was done with school.

– We'll see what your father has to say about this, Serena Johns!

– He already *knows*, Mammy!

Dada and her had already discussed it. God, I was sick to my stomach of always being bloody second best! What right did *he* have to decide anything about her future? She was mine, mine alone. I had given up my life because of her. Because it's a tradition, I burst into tears instead of coming up with any of the thousand reasons racing through my head why she should do what I had failed to do. She had a place in Belfast's Jordanstown to do a foundation course in art and I was immediately terrified about how safe it would be but she couldn't be put off.

I was quickly on to how worried I was about 'art' as a good career choice. She moved closer to John and they both looked at me with pity. I knew nothing that could be of any use to her … or him. He stood by her decision when I was panicking that she wouldn't be able to make a living; surely she should be a teacher or something sensible? Jesus, *sensible*! Sensible was the worst word I could have picked; they both looked at me as if I'd just crawled out of a cave.

She leaned into him, her protector from day one. He said no, no, she was to do what she wanted and anyway he at least had been to London and I hadn't been past the front stoop even though the door wasn't *exactly locked*. I felt a fine needle of resentment for him push its way through my shoulder blades but I managed not to scream from the rooftops that she wasn't his. Apart from anything else, the boys didn't know and the dawn of a new year wasn't a good date to find out that your mother was a tramp. My darling family rode to the rescue over the next few months.

- What odds as long as she's happy? says Kathleen.
- That child will do well whatever she does, so stop worrying yourself sick about her! says Eileen.
- Isn't it great she knows what she wants? says Bridie.
- I'm not surprised she's let you down! says Mammy. What did you expect of such weak material? After all, she's *your* daughter!

She started that September and came home often with tales of how 'boring' it was, stuck away outside Belfast. The only great thing was a pile of second-hand clothes shops. She took to wearing stuff that was ripped and reeked worse than Granda Ban in his day. Bernie would give her a good smelling and shake her head and wag her finger! We laughed along but I was only pretending to join in. That she wore horrible collarless shirts and waistcoats from some old dead man's wardrobe in Belfast made me itch. They might be the clothes of someone shot in the head.

I fought back the tears every time she left the street. I couldn't bear to ride into town and see her on to the bus. The twice-daily service went from Carncloon to Omagh, then she had a thirty-minute wait for the Belfast Express. Every time John came back from dropping her off he was quieter. We had been stitched together because of our daughter and her absence was allowing us to tear apart. Every night when he rolled back to his side of the bed, he took his thoughts with him.

Serena had been gone for six months when I saw him standing at the door staring out at the orchard. It was pouring down, the wild greens of the trees were being blown this way and that, and I drew level with him to see what was so exciting. One of our auld hens, Gerty, was standing out in the terrible weather, her feathers rippled so much she was soaked down to her bones. We had put a setting of duck eggs under her when she was clocking and the six ducklings were having a great time in the puddles springing up. She wouldn't leave them.

– Look, Mary.

– Poor Gerty.

- It's like watching you, Mary. She doesn't know when to give up!
- She can't give up! What would they do without her?
- Get sense, Mary, she'll be dead in a week. Then they'll carry on growing without her!

Things can only get better.

2004

UNTIL WE MEET AGAIN

28

Serena had just finished her fourth year at Manchester University and was moving on to London when we lost Bridie. It was early, 5am and I struggled awake. I thought there was someone on the street and when I looked out Bridie was walking through the gate to the river field. She was moving smoothly, no limp or stoop, and I was washed with joy that she was no longer in pain. But where was she heading at this hour when it was barely light? Then I saw auld Brandy dog walking at her heel like he always had. When he turned his head and his rheumy eyes locked with mine, my heart stopped.

I ran to the kitchen and she was there as usual in the chair by the range. But it wasn't lit and the kettle was cold and so was she. She had her ankles crossed and a work apron pulled over her ancient dressing gown. I sat beside her, held her slack hands and cried my fill over the best mother I had ever had. With her passing the true heart would go out of the house. The boys would be destroyed and Serena would be broken to bits; they all loved Bridie for the kind, decent, funny soul she was. And John?

How would I tell him and how would he react? He would be down in five minutes and then we'd both find out.

– John, it's Bridie. She's gone!

He went to her and felt her face and it looked for all the world that he was anointing her. A big fat tear had time to hit the cement floor before he got away.

– I'll get the priest, says John.

– Alright, alright. I'll tell the boys.

He left me alone with her and I had to try and avoid looking at her poor old feet crossed at the ankles in their tights and socks and pink bedroom slippers. Serena had bought her those with a matching nightie. Bridie, always full of craic, had come into the kitchen and pirouetted and preened in front of the boys. They all squirmed and screamed for her to get away and she laughed and laughed at them dodging out from under her kisses.

– What's wrong with ye? Don't ye have a kiss for your auld granny? Come here and we'll see, we'll soon see who has a kiss for me in my brand-new nightie! Sure, aren't I *gorgeous*?

I pulled myself together and rang Kathleen in Derry, Auntie Eileen and Lizzie Magee who was in town. I would let John Johns call in and tell Mammy on his way to the priest but I could do without *her* interfering in my house as we got it ready for the wake. Lizzie being home was a godsend; I had always liked Auntie Eileen around in a bad time but I needed Lizzie to get me through this one.

The two of them with Bernie in tow got to me around mid-morning. I'd sent the boys, dry-eyed in shock, up to The Hill to make sure that Mammy would stay put with her flashy rosary beads and Lourdes water. I waited alone for the priest and Junior O'Carolan to show up, keeping my back to Bridie so she couldn't see my face. It had always broken her heart to see me crying.

I prayed for the sound of the cars on the river to save me from the despair choking my lungs. Auntie Eileen and Lizzie were all solemn looks and heartfelt hugs 'til they got inside and Lizzie nearly keeled over.

- Holy Mother of fu—! She's still *there*. Just sitting there!
- Well, the priest is on his way, I hope, and O'Carolan. Where did you think she was going to be?
- I don't bloody *know*, Mary! In a bed or something! Jesus, that's put the heart right across me, that has, seeing her by the range. Can you not *move* her?
- Where would you like her? Pegged out on the washing line? That's when we fell apart, laughing fit to burst!
- Behave now, you pair, says Eileen. You're confusing Bernie. She doesn't even know what's wrong!

Bernie was sitting beside Bridie, looking like she was waiting for a mug of tea. We howled some more 'til we heard the priest's car draw up and right behind it the sound of John Johns's tractor and O'Carolan's hearse. Far too soon, she was laid out in her room full of blue roses. Remember, man, that thou art but dust, and unto dust thou shalt return.

The wake was packed to the rafters. I saw people that I hadn't seen in twenty years. Why did people make a bigger effort for the dead than the living? Even my friend Scrumptious Connolly from schooldays showed up already pissed. His hair was still blond but his beautiful face was purple; what a waste, I thought, as he hugged me and a whiff of old sweat and drink soured the very air around him. I caught Lizzie looking at him with something akin to regret. The road not taken. We had made a mountain of ham sandwiches and had bought another mountain of fruitcake. John had ordered there was to be no scrimping.

He came with crates of whiskey and beer and Lizzie had come back with wine. Serena must have wept the whole way home; her face was the size of a football by the time we got her in and settled with cold teabags on her eyes.

We had a great couple of jolly days and nights. The place never emptied and the smell of cigarette and pipe smoke soaked away the nervy air. Scrumptious came both nights because there was free drink – he had no shame at all, God love him, not a shred. We drank and we talked and we laughed 'til we cried over all the old stories. Bridie getting trapped in the auld outhouse by a herd of stray cows; Bridie pretending she wasn't lifting up her backside to fart after every meal; Bridie arguing that it was *not* possible to use too much lily-of-the-valley talcum powder, we were all too allergic for our own good.

Bridie shouting 'Bingo' instead of 'House' because she was so overexcited, Bridie encouraging all five of the waynes to get in beside her in bed at the same time so that they could heat her back and her front, Bridie chasing us in a nylon nightie 'til we nearly peed ourselves. I thought my heart wouldn't stand the pain. She would have just *loved* it: the company, the craic, the chocolate biscuits.

The funeral was the worst day. When O'Carolan had come to screw the lid on the coffin I felt a bit of myself slipping inside with Bridie. The rosary beads she had thrown aside so often wrapped now around her cold fingers for evermore. The tears could not be stemmed; the thought that I would no longer have her by my side was too much.

Mammy had sniffed and told me to offer it up; it wasn't seemly for a grown woman with children of her own to be carrying on like a baby. Did I think she was going to live forever to coddle me? But it's always the worst part when they disappear; you know it's forever. Bridie had been wearing her favourite dress; every colour of the rainbow it was and all the brightness went out with her, feet first.

It rained so hard that we couldn't walk the coffin to the end of the house; she went in the hearse all the way. The chapel was full to overflowing. I even spotted Doctor Dermot Darling Loughrey about halfway down the centre aisle. At John's command I – and no other – was to grace the altar and do the first reading, Psalm 23, and the Responsorial Psalm, and when I looked up from the pulpit by mistake, it seemed that the whole townland was looking back.

The Lord is my shepherd; I shall not want. He maketh me to lie down in green pastures; he leadeth me beside the still waters. He restoreth my soul: he leadeth me in the paths of righteousness for his name's sake. Yea, though I walk through the valley of the shadow of death, I will fear no evil: for thou art with me; thy rod and thy staff they comfort me.

Thou preparest a table before me in the presence of mine enemies: thou annointest my head with oil; my cup runneth over. Surely goodness and mercy shall follow me all the days of my life: and I will dwell in the house of the Lord forever.

The grave was a mudbath. Marius and Eugene were at the front, Shane and Daniel at the back carrying her on their fine, wide shoulders, but they were slipping and sliding when they had to lower her in and our hearts were in our mouths in case there was a mishap. That she was going in beside her boys was cold comfort. John held up 'til they started to fill the mud in on top and then he lost it. The wet earth thumped on the lid, splat after splat, and with each shovelful the tears rolled silently down to his chin. None of us knew what to do. I looked at Lizzie Magee and she looked back, stuck for words when I needed her most. John's no good with *loss*, says Bridie from a different life.

The boys stood with him, a strict unit of grief, and Serena stood with me. My mother looked utterly disgusted by a grown man crying; she was chewing the lemon lips off herself. She was wearing the same green felt hat that she had worn to my wedding. In the end it was Bernie who saved him. She stepped up and held his hand.

I regretted not going over to him myself as soon as my feet turned away. I couldn't make myself move closer to him or to her grave; I didn't want to look down and see Bridie's name on the lid picked out in brass. I didn't want to feel his pain. When he got to the parish hall with Bernie on his arm, he was ready to accept another round of 'I'm sorry for your troubles.' He looked stunning in a brand-new black suit and white shirt. His beauty could still take my breath away.

- God alive, you must be ridin' him twice a night at least?
- Jesus, Lizzie! What are you like? At a funeral? At *his* mother's funeral?
- Oh alright, Modest Mary, I'll shut my trap. It is such a shame about Bridie. Things are going to be a bit different at Johns Farm without her, aren't they?
- Yes, they are.

We went our separate ways as the early evening drew in, Eileen guaranteeing more visits and Lizzie with promises of phone calls and keeping track of Serena. I hoped she would keep her word; it had been three years since the Real IRA had bombed the BBC's building and Ealing Broadway but you never know when madness might strike again. When I saw the pictures of the glass buildings in London all I could think of was the shards they'd make if broken, shards that could hurt my girl.

The lane down to Johns Farm had never seemed as long but it still took us home. I couldn't go in at first and sat by Bridie's roses at the front door. I was officially the woman of the house now and I didn't want to be.

Ginger jumped on to my knee and looked just as sad as I felt. Not really sure what to do, the children all went to get changed and pretend that we were going to carry on as normal. The boys didn't come back into the kitchen and nor did Serena but when I did, I noticed that John had taken Bridie's armchair away. I hunted about and found that he had put it in the corner of her room, the blue roses still in bloom after a decade.

He was getting changed out of his suit: a farmer's work is never done. He was so still, standing with his bare back to me rolling his tie into a ball, that I couldn't help but touch him. I put my arms around his waist and laid my cheek against his back. I knew he wouldn't take it the wrong way. I just reached to below his shoulder blades where his skin felt tender and smooth. He pulled my arms tighter and kissed the tips of my fingers before putting my left hand over his heart and we swayed like that for a little. I heard lovely Bridie's voice ringing in my ears as if she was still sitting happy as a lark in the kitchen.

– John's a good man, y'know, Mary? There's worse men. Mary? I say, there's worse men?

– I know, I know, a lot worse. I could have done a lot worse. Drink your tea, Bridie.

Her cup always did runneth over. I felt my heart open and an ember of light curled towards my husband. I breathed against his skin and wished myself laid along the length of it. If he even *looked* at the bed I would be there before him. Could he feel the thaw in me without me having to declare it?

He had Bridie's wedding band in his palm. He rubbed the old gold between his fingers before he reached for my left hand and the light at my heart swelled and fluttered. I held my breath.

Could this be the day we finally met? Could this be the day when what lay between us could be named? I smiled my brightest smile; I couldn't keep it in. If he'd changed his mind, if he was in the market for a wife, I was ready.

– Give this to Serena for me, will you? he says. She's the best granddaughter Bridie could have had.

The light went out. My heart snapped shut and I reminded myself for the thousandth time not to forget my place. I was a charity case: nothing more, nothing less. I swallowed the disappointment. I wasn't *his* and he wasn't *mine*. He didn't want to see me or hear from me. I'd failed to keep the promise I'd made myself – don't drop your guard ever again. I carried his mother's ring to my daughter, his girl, the only girl he'd ever have, without another word. The freeze was back on.

Bridie was always going to be an absence, a pair of pink bedroom slippers that could never be filled, but life moves forward. Serena went back to London after a week and the twins left for college in Leeds, two more holes for me to fall in. My body felt tender as they pulled off the street waving and waving from the back of the car, it was like being kicked in the stomach. At least they'll be together, I consoled myself. I felt as if my head was full of wool; I couldn't think straight but I kept going, a robot – make the dinner, wash the plates, repeat – feeling nothing.

John was no better; he had a scowl that only lifted when Shane or Daniel talked to him, then he would force a smile and give them an auld hug or two. But with me, he was even more withdrawn than usual; we danced around each other in separate ballrooms. When we made love it was all about the battle to get there rather than the joy of being on the road. We were both bruised by it but we kept at it, night after lonely night, every kiss another goodbye. And bad though it was, even that wasn't the worst side effect. With Bridie ousted at last, my mother had taken to visiting.

She had hardly left my kitchen since the funeral. I couldn't stand it, it was a double blow, no Bridie at all and twice as much of bloody *her*. Didn't she know that I had work to do? Didn't she know I wasn't listening? Why didn't *she* have work to do? She must want something, something more than doing my head in?

- Was there something you wanted, Mammy, only I have to get on?
- Ah Mary, you're back from the fairies! Well now, well now … there is something I need to talk to you about. A *private matter* – maybe we should walk a little?
- Walk?
- Yes, *walk*.
- Where?
- The river?

We set out, me in my wellies, she in Daniel's, even though he made a face that looked like someone had been sick straight into his mouth when she slipped her American Tans into them. By the by, she did something even stranger than seeking my company, she linked arms with me and drew me near. I got a whiff of the warm-elastic smell of her, felt the fierce grip, the sheer strength of her after a lifetime of work and wallops even though she was nearly eighty. A tough old bird with a lifetime of bugbears stuck in her craw.

– Well? Are you going to spit it out?

– Mary! Really! You're so cold sometimes it's shockin'!

– *I'm* cold? What do you *want*?

– Well, if you must know, I'm having a bit of a problem ... you know, ah, down below.

– Down below?

– Down below.

– Down below where? Front or back?

– Front. Something's definitely wrong.

– Have you been to the doctor?

– Well no, I thought it might get better but it hasn't and I think I might have to go away for a few days to get things sorted ...

I couldn't quite believe that I was having a conversation about my mother's private parts. She was so private it seemed impossible that she would *have* private parts. I swallowed a smirk and bemoaned the fact that I would never get to tell Bridie that Sadie Rattigan had taken her front down below for an airing in the river field! She'd have split her sides! The whole kitchen would have been sprayed with cake crumbs!

- Could you be a bit more specific, Mammy? Is it an infection, an itch or something else?
- It's the same as Mrs Calhoun across the way, needs an operation.
- You think you have a prolapsed womb?
- KEEP YOUR VOICE DOWN!
- We're in the middle of a *field*?
- The point is *I'll* be needing help up at The Hill and now Bridie Johns is out of the picture you might remember who had the *trouble* of rearing you ... who sorted you out when *you* had *your* little problem ...
- Don't even say her name! You horrible, horrible old woman! Why would I want to help *you*? WHY?
- Because I'm *asking* you for help, Mary. *You!* You should be grateful!

I pushed her arm away from me then and started the stomp back towards Johns Farm. Grateful? Grateful? She wanted me to be grateful that she'd marooned me with my baby girl? She wanted me to be grateful for the fact that she had no one else to ask! I was the last chance saloon! I had never been good enough for her, she had rubbished me from day one with her 'weak material' and 'bad blood' and 'nothing', and now that I was red raw from the loss of my real mother she'd decided it was time I started playing the Duty Game? She was not getting *me* back!

I would *love* to have Daddy, have him to myself for a few days without her hovering like a vulture at his back, but *she* wasn't getting a leash on her favourite dogsbody, No Siree Bob. The blood boiling in my ears and across my face made me feel better than I had for months:, where there's blood there's life.

- Call me when you're leaving and I'll go up and make Daddy's tea! I might even show him how to fry a SHAGGIN' egg for himself!
- Mary Rattigan! Honour thy mother and thy father! What is wrong with you? What? Sometimes I swear you've never moved beyond being sixteen! Mary, do you hear me, I swear you've never moved beyond being *sixteen*?
- It's Mary *Johns*, Mammy, don't make me tell you again.

29

The months were rolling past, flying over the hills quicker than clouds on a breezy day. I waited for the wound of Bridie to heal. I missed her from minute to minute, her and Serena and Marius and Eugene, all lost to me in their various ways. I tried not to fuss over Shane and Daniel, especially when their father was watching. His black eyes bored into me when I left my fingers too long on their cheeks.

If I did speak to John he looked put out, like I was someone who wanted something from him, something he didn't have. He was angry over his mother's death and surely angry that he was left with me, just me, the rattling bag of bones and nerves Bridie had held together for the guts of thirty years. She had always had my back, interpreting what I meant, what I said, what I did and setting it out in terms that he could understand. She could make him see that I wasn't all bad. Without Bridie between us, daytime relations between John Johns and me would deteriorate nicely. We might not even hit our low goal of civilities.

We have to be outside the granite walls of Johns Farm, have to be away from its street, before we can relax in each other's company. He hates how I can drift off when I have the four walls of Johns Farm as my horizon; I've been caught a few too many times just staring. Then he'll snap at me and I jump to, embarrassed. Outside we can be companionable. As we move together cutting the corners on the golden bags of wheat, we never speak, we don't need to we've done it so often, muscle memory. We let the dusty cows nudge us this way and that in the fading light and some of its golden peace falls on both our shoulders. But we always have to go home.

Shane went off to university in the September – only to Belfast, thank God. Johns Farm seemed to be expanding: walking across the big concrete floor took an age. The stairs were as steep as the road to The Hill. Every bedroom gaped empty, the blue roses in Bridie's room lost their charm but I couldn't find the strength to paper over them. We got through the winter with just Daniel to keep us company, but the atmosphere in the kitchen had our son running for his bedroom. We spoke through him, pulling him between us 'til he frowned at us to be left alone.

Spring came as a relief, with endless work and toil needed to get the farm ready for another year, but by summer we were scratchy again and worn. In desperation, Daniel told us to GET OUT, we needed to get out more! We were driving him potty and that's how we came to agree – reluctantly – that we'd have another night in the Long Lounge. And we'd do it before the other three boys all came home that weekend.

I called Auntie Eileen to make sure I'd have someone to talk to when we got there. I'd already spent a few nights in there watching other women pant over my husband as he went to the bar, stopping here and there to chat. The way their eyes followed him around the room made me fume. Once, a drunk girl had even pulled him up out of his seat and on to the dance floor and I'd had to sit with my face on fire as they lurched about. She did her best to get her arms around his neck, the better to get her boobs on his chest, but he'd managed to keep hold of her hands right up until she just threw shame out the door and wrapped herself around his waist. She was nothing short of a T.R.A.M.P.

As luck would have it Lizzie Magee was home again. John called her Saint Lizzie, short for Saint Lizzie of the Polished Nails, and she was going to have to stop guffawing every time he said it or I'd punch her. Her behaviour around dishy men hadn't improved much since we were girls, she still had no idea when to back off.

I'd made a fairly good job of myself. Being such a natural person himself, John doesn't like too much make-up so I concentrate on my hair, brushing it until it shines and trying not to notice the silver streaks. I'm still lean as a greyhound even though I eat like a horse, something that makes Lizzie rage. She watches me put on a slick of red lipstick.

- I actually fucking hate you, Mary Rattigan! Have you a portrait in the attic or wha'?
- There might be an auld Polaroid curling up somewhere now!

She was ensconced at the kitchen table, dressed to the nines and in full make-up. Just seeing her pick her way from the hire car through the cowshit was enough to keep me going for another year. She was full of chat. I dreaded it as much as I

299

loved it, yearned for it, for her company and her stories. She had a habit of bringing me stones from lands I would never walk on and she handed me one as she talked. She'd been to Namibia this time – in Africa, as she kept telling me, as if I mightn't know.

She told me about the colours: pink, orange, the bluest sky she'd ever seen, the blackest sky at night, the brightest stars, the dust, and the light, ah, the light. It seemed to have got inside her, opened up a huge space inside where colours were brighter and more vivid than it seemed possible, it shone from behind her eyes. I was glad, Lizzie had been having a bad time of it recently.

Auntie Eileen bowled in, a bottle under each arm and a bag of crisps in each hand. She was rarin' to go, this was going to be her lucky night. She wanted to come home with a rich farmer under her belt. We laughed and drank as if we didn't have a care in the world between us. John found us like that, squealing and teary-eyed, and he just shook his head and carried on to the bedroom to get changed. I knew he was smiling. It had been too long since the house had heard a bit of happiness.

We went to the Long Lounge and sang and drank our fill. Every time the band finished 'The Fields of Athenry' we demanded it again and every time the small free birds flew we cried harder and sang louder 'til our throats were raw. Lizzie managed to drag John up for a dance and she was *definitely* trying to get her boobs on his chest but I let it go. I owed her one for Jacques Bernier.

The next morning she phoned up with a hangover shocking enough to match my own but says she needs to chat. John Johns was already up and away to Arthur Rowley's. I boiled the kettle. It was still only nine o'clock, it was unusual that

Lizzie was awake at all, never mind up and dressed and on the road. I took a cup of tea out to the stoop and the sunshine and waited for her.

Lizzie lands after a while, my tea is cold and I sling it into the bushes at the side of the half-door as she gets out of her car. As I make tea, mashing some leaves in Bridie's old brown pot, I can hear her sighing. She's thoughtful, miles away and angry, and I can see a muscle twitching in her jaw when she bends too quickly to hide it. Should I bring the ghost of it into the house? Yes, yes it's time I conjured the one stillborn dream of Lizzie Magee's life.

– Listen ... is there any news?

I always dreaded asking her about the baby thing. She and Kenny had been trying for years, had thrown money at it, a lot of money, but nothing. She's too old but she won't give up. She can't face life without a family. She looked down now to hide her face. We'd been friends since we were four – thirty-five years – but still we hid the worst of things from each other. She pretended that she would be far better off without children. We laughed when we had the courage to talk about how it would ruin her figure, a figure fleshed out with too many drinks and prescription drugs.

With her head down she told me that the last batch of IVF was another failure. The doctors were trying to get her to forget all about it. Kenny was, too, he couldn't take much more. It made Lizzie feel like a failure. Dessie refused to stay in the room if her 'women's troubles' were being discussed. It was just one of those things, God's will or God's joke. She sniffed and then laughed.

– Nearly the worst of it is coping with Sheila ... she's *so angry*!

– Your mammy's a diamond. She'll get over it, so will you …

– I'm not so sure she will, she's all for going again! You'd think sticking needles in yourself for weeks was the best craic in town!

I dabbed my eyes on the edge of my work apron and Lizzie fetched out a packet of paper hankies from her posh handbag. She was always drenched in some expensive perfume; it was out of place with its musky sweetness. Her life was not something I would ever understand. She had total freedom; Kenny didn't really care what she did or where she went. They had a big house in London where they could walk to all sorts of fancy restaurants. Her job was a success – she was a lawyer, for heaven's sake! She took *three* holidays a year, though both of us knew that the trips weren't filling the space that she and Kenny needed filling most.

Would she be able to understand the kind of life I had built with John Johns? I had never burdened her or anyone with the whole truth of what went on at Johns Farm. I had a man who could block out the fact that I was in the room unless that room was the bedroom. A man who was tired of me but who wouldn't let his own father know what he'd taken on. A man who made the decisions that affected us both: more cows, more children, different cows, no more children. A day at the seaside maybe once a year when I got to eat something that I hadn't planted, grown, dug, washed and cooked myself.

I had lost my nerve. I had lost myself. I had been hiding for so long, breaking cover for any reason seemed impossible. No one knew us better than each other and we didn't know each other at all. It was an authentic Northern Irish friendship. Lizzie pulled herself together as she hadn't any other option but she did have other news.

– So, Joe Loughrey's back in town. He's going to take over the surgery. Dermot Darling is retiring!

I'd always had a strange notion that I would somehow *feel* Joe Loughrey if he came back again, feel his presence like someone walking on my grave. We were unfinished business.

– Mary? Are you alright?

– How long?

– Two weeks already. He's bought that big house out past Brooky Hay.

– Is he married?

– He was married at a time but there's no wife now. Imagine the scandal? A divorced doctor in Carncloon! The auld wans'll have to bless themselves before they drop their drawers!

– Lizzie! Behave! Have you seen him?

– I have. He's a very different boy from the one we knew. He has quite the high opinion of himself these days! Kenny was *not* keen. I think his exact phrase was 'an out-of-this-world wanker'?

All the air in my body was leaking out and I couldn't breathe any back in. I could nearly hear it, hissing in my ears.

– Mary, are you alright? Jesus, you've gone a terrible colour! Sure, it's all ancient history anyway? Mary, can you hear me? Isn't it all ancient history?

– Ancient, yeah. Thanks, Lizzie.

She wasn't gone five minutes before the door was darkened by my mother again. She must have set out at quite a pace when she saw Lizzie's car. She came in gasping and throwing herself down on a kitchen chair, clutching at her arthritic hip.

– I see that flash car of Lizzie Magee's was here again but that last was a flying visit.

303

– Yes, she's away tomorrow.

– Hmmm, I suppose you know by now then, he's back? *Your lovely boy?*

– Who?

– Ach, who indeed! As if you didn't know! Pah! The lovely Joe Loughrey back from his doctoring in America to settle in that big barracks of a house that Eddie Connolly threw up and put a roof on! He's a man in need of a lot of space for a man on his own. Maybe he's planning on a big family?

– Maybe.

– Hmm. … maybe, maybe indeed. You make sure you have nothing to do with him – do you hear me, Mary Rattigan?

– I'm Mary Johns, Mammy. *Why can't you remember that?*

I must stand up now, stand up and start moving. I must make a start on the special dinner for tomorrow when the boys arrive. I imagined that one day when we'd been alone for too long, John would come home and decide at last that he was tired of being hitched to me. He would get a bulldozer and charge the house, smashing the half-door and the ancient lintels. Tumbling the chimneys and breaking the glass at the windows and the first brick to hit my head would stun me just enough so that I would know I was being buried alive.

I found myself listening for machines and checking the walls for cracks before I shook it off and snorted at my own madness! The very thought! That John Johns would waste money or time hiring a bulldozer and driving it all the way down the lane, when we both knew all he had to do was walk into the house, take me by the hand and silence me with a well-chosen word or two, something loaded like 'Come'.

– What news did Sadie have?

– Jesus, John! How do you *do* that?

– Well? What news?

– Nothing! Nothing at all!

I turned back to the dark kitchen and walked dry-eyed to the yellow range. The terrible palpable silence and distance that was always between me and him in the heart of the house settled itself in the concrete corners of the room. He'd know, of course, that Joe Loughrey had reappeared. I felt him move to stand behind me. An inch away at most – not touching me but still somehow *inside* me. It took all my strength not to sink against him and let him take me down and down to our meeting place. He was right, some nights *I couldn't be more his.*

He was breathing slow, I was hardly breathing at all, but both our hearts were smashing at their ribcages. After minutes he moved away and out into the hall. He closed the glass door into the back scullery gently behind him and I turned around in time to see his big shape picked out in glass flowers before he stepped into the orchard.

30

I climbed the hill the next day to meet my first three boys from the bus, leaving Daniel to sleep. John Johns was away early again to Omagh but he wouldn't be too late as he couldn't wait to see them either. All four of them would be at home – all of them together! – and my chest swelled at the thought of all the noise and bother that I would *yearn* to endure for another twenty years.

Marius and Eugene were coming back from Leeds after a week's trip to see Serena in London, Shane was meeting them in Belfast. They had stayed with a pal in Derry overnight and they would take the same workers' bus together that I had to the end of the Hill Road.

I stopped for a while at the turn in the lane, looking down at Johns Farm: the red tin roofs still on the big white barns; the river field full of buttercups; the prize Charolais grazing; Serena's old pony, Bantree, standing stock-still. All of it framed in the greenest of green. John wouldn't sell the little pony, although he cost a small fortune in vet's fees and feed. Bantree was safe and sound and waiting for her anytime, his girl.

They came pushing and shoving and noisy along the lane just as I got past the big hayfield that ran along the side of the road. I got a smattering of kisses and hugs and far too many tickles to make me scream and threaten them with a good slap. That made them laugh; they'd never been smacked in their whole lives. Their beautiful faces were his, the big shoulders and long legs all his, and I loved them so, loved the perfection of them, I had to stop myself kissing them half to death. When we were in sight of the red roof on the milk house, Eugene took off and started running for the door with me among them, all of us like children.

It was a sight to see when all four of them collided on the street, hugging and shouting and ragging each other. Before he knew it, poor Daniel was lifted shoulder-high and run at some speed towards the river. He managed to wriggle free and I could see him pretending to throw punches and karate kicks before they all piled in on top of him again. All I could hear was laughter, even though every face was under someone else's backside! I ran down to break them up, picking up a stray shoe here and there as they scattered and ran for the water. Buck naked to a man, they jumped in screaming.

I stayed a safe distance from the bank and soaked up their enjoyment and love. Shane climbed out and grabbed for his shirt to cover himself.

– Where's Da? Did he say when he would be here?

– He's at the mart, said he wouldn't be too late.

We stayed down by the water for an hour or so, lying around, chatting about Serena mostly, how well she was doing, how happy. Marius said her paintings were great, huge monochrome flowers. Eugene said they were shite. The other two laughed along, the twins could argue over what way the world was turning. There was still no sign of a boyfriend to replace the last one but it wasn't bothering Serena too much. She had sent me a present, they said, and so we headed up the river field through the delicate stalks of white cow parsley and purple heads of wild angelica.

Marius handed me a cardboard tube before he walked away with his holdall to the bedroom at the back of the barn he had shared with Eugene. I pulled out a heavy paper roll and unfurled it to see myself. She had drawn me with my back against the wall of Johns Farm but I was staring off to the side. It was a striking resemblance, right down to the nervous meeting of the tips of my fingers. I touched it and some of the charcoal came away. I would fade with time.

As the evening drew in, John didn't appear so we ate without him. The boys were calling him but got no answer. I made them pasta with a tomato sauce from my own tomatoes which were sweeter than life itself. My developing set of green fingers cheered me, the beauty of my garden was just beginning to knit the break of Bridie.

We opened some wine and saved a glass for John; when he didn't come we opened some more wine and saved him a glass from that. He was never late and it wasn't long 'til we took ourselves out on the street to listen for his car. We were all beginning to fret so I occupied them with jobs: I had them check the gates, walk the fences and give the beasts an extra feed.

John Johns hadn't come back by dusk; it was way past his time. I didn't worry now that the days of the RUC on the prowl were long over; they were the PSNI now, the Police Service of Northern Ireland who were going to look after us without bias or bile. Daniel hung close to me as I moved around the kitchen. Shane was gassing with Serena on the phone; the twins were kicking a ball outside as it grew dark, their voices carrying high and happy, carefree. But something was niggling me, John Johns would have set out for home early, knowing the boys would be waiting.

After an age I heard a vehicle coming. The sound carried easily on the river, it was so still; and I knew it wasn't him, his engine was different. I was standing at the end of the house waiting for whoever it was when a red tractor turned the bend. The boys were all around me before it came to a stop on the street. Wordy Clarke was behind the wheel so it wouldn't be a long story. He got out and tipped his cap before he threw his fag over the hedge.

– Missus.

– Wordy.

– Himself's had an accident.

– What kind of accident?

– Fall. Been took to Omagh.

– Wordy, HOW DID HE FALL?

– Off a baler, cab jolted.

– AND?

– He's in Omagh.

– Jesus wept! Thanks, Wordy, you're a star turn as always!

I roared at my waynes to get me the phone book as we all ran for the kitchen. My heart was in a panicky beat of worry as I dialled the number for the hospital. I got through to the men's ward where no one seemed to know much. He wasn't badly cut up but his back was bruised so he'd been sedated for now and they'd know more tomorrow. We had no car; it was at the mart.

Rattling the nerves and doors at The Hill seemed too dramatic and Bernie would be fast asleep so Eileen was not an option. We decided John would have to keep for one night.

The boys were worried so I set about reassuring them. I reeled off one of my lists. Your father is made of strong stuff. He hates fuss of any kind. He heals fast, bouncing back from cuts that would have slowed a normal man down. He once gaffer-taped a wad of bandages around a sliced forearm that had to be stitched two days later; he could survive without us and anyway he was asleep. They sloped back to their film and I took a shaky cuppa out to drink under the stars. Wordy was still on the street, leaning against his tractor. Why?

– Wordy, was there something else?

– No.

– Well *goodnight* then, safe home!

With that he swung up into the cab and started away. Wordy was just one among many misfits that John had looked out for over the years; he was known as a bit simple even by people who knew his mother had taken too much drink through all four of her pregnancies. The Plough hung just above my head and I tracked my eye up to the North Star and hoped it could be seen in Omagh if anyone was gazing out of a hospital window.

During the night, after falling asleep as soon as my head touched the pillow, I woke up with sweat running down my back and between my breasts and realised that I was on his side of the bed, tangled in a knot of sheets and worry. I was alone but I was not on my own. When I swung my legs out, Granny Moo was standing by the window, she was looking at the stars. I kept my eyes glued to her for as long as I could but with the first blink she was gone. That was the end of sleep. Rising at 5am, I went through several changes of clothes. I had a lot of stuff brought to me over the years. Posh stuff from all over the world from Lizzie Magee: perfume, high heels, leather handbags in every colour of the rainbow. I love buying clothes for you, Mary Rattigan, she says, I get to pretend that I'm thin and gorgeous. She's a card!

The thought I had to fight most was the one where I knew it was important to me to look good when I went to the hospital; I wanted to look out-of-this-world. I hadn't felt like this since I went to the school disco in the parish hall! I picked a sober black trouser suit from the Magee collection and a soft red jumper that I had to pull from its tissue paper. Red was still my colour and it gave me some sort of life as it bounced against the white of my skin. I wiped a lot of the make-up off and brushed my hair again.

– How do I look?

– Fine, Ma, just fine!

– And remember, do NOT tell your sister! Later is always time enough for lousy news! Especially when it's Serena!

I smiled as all their eyes followed me to the hall. I had told them to get on with the feeding and milking while I went alone to find out how their father was. I stuffed a pair of dangerously high-heeled black boots in a bag while I rooted around for my wellies. The hall mirror let me know I didn't look half bad for a hard-worked mother of five.

I set off early so that I could drop into Mammy's and explain the situation. She was all questions and hand-wringing and Ave Marias and asking me about money, which I had plenty of, but the purse was still opened with a maximum of fuss.

The bus was set up exactly as it was in my time. The loud, pretty children sat at the back, safe in their numbers. The bespectacled and greasy few sat here and there in the middle of the bus and the workers sat at the front. The only thing that was different was the fact that the uniforms were mixed now – there no longer was a bus just for Catholics and another one just for Protestants. Public transport was shared since peace broke out: one giant leap for Northern Irish mankind.

As Carncloon rolled away I realised how much everything else had changed too. The same green fields, the same tumble-down stone walls and the same derelict cottages now had *Dallas*-style houses sitting back from the road with pillars at the gate. Some of them hadn't even bothered to hang a curtain to hide the perfect cream interiors.

I walked into the hospital and found the ward, already feeling sick from the smell of disinfectant and what it was devised to mask. The Sister asked me to wait – my husband was in the bed that had the curtains round it, could I just wait a few minutes more so that the nursing staff could finish their jobs?

– Is he bad, y'know? Badly cut or what?

– You'd hardly know by looking at him that there was much wrong, God bless him anyhow!

It seemed hours until they drew the curtains and asked me to go on up. He was at the end of the ward, by the window.

– Mary! I thought you'd never come!

– I only heard last night, late last night at that, so I couldn't make my way here.

I was startled by the big hand that he'd flung out for me before I realised it was for me to hold. I'd never held his hand in public.

It was warm and dry and something deep inside me rattled, a feeling of ... *belonging.*

– Well, you don't *look* too bad. What have they said about you?

– Oh, Mary, I can't move my legs! They've X-rayed and I might've broke my back but they don't know if the spine is gone too 'til the swelling goes down! What'll we do if I'm off my legs, Mary?

I snapped to. What was he saying? He couldn't walk? I just sat there with my lip hangin'. Why had I just sailed in here unprepared? Sometimes my own stupidity took my breath away. A jagged cut ran from his wrist to his elbow. It looked raw and sore and I was moved to kiss it, leaving my lips on it while big salty tears ran silently down my face.

– We'll manage, I managed to say at last. We'll manage.

I sat with him for the next few hours while he slept. A nurse had given him something to make sure he lay still. I tried not to look at the shadows his eyelashes cast on his cheeks, at the thick dark hair of his arms and his big hands curled, helpless as a baby. I curled my own hand inside his but there was nothing, not even a flicker, and I had to push his fingers over mine to make him hold me. The callouses were starting to soften and he'd only been out of the fields a matter of hours.

The doctor came round in the afternoon and explained why John had to go to the Mater Hospital in Belfast. They had a specialist spine-injury unit there and my husband would receive the best of care, although it would be more of a journey for me to make when I wanted to visit. My top lip was stuck to my teeth and I kept licking its underside to set it free so that I could hold my mouth in a steady line.

He came to when they shifted him from the bed to the trolley. He didn't speak but fixed me with a stare that made me feel as if I was being memorised. When I had turned from red to white and back again, he spoke.

– I know you won't come.

– I will, I promise.

I stayed 'til he was transferred to the ambulance and I explained to the doctor that I couldn't go with him because I had children and must be home. Children were always more important than husbands so they understood, though I could tell they thought I was a quare wan, letting an injured man go so far, so alone. I didn't mention the cows, though their hooves were practically sticking out of my mouth. John Johns held my eyes the whole time because I couldn't get close enough for him to hold anything else, and I looked back because I needed to prove that I could stand on my own two feet even though my legs were wobbling like jellies. They were not strong enough to let me jump in beside him, to console him, before it was too late.

As the doors of the ambulance closed I saw one big tear roll down his face before I was shut out completely. I waited as it left the car park and turned at the roundabout with a couple of warning whoops to take him to the other side of the Six Counties and all I felt was forsaken. He was lost to me for the sake of one step in the right direction.

I didn't want to phone Serena and listen to her howling, she cried if I told her I'd just dug a thorn out of his finger. I didn't want to go home and face our boys, and anyway there was only one bus, same as when I was at school. Instead I wandered into Omagh town and detoured past to the garden of remembrance for the bloody Real IRA bomb. It was still, just a sweet packet fluttered at the bottom of a bush. I thought again of the woman who had died when she was pregnant with twins. Her mammy, them and her little girl all gone in a flash.

At the time the loss of her and them seemed more terrible than everyone else's loss, but now all five of them were just part of the Northern Irish dead: lives lost, lives never lived. We have a great word here for that kind of act, indiscriminate. How could anything, *anything* be worth parking a car loaded with explosives in a busy market town on a fair day? Twenty-nine families of both creeds would be asking that question for the rest of their time.

Was John's ambulance on the motorway yet? The umbilical between it and me was tearing at my guts, one more inch and I'd unravel. I wandered around the shops looking at stuff that I'd never want, thoughts of John and his words, *I know you won't come*, ricocheting around my head. *I'm yours* – that's what I should have said while I still had the chance, damn being embarrassed, damn being scared. You were right, John, I *couldn't be more yours*.

The Ulsterbus rolled in at six thirty to Carncloon. I changed to the other bus which was ticking over at the stop and waited for it to start its climb to The Hill. I didn't get as far as home. The boys were all in Mammy's. I could imagine the clack of the rosary beads for an occasion such as this. The Angelus bell still crowed three times a day for Sadie and her increasingly painful knees. Eugene speaks for them all.

– How is he?

– Well, he's gone to Belfast, the Mater. He might have broken his back.

– Jesus, don't soften it, Ma! says Eugene. What does that mean for him?

– They don't know yet. There's a chance that he'll be okay but they have to wait and see if his spine is damaged too when the swelling goes down.

– What'll we do now? When can we go and see him?

– We'll go home for now and I'll ring the Mater. Then we'll know exactly when we can go and see him, alright?

They looked away, not sure what to feel or think, torn between being men and boys. They loved him so dearly, it was tattooed on them. Mammy could hang back no longer. She loved bad news more than altar wine, thrived on it.

– Oh, Mary! Will we see if Father O'Brien can offer up tonight's Mass for him?

– Maybe we'll just pin most of our hopes on the surgeons at the Mater, what about that for a radical idea?

– Well now, isn't it just like you to be facetious at a time like this! There's never any point in giving up on God, Mary, you'll come to know that yet!

– Mammy, I'm tired, I'm stressed and so are my boys. I just want to get past you and your fu— effing rosary beads and into my own home so that I can phone the hospital, alright?

– Hmmm, well, I suppose it'll have to be. But I've made stew, enough for all of you, so I don't know what's going to happen now …

Ah, I love Ireland. It's the only country in the world where a plate of spuds and some overboiled beef brisket can compete for importance with any major life event. That a pot of stew might have to be put out to the hens was a moral dilemma no one could sanction.

- That's very *kind* of you, the boys can wait here. I'm going to get changed and make my call and then I'll be back. Does that suit?
- That suits, that suits, whatever suits *you* is best, Mary darlin'!
- Jesus!
- Don't take the Lord's name in —
- SHUT UP, MAMMY!

Everyone jumps, including Daddy who spills his tea. I fix my boys with a stare that says don't question me or my decision or I may just explode and they all duly back off. As I walk away, I feel something hitting me and look back just in time to see Mammy recork her really big bottle of Holy Water from Lourdes. So, I'm blessed once more.

I walk on and down the long lane. The whitewashed wall that runs along the side of the orchard is ahead and to every side the animals are carrying on with their lives. I notice that the Charolais need to be moved to the next section of the hill field, because they have grazed it down to lime green, and bend double with a glancing pain in my stomach when I realise that I won't be telling John, I'll be doing it myself. I stumble on for the house. I'm glad for Bridie that she's not here to suffer this.

The phone rings and it's Auntie Eileen. Seems Mother Dear has been extremely busy spreading the bad news as far and as wide as she can in one short day and she's not exactly been shaving the truth. I tell Eileen I can't talk right now because there's a lot of words I can't force out of my mouth – broken, disabled, alone, *love* – and she says she understands.

I put the phone down and lift it quick before anyone else gets through. I've never rung a big hospital before and the many silences and clicks it takes to get through to the right ward stretch out the minutes before I speak to a nurse. My husband is

317

comfortable, I cannot talk to him because he's been sedated. We can visit any time we want but he may be missing from the bed a lot as he's due for many more X-rays and other tests.

I mustn't worry. They can work miracles these days. *Miracles?* Does she know she's talking to a woman who's just had Holy Water lobbed at her by a hyper-religious lunatic who wouldn't be familiar with kindness or love or hope if it punched her in the face? I say thank you and I hang up, spinning around suddenly in the silence as if someone is standing between my shoulder blades. I cannot form a single thought except that on this day, of all days, I do not want to see Granny Moo.

I shove off my good clothes and pull on my ancient track bottoms and an old sweatshirt and wellies and run all the way back up the hill. The blisters on my heels don't even slow me down. I want my lungs to burn. I want to feel the blood pump around my body, my body that could still move.

Perhaps I should have waited outside because bursting into a house completely out of puff and red in the face is not what people waiting for bad news necessarily want to see.

- What is it, Mary? Oh Good Holy God and His Blessed Mother, he's dead! He's dead! Isn't he, Mary? Don't lie to us! HE'S DEAD!
- He's *not dead*, Mammy! Get a grip! He's fine, comfortable, sedated, we can go and see him tomorrow. Daddy, can you get me a drink of water?
- Why were you runnin'?
- I don't *know*, Daddy, I just took a fit of running!
- Oh.
- I'll put the dinner out, says Mother Hen. That's what we all need: a good home-cooked dinner to heat our gizzards!

Mammy's loving the fact that she has a full house, that she can grumble about how unused she is to having to get a dinner up for *seven people* but how it's all no trouble, *really*, no trouble. She wouldn't have chosen to do anything else in the circumstances, though her hands are aching a bit from peeling all those spuds, but it was *no trouble at all*. The boys push the food into their mouths as silent as their grandfather while I bat answers back to my mother's mundane questions.

– So, was Omagh busy?

– Average.

– Did you walk down to the Memorial Garden?

– Yes.

– Did you say a prayer?

– Why would I?

Daddy raises an eyebrow. The eyebrow said don't push her, don't start a row, don't you think we've had enough of those over the years? I voted with my feet and said we needed to get going. Mammy – who in over two decades had hardly asked me if I was alright – started up in her best pretend-fret, would we be warm enough, would we be able to see our way, would we be able to cope down there all *alone*? She had the makings of a solution. As we all pushed to get past each other and out the back door, she showered us with Holy Water. We all stopped just long enough to realise that it wasn't raining and then set off, covered in irritation.

Halfway down the hill, Eugene let rip an enormous fart to dispel the gloomy silence and, to be fair, he did make us all laugh.

– There's nothing like a bit of home-cooked stew to heat your gizzards! he says.

*

We set off early the next morning. Daddy was going to drop us into Carncloon as a way of making the journey seem shorter and we would pick up the Belfast bus in Omagh. Watch yourself, he says, and I nod that I will. I sit with Daniel beside me, Marius and Eugene behind and Shane behind them, all my little ducks lined up. I couldn't get my mind to stretch as far as the Mater, trying to imagine what I would see, what I would hear, what I would feel.

The bus steamed up with the wealth of early-morning breath mixed in with cold rubber. From habit I cleared a little sweaty patch in the window with my hand. And there he was. Joe Loughrey – sorry, Doctor Joseph Loughrey – instantly recognisable and standing on the pavement opposite, looking straight past me.

Jeepers! Why didn't Lizzie Magee mention that he was as bald as an egg? I was looking at a face that I used to know better than my own. It was altered by a sort of sneer, as if he was a doctor who had had to deal with too much toe fungus or one haemorrhoid too far in his career. Mind, the face also used to have a fringe. The years in between melted like butter in a pan. I was sixteen again and listening to our friends slagging us as we went off for a snog in the bombed-out Long Lounge. I'd pinned so many hopes and dreams on him, thinking that we would make it out of Carncloon together, thinking that he would be the answer. Joe Loughrey, my magic-carpet ride that never got off the ground.

– Ma! Ma!

– *What?*

– You were off in your own little world again!

– Sorry, Daniel! I'm all at sixes and sevens!
– We'll be in Belfast soon, you'll feel better when you've seen
  Da for yourself?
– Yes, yes, I'll feel better then.

31

The waiting room at the Mater Hospital in Belfast was green, the carpet was blue, the air was dry and the magazines were a year out of date. A man with a badly burnt face, another man with an eyepatch and a few limping ladies came in and went out and still we waited to be called. John was off somewhere having tests; the boys were restless, shuffling about on the plastic chairs and flicking through the mags without even seeing the pictures.

– Mrs Johns? Mrs Mary Johns?

– That's me, I say, raising my hand like a schoolgirl.

I must have stood up, I must have tried to move forward, but all of a sudden the whole room tipped. The blue and the green swirled faster and faster and I was thrown down, a black wave washed over my head and I was gone.

I came to in a recovery room, with only Daniel beside me, looking pale and worried. The curtain is pulled back by the other three who've just seen their daddy for the half hour he'll be awake today.

– What did they say about him?

– They don't see a break, but his back is still badly swollen so they're keeping him drowsy so he doesn't move too much.

John is lying at the far end of a ward with four beds. The gash on his arm is a mottled purple but already healing. A urine bag hangs on the side of the bed and a beaker with a straw in it is on his tray table. Daniel does what I should and moves to him, holding his hand and talking to him, but I can't. I can't touch him, I can't speak. I'd watched him sleep a thousand times but this, *this was different*, he was too still, too vulnerable. I couldn't stand it. I couldn't learn to live without this man. A bitter lump of tears is bobbing at the back of my throat. I want to hold his head against my breast and tell him he's going to be okay. *We* are going to be okay.

Little pins of light start swirling behind my eyes and I fear that I'm going to faint again. When I sway backwards Marius grabs my arm and takes me back to the waiting room, he gets me a Fat Coke from the vending machine and I throw caution and my fillings to the wind and drink the lot. When I've chugged it back, he hands me a chocolate bar without a word and I scoff that too, ashamed that I'm supposed to be looking after *him* not vice versa. He hugs me when he sees that I feel bad *again*; he's such a beautiful boy. *You're a diamond, you know that, Ma?* I'm glad of his arm around my shoulders when the nurse tells us we've had our lot for the day; John won't be woken up again until tomorrow.

Marius and Eugene decide to stay up in the city for a couple of days to see how things pan out and Shane, Daniel and me go home: Johns Farm must be tended. Serena has to be told now, so she and my Auntie Eileen are first on my list of people to call after I ride the gauntlet of getting past my mother. My brain is a pea rolling on a plate but my feet keep moving because I'm concentrating on putting one of them in front of the other – to get the bus home, to get off the bus, to walk the mile to The Hill, to walk the other two miles to Johns Farm.

I'll be fine as soon as I get to my kitchen, get to the auld yellow range, get the fire up to boil the kettle, get a mug of tea to take out to the stoop and surely soon the hole in my chest will start to fill up? I am back before I know what's hit me and facing down another night at Johns Farm without him.

Serena is inconsolable. She cries and cries and the sound of it scours my brain. She wants to come home straight away and, much as I'd love to have her beside me, she'd undo me totally. I need all the energy I have to stop myself from falling to pieces. Auntie Eileen is quiet. I hear the smoke being blown slowly out of her mouth as I relay the news. I'll be there tomorrow, she says, sit tight.

I make a grand performance of feeding my boys. I crack eggs and mix flour and drop twenty scones into the sizzling butter in the pan. They know that drop scones are one of John's favourites and ask me to save some for him. I try to nod but the muscles at the back of my neck are rock-hard. My back feels brittle, my legs like spindles held too long on the lathe. *I miss him.* He would have robbed a scone straight out of the pan by now even if it meant burning his fingers.

Good job there'll be so much to do, the cows must be fed, the chickens too. Matthew is coming to take off the first crop of silage, I'll get him to stack some bales down by the side of the river field. I'll have to see to the garden; the vegetables and fruit bushes are all growing wild. I'll stoke the fire high tonight and watch the flames burst and leap.

I could hear the boys in the river field calling to the cows, hep, hep, hep as they threw the hay into the feeders, the sounds of their father. I hope he wasn't fretting if he was awake at all. I hope he knew he was on my mind. I hope he knew that a flame of hope blazed once more in my eggshell heart.

I have Eileen down at Johns Farm to comfort me and she's checking the cupboards to make sure I have enough cups to cater to a wake house 'if the worst happens'! How I love that reassuring aunt of mine!

The boys were off doing the feeding and other chores while I saw to the hens. A faint breeze ruffled their red feathers as they chooked and scratched about in the handfuls of barley that I was throwing down. Was he feeling lonely up there in Belfast? He would hate the lights inside and outside the hospital; he was such a natural person, almost a part of the land. I could not *picture* Johns Farm without him.

For years I thought he had resisted electricity because of the cost, but I had come to learn that he liked the softer light and life that comes with gas lamps. I had missed them myself the first time the naked bulb had sprung into life in the kitchen, even though Bridie and me had danced about and declared that this was the only way forward. John had looked sad, like he had given in. He still made us boil the kettle on the range, though, and never buckled on having a toaster.

– Why do you need a toaster when you have a fire going all day? You can toast all the bread you want.

He had a point. I'm not sure I'd ever give up sitting in front of the fire with the waynes toasting their bread on the ends of forks to have with their cocoa. It gave us all a minute to look at each other in a timeless light.

*

I phoned Marius and Eugene first thing – John was resting – and spent the rest of the morning analysing what I'd been told. There was still no news about his back or his spine. So it was no surprise that he was a bit gloomy, a bit *odd*. He had asked them if I'd made it to the hospital yet, so they reported the fainting, the crying, the standing by the bed like a gom, the having to be fed chocolate. The fact that I hadn't hesitated for a second when a decision had to be made about who would stay with him, who would go back to Johns Farm.

It sounded even worse when I heard my fantastic attempt at being a good wife summarised. I had abandoned him. He had nodded and said something peculiar. *She never was one for grasping the nettle.* The boys didn't really understand what he meant so they didn't have the sense to keep it from me.

The problem was that John had been right: I wouldn't go, I couldn't go, he knew me so well. I was weak material and getting weaker. That he was not here was about as much as I could bear – what would I do if he could never come home? What if he couldn't walk? What if I reached out to him *at last* to keep him from falling and he was still determined to push me away?

The wool in my head was getting wetter, heavier, it was pushing at the back of my throat threatening to choke me. I kept swallowing and swallowing but something was bubbling up inside me, something desperate to break *free*. Eileen was feeling my forehead again – it's as well if we won't have both of them in the hospital at this rate, she tutted to Bernie. I was saved by the sound of a tractor on the lane.

My father was rounding the bend when I got to the half-door. He'd come to see if I needed anything, he wanted to help. He'd already done a few novenas, he says, embarrassed because he knew I'd given up on God. A few auld grey hairs poked out of his work shirt and the bristles on his face shone silver and there was only one thing that could be done for me.

– Give me a hug, Daddy, before my actual heart breaks?
– Come here, Mary girl, I've got you.

John refused to come to the phone. Every day for four days I called Eugene and Marius and begged to speak to him but he waved our boys away. I could hear them hissing at him to just *speak*, say *something*, but he didn't. All I could hear was no, no, no, like a child being spoon-fed cabbage. He was not biting. So, he was there and I was here, refusing to leave Johns Farm. Daddy, Eileen and Matthew all offered lifts to town to get the bus to Omagh and then to Belfast. I shook my head, no, no, no. There was no point. I had already confirmed to John that I was a coward. I had left him alone in his hour of need. I was too scared to hear him say it out loud. I had broken my promise to stay by his side in sickness and in health.

There were several worried faces to dodge, a gallon of tea undrunk, sin of sins, food pushed around a plate then set aside for the hens. My sons and my aunt stopped whispering when I came into the room. Daddy stayed on the stoop smoking his pipe in case he was needed again. Mammy showed up with a Lemon Madeira, though she hadn't been invited, and the air in the kitchen was so tense that her and Auntie Eileen didn't even bother having a fight. I found them at either end of the table looking ill at ease over this unexpected turn of events.

Serena *had* been speaking to John Johns and was demanding to know what was going on between us *now*? When would we both just *grow up*? Nothing's going on, I told her, nothing!

You're as bad as each other, she roared before hanging up. It would only be a matter of time before Kathleen 'just popped by' doing her finest impersonation of a woman who hadn't been phoned, who hadn't been told to get her backside home because her baby sister was in the clabber again.

I wanted to tell them that a door had closed. It was the door of the ambulance closing over and over again to shut John Johns away from me. The metallic click played even while I slept. I hadn't recovered because my heart had been inside the ambulance when it drove off, but that was too fanciful for County Tyrone, too far-fetched for a grown woman to say she couldn't leave a house because she felt cut open and left raw.

I rushed at my work instead: ripping up and plaiting the onions, retying peas and beans, digging potatoes, scrubbing the hen-house roof and repainting it. And though I dropped into bed every night exhausted I had the overwhelming sensation of standing stock-still.

All of the thoughts bombarding my head had hard edges which jarred and hurt. I tried to blink them away but it was like dragging my eyelids over sand. I wanted to pull myself together, to get a bit done up, to get up the lane and to the bus. I wanted to do it but it was like wanting to know if there was a monster under the bed. I'd have to risk having my head torn off to find out. No matter how much I wished myself in Belfast I just couldn't go there.

On day five Kathleen breezed in with flowers and vegetables as if we might be short of those things on a farm. She gets a kind of fixed little smile when she's nervous and she only gets nervous when I'm behaving oddly. She wants to know what's going on with John and me and I wish with all of my heart that

I could tell her. Instead I say *nothing's going on*, will you take tea? She lays the back of her hand on my head. You're on fire, Mary, she says.

I changed tack and called the hospital direct every day but John was 'not in his bed' when the nurses went looking. Getting the phone out of the cradle and punching in the number was like running a marathon; I had to sit down afterwards to steady my legs. How could a man who couldn't walk get so far away that he couldn't speak to his wife? The panic set in. It had only taken him five days of freedom to let him see he wanted more. He'd got away.

I was kept up to date with his progress by Eugene and Marius who were still there. They were embarrassed, stumbling over their excuses for his absence now that he'd let them see he wasn't keen on contact. After a whole week had flown by, they called me, clearing their throats and trying to make light of a heavy body-blow. John Johns had put in a request that I was not to try phoning him again 'til I was contacted. *He* would let *me* know when I was wanted. I was not to get on a bus, I was not to come anywhere near him, until he had fully recovered his strength.

It was good news about his back: it wasn't broken and his spine was fine now that the bruising had gone down. He was going to stay away for a while because there were other things he had to sort out, physiotherapy and such. I was to send Shane and Daniel up as soon as I could spare them, John needed to talk to his boys. Swallowing the salty disappointment of being stood down after only seven days was not easy. Swallowing anything wasn't easy, the razor blades in my throat cut a bit deeper. I felt like I'd had a good hard slap, one that I didn't see coming, and the sting of it stayed with me.

– That's all good news, isn't it, Mary? says Eileen. Mary? Mary? Where are you *going*?

I had nowhere to go but the vegetable patch. I sank down in its rich dark earth and gathered handfuls of the clay in my fists. I'd lost Roisin out here, her spirit was in this soil. How I wish she had grown. He would have stayed for her, she would only be nine now, she'd need her daddy. Then the answer came to me, burning through the fog in front of my eyes. I hadn't atoned enough for my sin! My Serena and how she came to be was the starting pistol for the race I'd been running for decades! Only Joe Loughrey could let me rest. He was always going to be my key. I would walk to Brooky Hay. I needed to say I was sorry.

Little dots of purple orchids stood proud at the foot of the hollow. They swam in and out of focus as I tried to steady myself against the trunk of the oak tree. The top of it swayed, sending ripples through the ferns as I looked up. I was dizzier still as I let my feet turn for the house that Joe Loughrey had bought.

It was a two-storey, yellow-painted affair ringed all around with a tarmac moat, a strip of what would be a flower bed and some stark metal fences. The ground had been dug up and left ready for a lawn but so far only one hopeful thistle bloomed. Enormous windows showed featureless beige rooms with acres of beige carpet. I could imagine his mammy wafting from room to room with a can of roses holstered in each cardigan pocket like a demented gunslinger. The breath rasped painfully in my throat at the memory of it.

When I walked on up, he was at his car, rummaging in the boot for something among a pile of boxes.

– Hello, Joe.

He banged his baldy head hard on the boot lid when he stood up and that made him blush. I had taken him quite by surprise. The once-beloved blue eyes were cold enough to make me shiver. He wetted his pale lips with the tip of his tongue and leaned back to take all of me in.

– Well, well! If it isn't the auld woman who lived in a shoe! What's up?

– I needed to see you.

– Well, I'm busy and you look like you should be in bed.

He slammed the boot and made for his house, trying not to run. He didn't look back. Were his shoulders always that narrow? What was wrong with him? Didn't he realise that I wanted to *explain*? I wasn't a bad girl. I wasn't a tramp. I just needed his forgiveness so that I could draw a line under our time together and get back to the life I had built. I hadn't thrown away my one chance at happiness. I was a mother, a farmer's wife. And now that farmer was far away, out of my reach, learning to walk again without me by his side. I could make him understand but I'd pick a day when I wasn't being licked by flames. I turned for home in a daze, disregarded.

It was stumbling through the sunny leaves on the floor of Brooky Hay that made me realise Joe just hadn't given me a fair chance, hadn't allowed me the five minutes it would take to say that I'd never set out to hurt him. I was done with being put to one side. He'd have to listen. I dragged myself back to his street and knocked and had to knock again when the doctor took his time to answer my call.

– I need to talk to you about us, you and me ...

– There *is* no us, Mary! There never really was an 'us' because of you!

– I *thought* I loved you, you see, but ...

331

– What would *you* know about love, you lousy little *tramp*?

I had the sudden and unpleasant sensation that I was standing on his doorstep with no knickers on. I was still sixteen, but not sweet – soured. I couldn't speak, and luckily he seemed to be all out of words, but I could tell from his face that I looked a very sorry state. It wasn't concern but disgust; I repulsed him. I had wounded the doctor's son by making him think he was not good enough, when he *knew* in his heart of hearts that he was a darling. His mammy had told him a million times plus one that he was the top of the pile.

He had no intention of softening the blow he'd just delivered and he'd half turned to walk away from me again when he changed his mind. I didn't like the scowl he turned back with. He pulled me into the open garage and pushed me ahead. He was going to show me the error of my ways. There's a kind of calm that descends before someone wants to hurt you badly. I could feel it move towards me, like an old childhood friend. I looked to see if there was another way out and didn't get a chance to look back.

He yanked the waist of my jeans down and kicked my feet apart. He was determined, unaware that he didn't need to use such force. I was as weak as a kitten. I turned my face away and put my hand over it to block out the fluorescent tube humming on the ceiling. I steadied myself against a shelf with the other one, wedged against the side of an old tin bath. It was dusty in here, cobweb streamers swayed from every corner. A small grey feather caught my eye as it danced in a draught from the open door. Pigeon?

Joe was silent bar breathing heavily in and out of his nose. My head hit against the bath's side and made a rhythmic muffled sound. There was only one other: the dry push, the dryer pull.

It didn't take long – a matter of minutes. He took what had been promised to him all those years ago when we were both innocent. When he was finished, I didn't look. I didn't want to see how my legs had been arranged. With the one hand still over my eyes I reached down and pulled my clothes back into place. I dropped to my knees and let my whole body flop over 'til I was looking at a blank wall. When I finally breathed back in after minutes, the smell of motor oil and cement dust came with it. I was cold to the bone; all the heat was in my face.

The pain I felt was in my throat; it had travelled up my body as it was being administered and lodged there, gagging me. I heard him step away, and when he had his back to me he zipped his fly. He spat out the last of his rage.

– That's all the 'us' you deserve. Don't forget it was *you* who wanted this, not *me*.

The fluorescent tube pinged off when he slapped the switch and made for the kitchen. He would wash his hands with fresh soap and dry them on a beige towel. I'd never felt like an animal before – not once in all the years of making love with John Johns, not even while I was giving birth. Now I was meat: butchered and torn.

It was a short walk once I got as far as Brooky Hay but after I had tripped for the third time I knew I was coming down with something. The signs were all there: the pounding head, the scorching eyes, the chest that felt like it had a gravestone lying on top of it. I would be in bed for at least a week. The last time I had been bedridden with a fever was when Serena had left home and John Johns had slept beside me in a chair; this time I'd have to burn alone.

I don't remember reaching home but that's where I woke up, under the eaves. It must have been Auntie Eileen who called the doctor. She was there when I came round, with an anxious Daniel and Bernie hovering behind her. Doctor Loughrey Senior had been in attendance – dear auld Dermot – and I hadn't even recognised him I was so doolally! I picked the plaster from the top of my hip where he'd injected the dose of antibiotic needed to get my temperature down. The little bruise was already yellow. I didn't dwell on my other bruises.

My ankles ached, my knees, my dignity. I had never felt more ugly. I had hurt myself again. I had pulled one of my walls down and had it land squarely on my shoulders. Kathleen 'just popped by' that evening and she set about fussing and bothering and making batches of disgusting chicken soup. I begged her to help me into the shower so that I could scald my skin, modesty be damned.

When she was drying me off, she touched a tender spot at the back of my neck about the size of a thumb pad, but she said nothing. I had always marked easily.

There had been no further word from Belfast. My mother was ringing, despite being asked not to, but John was taking no word from Carncloon. She'd thought that the news of my illness would bring him to the phone but it had not. Having nothing to report in the bingo hall must be doing her head in.

Dermot didn't come back to check that I was alright but I had his prescription filled. Would he ever guess that it was his darling who had helped lay me so low? I imagined myself stopping at the crest of Brooky Hay and turning back for home before any damage is done. Every time I manage to walk myself all the way, with only the dappled leaves bearing witness, John is standing at the half-door waiting for me.

With Eileen, Kathleen and Bernie to take over the feeding and milking, Daniel and Shane went off to see their father. Matthew came to help the women and Daddy walked around the end of the house with his pipe in his teeth and parked himself in front of the range. He asked Eileen how I was doing and I heard her tell him that I would live to fight another day. Grand, grand, he says. He put a half bottle of medicinal poteen on the kitchen table and Kathleen carried it to me in mugs of hot water and sugar 'til I was punch-drunk. He brought the other half when he was told I was knocking it back like tap water and crying out for more. Ginger crept in and slept beside me, purring like an engine because the heat off me was raging through the whole bed.

Mammy drifted in and out of the feverish proceedings, tutting and sucking her dentures at the end of my bed. She was at a loss as to why I was such an attention-seeker when there was a good farm to run. I would never learn when I was well off.

    – I hope the door doesn't hit her too hard on the arse on the
      way out, says Eileen.

After another week, Eugene and Marius thought it was safe enough to leave the hospital. Eileen made dinner to welcome them home and when I sat with my plate of lovely golden chips swimming in salt and vinegar in my lap and my boys all sitting around my bed to keep me company, flowers on the stand from Serena, I felt that I was going to make it somehow.

Johns Farm hadn't killed me, it had only fenced me in while I grew up. I saw the faultlines develop in the story that I had told myself from day one, the sad story of poor abandoned me. I'd had myself on repeat talking nonsense for years. I was well off, well cared for and well loved. There were worse men than John

Johns, a lot worse. I knew he would not use his body as a weapon if there was no other way to hurt me.

There's no point in dwelling on the past: it's gone, gone forever, never to be revisited. Bridie had never preached at me about life but she had shown me the way. Get up every morning, get to your work, do the best you can for your waynes, see your man for the catch he is, take everything else with a pinch of salt and a side order of good strong tea and plenty of biscuits.

I thought of Lizzie Magee sitting in her gilded empty nest and rattled my brains to figure out why I had ever been envious. I had five children, five green hills, eighty good acres and time enough left to put things a bit more right with the world. It never does to give up on God!

Lizzie had asked me on the phone what I had *expected*? She didn't know the full extent of my reunion with Joe Loughrey. I would never tell her. I would never tell anyone. I could hardly say the words to myself.

What *had* I expected? Joe Loughrey hadn't *got away* – he'd been banished. He'd lost everything he'd known overnight in much the same way I had. I didn't feel sorry for him or for anything he had suffered. All my debts to him were paid in full. I was a clean slate.

32

John Johns has finally called. I was feeling stronger. I was clearer in my mind than I had been for years. The fever burned a loftful of fluff from between my ears. I knew what I wanted. Now all I had to figure out was how to get it. I was sitting up against my pillows when Auntie Eileen brought the phone in. Her face is straight, no fake smile or worrying frown, but I know her too well. When it's really bad news she hangs a fag on her bottom lip to waste no time in getting it lit. I'm still holding the phone when I hear her strike a match just outside the bedroom door. I clear my throat and try to stop feeling sick. I must make sure there's no wobble in my voice when this is the first time I've spoken to my husband in over two weeks.

I had good news, if I could get it delivered! I wanted to be *his*, I wanted him to be *mine*! He'd be *delighted* with my change of heart, surely? Catherine was gone, Joe Loughrey might well have never existed. We couldn't go on like this, a man and a woman only bound together under a patchwork quilt? We could be equals, we could try talking to each other, we could live out our days in the beauty of Johns Farm.

I had my speech all planned. It was glossy – a brilliant summary of all the things that I had got wrong since I became Mrs Mary Johns. A sudden memory of him running out of ten-pence pieces when he was in the horrible digs in London popped up. He had been working to save money to build a bigger, better Johns Farm, one that had kept us all cosy and warm. All he ever asked me before the pips went was if I needed anything. Well, I did need something now: I needed him. I needed him to come home. I held the phone tight against my chest to protect him, because there was something I had to shout out loud and clear before me and him got down to business.

– Auntie Eileen! Get away from that door, you nosy old
  woman!
– Spoilsport!

The sound of her finally clip-clopping down the stairs leaves me no option but to plunge in. This is the moment I reach out and ask for what I want. This is the moment I paint all the colour that I can bring now that the sun is high in the cloudless sky.

– Hello ...
– Mary?
– John!
– Mary, I'm not planning on coming back. I wanted you to
  hear it from me before I tell the children. There's nothing
  there for me now, nothing. I'll decide what to do about the
  farm and let you know later.
– What about me?
– I'll decide what to do about you, too.

The phone clicked in my hand. My husband always was a man of few words. Had he known all along that I was nothing? My speech gave a few little death throes in my breast before it croaked. He was gone and all I had to chew on was dust.

I stared at the dead phone for a good long while. When that got old, I collapsed back on the bed and stared at the ceiling for a longer while. I willed Granny Moo to appear with the flimsiest of signs on what turn to take next but even she let me down. I would have to find my own way. I grasped the nettle. Minds can be changed, hearts too – I was proof. I roped in Serena; she was going to make the first approach then the boys were all going to have a go. They smiled like indulgent parents at my grand scheme to turn their father round when he'd already made his feelings clear. We all knew he wasn't easily turned.

Never one to take a hint, the more I thought about it, the better it got until it shone on the horizon, a huge gold dome where all my worries would disappear. John would let me have my say, *he'd* understand why I couldn't open my own mouth and why the children would be so eloquent on my behalf – he'd always been a reasonable man.

John had taken his sons out in Belfast. They had told all the old tales of Bridie over pizzas and beers and laughed 'til they cried. They still missed her. I had a flashback to the man I had seen weeping in Omagh, the man who wanted me to hold his hand, the man who had worried about me in case he never came back, the man who made me promise that I would visit. The man who had looked at me with ... what on his face? What *was* that on his face? Why could I still not read him?

Oh! They had so much news! I breathed in, my chest rattled in protest, but there was something I needed to know, something I was quite *desperate* to know. I'd given them their lines. They'd carried my message straight to him like good little pigeons. I wasn't put off by the fact that Serena hadn't been hopeful. Hope was my friend! Hope was my harbour! Hope was the only nail not in the coffin.

- Tell me ... did he ask about me at all? About how I was doin'?
- No.
- Did he say he wanted to give us another go?
- No.
- Is he comin' home?
- No.

33

One by one my sons went back to their lives. Their father was not coming home. He had told them not to wait, he wasn't going to change his mind.

You should get *out* more, says Number One son. You shouldn't *fret* so much, Ma, says Number Two son. You're too *sweet* for this world, says son Number Three. Daniel thought he might as well sign on with Darragh Magee who was thinking of starting up a taxi business. I was back on my feet and able to work, after all. He would be home every night to keep me company. Ma, I'll not be leaving you for *months*, he says.

The little house emptied out and the range went cold. I left it like that for days 'til I was pig sick of waiting for an electric kettle to boil. John didn't come home, he didn't call, he stayed true to his word as always. Serena tells me she'd never experienced him so tight-lipped. Your mother and me chose silence over sense, he told her, that's all there is to tell. Her and the boys aren't showing any signs of distress over the fact that we've parted company. Auntie Eileen just broke out laughing when I wondered aloud why they weren't at least shocked. For God's sake, Mary, she says, those waynes were brought up in a house on fire!

The greenery outside mocked my blackest blues. I pulled myself together and went back to the fields. There's nothing like having no choice to focus the mind.

John Johns had left the hospital after about ten days and had moved into a Catholic retreat run by nuns. I was summoned by post after another month, given very little information other than the address and the date that would suit *him*, so I headed up the long lane once more to get the bus to town. He was determined to make me come to him, one last time.

I changed to the Belfast bus in Omagh and rolled through the hills and motorways and got snared in traffic a few times before it rolled into the grimy Europa Bus Centre. My first thought was how dearly I wanted to be back in Johns Farm, with its high hedges throwing out the scent of honeysuckle and whinbush, its vast piece of sky draped over the green fields, its animals and *life*. My second thought was how much I didn't want to go back without John Johns, but he might, just *might*, take the opportunity to come home with me?

The sanctuary of Froughlagh smelt exactly like the convent: floor polish and stale dinner mingling unpleasantly with a huge display of lilies on the desk where a nun was waiting to direct people. I asked for John and the Sister sent me along the corridor where he'd be outside. He'd been a dream come true for the roses!

I found him where she said, in the big formal gardens at the back of the house. He seemed even bigger than usual as he'd picked up a little bit of weight and looked ridiculously hale and handsome. He didn't stand up but sat and waited for me to make my way to him.

   – Hello.

   – Hello, Mary. You've *finally* made it, I see ...

   – I'm sorry I wasn't here before!

He just laughed. The boys were right: he was different, lighter. He was a man who had halved his troubles when he shared them; the frown line between his eyebrows was smoother, his black eyes clear. He was still smiling when he confirmed he was leaving me for good.

> – Mary, I'm going to miss you, believe it or not. I've plans to go abroad for a while at the end of the year. I've not told the boys yet.
>
> – You're really leaving me?
>
> – To be fair, I've never really been with you. You were never mine. And getting away from me is all you have ever wanted, so chin up, Mary darlin'! All your dreams have come true at once.

He looked sad but not sad enough to change his mind. Why won't my stupid mouth *for once* let me say the right thing at the right time? *I want you, only beautiful you* – such a simple thing to say. But because I'm *me*, things don't trip off my tongue easily and I start to cry. Salt water is always going to be the bane of my life.

> – Why the tears, Mary? Is it relief?
>
> – No, it's not relief! Why would you give up on me now? Now, when we've come so far? We could be ... happy?
>
> – You can't allow yourself to be happy! And what about me? Did you ever think about what *you* did to *me*? I *waited* five years for you to love me, Mary, and every day you looked at me like I was the bogeyman!

– What did you expect?

– I expected that you'd come to understand that you were well off!

John sat still in front of me, a rock. He needed to hear from me but I had built too many walls, they wouldn't all come down in a short afternoon. I was dumb. When I opened my mouth only a sob sailed out. In the end, he gave in to his exasperation.

– I know you think I robbed your life, Mary, but what would you have *done*? You were only sixteen, but you were only sixteen and pregnant. Bridie'd had a terrible time in Carncloon and she was more than twice your age and married before. What do you think would have happened if I hadn't stepped in? I never demanded to know whose child I was rearing at the time – is she Joe Loughrey's?

– No. She's not Joe Loughrey's. She belongs to a French teacher we had at the convent and, before you ask, he didn't force me. I wanted to *make love*!

John nodded, he understood, he understood me and perhaps he's understood me all along without the use of words. He'd never talked to me because he knew I wouldn't grace him with my interest. I never talked to him because I was busy holding myself together, holding myself as far away from him as possible. I had been holding in the damage gifted by Mammy and its toleration by Daddy forever, from even before I had got myself into trouble, and I was tired, so tired with the burden of it, it threatened to crush me.

– I have to go to sleep, I haven't been well. I need to sleep right now.

– You can sleep here. It's early yet.

344

We followed a long cool corridor to a priest's cell. His bed was made, a brown coverlet folded back to show the starched white sheets underneath. A crucifix with an accepting Jesus hung above. John's bags were new, brown leather, very smart, suitable for going overseas. I took off my jacket and shucked off my shoes to discover that I had mismatched socks on: one yellow, one green. Jesus, I couldn't even pair socks! I climbed into the bed fully clothed. I had time to register the slight chill of the linen and my husband's familiar mossy smell before I fell into a black sleep.

He was in the chair beside me when I woke up, dozing too. Would that he had climbed in beside me and kissed it better! I could feel the life of the retreat carrying on outside, the shadows of nuns moved as if on casters across beneath the bottom of the door. It was cosy, so I snuggled down in the bed a bit further and stretched like a cat before I could get off to sleep again.

– Oh no, you don't, Mrs Johns! I'm starvin' and thanks to your ability to pass out for hours at a time we've missed lunch with the good Sisters. Get up, I'll get us a taxi!

He was immaculate – every stitch he had on was new and had been laundered and ironed by nuns eager to please, his leather shoes gleamed as he walked; aside from a slight limp in his left leg he was every inch the man I knew. His dark head was closely shaved and his lips were red enough to make me swallow.

I had a pillow mark the length of my right cheek, juicy eyes from all the wailing I'd done, hair that had a bit of water flicked at it and it still only managed to set off how rumpled the rest of me was. We ventured forth anyway, two people with nothing in

345

common except for five children, two little angels, a farm, a mother, a lifetime and a pair of plain gold bands.

I looked at the Victorian buildings flashing by and smiled like a tourist. The city looked lovely and grand in the muted light of afternoon. We sat in the window of a restaurant called Arancia so that I could look some more.

Now I was with my husband of twenty-five years who was about to walk away and leave me in the place I dreaded, alone with myself. I felt giddy; the wave of pain that would dump me on to the beach was getting closer and closer and I knew I couldn't outrun it. My legs were twitching under the table as I struggled to keep my feet still on the floor. I ignored the list of lovely things to eat and ordered chips and a bottle of champagne, hoping it wasn't going to be too dear when the bill came.

I had never sat across from him alone in a restaurant; it was difficult to avoid his icy stare. I couldn't stand it. I didn't feel that bringing up the detailed horror of the years with yards of red gingham between us was appropriate, but I had to say something, *anything*, before I froze to death!

– Serena told me about poor Catherine and the little baby. I'm sorry. It must have been desperate.
– First love always leaves its mark. First loss, too.
– I'll take your word for it. I think you could easily substitute it with chewing razor blades while someone was reversing over your head in a bus!
– Ah! I take it your reunion with Joe Loughrey did not go well?

Of course he knew I would trail my sorry carcass back to Joe Loughrey, looking for forgiveness, when I finally had a chance to put my teenage heart to bed. I would never tell him how much that had cost me, how the disgrace rotted my guts.

I had to get back to my life at Johns Farm. Being away from the street and the sound of the river was making me homesick for myself, for the woman that I had become: the wife, the mother, maybe even the daughter I had always wanted to be. I had to get him to understand that I knew where I belonged.

– Why did you do it?

– Do what?

– Marry me? You could have had anybody! What possessed you to pick *me*?

– I *knew* you and I knew you had a rough road ahead. You had a smile that could break any heart. I latched on to that smile when I couldn't see anything else. It was such a shock when I realised that I loved you. I never thought I'd feel like that again after Catherine. The loss of her and the baby was an open wound. I thought for a while it was just Serena but the truth is I fell for you the night she was born. When I came home and saw her in your arms I thought my heart would burst. You were lit up! You had no idea how exquisite you were – still are, for that matter, though you've always been blind to the fact and a thousand others.

The word 'loved' landed on me like a slap that I didn't see coming. He made it sound so simple. He was telling me he had wanted me all along, stupid *me*. He had looked out for me, he had found me. His was no silly schoolboy crush; his was a feeling as constant as the Cloon flowing past our house.

I had made a fool of my precious time with him. You never miss the water until the well runs dry, says Auntie Eileen when she's sad but needs to say something as she fires up the cigarette that will make it better. I tried to open my mouth but a decades-old fear of just not being good enough squeezed my throat like a vice. John had no such troubles.

- I understood how young you were, how unformed, how naive. But at least *try* to imagine what my life was like? Please tell me that you at least thought about *me*? Once? I had another man's child under my roof and you looking at me like I was the Devil himself? I was in a pit again just after I'd managed to get myself out of one. Every day I thought it would get better but every day I was wrong. Can you imagine being locked out by the person you love? What would you have had me *do*?
- I *don't know*. And stop shoutin', you're making people look!
- Well, Jesus! We don't want to risk something *so terrible*, Sadie!

He was angry, fed up dealing with an idiot, an idiot with my mother. My head was light. The last few days and weeks had pulled everything I thought I had buried up by the roots and it left me feeling exposed, displaced. I was sitting with a man I could talk to, one who would understand my life if only I could find the words and time to tell him. I was sitting with the man I loved.

I considered the lie I had spun myself all these years that I had given in to his love-making with a martyr's grace, when in truth I had longed for the moments he had made me feel alive over and over and over again in the pitch-dark of Johns Farm. Right this minute I would give *anything* to be back in his priest's cell with him and the cold linen sheets on my naked skin. He touched my arm but it was my heart that leapt.

- Mary, are you going to mention the fact that I've told you I love you?
- Stay with me then!
- It's too late!
- Give me a chance, I'll stop being scared!
- You came to me scared! Christ alive, you were a wreck – not that I blame you when you had that bloody auld bitch to deal with! You were determined to hate me, you never gave me a chance, not one! But remember, Mary, it wasn't me who stunted your life, it was you. When are you going to realise that? When are you going to grow up?

He was clenching his jaw, willing me to give voice to the words that might save me. Nothing happened, I didn't even manage a whimper.

- It's time we put this marriage out of its misery. That way we'll both find some peace. Let's go …

The urban daylight was blinding, the few flowers all growing to their death in sad little plastic pots and baskets. He raised his arm to stop a taxi and I knew it was for me. I was being set free. I grabbed at a street light to slow the horror of it down but he yanked me away from it by the arm.

- Get in the taxi, Mary! *Now!*
- I'm not going back to Johns Farm on my own, I'm not!
- You can go where you like! I'm past caring.
- Don't say that! Say you'll stay!
- I can't stay! I need to get away from you before you drown me! You're a miracle of self-pity! Do you know that? No one could feel sorrier for you than you do for yourself!

That shut me up at last. As he pushed me into the back of the car, he only had one thing to add before his voice broke.

– I've had the living of a dog from you, Mary Rattigan!

He didn't wait to see me go. His big back was turned to me forever. I'm *Mary Johns* now, I said but there was no one left to hear me.

2007

THE PALM OF GOD'S HAND

34

I've lived through another autumn, a harsh winter, a spring that seemed to appear one day and be replaced overnight by summer. Mammy has soured every one of those seasons. I have evidence. The arthritic hip has been replaced and she makes the most of soaking up every spare moment I have by playing the patient. This morning she needs Deep Heat. Could I 'just' nip up and rub it in *this very minute* and she won't bother me again for the rest of the day? Her neck is killing her!

   – Where's Daddy?

   – What do you want with *him*?

   – If *he* was there *he* could do it, surely?

   – MARY RATTIGAN! Are you ever going to stop being MUCKY?

How did she ever get pregnant? Was *she* in fact the Virgin Mother? Daddy and her were two people who should not have met, never mind married, never mind having nine children, seven of whom lived. Would the little dead boys have made her happy?

Though I never knew them, I feel their absence myself. They pull at me like my own little Roisin-that-never-was – we have that in common, only that. How much worse must it be for her when they grew whole right under her heart? We didn't have depression in my day, she says, we offered it up to Good Holy God. Was it their passing which set her in stone? Auntie Eileen doesn't care.

– You don't have to look after that fuckin' rancid auld bitch, she says, just because you're the only unfortunate on the doorstep! Oh no, no, no, no! She can go to Hell where she belongs!

She's right. But you only get one mammy in this life, presumably because two would kill you, so I go while I still have strength enough to take her on, warts and all.

– I'm not being MUCKY! I'm being practical!

– Well, if you're too busy *doing whatever it is you think you're doing* then I'm sorry I bothered you! Truly! I'll manage on my own!

– Jesus, Mammy! I'll be there in five minutes!

Pick a saint, any saint, and she could try their patience. She doesn't like that I've set myself up a little business; it smacks of pride, of a girl with ideas above her station. She is doing everything she can to tear me down from my pedestal. I get the range up to boil the kettle and make a pot of tea. I won't rush myself to please her, No Siree Bob! I have postcards to read, three postcards that were lying on the mat inside the half-door this morning and each one is *screaming* to be read.

The first is from darling Kathleen. She's been gone for five months already – took to travelling when she'd got in her thirty-five years of nursing in Derry. The second is from Lizzie Magee.

She's in Africa for the third time. She's obsessed with the place. Poor Kenny McGuckin: he hates the heat. The rashes race from his toes to the top of his head.

The third is from him, the lost husband. The slope and loops of his handwriting scald me before I have the sense to stuff it into my pocket. So, he's made his decision?

I hope today is not one of the days that Mammy wants to *talk*. My heart won't take it. The blasted TV is to blame. It has cut more corners off my mother in a matter of months than a whole herd of Catholic clergy did in a lifetime. She's been trapped in front it with her new hip and the overexposure has finally hit home. She has come to understand that everyone outside The Hill can *talk* and she doesn't like being behind the times.

– I used to mazurka with Malachy McCullen! It was a great dance, very fast and you had to really move from corner to corner! Those were the days!

This is the kind of guileless opener offered by the woman who did not dance with my father in nearly fifty years of marriage, abandoning him to widows and aunts for the waltzes he loved at weddings because she thought taking to the floor was 'nonsense, ridiculous nonsense' and he was no less than an eejit? She always mouthed the word 'eejit' because he was, after all was said and done, her husband and deserving of a modicum of respect.

The mazurka is not the worst bomb Mammy's dropped but somehow it's the one that bounces around my head from corner to corner. Every time she wheels past me, in Malachy McCullen's arms, her skirts are higher, her smile is wider and her hair, always rollered weekly into submission in my lifetime, is flying in damp ribbons.

355

I know Malachy McCullen. I still see him at the post office collecting his pension, smelling to high sheep heaven in a wet wool coat and barely able to push one foot in front of the other. His nose is long, the dark hairs racing each other to get out of it are long and his earlobes graze the collar on his coat. He looks like he's melting. I offer her these details to verify we are talking about the Maestro of Mazurka.

– He was quite a dish back in the day! she says.

– Your mother wasn't always your mother, sighs my father.

The walk to The Hill is a welcome buffer between me and his postcard. The hedges are alive with small birds; the many pigeons and rooks keep to the high branches of the trees and take off for a quick nervous circle as I pass by. The lush slopes of Dergmoy climb to meet the other hills. The stone walls are bleached white in the sunshine. I see that the pink rhododendron hedge over at Arthur Rowley's farm is in full bloom as I get to the top and turn for the house where I was born and battered.

The whole place is taking on a disused air; the lack of children or the lack of love is dragging it down. It would be easy to think it had been abandoned, until the sound of the television carries down the hall. Mammy will stay put with her game-show hosts and quizmasters until she's administered to.

I meet my father in the back pantry. He's getting thinner and more precious with every day that passes. Two big sinews stick out on his neck and even one day's silvery beard growth makes him look vulnerable, like a much older man. I want to reach out and pull him to me, to rock him like a baby, but he'd only die of embarrassment. Instead I offer him the Irish substitute for love.

356

– Tea?

– Aye, tea would be grand.

I make them both mugs of tea, lumps of scone bread that I bake myself and pile it high with my home-made jam. He likes to take his in the tick-tock of the kitchen so he doesn't have to struggle out of his wellies.

– How's the waynes?

– Grand, Daddy, they're all grand.

– Good, good … ah … Mary?

– Yes?

– I heard at the mart that John's about.

– Aye, I got a postcard off him just this morning.

– Is he … is he …

– He says he'll call this way at some point.

– Good, good.

– There's no need for you to tell Mammy?

– No need, no need at all.

She reaches for her tea in the Good Room without taking her eyes off the television and doesn't burden me with thank yous.

– Ah, finally! I thought you were going to keep me waiting *all* day?

– Hello, Mammy!

While I'm rubbing in the Deep Heat, she has a sudden rush of blood to the head and lets slip a kind word before she can snatch it back.

– This jam isn't terrible, she says.

My eyes fill up in spite of myself. Suddenly her papery skin is a reminder that even she will slip away from me one day and I know there will be more sadness to swallow. She's a monster but she's *my* monster. A whiff of sweat rises above the menthol

357

cloud and I lunge at it like a drowning man for a twig. I ask her straight out if she was able to look after herself properly without my help. Well! I might as well have pulled the pin from a grenade. For a woman who was supposed to ease herself in and out of chairs for six weeks she was up and in my face before I had time to flinch.

- How dare you! I'm not going to take bloody insolence from YOU!
- I'm not being insolent! I'm being kind ...

This truth took us both by surprise. She settled down and cleared her throat to nearly out-mazurka me for the second time in a week.

- I can't manage the bath but I have a system.
- A system?
- Aye, a system. *My own system!*
- What kind of a system?
- Well ... I stand at the sink ... and I start with my hands and wash down as far as possible then I wash my feet and wash up as far as possible ... and then when I'm done, I wash the possible.
- The poss—
- That's right ... *with a flannel*, so don't you go getting sniffy with me! I'm clean because I make sure I'm clean inside *and* out! Which is more than can be said about *you*, Yes Siree Bob!

35

Disquieting days bring strange nights. I lay for hours in the pitch-dark, knowing that the eaves were above me but not able to make out their shape. I had his postcard under my pillow. *Mary, I may call that way at some point. John.* No frills, no dates, no times, no hope. I knew he'd get sick of wandering about eventually. The place is part of him: he loves it like I love it, with all of his heart. I will the words under my head to re-arrange themselves and say something different. They might speak at any moment so I wait and wait but they still don't tell me what I want to hear. He is coming back for his land, his fields, his trees and ditches, the bone-chilling Cloon waters. And nothing else.

The sun rose at five-thirty and I rose with it, aching and tired. Mammy calls around midday and I walk up, get the Deep Heat on and get out. The big white wall of the orchard welcomes me home. I cross the floor to the range and put the kettle on to boil. The silence soon drives me back out to the front stoop. I can breathe easier outside my empty house than in.

Inside smells like him, my errant husband, it's like choking on nectar. And I can sit against the ancient granite wall, warmed by the heat of the day, and be able to feel for five minutes that nothing can harm me when I have solid rock at my back. I watch the river field, jumping with heavy cream meadowsweet, the lilac of cuckooflowers, the yellow dots of buttercups and the ball dance of midges.

For decades it had seemed to me that my life was a truck that roared past showering me with muck, then I realised that I was *driving* the bloody truck! It's because I'm a different girl now; I grew up about a year ago! Whoosh! Bam! The scales flew clean off my eyeballs and I could see that I had my hands on the wheel all along! What a fool! Soon I would be a fool without a home because he's coming back, coming back to winkle me out.

Will I be able to secure myself just one more chance? My lungs or is it my heart plays up when I allow myself that question, flapping about like a fish on a riverbank taking in the horror with its right-side-up fish eye that it's just air between it and the sky for evermore.

Ginger looks up at me from the sunlight dancing on the granite slab we laid down to mark Brandy dog's grave and shows me the back of his dark little throat with an extra-wide yawn. I'm not leaving you behind, I tell him with a sob.

After John binned me in Belfast, he wrote to say he was going to lease the herd as he knew that the beasts would be too much work for me when all the boys would soon be gone. *Waynes don't last forever, Mary, you need to find something else to do with your life!* True to his word, he set the wheels in motion within days and Scrumptious Connolly – who had dried out and rediscovered God all in the same afternoon – showed up to appraise the cows and walk the fields and inspect the drains and inform me it was never too late to go back to Jesus. *Jesus!*

The decision was made to leave me with the hill field, the river field and the back field. All I could see was a lot of space opening up around me. Johns Farm and The Hill always seemed small, like fields that could be gathered in one hand; now they were vast, green spaces rolling forever in front of me. Auntie Eileen took a leaf out of John's book and leased her farm in the same week. Two of us can play at this retirement lark, she said.

I wept when the last of the cattle were walked past the half-door of Johns Farm on their way to greener grass on Aghabovey. At least this time I said goodbye.

When Daniel went to university in Liverpool the September after John left me, I cried so much that I thought I would drown. Until then I had had Son Number Four to focus on, him to cook for, him to love. He had to prise my arms from around his neck at Belfast airport. I had never been on a plane and the thought of him being lifted up, up and away was brutal.

I cried all the way down the M1 while Eileen roared at me to for God's sake, get a grip, it was only fucking England not fucking Mars! We wouldn't have to get on a rocket ship to see him, just a plane which took sixty minutes! *Only sixty fucking minutes!* Bernie kept passing the tissues through from the back seat 'til the box was empty. When she growled at me and gave me a good hard bang on the head with the empty box I howled some more.

His father had gone straight from Belfast to Serena in London and after a fortnight sightseeing he had taken off for Australia.

361

The twins followed him within weeks 'just to see how it was'. I cried and cried and cried. When I stopped crying for five minutes I found enough energy to cry some more. My face was like a baboon's backside.

Auntie Eileen threatened to get Doctor Joe Loughrey to have a look at me and the shock of that finally stopped my nonsense. Joe Loughrey listening to my heart? Joe Loughrey shining a light in my eyes? Joe Loughrey trying to ascertain the state of my mental health? No Siree Bob! I snapped to and came up with a plan of sorts on how to survive on my own.

I had all this land lying around me going to waste so I started growing ever more vegetables and fruit. The orchard was always great for apples and plums, Victoria and damson, but I have low fruit too: gooseberries, blackcurrants, redcurrants all planted now and ready to give up a fine crop next year. I had such plans for that harvest. I conserve it and distribute it to the shops in a thirty-mile radius, but not by myself. Auntie Eileen and Bernie are here three days a week and we have become Bridie's Jams & Pickles. I think Bridie would love having her name put to such a sweet joke. I hope I've done her proud. I am still hers and always will be. The thought of her makes the possibility of having to return to The Hill a hundred times worse. At least here I feel she's still near me, still able to eat me up and not even need sugar.

We have huge boiling pans set up in the milk house; Eileen and me wash and rinse and cook and bottle and Bernie puts the labels on like she has an internal spirit level – she's a pure angel out of Heaven. Daddy drops in every day as he likes to feel he's on hand for any heavy work and us only stewing fruit. I feed him up and he sits on the stoop and smokes himself blind while Ginger purrs fit to burst at his feet.

- Will I empty this into that, Mary?
- That would be a great help, thanks, Daddy. Sure, I don't know what I'd do without you!
- Have you anything to lift, Eileen?
- No, Frank! But I could lift a mug of tea to my lips now that you've mastered boiling the kettle!
- I'll make a pot.

He knows he'll never be seen down here in the hollow of Johns Farm doing such a cissy thing so it's safe enough for him to venture into the kitchen. Serena designed the labels for the jars with a white longhouse with a red tin roof and all the front of the house is covered in red fruits. I finish them off with red gingham cloth covers. Red is still my colour. I'm waiting to hear from a big distributor in Belfast who supplies supermarket chains with 'niche organic foodstuffs', or jam as we call it in County Tyrone. It'll be hard to tell them my plans have changed.

That's all the postcard said: *Mary, I may call that way at some point. John.* What if I have to give up my little business and get a job? A job in a shop or a hospital? I'm not qualified. I've never worked a day in my life closeted in one of those horrible airless places.

Lizzie Magee will give me pointers on how to survive if that happens. I'm so glad she'll be home soon, though the last time she was here wasn't easy on either of us. She wanted to surprise me and she certainly did. She'd found me howling like a banshee in the vegetable patch. Every time I thought about my little Roisin-that-never-was the blue waves of longing would crash over my head and nearly drown me. Lizzie knew about her but I'd never been able to put into words how much I missed her. She had been so real, so complete in my mind, that I could never put her from it.

After a stiff whiskey each, with an even stiffer whiskey chaser, Lizzie found the strength to tell me something, a thing she has wanted to be able to say out loud for what feels like a hundred years. She does know how I feel. She also knows why she's childless. She's always known.

She had had an abortion. Dessie had driven her to the boat and given her a handful of money covered in engine oil. She'd never seen so much cash, it must have been a whole month's takings at the garage. After the terrifying boat ride from Larne to Stranraer and the never-ending coach trip to London overnight, she'd found the place and committed the sin of all sins. All alone with nothing but a packet of painkillers she'd done the return journey in under three days. She forced herself to eat Mars Bars and Twixes at every service station because it was still a day out.

She was eighteen and hadn't found the 'man of her dreams'. It was the week after she'd driven up to Johns Farm and I had Serena on my hip and tall tales of how *great* married life was. I had looked so happy, she tells me, looked so lovely standing outside my little house with my gorgeous girl and with John Johns in the bag; she thought she would die of jealousy. She'd been feeling sorry for me and missing me and all along I'd been doing more than fine without her. I was living our schoolgirl dream of being in love and having a husband.

She just couldn't wait another day to catch me up. She couldn't wait any longer for a ride! If she waited *one minute* more she'd be on the shelf forever. She was behind the times; no one was a virgin any more. Green with envy, she went off to Bundoran with none other than Scrumptious Connolly. She kept him out of the bar long enough to get herself and him into a caravan in the Star of the Sea camping site and took every precaution known to womankind, rubber johnnies included, and still got herself knocked up.

Sheila and Dessie sent her to England for 'the treatment' when she went crying to them. They turned into strangers, into statues; she couldn't get through to them! She kept telling them it was okay, Mary had a baby and it's okay, I saw her! But it was not okay for Sheila and Dessie, not okay at all.

They had only been letting on that they didn't mind because I was nothing to do with them. The muck all stuck on me. She had never even seen them in a bad temper before; she was so shocked, she could hardly believe what they were telling her to do. It has never been discussed since.

All through the IVF, the constant heartache and the little babies who only stayed for a few weeks, it was never referred to: a non-event. Sheila and Dessie blamed Lizzie for her stupidity and never took an ounce of responsibility for their part in covering it up.

 – I'm surprised John Johns didn't tell you, she says, he took me home when he found me doubled up with cramps at the bus station. I nearly bled to death. I had on white jeans, can you bloody believe that? I wanted to look nice on the boat!
 – Oh, Lizzie!
 – I was so mortified. John had to half-carry me to the front door. He never said a word but he knew exactly what was going on.

My husband would never have given her away, even to me. There's no one who doesn't make a mistake at some point or another, he often said to the children. I never agreed or disagreed, too busy agitating the shadows. No, he would never dob her in, his Saint Lizzie of the Polished Nails.

That's all the postcard said: *Mary, I may call that way at some point. John.* In the end Serena calls. She's heard from Dada and he *does* want to look over the farm. He's not sure what the future holds for him. He's really loved being away in Australia; Marius and Eugene and him did a bit of travelling, camping out and such. Her Uncle Mick joined them at some stage but he didn't take to the auld camping; he's a vet who doesn't like bugs and prefers the air-conditioned comforts of his surgery and home.

The bugs there are huge and the spiders are monstrous, Dada told her, enough to make a grown man run for cover. *Imagine Dada being afraid of something!* she roars. It's too preposterous. Seems Mick has a very nice man living in his house, not that he verified anything. I'm glad he has someone to keep his night terrors away, someone to hold him.

Australia also has something called Blue Sky Syndrome which sounds bloody awful! What good is a pure blue sky to anyone? Why is half of Ireland's youth there getting bitten and burnt when we have a perfectly good country here which is practically empty? And no bombs, bullets or ballots flying? Sometimes it seems we were all just fighting to clear the blockades on the road to the airport. Anyway, Dada is now considering his options, one of those options being to put me out on the street when he comes to view *his* farm. She doesn't say this last part but I hear it anyway.

– What are you going to do, Ma?

– About what?

– About him!

- What about him?
- He's coming *home*, Ma, he's going to be landing on the street any day now, you'd better have something to say for yourself!

John and me hadn't spoken for three hundred and seventy-three days now and counting. I had no clue what was in his mind or his heart. I needed Lizzie Magee to stop hoovering up the local wildlife in Africa and to get her ass back to Carncloon right away, we needed a pow-wow! We needed to compare notes, we needed to come up with a plan, we needed to make sure we got it right this time. I didn't know where to start without her. The clock was ticking. No matter how hard I pushed it down, the hope that he wouldn't hate me outright rose up in my breast, the eternal flame to my sacred heart.

36

The night closes in around Johns Farm softly. A pink haze hovers over the river field to one side of the house and to the other the high slope of the hill field takes on the shadows of the lofty sessile oaks in the far hedges. Soon it will be autumn and the precious leaves will burn red and yellow before they disappear. When I was a little girl, I could see the evening turf smoke from Bridie's chimney from our street. The sight of its white plumes would make Mammy rage and run for the rosary beads. All the novenas she could fire off could hardly keep the pure badness of Bridie Johns away.

The river runs on in its course, the lovely cold clear Cloon rising and falling, smoothing the stones and taking a few inches here and there to leave me less of Johns Farm each year. I must go in, I must go in and face the empty house, but not yet. I sit in the glow of the windows on my stoop. I have night stock planted in the hedges now and its fragrance is curled about me when I hear the splash. It's soft but I hear it and I know he's coming from the river field. The cup of tea starts to shake in my hands and I put it down and link my fingers around my knees to wait.

Will he throw me straight out? This very night could be the last I have a beloved roof over my head. The last time I stoke the auld yellow range before I go to bed. Walking past pictures of my children in Christening robes, Holy Communion outfits, Confirmation suits that I've nailed all along the kitchen wall, Eugene frozen forever with a black tooth he got when he fell face first from the barn steps.

Marius and him were daring each other to jump from higher and higher up, even though the barn steps were forbidden ground. Twelve steps of solid stone covered in moss even at the height of the summer. He had begged me and John to please get the tooth pulled before his Holy Communion photo! The precious Holy Communion photo that he knew would *haunt* him for the rest of his days. I knew what he was going through but records have to be kept.

On the very day that I had received the Body of Christ my scabby knees had hurt when I knelt down, my poorly lip had torn open a bit when I put my tongue out to receive the Host. The photo's still nailed to the wall in the Good Room at The Hill in a brown wood frame.

- We'll leave it in 'til you learn to put your hands out to save yourself! said John.
- Just keep your mouth closed for the photo, I said. Don't smile with your teeth and you'll be grand. Anyway, Marius has no teeth at all so I don't know what you're worrying about!

Great consolation there from the Mammy of the Year! There's always someone worse off than yourself if you would just open your eyes to it.

The blackbirds sound off a few chirrups of alarm as he comes past the row of oaks in the border of the river field. Would that be the song to haunt me? The gate whines open and clangs shut and the bats take off in a black cloud. The soft crunch of his step comes closer.

– Hello, Mary.

– John.

He has grown his hair again; it is down to his shoulders. A small rucksack tells me he isn't staying long. He's brown as a nut and even from a safe distance I could tell he's as clean as he had always been. I bet he smells light, natural, tender. The tears started to boil up from my secret reservoir, gathering in a choking lump at the back of my throat. I swallow them down and speak.

– How was Australia?

– I missed the rain.

– Well, you're back now, you can stand out in it!

– I might just do that!

– How are the boys? Do you think they'll ever come home?

– They're not far away, Mary, nothing's far away these days ...

Why did it feel like the moon? He went into the house then, stooping at the half-door as he'd always done. I hear him walk the length of the kitchen and put the kettle on. He would be looking around, figuring out what changes he would make. I hear him talking to Ginger who's under his feet already looking for a scratch. I'd lived long enough to be jealous of a cat.

The bats regroup in the branches of the first big sycamore, so close I can hear their tiny clicks. I would miss the quivering velvety mass of them. I would miss sitting in the square of light from my kitchen. Would miss the milk house with its solid walls and red tin roof. Would miss the joy of pans of fruit bubbling to a golden syrup. Would miss the shush of the river as it rounded the bend. Would miss the sweep of Combover Hill as it wound its way over the horizon. Would miss every blade of grass like I missed every hair on my children's heads.

I would miss my husband every second of every minute of every hour of every day 'til I died. Growing up was bloody over-rated. If I could have my time over again, I'd be more careful with it. I wouldn't let it slip through my careless fingers like flour. Please Good Holy God and Bo Derek, can you hear me begging? Let this cup pass over me.

He was behind me before I knew it. Perhaps he would offer to drive me up the back lane and give me an hour some other day to return for the things I couldn't live without. The photo of Bridie being kissed by all five of our children at once, her eyes sealed with laughter? Some seashells from various Sundays at Bundoran, a hairclip made of small misshaped pearls from Lizzie Magee, my postcards from all the countries I would never set foot in? The small gold band I had slipped off my finger a year ago because I knew I didn't deserve it? It was hanging on a silken ribbon that I had tacked to the bedpost.

I was shaking so much I should have been giving off a sound. His big hands came down on my shoulders to steady me, rest-ing lightly at first before he traced my collarbones and ran his fingers down my arms. He lifted me from the chair and turned me round so he could see what kind of animal he was going to have to deal with. Would he give me time to hug Ginger

goodbye? I couldn't take him with me, a cat would not be tolerated at The Hill.

I looked like sin, as usual! I had dark hollows under my eyes
and a sore lip where I'd bitten straight through it, trying to stem
the heartbreak. He traced the shape of it with his thumbs, wip-
ing away my tears. His face was impossible to read as he stood
with his back to the glow of Johns Farm but his body was an
open book.

   – I've missed you, Mrs Johns.

   – I've been here all along ...

   – Could I stay, d'you think?

My God! What was he saying? Was he saying he wanted to
stay for the night? Was he asking me if it was alright if he bunked
out in the milk house? Did he want to stay here but without me?
Did he want me to join him under the eaves – because I would,
I would in an instant?

   – I could think of worse men! A lot worse!

   – So, you can see your way clear to giving me a place to lay
     my weary head?

   – You can lay it on my heart where it *belongs*.

   – For how long?

   – How long have we got?

The touch of his lips and tongue went all the way to my toes,
smoothing my frayed nerve endings as it went. I was going to
burst my banks! My cup runneth over! Surely goodness and
mercy shall follow me all the days of my life? I pushed against
him, trying to grind his bones into mine. I wanted us to be one.
I wanted us to have hard-fought peace in our day.

I wanted 'us' to just be us. I wanted us to be the 'Song of
Ruth'. *Wherever you go, I will go. Wherever you dwell, I will*

dwell. Your people will be my people. And your God will be my God. Wherever you die, I will die. And there will I be buried beside you. We will be together forever, and our love will be the gift of our life. I breathed him in, I couldn't not. He was *mine* and I was *his*. We belonged together. We'd found each other at last. When he held out his hand for me, I took it and let him lead me home. Love doesn't make itself, y'know?